Nora Roberts is the *New York Times* bestselling author of more than one hundred and ninety novels. A born storyteller, she creates a blend of warmth, humour and poignancy that speaks directly to her readers and has earned her almost every award for excellence in her field. The youngest of five children, Nora Roberts lives in western Maryland. She has two sons.

Visit her website at www.noraroberts.com.

Nora Roberts

Mistletoe and Snow

MILLS BOON

First Impressions

To Georgeann, neighbour and friend

Chapter 1

The morning sun shot shafts of light over the mountains. It picked up the hints of red and gold among the deep green leaves and had them glowing. From somewhere in the woods came a rustling as a rabbit darted back to its burrow, while overhead a bird chirped with an insistent cheerfulness. Clinging to the line of fences along the road were clumps of honeysuckle. The light scent from the few lingering blossoms wafted in the air. In a distant field a farmer and his son harvested the last of the summer hay. The rumble of the baler was steady and distinct.

Over the mile trek to town only one car passed. Its driver lifted his hand in a salute. Shane waved back. It was good to be home.

Walking on the grassy shoulder of the road, she plucked a blossom of honeysuckle and, as she had as a child, drew in the fleetingly sweet aroma. When she crushed the flower between her fingers, its fragrance briefly intensified. It was a scent she associated with summer, like barbecue smoke and new grass. But this was summer's end.

Shane looked forward to fall eagerly, when the mountains would be at their best. Then the colors were breathtaking and the air was clean and crisp. When the wind came, the world would be full of sound and flying leaves. It was the time of woodsmoke and fallen acorns.

Curiously, she felt as though she'd never been away. She might still have been twenty-one, walking from her grandmother's to Sharpsburg to buy a gallon of milk or a loaf of bread. The busy Baltimore streets, the sidewalks and crowds of the last four years might have been a dream. She might never have spent those four years teaching in an inner-city school, correcting exams and attending faculty meetings.

Yet four years had passed. Her grandmother's narrow two-story house was now Shane's. The uneven, wooded three acres of land were hers as well. And while the mountains and woods were the same, Shane was not.

Physically, she looked almost as she had when she had left western Maryland for the job in a Baltimore high school. She was small in height and frame, with a slender figure that had never developed the curves and roundness she'd hoped for. Her face was subtly triangular with its creamy skin touched with warm color. It had been called peaches and cream often enough to make Shane wince. There were dimples that flashed when she smiled, rather than the elegant cheekbones she had wished for. Her nose was small, dusted with freckles, tilted up at the end. Pert. Shane had suffered the word throughout her life.

Under thin arched brows, her eyes were large and dark. Whatever emotion she felt was mirrored in them. They were rarely cool. Habitually, she wore her hair short, and it curled naturally to frame her face in a deep honey blond. As her temperament was almost invariably happy, her face was usually animated, her small, sculpted mouth tilted up. The adjective used most to describe her was *cute*. Shane had grown to detest the word, but lived with it. Nothing could be done to alter sharp, vital attractiveness into sultry beauty.

As she rounded the last curve in the road before coming into town, she had a sudden flash of having done so before—as a child, as a teenager, as a girl on the brink of womanhood. It gave her a sense of security and belonging. Nothing in the city had ever given her the simple pleasure of being part of the whole.

Laughing, she took the final yards at a run, then burst

through the door of the general store. The bells jingled
fiercely before it slammed shut.

"Hi!"

"Hi, yourself." The woman behind the counter grinned
at her. "You're out early this morning."

"When I woke up, I discovered I was out of coffee."
Spotting the box of fresh doughnuts on the counter,
Shane rolled her eyes and headed for them. "Oh, Donna,
cream filled?"

"Yeah." Donna watched with an envious sigh as Shane
chose one and bit into it. For the better part of twenty
years, she'd seen Shane eat like a linebacker without
gaining an ounce of fat.

Though they had grown up together, they were as different as night and day. Where Shane was fair, Donna
was dark. Shane was small; Donna was tall and well
rounded. For most of their lives, Donna had been content
to play follower to Shane's leader. Shane was the adven-
turer. Donna had liked nothing better than to point out
all the flaws in whatever plans she was hatching, then
wholeheartedly fall in with it.

"So, how are you settling in?"

"Pretty well," Shane answered with her mouth full.

"You've hardly been in since you got back in town."

"There's been so much to do. Gran couldn't keep the
place up the last few years." Both affection and grief
came through in her voice. "She was always more in-

terested in her gardening than a leaky roof. Maybe if I had stayed—"

"Oh, now don't start blaming yourself again." Donna cut her off, drawing her straight dark brows together. "You know she wanted you to take that teaching job. Faye Abbott lived to be ninety-four. That's more than a lot of people can hope for. And she was a feisty old devil right to the end." ·

Shane laughed. "You're absolutely right. Sometimes I'm sure she's sitting in her kitchen rocker making certain I wash up my dishes at night." The thought made her want to sigh for the childhood that was gone, but she pushed the mood away. "I saw Amos Messner out in the field with his son haying." After finishing off the doughnut, Shane dusted her hands on the seat of her pants. "I thought Bob was in the army."

"Got discharged last week. He's going to marry a girl he met in North Carolina."

"No kidding?"

Donna smiled smugly. It always pleased her, as proprietor of the general store, to be the ears and eyes of the town. "She's coming to visit next month. She's a legal secretary."

"How old is she?" Shane demanded, testing.

"Twenty-two."

Throwing back her head, Shane laughed in delight.

"Oh, Donna, you're terrific. I feel as though I've never been away."

The familiar unrestricted laugh made Donna grin. "I'm glad you're back. We missed you."

Shane settled a hip against the counter. "Where's Benji?"

"Dave's got him upstairs." Donna preened a bit, thinking of her husband and son. "Letting that little devil loose down here's only asking for trouble. We'll switch off after lunch."

"That's the beauty of living on top of your business." Finding the opening she had hoped for, Donna pounced on it. "Shane, are you still thinking about converting the house?"

"Not thinking," Shane corrected. "I'm going to do it." She hurried on, knowing what was about to follow. "There's always room for another small antique shop, and with the museum attached, it'll be distinctive."

"But it's such a risk," Donna pointed out. The excited gleam in Shane's eyes had her worrying all the more. She'd seen the same gleam before the beginning of any number of outrageous and wonderful plots. "The expense—"

"I have enough to set things up." Shane shrugged off the pessimism. "And most of my stock can come straight out of the house for now. I want to do it, Donna," she went on as her friend frowned at her. "My own place, my own business." She glanced around the compact, well-stocked store. "You should know what I mean."

"Yes, but I have Dave to help out, to lean on. I don't think I could face starting or managing a business all on my own."

"It's going to work." Her eyes drifted beyond Donna, fixed on their own vision. "I can already see how it's going to look when I'm finished."

"All the remodeling."

"The basic structure of the house will stay the same," Shane countered. "Modifications, repairs." She brushed them away with the back of her hand. "A great deal of it would have to be done if I were simply going to live there."

"Licenses, permits."

"I've applied for everything."

"Taxes."

"I've already seen an accountant." She grinned as Donna sighed. "I have a good location, a solid knowledge of antiques, and I can re-create every battle of the Civil War."

"And do at the least provocation."

"Be careful," Shane warned her, "or I'll give you another rundown on the Battle of Antictam."

When the bells on the door jingled again, Donna heaved an exaggerated sigh of relief. "Hi, Stu."

The next ten minutes were spent in light gossiping as

Donna rang up and bagged dry goods. It would take little time to catch up on the news Shane had missed over the last four years.

Shane was accepted as an oddity—the hometown girl who had gone to the city and come back with big ideas. She knew that to the older residents of the town and countryside she would always be Faye Abbott's granddaughter. They were a proprietary people, and she was one of their own. She hadn't settled down and married Cy Trainer's boy as predicted, but she was back now.

"Stu never changes," Donna said when she was alone with Shane again. "Remember in high school when we were sophomores and he was a senior, captain of the football team and the best-looking hunk in a sweaty jersey?"

"And nothing much upstairs," Shane added dryly.

"You always did go for the intellectual type. Hey," she continued before Shane could retort, "I might just have one for you."

"Have one what?"

"An intellectual. At least that's how he strikes me. He's your neighbor too," she added with a growing smile.

"*My* neighbor?"

"He bought the old Farley place. Moved in early last week."

"The Farley place?" Shane's brows arched, giving Donna the satisfaction of knowing she was announcing fresh news. "The house was all but gutted by the fire. Who'd be fool enough to buy that ramshackle barn of a place?"

"Vance Banning," Donna told her. "He's from Washington, D.C."

After considering the implications of this, Shane shrugged. "Well, I suppose it's a choice piece of land even if the house should be condemned." Wandering to a shelf, she selected a pound can of coffee then set it on the counter without checking the price. "I guess he bought it for a tax shelter or something."

"I don't think so." Donna rang up the coffee and waited while Shane dug bills out of her back pocket. "He's fixing it up."

"The courageous type." Absently, she pocketed the loose change.

"All by himself too," Donna added, fussing with the display of candy bars on the counter. "I don't think he has a lot of money to spare. No job."

"Oh." Shane's sympathies were immediately aroused. The spreading problem of unemployment could hit anyone, she knew. Just the year before, the teaching staff at her school had been cut by three percent.

"I heard he's pretty handy though," Donna went on. "Archie Moler went by there a few days ago to take him some lumber. He said he's already replaced the old porch. But the guy's got practically no furniture. Boxes of books, but not much else." Shane was already wondering what she could spare from her own collection. She had a few extra chairs… "And," Donna added warmly, "he's wonderful to look at."

"You're a married woman," Shane reminded her, clucking her tongue.

"I still like to look. He's tall." Donna sighed. At five foot eight, she appreciated tall men. "And dark with a sort of lived-in face. You know, creases, lots of bone. And shoulders."

"You always did go for shoulders."

Donna only grinned. "He's a little lean for my taste, but the face makes up for it. He keeps to himself, hardly says a word."

"It's hard being a stranger." She spoke from her own experience. "And being out of work too. What do you think—"

Her question was cut off by the jingle of bells. Glancing over, Shane forgot what she had been about to ask.

He was tall, as Donna had said. In the few seconds they stared at each other, Shane absorbed every aspect of his physical appearance. Lean, yes, but his shoulders were broad, and the arms exposed by the rolled-up shirtsleeves were corded with muscle. His face was tanned, and it narrowed down to a trim, clipped jaw. Thick and straight, his black hair fell carelessly over a high forehead.

His mouth was beautiful. It was full and sharply sculpted, but she knew instinctively it could be cruel. And his eyes, a clear deep blue, were cool. She was certain they could turn to ice. She wouldn't have called it a lived-in face, but a remote one. There was an air of arrogant distance about him. Aloofness seemed to vie with an inner charge of energy.

The spontaneous physical pull was unexpected. In the past, Shane had been attracted to easygoing, good-natured men. This man was neither, she knew, but what she felt was undeniable. For a flash, all that was inside her leaned toward him in a knowledge that was as basic as chemistry and as insubstantial as dreams. Five seconds, it could have been no longer. It didn't need to be.

Shane smiled. He gave her the briefest of acknowledging nods, then walked to the back of the store.

"So, how soon do you think you'll have the place ready to open?" Donna asked Shane brightly with one eye trained toward the rear of the store.

"What?" Shane's mind was still on the man.

"Your place," Donna said meaningfully.

"Oh, three months, I suppose." She glanced blankly around the store as if she had just come in. "There's a lot of work to do."

He came back with a quart of milk and set it on the counter, then reached for his wallet. Donna rang it up, shooting Shane a look from under her lashes before she gave him his change. He left the store without having spoken a word.

"That," Donna announced grandly, "was Vance Banning."

"Yes." Shane exhaled. "So I gathered."

"You see what I mean. Great to look at, but not exactly the friendly sort."

"No." Shane walked toward the door. "I'll see you later, Donna."

"Shane!" With a half laugh, Donna called after her. "You forgot your coffee."

"Hmm? Oh, no thanks," she murmured absently. "I'll have a cup later."

When the door swung shut, Donna stared at it, then at the can of coffee in her hand. "Now what got into her?" she wondered aloud.

As she walked home, Shane felt confused. Though emotional by nature, she could, when necessary, be very analytical. At the moment, she was dealing with the shock of what had happened to her in a few fleeting seconds. It had been much more than a feminine response to an attractive man.

She had felt, inexplicably, as though her whole life had been a waiting period for that quick, silent meeting. Recognition. The word came to her out of nowhere. She had recognized him, not from Donna's description, but from some deep inner knowledge of her own needs. *This was the man.*

Ridiculous, she told herself. Idiotic. She didn't know him, hadn't even heard him speak. No sensible person felt so strongly about a total stranger. More likely, her response had stemmed from the fact that she and Donna had been speaking of him as he had walked in.

Turning off the main road, she began to climb the steep lane that led to her house. He certainly hadn't been friendly, she thought. He hadn't answered her smile or made the slightest attempt at common courtesy. Something in the cool blue eyes had demanded distance. Shane didn't think he was the kind of man she usually liked. Then again, her reaction had been far removed from the calm emotion of liking.

As always when she saw the house, Shane felt a rush of pleasure. This was hers. The woods, thick and touched with the first breath of autumn; the narrow struggling creek; the rocks that worked their way through the ground everywhere—they were all hers.

Shane stood on the wooden bridge over the creek and looked at the house. It did need work. Some of the boards on the porch needed replacing, and the roof was a big problem. Still, it was a lovely little place, nestled comfortably before woods, rolling hills and distant blue mountains. It was more than a century old, fashioned from local stone. In the rain, the colors would burst out of the old rock and gleam like new. Now, in the sunlight, it was comfortably gray.

The architecture was simple—straight lines for durability rather than style. The walkway ran to the porch, where the first step sagged a bit. Shane's problem wouldn't be with the stone but with the wood. She overlooked the rough edges to take in the beauty of the familiar.

The last of the summer flowers were fading. The roses were brown and withered, while the first fall blooms were coming to life. Shane could hear the hiss of water traveling over rocks, the faint whisper of wind through leaves, and the lazy drone of bees.

Her grandmother had guarded her privacy. Shane could turn a full circle without seeing a sign of another house. She had only to walk a quarter mile if she wanted company, or stay at home if she didn't. After four years of crowded classrooms and daily confinement, Shane was ready for solitude.

And with luck, she thought as she continued walking, she could have her shop open and ready for business before Christmas. Antietam Antiques and Museum. Very dignified and to the point, she decided. Once the outside repairs were accomplished, work could start on the interior. The picture was clear in her mind.

The first floor would be structured in two informal sections. The museum would be free, an inducement to lure people into the antique shop. Shane had enough from her family collection to begin stocking the museum, and six rooms of antique furniture to sort and list. She would have to go to a few auctions and estate sales to increase her inventory, but she felt her inheritance and savings would hold her for a while.

The house and land were hers free and clear, with only the yearly taxes to pay. Her car, for what it was worth, was paid for. Every spare penny could go into her projected business. She was going to be successful and independent and the last was more important than the first.

As she walked toward the house, Shane paused and glanced down the overgrown logging trail, which led to the Farley property. She was curious to see what this Vance Banning was doing with the old place. And, she admitted, she wanted to see him again when she was prepared.

After all, they were going to be neighbors, she told herself as she hesitated. The least she could do was to introduce herself and start things off on the right foot. Shane set off into the woods.

She knew the trees intimately. Since childhood she had raced or walked among them. Some had fallen and lay aging and rotting on the ground among layers of old leaves. Overhead, branches arched together to form an intermittent roof pierced by streams of morning sunlight. Confidently she followed the narrow, winding path. She was still yards from the house when she heard the muffled echo of hammering.

Though it disturbed the stillness of the woods, Shane liked the sound. It meant work and progress. Quickening her pace, she headed toward it.

She was still in the cover of the trees when she saw him. He stood on the newly built porch of the old Farley place, hammering the supports for the railing. He'd stripped off his shirt, and his brown skin glistened with a light film of sweat. The dark hair on his chest tapered down, then disappeared into the waistband of worn, snug jeans.

As he lifted the heavy top rail into place, the muscles of his back and shoulders rippled. Totally intent on his work, Vance was unaware of the woman who stood at the edge of the woods and watched. For all his physical exertion, he was relaxed. There was no hardness around his mouth now or frost in his eyes.

When she stepped into the clearing, Vance's head shot up. His eyes instantly filled with annoyance and suspicion. Overlooking it, Shane went to him.

"Hi." Her quick friendly smile had her dimples flashing. "I'm Shane Abbott. I own the house at the other end of the path."

His brow lifted in acknowledgment as he watched her. What the hell does she want? he wondered, and set his hammer on the rail.

Shane smiled again, then took a long, thorough look at the house. "You've got your work cut out for you," she commented amiably, sticking her hands into the back pockets of her jeans. "Such a big place. They say it was beautiful once. I think there used to be a balcony around the second story."

She glanced up. "It's a shame the fire did so much damage to the inside—and then all the years of neglect." She looked at him then with dark, interested eyes. "Are you a carpenter?"

Vance hesitated briefly, then shrugged. It was close to the truth. "Yes."

"That's handy then." Shane accepted the answer, attributing his hesitation to embarrassment at being out of work. "After D.C. you must find the mountains a change." His mobile brow lifted again and Shane grinned. "I'm sorry. It's the curse of small towns. Word gets around quickly, especially when a flatlander moves in."

"Flatlander?" Vance leaned against the post of the railing.

"You're from the city, so that's what you are." She laughed, a quick bubbling sound. "If you stay for twenty years, you'll still be a flatlander, and this will always be the old Farley place."

"It hardly matters what it's called," he said coldly.

The faintest of frowns shadowed her eyes at his response. Looking at the proud, set face, Shane decided he would never accept open charity. "I'm doing some work on my place too," she began. "My grandmother loved clutter. I don't suppose you could use a couple of chairs? I'm going to have to haul them up to the attic unless someone takes them off my hands."

His eyes stayed level on hers with no change of expression. "I have all I need for now."

Because it was the answer she had expected, Shane treated it lightly. "If you change your mind, they'll be gathering dust in the attic. You've got a good piece of land," she commented, gazing over at the section of pasture in the distance. There were several outbuildings, though most were in desperate need of repair. She wondered if he would see to them before winter set in. "Are you going to have livestock?"

Vance frowned, watching her eyes roam over his property. "Why?"

The question was cold and unfriendly. Shane tried to overlook that. "I can remember when I was a kid, before the fire. I used to lie in bed at night in the summer with the windows open. I could hear the Farley cows as clearly as if they were in my grandmother's garden. It was nice."

"I don't have any plans for livestock," he told her shortly, and picked up his hammer again. The gesture of dismissal was crystal clear.

Puzzled, Shane studied him. Not shy, she concluded. Rude. He was plainly and simply rude. "I'm sorry I disturbed your work," she said coolly. "Since you're a flatlander, I'll give you some advice. You should post your property lines if you don't want trespassers."

Indignantly, Shane strode back to the path to disappear among the trees.

Chapter 2

Little twit, Vance thought as he gently tapped the hammer against his palm. He knew he'd been rude, but felt no particular regret. He hadn't bought an isolated plot of land on the outskirts of a dot on the map because he wanted to entertain. Company he could do without, particularly the blond cheerleader type with big brown eyes and dimples.

What the hell had she been after? he wondered as he drew a nail from the pouch on his hip. A cozy chat? A tour of the house? He gave a quick, mirthless laugh. Very neighborly. Vance pounded the nail through the wood in three sure strokes. He didn't want neighbors. What he wanted, what he intended to have, was time to himself. It had been too many years since he had taken that luxury.

Drawing another nail out of the pouch, he moved down the rail. He set it, then hammered it swiftly into place. In particular, he hadn't cared for the one moment of attraction he had felt when he had seen her in the general store. Women, he thought grimly, had an uncanny habit of taking advantage of a weakness like that. He didn't intend for it to happen to him again. He had plenty of scars to remind him what went on behind big, guileless eyes.

So now I'm a carpenter, he mused. With a sardonic grin, Vance turned his hands palms up and examined them. They were hard and calloused. For too many years, he mused, they had been smooth, used to signing contracts or writing checks. Now for a time, he was back where he had started—with wood. Yes, until he was ready to sit behind a desk again, he was a carpenter.

The house, and the very fact that it was falling to pieces, gave him the sense of purpose that had slipped from him over the last couple of years. He understood pressure, success, duty, but the meaning of simple enjoyment had become lost somewhere beneath the rest.

Let the vice-president of Riverton Construction, Inc., run the show for a few months, he mused. He was on vacation. And let the little blonde with her puppy-dog eyes keep on her own land, he added, pounding in another nail. He didn't want any part of the good-neighbor policy.

When he heard leaves rustling underfoot, Vance

turned. Seeing Shane striding back up the path, he muttered a long stream of curses in a low voice. With the exaggerated care of a man greatly aggravated, he set down his hammer.

"Well?" He aimed cold blue eyes and waited.

Shane didn't pause until she had reached the foot of the steps. She was through being intimidated. "I realize you're *extremely* busy," she began, matching his coolness ice for ice, "but I thought you might be interested in knowing there's a nest of copperheads very close to the footpath. On *your* edge of the property," she added.

Vance gave her a narrowed glance, weighing the possibility of her fabricating the snakes to annoy him. She didn't budge under the scrutiny, but paused just long enough to let the silence hang before she turned. She'd gone no more than two more yards when Vance let out an impatient breath and called her back.

"Just a minute. You'll have to show me."

"I don't *have* to do anything," Shane began, but found herself impotently talking to the swinging screen door. Briefly, she wished that she'd never seen the nest, or had simply ignored it and continued down the path to her own home. Then, of course, if he'd been bitten, she would have blamed herself.

Well, you'll do your good deed, she told herself, and that will be that. She kicked a rock with the toe of her shoe and thought how simple it would have been if she'd stayed home that morning.

The screen door shut with a bang. Looking up, Shane watched Vance come down the steps with a well-oiled rifle in his hands. The sleek, elegant weapon suited him. "Let's go," he said shortly, starting off without her. Gritting her teeth, Shane followed.

The light dappled over them once they moved under the cover of trees. The scent of earth and sun-warmed leaves warred with the gun oil. Without a word, Shane skirted around him to take the lead. Pausing, she pointed to a pile of rocks and brown, dried leaves.

"There."

After taking a step closer, Vance spotted the hourglass-shaped crossbands on the snakes. If she hadn't shown him the exact spot, he never would have noticed the nest…unless, of course, he'd stepped right on it. An unpleasant thought, he mused, calculating its proximity to the footpath. Shane said nothing, watching as he found a thick stick and overturned the rocks. Immediately the hissing sounded.

With her eyes trained on the angry snakes, she didn't see Vance heft the rifle to his shoulder. The first shot jolted her. Her heart hammered during the ensuing four, her eyes riveted to the scene.

"That should do it," Vance muttered, lowering the

gun. After switching on the safety, he turned to Shane. She'd turned a light shade of green. "What's the matter?"

"You might have warned me," she said shakily. "I wish I'd looked away."

Vance glanced back to the gruesome mess on the side of the path. That, he told himself grimly, had been incredibly stupid. Silently, he cursed her, then himself, before he took her arm.

"Come back and sit down."

"I'll be all right in a minute." Embarrassed and annoyed, Shane tried to pull away. "I don't want your gracious hospitality."

"I don't want you fainting on my land," he returned, drawing her into the clearing. "You didn't have to stay once you'd shown me the nest."

"Oh, you're very welcome," she managed as she placed a hand on her rolling stomach. "You are the most ill-mannered, unfriendly man I've ever met."

"And I thought I was on my best behavior," he murmured, opening the screen door. After pulling Shane inside, Vance led her through the huge empty room toward the kitchen.

After a glance at the dingy walls and uncovered floor, Shane sent him what passed as a smile. "You must give me the name of your decorator."

She thought he laughed, but could have been mistaken.

The kitchen, in direct contrast to the rest of the house, was bright and clean. The walls had been papered, the counters and cabinets refinished.

"Well, this is nice," she said as he nudged her into a chair. "You do good work."

Without responding, Vance set a kettle on the stove. "I'll fix you some coffee."

"Thank you."

Shane concentrated on the kitchen, determined to forget what she'd just seen. The windows had been re-framed, the wood stained and lacquered to match the grooved trim along the floor and ceiling. He had left the beams exposed and polished the wood to a dull gleam. The original oak floor had been sanded and sealed and waxed. Vance Banning knew how to use wood, Shane decided. The porch was basic mechanics, but the kitchen showed a sense of style and an appreciation for fine detail.

It seemed unfair to her that a man with such talent should be out of work. Shane concluded that he had used his savings to put a down payment on the property. Even if the house had sold cheaply, the land was prime. Re-membering the barrenness of the rest of the first floor, she couldn't prevent her sympathies from being aroused again. Her eyes wandered to his.

"This really is a lovely room," she said, smiling. The

faintest hint of color had seeped back into her cheeks. Vance turned his back to her to take a mug from a hook.

"You'll have to settle for instant," he told her.

Shane sighed. "Mr. Banning… Vance," she decided, and waited for him to turn. "Maybe we got off on the wrong foot. I'm not a nosy, prying neighbor—at least not obnoxiously so. I was curious to see what you were doing to the house and what you were like. I know everyone within three miles of here." With a shrug, she rose. "I didn't mean to bother you."

As she started to brush by him, Vance took her arm. Her skin was still chilled. "Sit down…Shane," he said.

For a moment, she studied his face. It was cool and unyielding, but she sensed some glimmer of suppressed kindness. In response to it, her eyes warmed. "I disguise my coffee with milk and sugar," she warned. "Three spoonsful."

A reluctant smile tugged at his mouth. "That's disgusting."

"Yes, I know. Do you have any?"

"On the counter."

Vance poured the boiling water, and after a moment's hesitation, took down a second mug for himself. Carrying them both, he joined Shane at the drop-leaf table.

"This really is a lovely piece." Before reaching for the milk, she ran her fingers over the table's surface. "Once it's refinished, you'll have a real gem." Shane added three generous spoons of sugar to her mug. Wincing a little, Vance sipped his own black coffee. "Do you know anything about antiques?"

"Not really."

"They're a passion of mine. In fact, I'm planning on opening a shop." Shane brushed absently at the hair that fell over her forehead, then leaned back. "As it turns out, we're both settling in at the same time. I've been living in Baltimore for the last four years, teaching U.S. history."

"You're giving up teaching?" Her hands, Vance noted, were small like the rest of her. The light trail of blue veins under the pale skin made her seem very delicate. Her wrists were narrow, her fingers slender.

"Too many rules and regulations," Shane claimed, gesturing with the hands that had captured his attention.

"You don't like rules and regulations?"

"Only when they're mine." Laughing, she shook her head. "I was a pretty good teacher, really. My problem was discipline." She gave him a rueful grin as she reached for her coffee. "I'm the worst disciplinarian on record."

"And your students took advantage of that?"

Shane rolled her eyes. "Whenever possible."

"But you stuck with it for four years?"

"I had to give it my best shot." Leaning her elbow on the table, Shane rested her chin on her palm. "Like a lot of people who grow up in a small, rural town, I thought the city was my pot of gold. Bright lights, crowds, hustle-bustle. I wanted excitement with a capital *E*. I had four years of it. That was enough." She picked up her coffee again. "Then there are people from the city who think their answer is to move to the country and raise a few goats and can some tomatoes." She laughed into her cup. "The grass is always greener."

"I've heard it said," he murmured, watching her. There were tiny gold flecks in her eyes. How had he missed them before?

"Why did you choose Sharpsburg?"

Vance shrugged negligently. Questions about himself were to be evaded. "I've done some work in Hagerstown. I like the area."

"Living this far back from the main road can be inconvenient, especially in the winter, but I've never minded being snowed in. We lost power once for thirty-two hours. Gran and I kept the woodstove going, taking shifts, and we cooked soup on top of it. The phone lines were down too. We might have been the only two people in the world."

"You enjoyed that?"

"For thirty-two hours," she told him with a friendly grin. "I'm not a hermit. Some people are city people, some are beach people."

"And you're a mountain person."

Shane brought her eyes back to him. "Yes."

The smile she had started to give him never formed. Something in the meeting of their eyes was reminiscent of the moment in the store. It was only an echo, but somehow more disturbing. Shane understood it was bound to happen again and again. She needed time to decide just what she was going to do about it. Rising, she walked to the sink to rinse out her mug.

Intrigued by her reaction, Vance decided to test her. "You're a very attractive woman." He knew how to make his voice softly flattering.

Laughing, Shane turned back to him. "The perfect face for advertising granola bars, right?" Her smile was devilish and appealing. "I'd rather be sexy, but I settled for wholesome." She gave the word a pained emphasis as she came back to the table.

There was no guile in her manner or her expression. What, Vance wondered again, was her angle? Shane was involved in studying the details of the kitchen and didn't see him frown at her.

"I do admire your work." Inspired, she turned back to him. "Hey listen, I've got a lot of remodeling and renovating to do before I can open. I can paint and do some of the minor stuff myself, but there's a lot of carpentry work."

Here it is, Vance reflected coolly. What she wanted

was some free labor. She would pull the helpless-female routine and count on his ego to take over.

"I have my own house to renovate," he reminded her coolly as he stood and turned toward the sink.

"Oh, I know you wouldn't be able to give me a lot of time, but we might be able to work something out." Excited by the idea, she followed him. Her thoughts were already racing ahead. "I wouldn't be able to pay what you could make in the city," she continued. "Maybe five dollars an hour. If you could manage ten or fifteen hours a week..." She chewed on her bottom lip. It seemed a paltry amount to offer, but it was all she could spare at the moment.

Incredulous, Vance turned off the water he had been running, then faced her. "Are you offering me a job?"

Shane flushed a bit, afraid she'd embarrassed him. "Well, only part-time, if you're interested. I know you can make more somewhere else, and if you find something, I wouldn't expect you to keep on, but in the meantime..." She trailed off, not certain how he would react to her knowing he was out of work.

"You're serious?" Vance demanded after a moment.

"Well...yes."

"Why?"

"I need a carpenter. You're a carpenter. There's a lot of work. You might decide you don't want any part of it. But why don't you think about it, drop by tomorrow and take a look?" She turned to leave, but paused for an instant with her hand on the knob. "Thanks for the coffee."

For several minutes, Vance stared at the door she had closed behind her. Abruptly, he burst into deep, appreciative laughter. This, he thought, was one for the books.

Shane rose early the next morning. She had plans and was determined to begin systematically. Organization didn't come naturally to her. It was one more reason why teaching hadn't suited her. If she was to plan a business, however, Shane knew an inventory was a primary factor—what she had, what she could bear to sell, what she should pack away for the museum.

Having decided to start downstairs and work her way up, Shane stood in the center of the living room and took stock of the situation. There was a good Chippendale fireplace seat in mahogany and a gateleg table that needed no refinishing, a ladderback chair that needed new caning in the seat, a pair of Aladdin lamps, and a tufted sofa that would require upholstering. On a Sheridan coffee table was a porcelain pitcher, circa 1830, that held a spray of flowers Shane's grandmother had dried. She touched them once briefly before she picked up her clipboard. There was too much of her childhood there to allow herself the luxury of thinking of any of it. If her grandmother had been alive, she would have told Shane to be certain what she did was right, then do it. Shane was certain she was right.

Systematically, she listed items in two columns: one for items that would need repairs; one for stock she could sell as it was. Everything would have to be priced, which would be a huge job in itself. Already she was spending her evenings poring through catalogs and making notations. There wasn't an antique shop within a radius of thirty miles she hadn't visited. Shane had taken careful account of pricing and procedure. She would incorporate what appealed to her and disregard what didn't. Whatever else her shop would be, she was determined it would be her own.

On one wall of the living room was a catchall shelf that had been built before she'd been born. Moving to it, Shane began a fresh sheet of items she designated for the museum.

An ancestor's Civil War cap and belt buckle, a glass jar filled with spent shells, a dented bugle, a cavalry officer's sabre, a canteen with the initials JDA scratched into the metal—these were only a few pieces of the memorabilia that had been passed down to her. Shane knew there was a trunk in the attic filled with uniforms and old dresses. There was a scrawled journal that had been kept by one of her great-great-uncles during the three years he fought for the South, and letters written to an ancestral aunt by her father, who had served the North. Every item would be listed, dated, then put behind glass.

Shane might have inherited her grandmother's fascination for the relics of history, but not her casualness. It was time the old photos and objects came down from the shelf. But as always when she examined or handled the pieces, Shane became caught up in them.

What had the man been like who had first blown that bugle? It would have been shiny then, and undented. A boy, she thought, with peach fuzz on his face. Had he been frightened? Exhilarated? Fresh off the farm, she imagined, and sure his cause was the right one. Whichever side he had fought for, he had blown the bugle into battle.

With a sigh, she took it down and set it in a packing box. Carefully, Shane wrapped and packed until the shelves were clear, but for the highest one. Standing back, she calculated how she would reach the pieces that sat several feet above her head. Not bothering to move the heavy ladder from across the room, she dragged over a nearby chair. As she stood on the seat, a knock sounded at the back door.

"Yes, come in," she called, stretching one arm up while balancing herself with a hand on one of the lower shelves. She swore and muttered as her reach still fell short. Just as she stood on tiptoe, teetering, someone grabbed her arm. Gasping as she overbalanced, Shane found herself gripped firmly by Vance Banning. "You scared me to death!" she accused.

"Don't you know better than to use a chair like that?" He kept his hands firmly at her waist as he lifted her down. Then, though he'd had every intention of doing so, he didn't release her. There was a smudge of dust on her cheek, and her hair was tousled. Her small, narrow hands rested on his arms while she smiled up at him. Without thinking, Vance lowered his mouth to hers.

Shane didn't struggle, but felt a jolt of surprise. Then she relaxed. Though she hadn't expected the kiss then, she had known the time would come. She let the first stream of pure pleasure run its course.

His mouth was hard on hers, with no gentleness, no trace of what kissing meant to her—a gesture of affection, love or comfort. Yet instinct told her he was capable of tenderness. Lifting a hand to his cheek, Shane sought to soothe the turbulence she sensed. Immediately, he released her. The touch of her hand had been too intimate.

Something told Shane to treat it lightly no matter how her body ached to be held again. Tilting her head, she gave him a mischievous smile. "Good morning."

"Good morning," he said carefully.

"I'm taking inventory," she told him with a sweeping gesture of the room. "I want to list everything before I haul it upstairs for storage. I plan to use this room for the museum and the rest of the first floor for the shop.

Could you get those things off the top shelf for me?" she asked, looking around for her clipboard.

In silence, Vance moved the ladder and complied. The fact that she'd made no mention of the turbulent kiss disconcerted him.

"Most of the work will be gutting the kitchen and putting one in upstairs," Shane went on, giving her lists another glance. She knew Vance was watching her for some sort of reaction. She was just as determined to give him none. "Of course, some walls will have to be taken out, doorways widened. But I don't want to lose the flavor of the house in the remodeling."

"You seem to have it all plotted out." Was she really so cool? he wondered.

"I hope so." Shane pressed the clipboard to her breasts as she looked around the room. "I've applied for all the necessary permits. What a headache. I don't have any natural business sense, so I'll have to work twice as hard learning. It's a big chance." Then her voice changed, became firm and determined. "I'm going to make it work."

"When do you plan to open?"

"I'm shooting for the first part of December, but..." Shane shrugged. "It depends on how the work goes and how soon I can beef up my inventory. I'll show you the rest of the place. Then you can decide if you want to take it on."

Without waiting for his consent, Shane walked to the

rear of the house. "The kitchen's a fairly good size, particularly if you include the pantry." Opening a door, she revealed a large shelved closet. "Taking out the counters and appliances should give me plenty of room. Then if this doorway is widened," she continued as she pushed open a swinging door, "and left as an archway, it would give more space in the main showroom."

They entered the dining room with its long diamond-paned windows. She moved quickly, he noted, and knew precisely what she wanted.

"The fireplace hasn't been used in years. I don't know whether it still works." Walking over, Shane ran a finger down the surface of the dining table. "This was my grandmother's prize. It was brought over from England more than a hundred years ago." The cherrywood stroked by sunlight, gleamed under her fingers. "The chairs are from the original set. Hepplewhite." Shane caressed the heart-shaped back of one of the remaining six chairs. "I hate to sell this, she loved it so, but..." Her voice was wistful as she unnecessarily straightened a chair. "I won't have anywhere to keep it, and I can't afford the luxury of storing it for myself." Shane turned away. "The china cabinet is from the same period," she continued.

"You could keep this and leave the house as it is if you took a job in the local high school," Vance interrupted.

There was something valiant and touching in the way she kept her shoulders straight while her voice trembled.

"No." Shane shook her head, then turned back to him. "I haven't the character for it. It wouldn't take long before I'd be cutting classes just like my students. They deserve a better example than that. I love history." Her face brightened again. "*This* kind of history," she said as she walked back to the table. "Who first sat in this chair? What did she talk about over dinner? What kind of dress did she wear? Did they discuss politics and the upstart colonies? Maybe one of them knew Ben Franklin and was a secret sympathizer of the Revolution." She broke off laughing. "That's not the sort of thing you're supposed to teach in second-period eleventh-grade history."

"It sounds more interesting than reciting names and dates."

"Maybe. Anyway, I'm not going back to that." Pausing, Shane watched Vance steadily. "Did you ever find yourself caught up in something you were good at, something you'd been certain was the right thing for you, then woke up one morning with the feeling you were locked in a cage?"

The words hit home, and he nodded affirmatively.

"Then you know why I have to choose between something I love and my sanity." She touched the table again. After a deep breath, Shane took a circle around the room. "I don't want to change the architecture of this room except for the doorways. My great-grandfather built the chair rail." She watched Vance walk over to examine it. "He was a mason by trade," she told him, "but he must have been handy with wood as well."

"It's a beautiful job," Vance agreed, admiring the workmanship and detail. "I'd have a hard time duplicating this quality with modern tools. You wouldn't want to touch this, or any of the woodwork in this room."

In spite of himself he was becoming interested in the project. It would be a challenge—a different sort than the house he had chosen to test himself on. Sensing his change of attitude, Shane pressed her advantage.

"There's a small summer parlor through there." Indicating another door, she took Vance's arm to draw him with her. "It adjoins the living room, so I plan to make it the entrance to the shop, with the dining room as the main showroom."

The parlor was no more than twelve by twelve with faded wallpaper and a scarred wooden floor. Still, Vance recognized a few good pieces of Duncan Phyfe and a Morris chair. On the brief tour, he had seen no furniture less than a hundred years old, and unless they were excellent copies, a few pieces of Wedgwood. The furniture's worth a small fortune, he mused, and the back door's coming off the hinges.

"There's a lot of work here," Shane commented, moving over to open a window and dispel the faint mustiness.

"This room's taken a beating over the years. I suppose you'd have a better idea than I would exactly what it needs to whip it into shape."

She watched his frowning survey of chipped floorboards and cracked trim. It was obvious to her that his professional eye missed little. It was also obvious the state of disrepair annoyed him. And, she thought, faintly amused, he hadn't seen anything yet.

"Maybe I shouldn't press my luck and take you upstairs just yet," she commented.

A quizzical brow shot up as he turned to her. "Why?"

"Because the second floor needs twice the attention this does, and I really want you to take the job."

"You sure as hell need somebody to do it," he muttered. His own place needed a major overhaul. Heavy physical work and a lot of time. This, on the other hand, needed a shrewd craftsman who could work with what was already there. Again, he felt the pull of the challenge.

"Vance..." After a moment's hesitation, Shane decided to take a chance. "I could make it six dollars an hour, throw in your lunches and all the coffee you can drink. The people who come in here will see the quality of your work. It could lead to bigger jobs."

He surprised her by grinning. Her heart leaped into

her throat. More than the tempestuous kiss, the quick boyish grin drew her to him.

"All right, Shane," Vance agreed on impulse. "You've got a deal."

Chapter 3

Pleased with herself and Vance's abrupt good humor, Shane decided to show him the second floor. Taking his hand, she led him up the straight, steep stairway. Though she had no notion of what had prompted the amused gleam or sudden grin, Shane wanted to keep him with her while his mood lasted.

Against his work-hardened hand, her palm was baby soft. It made Vance wonder how the rest of her would feel—the slope of her shoulder, the length of her thigh, the underside of her breast. She wasn't his type, he reminded himself, and glanced at the hairline crack in the wall to his left.

"There are three bedrooms," Shane told him as they came to the top landing. "I want to keep my own room, and turn the master into a sitting room and the third into my kitchen. I can handle the painting and papering after the initial work is done." With her hand on the knob of the master bedroom door, she turned to him. "Do you know anything about drywall?"

"A bit." Without thinking, Vance lifted a finger and ran it down her nose. Their eyes met in mutual surprise. "You've dust on your face," he mumbled.

"Oh." Laughing, Shane brushed at it herself.

"Here." Vance traced the rough skin of his thumb down her cheekbone. Her skin felt as it looked: soft, creamy. It would taste the same, he mused, allowing his thumb to linger. "And here," he said, caught up in his own imagination. Lightly he ran a fingertip along her jawline. He felt her slight tremor as his gaze swept over her lips.

Her eyes were wide and fixed unblinkingly on his. Abruptly, Vance dropped his hand, shattering the mood but not the tension. Clearing her throat, Shane pushed open the door.

"This—umm…" Frantically, Shane gathered her scattered thoughts. "This is the master," she continued, combing nervous fingers through her hair. "I know the floor's in bad shape, and I'd like to skin whoever painted that oak trim." She let out a long breath as her pulse began to level. "I'm going to see if it can be refinished." Idly, she touched a section of peeling wallpaper. "My grandmother didn't like changes. This room hasn't altered one bit in thirty years. That's when her husband died," she added softly. "The windows stick, the roof leaks, the fireplace smokes. Basically, the house, except for the dining room, is in a general state of disrepair. She never had the inclination to do more than a patch job here and there."

"When did she die?"

"Three months ago." Shane lifted a corner of the patchwork coverlet, then let it fall. "She just didn't wake up one morning. I was committed to teaching a summer course and couldn't move back permanently until last week."

Clearly, he heard the sting of guilt in her words. "Could you have changed anything if you had?" he asked.

"No." Shane wandered to a window. "But she wouldn't have died alone."

Vance opened his mouth, then closed it again. It wasn't wise to offer personal advice to strangers. Framed against the window, she looked very small and defenseless.

"What about the walls in here?" he asked.

"What?" Years and miles away, Shane turned back to him.

"The walls," he repeated. "Do you want any of them taken down?"

For a moment, she stared blankly at the faded roses on the wallpaper. "No... No," she repeated more firmly. "I'd thought to take out the door and enlarge the entrance." Vance nodded, noting she had won what must be a continuing battle with her emotions. "If the woodwork cleans off well," she continued, "the entrance could be framed in oak to match."

Vance walked over to examine it. "Is this a bearing wall?"

Shane made a face at him. "I haven't the slightest idea. How do—" She broke off, hearing a knock at the front door. "Damn. Well, can you look around up here for a few minutes? You'll probably get the lay of things just as well without me." With this, Shane was dashing down the steps. Shrugging, Vance took a rule out of his back pocket and began to take measurements.

Shane's instinctively friendly smile faded instantly when she opened the door.

"Shane."

"Cy."

His expression became faintly censorious. "Aren't you going to ask me in?"

"Of course." With a restraint unnatural to her, Shane stepped back. Very carefully, she shut the door behind him, but moved no farther into the room. "How are you, Cy?"

"Fine, just fine."

Of course he was, Shane thought, annoyed. Cy Trainer Jr., was always fine—permanent-pressed and groomed. And prosperous now, she added, giving his smart-but-discreet suit a glance.

"And you, Shane?"

"Fine, just fine," she said, knowing the sarcasm was both petty and wasted. He'd never notice.

"I'm sorry I didn't get by last week. Things have been hectic."

"Business is good?" she asked without any intonation of interest. He failed to notice that too.

"Money's loosening up." He straightened his tie unnecessarily. "People are buying houses. Country property's always a good investment." He gave her a quick nod. "The real estate business is solid."

Money was still first, Shane noticed with irony. "And your father?"

"Doing well. Semiretired now, you know."

"No," she said mildly. "I didn't." If Cy Trainer Sr. relinquished the reins to Trainer Real Estate six months after he was dead, it would have surprised Shane. The old man would always run the show, no matter what his son liked to think.

"He likes to keep busy," Cy told her. "He'd love to see you though. You'll have to drop by the office." Shane said nothing to that. "So…" Cy paused as he was wont to do before a big statement. "You're settling in."

Shane lifted a brow as she watched him glance around at her packing cases. "Slowly," she agreed. Though she knew it was deliberately rude, she didn't ask him to sit. They remained standing, just inside the door.

"You know, Shane, this house isn't in the best of shape, but it is a prime location." He gave her a light, condescending smile that set her teeth on edge. "I'm sure I could get you a good price for it."

"I'm not interested in selling, Cy. Is that why you came by? To do an appraisal?"

He looked suitably shocked. "Shane!"

"Was there something else?" she asked evenly.

"I just dropped by to see how you were." The distress in both his voice and eyes had an apology forming on her lips. "I heard some crazy story about your trying to start an antique shop."

The apology slipped away. "It's not a story, crazy or otherwise, Cy. I am going to start one."

He sighed and gave her what she termed his paternal look. She gritted her teeth. "Shane, have you any idea how difficult, how risky it is to start a business in to-day's economy?"

"I'm sure you'll tell me," she muttered.

"My dear," he said in calm tones, making her blood pressure rise alarmingly. "You're a certified teacher with four years' experience. It's just nonsense to toss away a good career for a fanciful little fling."

"I've always been good at nonsense, haven't I, Cy?" Her eyes chilled. "You never hesitated to point it out to me even when we were supposed to be madly in love."

"Now, Shane, it was because I cared that I tried to curb your...impulses."

"Curb my impulses!" More astonished than angry, Shane ran her fingers through her hair. Later, she told herself, later she would be able to laugh. Now she wanted to scream. "You haven't changed. You haven't changed a whit. I bet you still roll your socks into those neat little balls and carry an extra handkerchief."

He stiffened a bit. "If you'd ever learned the value of practicality—" he began.

"You wouldn't have dumped me two months before the wedding?" she finished furiously.

"Really, Shane, you can hardly call it that. You know I was only thinking of what was best for you."

"Best for me," she muttered between clenched teeth. "Well, let me tell you something." She poked a dusty finger at his muted striped tie. "You can stuff your practicality, Cy, right along with your balanced checkbook and shoe trees. I might have thought you hurt me at the time, but you did me a big favor. I *hate* practicality and rooms that smell like pine and toothpaste tubes that are rolled up from the bottom."

"I hardly see what that has to do with this discussion."

"It has *everything* to do with this discussion," she

flared back. "You don't see anything unless it's listed in neat columns and balanced. And I'll tell you something else," she continued when he would have spoken. "I'm going to have my shop, and even if it doesn't make me a fortune, it's going to be fun."

"Fun?" Cy shook his head hopelessly. "That's a poor basis for starting a business."

"It's mine," she retorted. "I don't need a six-digit income to be happy."

He gave her a small, deprecating smile. "You haven't changed."

Flinging open the door, Shane glared at him. "Go sell a house," she suggested. With a dignity she envied and despised, Cy walked through the door. She slammed it after him, then gave in to temper and slammed her hand against the wall.

"Damn!" Putting her wounded knuckles to her mouth, she whirled. It was then she spotted Vance at the foot of the stairs. His face was still and serious as their eyes met. With angry embarrassment, Shane's cheeks flamed. "Enjoy the show?" she demanded, then stormed back to the kitchen.

She gave vent to her frustration by banging through the cupboards. She didn't hear Vance follow her. When he touched her shoulder, she spun around, ready to rage.

"Let me see your hand," he said quietly. Ignoring her jerk of protest, he took it in both of his.

"It's nothing."

Gently, he flexed it, then pressed down on her knuckles with his fingers. Involuntarily, she caught her breath at the quick pain. "You didn't manage to break it," he murmured, "but you'll have a bruise." He was forced to control a sudden rage that she had damaged that small, soft hand.

"Just don't say anything," she ordered through gritted teeth. "I'm not stupid. I *know* when I've made a fool of myself."

He took a moment to bend and straighten her fingers again. "I apologize," he said. "I should have let you know I was there."

After letting out a deep breath, Shane drew her hand from his slackened hold. The light throbbing gave her a perverse pleasure. "It doesn't matter," she muttered as she turned to make tea.

He frowned at her averted face. "I don't enjoy embarrassing you."

"If you live here for any amount of time, you'll hear about Cy and me anyway." She tried to make a casual shrug, but the quick jerkiness of the movement showed only more agitation. "This way you just got the picture quicker."

But he didn't have the full picture. Vance realized, with some discomfort, that he wanted to know. Before he could speak, Shane slammed the lid onto the kettle.

"He always makes me feel like a fool!"

"Why?"

"He always dots his *i*'s and crosses his *t*'s." With an angry tug, she pulled open a cabinet. "He carries an umbrella in the trunk of his car," she said wrathfully.

"That should do it," Vance murmured, watching her quick, jerky movements.

"He never, never, *never* makes a mistake. He's always reasonable," she added witheringly as she slammed two cups down on the counter. "Did he shout at me just now?" she demanded as she whirled on Vance. "Did he swear or lose his temper? He doesn't *have* a temper!" she shouted in frustration. "I swear, the man doesn't even sweat."

"Did you love him?"

For a moment, Shane merely stared; then she let out a small broken sigh. "Yes. Yes, I really did. I was sixteen when we started dating." As she went to the refrigerator, Vance turned the gas on under the kettle, which she had forgotten to do. "He was so perfect, so smart and, oh… so articulate." Pulling out the milk, Shane smiled a little. "Cy's a born salesman. He can talk about anything."

Vance felt a quick, unreasonable dislike for him. As Shane set a large ceramic sugar bowl on the table, sunlight shot into her hair. The curls and waves of her hair shimmered briefly in the brilliance before she moved away. With an odd tingling at the base of his spine, Vance found himself staring after her.

"I was crazy about him," Shane continued, and Vance had to shake himself mentally to concentrate on her words. The subtle movements of her body beneath the snug T-shirt had begun to distract him. "When I turned eighteen, he asked me to marry him. We were both going to college, and Cy thought a year's engagement was proper. He's very proper," she added ruefully.

Or a cold-blooded fool, Vance thought, glancing at the faint outline of her nipples against the thin cotton. Annoyed, he brought his eyes back to her face. But the warmth in his own blood remained.

"I wanted to get married right away, but he told me, as always, that I was too impulsive. Marriage was a big step. Things had to be planned out. When I suggested we live together for a while, he was shocked." Shane set the milk on the table with a little bang. "I was young and in love, and I wanted him. He felt it his duty to control my more…primitive urges."

"He's a damn fool," Vance muttered under the hissing of the kettle.

"Through that last year, he molded me, and I tried to be what he wanted: dignified, sensible. I was a complete failure." Shane shook her head at the memory of that long, frustrating year. "If I wanted to go out for pizza with a bunch of other students, he'd remind me we had to watch our pennies. He already had his eye on this little house outside of Boonsboro. His father said it was a good investment."

"And you hated it," Vance commented.

Surprised, Shane looked back at him. "I despised it. It was the perfect little rancher with white aluminum siding and a hedge. When I told Cy I'd smother there, he laughed and patted my head."

"Why didn't you tell him to get lost?" he demanded.

Shane shot him a brief look. "Haven't you ever been in love?" she murmured. It was her answer, not a question, and Vance remained silent. "We were constantly at odds that year," she went on. "I kept thinking it was just the jitters of a long engagement, but more and more, the basic personality conflicts came up. He'd always say I'd feel differently once we were settled. Usually, I'd believe him."

"He sounds like a boring jackass."

Though the icy contempt in Vance's voice surprised her, Shane smiled. "Maybe, but he could be gentle and sweet." When Vance gave a derisive snort, she only shrugged. "I'd forget how rigid he was. Then he'd get more critical. I'd get angry, but I could never win a fight because he never lost control. The final break came over the plans for the honeymoon. I wanted to go to Fiji."

"Fiji?" Vance repeated.

"Yes," she said defiantly. "It's different, exotic, romantic. I was barely nineteen." On a fresh wave of fury, Shane slammed down her spoon. "He had plans for this—this plastic little resort hotel in Pennsylvania. The kind of place where they plan your activities, have contests and an indoor pool. Shuffleboard." She rolled her eyes before she gulped down tea. "It was a package deal—three days, two nights, meals included. He'd inherited a substantial sum from his mother, and I had some savings, but he didn't want to waste money. He'd already outlined a retirement plan. I couldn't stand it!"

Vance sipped his own tea where he stood and studied her. "So you called off the wedding." He wondered if she would take the opportunity he was giving her to claim the break had been her idea.

"No." Shane pushed her cup aside. "We had a terrible fight, and I stormed off to spend the rest of the evening with friends at this little club near the college. I had told Cy I wouldn't spend my first night as a married woman watching a tacky floor show or playing bingo."

Vance's lips twitched but he managed to control his grin. "That sounds remarkably sensible," he murmured.

On a weak laugh, Shane shook her head. "After I'd calmed down, I decided where we went wasn't important, but that we'd finally be together. I told myself Cy was right. I was immature and irresponsible. We needed to save money. I still had two more years of college and he was just starting in his father's firm. I was being frivolous. That was one of his favorite adjectives for me."

Shane frowned down at her cup but didn't drink. "I went by his house ready to apologize. That's when he very reasonably, very calmly jilted me."

There was a long moment of silence before Vance came to the table to join her. "I thought you told me he never made mistakes."

Shane stared at him a moment, then laughed. It was a quick, pure sound of appreciation. "I needed that." Impulsively, she leaned her head against his shoulder. The anger had vanished in the telling, the self-pity with the laugh.

The tenderness that invaded him made Vance cautious. Still, he didn't resist the urge to stroke his hand down her disordered cap of hair. The texture of her hair was thick and unruly. And incredibly soft. He wasn't even aware that he twisted a curl around his finger.

"Do you still love him?" he heard himself ask.

"No," Shane answered before he could retract the question. "But he still makes me feel like an irresponsible romantic."

"Are you?"

She shrugged. "Most of the time."

"What you said to him out there was right, you know." Forgetting caution in simple wanting, he drew her closer.

"I said a lot of things."

"That he'd done you a favor," Vance murmured as his fingers roamed to the back of her neck. Shane sighed, but he couldn't tell if the sound came from pleasure or agreement. "You'd have gone crazy rolling up his socks in those little balls."

Shane was laughing as she tilted her head back to look at his face. She kissed him lightly in gratitude, then again for herself.

Her mouth was small and very tempting. Wanting his fill, Vance cupped his hand firmly on the back of her neck to keep her there. There was nothing shy or hesitant in her response to the increased pressure. She parted her lips and invited.

On a tiny moan of pleasure, her tongue met his. Suddenly hot, suddenly urgent, his mouth moved over hers. He needed her sweetness, her uncomplicated generosity. He wanted to saturate himself with the fresh, clean passion she offered so willingly. When his mouth crushed down harder, she only yielded; when his teeth nipped painfully at her lip, she only drew him closer.

"Vance," she murmured, leaning toward him.

He rose quickly, leaving her blinking in surprise. "I've got work to do," he said shortly. "I'll make a list of the materials I'll need to start. I'll be in touch." He was out the back door before Shane could form any response.

For several moments, she stared at the screen door. What had she done to cause that anger in his eyes? How was it possible that he could passionately kiss her one second and turn his back on her the next? Miserably, she looked down at her clenched hands. She had always made too much of things, she reminded herself. A romantic? Yes, and a dreamer, her grandmother had called her. For too long she'd been waiting for the right man to come into her life, to complete it. She wanted to be cherished, respected, adored.

Perhaps, she mused, she was looking for the impossible—to keep her independence and to share her dreams, to stand on her own and have a strong hand to hold. Over and over she had warned herself to stop looking for that one perfect love. But her spirit defied her mind.

From the first instant, she had sensed something different about Vance. For the flash of a second when their eyes had first held, her heart had opened and shouted, *Here he is!* But that was nonsense, Shane reminded herself. Love meant understanding, knowledge. She neither knew nor understood Vance Banning.

With a jolt, she realized she might have offended him. She was going to be his employer, and the way she had kissed him…he might think she wanted more than carpentry for her money. He might think she intended to seduce him while dangling a few much-needed dollars under his nose.

Abruptly, she burst into laughter. As her mirth grew, she threw back her head and pounded both fists on the table. Shane Abbott, seductress. Oh Lord! she thought, wiping tears of hilarity from her eyes. That was rich. After all, what red-blooded man could withstand a woman with dirt on her face who tries to punch holes in walls?

She sighed with the effort of laughing. Her imagination, she decided, needed a rest. Shane went back to her inventory.

Chapter 4

Vance couldn't sleep. He had worked until late in the evening, sweating off anger and frustrated desire. The anger didn't worry him. He knew that emotion too well to lose sleep over it. Neither was he a stranger to desire, but having to acknowledge he felt it for a snippy little history buff infuriated him…and made him restless.

He should never have agreed to take the job, he told himself yet again. What devil had provoked him into doing it? Annoyed with himself, Vance wandered outside to stand on the porch.

The air had cooled considerably with nightfall. Overhead, the stars were spread in a wide, brilliant pattern around a white half-moon. Venus was as clear as he'd ever seen it. An army of crickets sent out their high,

monotonous signal while fireflies danced, tiny yellow
lights, over the fallow field to his right. When he looked
straight ahead, he could see to the edge of the trees but
no farther. The woods were dark, mysterious, secret.
Shane slept on the other side in a room with faded wallpaper and a Jenny Lind bed.

He imagined her cuddled under the wedding-ring quilt
he'd seen on the bed. Her window would be open to let
in the sounds and scents of night. Did she sleep in one
of those fussy cotton nightgowns that would cover her
from neck to feet, he wondered, or would she slip under
the quilt in solitary nakedness?

Furious with the direction of his thoughts, Vance
cursed himself. No, he should never have taken the damn
job. It had appealed to his ego and his humor. Six dollars an hour. He laughed shortly, startling an owl in a
nearby tree. Leaning on a post, he continued to stare into
the woods, seeing nothing but silhouettes and shadows.

When was the last time he'd worked for an hourly
wage? To answer his own question, Vance looked
back, trying to remember. Fifteen years? Good God,
he thought with a shake of his head. Had so much time
passed?

He'd been a teenager starting out at the bottom of his
mother's highly successful construction firm. "Learn
the ropes," she had told him, and he'd eagerly agreed.
Vance had wanted nothing more than to work with his

hands, and with wood. He'd had his share of youthful confidence—and youthful arrogance. Administration was for old men in business suits who wouldn't know how to miter a corner. He'd wanted no part of their stuffy business meetings or complicated contract negotiations. Shuffle papers? No, he was too clever to fall into that trap.

How long had it taken before he had been pulled in—chained behind a desk? Five years? he thought. Six? With a shrug, he decided it didn't matter. He'd gone beyond the time when a year made much difference.

Sighing, Vance walked the length of the porch. Under his hand, the rail he had built himself was rough and sturdy. What choice had there been? he asked himself. There had been his mother's sudden stroke and long painful recovery. She had begged him to take over as president of Riverton. As a widow with only one child, she had been desperate not to see her business run by strangers. It had mattered to her, perhaps too much, that the firm she had inherited, had struggled to keep during the lean years, stay in the family. Vance knew that she had fought prejudices, taken chances and worked nearly half her life to turn a mediocre firm into an exemplary one. Then she had been all but helpless, and asking him.

If he had been a failure at it, he could have delegated the responsibilities and stayed a figurehead without a qualm. He could have picked up his tools again. But he hadn't been a failure—there was too much of his mother in him.

Riverton Construction had thrived and expanded under his leadership. It had grown beyond the prestigious Washington concern into a national conglomerate. It was his own misfortune that he had the same knack with administration that he had with a hammer. He had bolted the lock on his own cage.

Then there had been Amelia. Vance's mouth tightened into a cynical smile. Soft, sexy Amelia, he mused, with hair like a sunset and a quiet Virginia drawl. She had kept him yapping at her heels for months, drawing him in, holding him off, until he had been mad to have her. Mad, Vance thought again. A very apt word. If he had been sane, he would have seen through that beautiful, cultured mask to the calculating scrambler she had been—before he had put the ring on her finger.

Not for the first time, he wondered how many men had envied him his lovely, dignified wife. But they hadn't seen the face unmasked—the perfect face with a rotted shell beneath. Cold. In all of his experience, Vance had known no one as cold as Amelia Ryce Banning.

The owl in the oak to his left set up a steady hooting: two short calls then a long—two short, then a long. Vance listened to the monotonous sound as he thought over the years of his marriage.

Amelia had spent his money lavishly those first

months—clothes, furs, cars. That had mattered little to him as he had felt her unearthly beauty demanded the finest. And he had loved her—or the woman he had thought she'd been. He had thought she was a woman made for diamonds, for soft, exotic furs and silks. It had pleased him to surround her with them, to see her sulky beauty glow. For the most part, he had ignored the excessive bills, paying them without a murmur. Once or twice he had commented on her extravagance and had received her sweet distress and apologies. He'd hardly noticed that the bills had continued to flow in.

Then he had discovered she was draining his bank account to feed her brother's teetering construction firm in Richmond. Amelia had been tearful and helpless when confronted with it. She had pleaded prettily for her brother. She had claimed she couldn't bear to have him almost facing bankruptcy while she lived so well.

Because he'd believed her familial concern, Vance had agreed to a personal loan, but he'd refused to siphon money from Riverton into an unstable and mishandled company. Amelia had been far from satisfied, had pouted and cajoled. Then when he'd remained adamant, she had attacked him like a crazed tigress, raking his face with her well-manicured nails, spewing out obscenities through her tinted cupid's-bow mouth. Her anger had driven her to strike out and tell him why she had married him—for his money and position, and what both could do for her and her own family business. Then Vance had looked beneath the beauty and the careful charm to see what she was. It had been only the first of many shocks and disillusionments.

Her warm passion had become frigidity; her adoring smiles had become sneers. She had refused to consider having children. It would have spoiled her figure and restricted her freedom. For more than two years Vance had struggled to save his failing marriage, to salvage something of the life he had planned to have with Amelia. But he had come to know that the woman he thought he had married was an illusion.

Ultimately, he'd demanded a divorce and Amelia had laughed and agreed. She would happily give him his freedom for half of everything he owned—including his share of Riverton. She had promised him an ugly court battle and plenty of publicity. After pointing out that she would be the injured party, Amelia had vowed to play her part of the cast-off wife to the hilt.

Trapped, Vance had lived with her for another year, keeping up the pretense of marriage in public, avoiding her privately. When he had discovered Amelia was taking lovers, he'd seen the first ray of hope.

He had felt no pain on being betrayed, for there had been no emotion in him for her. Slowly, discreetly, Vance had begun to compile the evidence that would give him his freedom. He was willing to face the humiliation and publicity of a messy court battle to free himself and his company. Then there had been no more need. One of Amelia's discarded lovers put a bullet through her heart and ended it.

It had been due to Vance's wealth and influence that the publicity hadn't been worse than it had been. Still, the whispers and speculation had been ugly enough. Yet there had been a staggering relief in him rather than grief. The guilt this had brought had caused him to bury himself even more in his work. There were condominiums to be built in Florida, a large medical complex in Minnesota, an addition to a university in Texas. But there had been no peace for him.

Determined to find Vance Banning again, he'd bought the dilapidated house in the mountains and had taken an extended leave of absence. Time, solitude and the work he loved had been his prescription. Then, just when he had thought he had found the answer, he had met Shane Abbott.

She was no smoldering hothouse beauty as Amelia had been, no poised sophisticate as were the women he had taken to his bed over the last two years. She was fresh and vital. Instinctively, he was attracted to her good-natured generosity. But his wife's legacy to him had been cynicism and distrust. Vance knew that only a fool fell for the innocent act twice. And he was no fool.

He had taken the job with Shane on impulse, and now

he would see it through. It would be a challenge to learn if he was still capable of the fine precision work she required. And he knew how to be cautious with a woman now. It was true her fresh looks and artless charm had appealed to him. He admired her way of dealing with her former fiancé. She'd been hurt, yet she had held her own and booted Cy out the door.

It might be interesting, he decided, to spend his vacation remodeling Shane's house and learning what she hid under her mask. Everyone wore masks, he thought grimly. Life was one long masquerade. It wouldn't take long to discover what went on behind her big brown eyes and bubbling laugh.

With a sound of disgust, Vance hurled himself back into the house. He wasn't going to lose any sleep over a woman. Nevertheless, he tossed and turned much of the night.

It was a perfect morning. In the west, the mountains rose into a paintbrush blue sky. Birds chattered in noisy jubilation as Shane tossed open the windows. The air that rushed in was warm, laced with the scent of zinnias. It was all but impossible for one of her nature to remain inside on such a day, cooped up with dust and a clipboard. But there were ways, Shane decided as she leaned on the windowsill, of doing her duty *and* having fun.

After dressing in an old T-shirt and faded red shorts,

she rummaged through the basement storage closet and unearthed a can of white paint and a roller. The front porch, she knew, needed more repair than her meager talents could provide, but the back was still sturdy enough. All it required was a coat or two of paint to make it bright and cheerful again.

Picking up a portable radio on her way, Shane headed outside. She fiddled with the tuner until she found a station that matched her mood; then, after turning the volume up, she went to work.

In thirty minutes, the porch was swept clean and hosed down. In the bright sun, it dried quickly while Shane pried the lid off the paint can. She stirred it, enjoying the day and the prospect of work. Once or twice, she glanced toward the old logging path, wondering when Vance would "keep in touch." She would have liked to have seen him coming down the path toward her. He had a long, loose-limbed stride she admired, and a way of looking as though he were in complete command of himself and anything that might get in his way. Shane liked that—the confidence, the hint of controlled power.

She had always admired people of strength. Her grandmother, through all her hardships and disappointments, had remained a strong woman right to the end. Shane would have admitted, for all their disagreements, that Cy was a strong man. What he lacked, in her opinion, was the underlying kindness that balanced strength and kept it from being hard. She sensed there was kindness in Vance, though he was far from easy with it. But the fact that the trait existed at all made the difference for Shane.

Turning away from the path, she took her bucket, roller and pan to the end of the porch. She poured, knelt, then took a deep breath and began to paint.

When Vance came to the end of the path, he stopped to watch her. She had nearly a third of the porch done. Her arms were splattered with tiny specks of white. The radio blared, and she sang exuberantly along with it. Her hips kept the beat. As she moved, the thin, faded material of her shorts strained over her bottom. That she was having a marvelous time with the homey chore was as obvious as her lack of skill. A smile tugged at his mouth when Shane leaned over for the bucket and rested her palm on the wet paint. Cheerfully, she swore, then wiped her hand haphazardly on the back of her shorts.

"I thought you said you could paint," Vance commented.

Shane started, nearly upsetting the contents of the bucket as she turned. Still on all fours, she smiled at him. "I said I could paint. I didn't say I was neat." Lifting her hand, she shielded her eyes against the sun and watched him walk to her. "Did you come to supervise?"

He looked down at her and shook his head. "No, I think it's already too late for that."

Shane lifted a brow. "It's going to be just fine when I've finished."

Vance made a noncommittal sound. "I've got a list of materials for you, but I need to make a few more measurements."

"That was quick." Shane sat back on her haunches. Vance shrugged, not wanting to admit he'd written it out in the middle of the night when sleep had eluded him. "There was something else," she continued, stretching her back muscles. Leaning over, she turned down the volume on the radio so that it was only a soft murmur. "The front porch."

Vance glanced down at her handiwork. "Have you painted that too?"

Correctly reading his impression of her talents, Shane made a face. "No, I didn't paint that too."

"That's a blessing. What stopped you?"

"It's falling apart. Maybe you can suggest what I should do about it. Oh, look!" Shane grabbed his hand, forgetting the paint as she spotted a family of quail bobbing single file across the path behind them. "They're the first I've seen since I've been home." Captivated, she watched them until they were out of sight. "There's deer too. I've seen the signs, but I haven't been able to catch sight of any yet." She gave a contented sigh as the quail rustled in the woods. All at once, she remembered the condition of her hand.

"Oh, Vance, I'm sorry!" Releasing him, she jumped to her feet. "Did I get any on you?"

For an answer, he turned his palm up, studying the white smear ironically.

"I really am sorry," she managed, choking on a giggle. He shot her a look as she struggled to swallow the irrepressible laughter. "No, really I am. Here." Taking the hem of her T-shirt, Shane lifted it to rub unsuccessfully at his palm. Her stab at assistance exposed the pale, smooth skin of her midriff.

"You're rubbing it in," Vance said mildly, trying not to be affected by the flash of skin or the glimpse of her narrow waist.

"It'll come off," she assured him while she fought a desperate battle with laughter. "I must have some turpentine or something." Though Shane pressed the back of her hand against her mouth, the giggle escaped. "I *am* sorry," she claimed, then dropped her forehead on his chest. "And I wouldn't laugh if you'd stop looking at me that way."

"What way?"

"Patiently."

"Does patience usually send you into uncontrollable laughter?" he asked. Her hair carried the scent of her shampoo, a faint tang of lemon. It was odd that he would think just then of the honey-sweetness of her mouth.

"Too many things do," she admitted in a strangled

voice. "It's a curse." She drew a deep breath, but left her hand on his chest as she tried to compose herself. "One of my students drew a deadly caricature of his biology teacher. When I saw it, I had to leave the room for fifteen minutes before I could pretend I disapproved."

Vance drew her away, unnerved by his unwanted, unreasonable response to her. "Didn't you?"

"Disapprove?" Grinning, Shane shook her head. "I wanted to, but it was so good. I took it home and framed it."

Suddenly, she became aware that he was holding her arms, that his thumbs were caressing her bare skin while his eyes watched her in the deep, guarded way he had. Looking at him, Shane was certain he was unaware of the gentle, intimate gesture. There was nothing gentle in his eyes. If she had followed her first instinct, she would have risen to her toes and kissed him. It was what she wanted—what she sensed he wanted as well. Something warned her against making the move. Instead, she stood still. Her eyes met his calmly, with no secrets to be seen in them. All of the secrets were his, and at that moment, they both knew it.

Vance would have been more comfortable with secrets than candor. When he realized that he was holding her, that he wanted to go on holding her, he released her.

"You'd better get back to your painting," he said. "I'll take those measurements."

"All right." Shane watched him walk to the door. "There's hot water in the kitchen if you want some tea."

What a strange man, she thought, frowning after him. Unconsciously, she lifted a finger to the warm spot on her arm where his flesh had touched hers. What had he been looking for, she wondered, when he had searched her eyes so deeply? What did he expect to find? It would be so much simpler if he would only ask her the questions he had. Shrugging, Shane went back to her painting.

Vance paused by the foot of the stairs and glanced at the living room. Surprised, he walked in for a closer look. It was clean as a whistle, with every vase, lamp and knickknack packed away in labeled boxes.

She must have really worked, he thought. That compact little body stored a heavyweight energy. She had ambition, he concluded, and the guts to carry it through. Whatever her former fiancé termed her, Vance would hardly characterize Shane Abbott as frivolous. Not from what he had seen so far, he reminded himself. He felt another flash of admiration for her as he mounted the stairs.

She'd been at work on the second floor as well, Vance discovered. She must move like a whirlwind, he concluded as he looked at the labeled boxes in the master bedroom. After taking his measurements and notations, he moved into Shane's room.

It was a beehive of activity, with none of the meticulous organization he had found in the other rooms. Papers, lists, notes, scrawled tablets and bills sat heaped on the open slant top of a Governor Winthrop desk. They fluttered a bit from the breeze through the open windows. On the floor beside it were dozens of catalogs on antiques. A nightgown—not the one he had envisioned her in, but a thigh-length chemise—was tossed inside out over a chair. A pair of worn sneakers sat propped against the closet as if they had been kicked there then forgotten.

In the center of the room was a large box of books, which he remembered seeing the day before. Then they had been in the third bedroom. Obviously, Shane had dragged them into her own room the night before to sort through them. Several were piled precariously on the floor; others littered her nightstand. It was apparent that her style of working and style of living were completely at variance.

Oddly, Vance thought of Amelia and the elegant order of her private rooms. They had been decorated in pinks and ivories, without the barest trace of dust or clutter. Even the army of bottles of creams and scents on her vanity had been carefully arranged. Shane had no vanity at all, and the bureau top held only a small enameled box, a framed photo and a single bottle of scent.

He noted the photo was a color snapshot of a teenaged Shane beside a very erect, white-haired woman.

So this is the grandmother, Vance mused. She had a prim, proper smile on her face, but he was certain her eyes were laughing out of the lined face. He observed none of the softness of old age about her, but a rather leathery toughness that contrasted well with the girl beside her.

They stood on the summer grass, their backs to the creek. The grandmother wore a flowered housedress, the girl a yellow T-shirt and cut-off jeans. This Shane was hardly different from the woman outside. Her hair was longer, her frame thinner, but the look of unbridled amusement was there. Though her arm was hooked through the old woman's, the impression was of camaraderie, not of support.

She was more attractive with her hair short, Vance decided as he studied her. The way it curled and clung to the shape of her face accented the smoothness of her skin, and the way her jaw tapered...

He found himself wondering if Cy had taken the picture and was immediately annoyed with the idea. He disliked Cy on principle, though he'd certainly employed a good many men like him over the years. They plotted their way through life as though it were a tax return.

What the hell had she seen in him? Vance thought in disgust as he turned away to take more measurements.

If she had tied herself up with him, she would be living in some stuffy house in the suburbs with 2.3 children, the Ladies Auxiliary on Wednesdays and a two-week vacation in a rented beach cottage every year. Fine for some, he thought, but not for a woman who liked to paint porches and wanted to see Fiji.

That buttoned-down jerk would have picked on her for the rest of her life, Vance concluded before he headed back downstairs. She'd had a lucky escape. Vance thought it was a pity he hadn't had one himself. Instead he had spent an intolerable four years wishing his wife out of existence and another two dealing with the guilt of having his wish come true.

Shaking off the mood, Vance walked outside to take a look at Shane's front porch.

Later, when he was measuring and muttering, Shane came out with a mug of tea in each hand. "Pretty bad, huh?"

Vance looked up with an expression of disgust. "It's a wonder someone hasn't broken a leg on this thing."

"No one uses it much." Shane shrugged as she worked her way expertly around the uncertain boards. "Gran always used the back door. So does anyone who comes to visit."

"Your boyfriend didn't."

Shane shot him a dry look. "Cy wouldn't use the back

door, and he's not my boyfriend. What do you think I should do about it?"

"I thought you'd already done it," he returned, and pocketed his rule. "And very well."

Shane eyed him a moment, then laughed. "No, not about Cy, about the porch."

"Tear the damn thing down."

"Oh." Gingerly, Shane sat on the top step. "All of it? I was hoping to replace the worst boards, and—"

"The whole thing's going to collapse if three people stand on it at the same time," Vance cut in, frowning at the sagging wood. "I can't understand how anyone could let something get into this condition."

"All right, don't get riled up," she advised as she held out a mug of tea. "How much do you think it'll cost me?"

Vance calculated a moment, then named a price. He saw the flicker of dismay before Shane sighed.

"Okay." It killed her last hope of holding on to her grandmother's dining-room set. "If it has to be done. I suppose it's first priority. The weather might turn cold anytime." She managed a halfhearted smile. "I wouldn't want my first customer to fall through the porch and sue me."

"Shane." Vance stood in front of her. As she sat on the top step, their faces were almost level. Her look was direct and open, yet still he hesitated before speaking.

"How much do you have? Money," he added bluntly when she gave him a blank look.

She drew her brows together at the question. "Enough to get by," she said, then made a sound of annoyance as he continued to stare at her. "Barely," she admitted. "But it'll hold until my business makes a few dollars. I've got so much budgeted for the house, so much for buying stock. Gran left me a nest egg, and I had my own savings."

Vance hesitated again. He had promised himself not to become involved, yet he was being drawn in every time he saw her. "I hate to sound like your boyfriend," he began.

"Then don't," Shane said quickly. "And he's not."

"All right." Vance frowned down at his mug. It was one thing to take on a job as a lark, and another to take money from a woman who was obviously counting her pennies. He sipped, trying to find a reasonable way out of his hourly wage. "Shane, about my salary—"

"Oh, Vance, I can't make it any more right now." Distress flew into her eyes. "Later, after I've gotten started…"

"No." Embarrassed and annoyed, he put a hand on hers to stop her. "No, I wasn't going to ask you to raise it."

"But—" Shane stopped. Realization filled her eyes. Tears followed it. Swiftly, she set down the mug and rose. Shaking her head, she descended the stairs. "No, no, that's very kind of you," she managed as she walked away from him. "I—I appreciate it, really, but it's not necessary. I didn't mean to make it sound as though—" Breaking off, she stared at the surrounding mountains. For a moment there was only the sound of the creek bubbling on its way behind them.

Cursing himself, Vance went to her. After a brief hesitation, he put his hands on her shoulders. "Shane, listen—"

"No, please." Swiftly, she turned to face him. Though the tears hadn't brimmed over, her eyes still swam with them. When she lifted her hands to his forearms, he found her fingers surprisingly strong. "It's very kind of you to offer."

"No, it's not," Vance snapped. Frustration, guilt and something more ran through him. He resented all of it. "Damn it, Shane, you don't understand. The money isn't—"

"I understand you're a very sweet man," she interrupted. Vance felt himself become tangled deeper when she put her arms around him, pressing her cheek to his chest.

"No, I'm not," he muttered. Intending to push her away and find a way out of the mess he'd gotten himself into, Vance put his hands back on her shoulders. The last thing he wanted was misplaced gratitude. But his hands found their way into her hair.

He didn't want to push her away, he realized. No, by God, he didn't. Not when her small firm breasts were pressed against him. Not when her hair curled riotously around his fingers. It was soft, so soft, and the color of wild honey. Her mouth was soft, he remembered, aching. Surrendering to need, Vance buried his face in her hair, murmuring her name.

Something in the tone, the hint of desperation, made Shane long to comfort him. She didn't yet sense his desire for her, only his trouble. She pressed closer, wanting to ease it while she ran soothing hands over his back. At her touch, his blood leaped. In a swift, almost brutal move, Vance pulled her head back to savage her mouth with his.

Shane's instinctive cry of alarm was silenced. Her struggles went unnoticed. A fire consumed him—so great, so unbearably hot, he had no thought but to quench it. She felt fear, then, greater than fear, passion. The fire spread, engulfing her until her mouth answered his wildly.

No one, nothing had ever brought her to this—this madness of need, terror of desire. She moaned in panicked excitement as his teeth nipped into her bottom lip. Along her skin, quick thrills raced to confuse and inflame. There was never a thought to deny him. She knew she was already his.

He thought he would go mad if he didn't touch her, learn just one of the secrets of her small, slim body. For countless hours the night before, his imagination had tormented him. Now, he had to satisfy it. Never stopping his assault on her mouth, he reached beneath her shirt to find her breast. Her heart pounded beneath his hand. She was firm and small. His appetite only increased, making him groan while his thumb and finger worked the already erect peak.

Colors exploded inside her head like a blinding, brilliant rainbow. Shane clutched at him, afraid, enthralled, while her lips and tongue continued with a demand equal to his. Against her smooth skin his palm was rough and callused. His thumb scraped her, lifting her to a delirium of excitement. There was no smoothness, no softness in him. His mouth was hard and hot with the stormy taste of anger. Crushed to hers, his body was taut and tense. Some raw, turbulent passion seemed to pour out of him to dare her to match it.

She felt his arms tighten around her convulsively; then she was free so quickly she staggered, grabbing his arm to steady herself.

In her eyes, Vance saw the clouds of passion, the lights of fear. Her mouth was bruised and swollen from the fierceness of his. He frowned at it. Never before had he been rough with a woman. For the most part, he was a considerate lover, perhaps indifferent at times but never ungentle. He took a step back from her. "I'm sorry," he said stiffly.

Shane lifted her fingers to her still-tender lips in a nervous gesture. Her reaction, much more than Vance's technique, had left her shaken. Where had all that fire and feeling been hiding all this time? she wondered. "I don't..." Shane had to clear her throat to manage more than a whisper. "I don't want you to be sorry."

Vance studied her steadily for a moment. "It would be better all around if you did." Reaching in his back pocket, he drew out a list. "Here are the materials you'll need. Let me know when they're delivered."

"All right." Shane accepted the list. When he started to walk away, she drew up all of her courage. "Vance..." He paused and turned back to her. "I'm not sorry," she told him quietly.

He didn't answer, but walked around the side of the house and disappeared.

Chapter 5

Shane decided she had worked harder over the following three days than she had ever worked in her life. The spare bedroom and dining room were loaded with packing boxes, labeled and listed and sealed. The house had been scrubbed and swept and dusted from top to bottom. She had pored through catalogs on antiques until the words ran together. Every item she owned was listed systematically. The dating and pricing was more grueling for her than the manual work and often kept her up until the early hours of the morning. She would be up to start again the moment the sunlight woke her. Yet her energy never flagged. With each step of progress she made, the excitement grew, pushing her to make more.

As the time passed, she became more convinced, and

more confident, that what she was doing was right. It *felt* right. She needed to find her own way—the sacrifices and the financial risk were necessary. She didn't intend to fail.

For her, the shop would be not only a business but an adventure. Though Shane was impatient for the adventure to begin, as always, the planning and anticipation were just as stimulating to her. She had contracted with a roofer and a plumber, and had chosen her paints and stains. Just that afternoon, in a torrent of rain, the materials she had ordered from Vance's list had been delivered. The mundane, practical occurrences had given her a thrill of accomplishment. Somehow, the lumber, nails and bolts had been tangible evidence that she was on her way. Shane told herself that Antietam Antiques and Museum became a reality when the first board was set in place.

Excited, she had phoned Vance, and if he were true to his word, he would begin work the next morning.

Over a solitary cup of cocoa in the kitchen, Shane listened to the constant drumming rain and thought of him. He had been brief and businesslike on the phone. She hadn't been offended. She had come to realize that moodiness was part of his character. This made him only more attractive.

The windows were dark as she stared out, with a ghostly reflection of the kitchen light on the wet panes.

She thought idly about starting a fire to chase away the damp chill, but she had little inclination to move. Instead, she rubbed the bottom of one bare foot over the top of the other and decided it was too bad her socks were all the way upstairs.

Sluggishly, a drip fell from the ceiling into a pot on the floor. It gave a surprising ping now and again. There were several other pots set at strategic places throughout the house. Shane didn't mind the rain or the isolation. The sensation of true loneliness was almost foreign to her. Content with her own company, the activity of her own mind, she craved no companionship at that moment, nor would she have shunned it. Yet she thought of Vance, wondering if he sat watching the rain through a darkened window.

Yes, she admitted, she was very much attracted to him. And it was more than a physical response when he held her, when he kissed her in that sudden, terrifyingly exciting way. Just being in his presence was stimulating—sensing the storm beneath the calm. There was an amazing drive in him. The drive of a man uncomfortable, even impatient, with idleness. The lack of a job, she thought with a sympathetic sigh, must frustrate him terribly.

Shane understood his need to produce, to be active, although her own spurts of frantic energy were patch-worked with periods of unapologetic laziness. She moved fast but didn't rush. She could work for hours without tiring, or sleep until noon without the least blush of guilt. Whichever she did, she did wholeheartedly. It was vital to her to find some way to enjoy the most menial or exhausting task. She concluded that while Vance would work tirelessly, he would find the enjoyment unnecessary.

The basic difference in their temperaments didn't trouble her. Her interest in history, plus her teaching experience, had given her insight into the variety of human nature. It wasn't necessary to her that Vance's thoughts and moods flow along the same stream as hers. Such comfortable compatibility would offer little excitement and no surprises at all. Absolute harmony, she mused, could be lovely, rather sweet and very bland. There were more... interesting things.

She'd seen a spark of humor in him, perhaps an almost forgotten sense of the ridiculous. And he was far from cold. While she accepted his faults and their differences, these qualities caused her to accept her own attraction to him.

What she had felt from the first meeting had only intensified. There was no logic in it, no sense, but her heart had known instantly that he was the man she'd waited for. Though she'd told herself it was impossible, Shane knew the impossible had an uncanny habit of happening just the same. Love at first sight? Ridiculous. But...

Impossible or not, ridiculous or not, Shane's heart was set. It was true she gave her affections easily, but she didn't give them lightly. The love she had felt for Cy had been a young, impressionable love, but it had been very real. It had taken her a long time to get over it.

Shane had no illusions about Vance Banning. He was a difficult man. Even with spurts of kindness and humor, he would never be anything else. There was too much anger in him, too much drive. And while Shane could accept the phenomenon of love at first sight on her part, she was practical enough to know it wasn't being reciprocated.

He desired her. She might puzzle over this, never having thought of herself as a woman to attract desire, but she recognized it. Yet, though he wanted her, he kept his distance. This was the reserve in him, she decided, the studied caution that warred with the passion.

Idly, she sipped her drink and stared out into the rain. The problem as Shane saw it was to work her way through the barrier. She had loved before and faced pain and emptiness. She could accept pain again, but she was determined not to face emptiness a second time. She wanted Vance Banning. Now all she had to do was to make him want her. Smiling a little, Shane set down her cup. She'd been raised to succeed.

The glare of headlights against the window surprised her. Rising, Shane went to the back door to see who'd come visiting in the rain. Cupping her hands on either side of her face, she peered through the wet glass. She recognized the car and immediately threw open the door. Cold rain hurled itself into her face, but she laughed, watching Donna scramble around puddles with her head lowered.

"Hi!" Still laughing, Shane stepped back as her friend dashed through the door. "You got a little wet," she observed.

"Very funny." Donna stripped off her raincoat to hang it over a peg near the back door. With the casualness of an old friend, she stepped out of her wet loafers. "I figured you were hibernating. Here." She handed Shane a pound can of coffee.

"A welcome home present?" Shane asked, turning the can over curiously. "Or a hint that you'd like some?"

"Neither." Shaking her head, Donna ran her fingers through her wet hair. "You bought it the other day, then left it at the store."

"I did?" Shane thought about it a moment, then laughed. "Oh, that's right. Thanks. Who's minding the store while you're out making deliveries?" Turning, she popped the can into a cupboard.

"Dave." With a sigh, Donna plopped onto a kitchen chair. "His sister's baby-sitting, so he kicked me out."

"Aw, out in the storm."

"He knew I was restless." She glanced out the window. "It doesn't seem as though this rain's ever going to let up." With a shiver, she frowned at Shane's bare feet. "Aren't you cold?"

"I thought about starting a fire," she said absently, then grinned. "It seemed like an awful lot of trouble."

"So's the flu."

"The cocoa's still warm," Shane told her, automatically reaching for another cup. "Want some?"

"Yes, thanks." Donna ran her fingers through her hair again, then folded her hands, but she couldn't keep them still. Suddenly, she gave Shane a glowing smile. "I have to tell you before I burst."

Mildly curious, Shane looked over her shoulder. "Tell me what?"

"I'm having another baby."

"Oh, Donna, that's wonderful!" Shane felt a twinge of envy. Hurriedly dismissing it, she went to hug her friend. "When?"

"Not for another seven months." Laughing, Donna wiped the rain from her face. "I'm just as excited as I was the first time. Dave is too, though he's trying to be very nonchalant." She sent Shane a beaming look. "He's managed to mention it, very casually, to everyone who came into the store this afternoon."

Shane gave her another quick hug. "You know how lucky you are?"

"Yes, I do." A little sheepishly, she grinned. "I've

spent all day thinking up names. What do you think of Charlotte and Samuel?"

"Very distinguished." Shane moved back to the stove. After pouring cocoa, she brought two cups to the table. "Here's to little Charlotte or Samuel."

"Or Andrew or Justine," Donna said as they touched rims.

"How many kids are you planning to have?" Shane asked wryly.

"Just one at a time." Donna gave her stomach a proud little pat.

The gesture made Shane smile. "Did you say Dave's sister was watching Benji? Isn't she still in school?"

"No, she graduated this summer. Right now she's hunting for a new job." With a contented sigh, Donna sat back. "She was planning to go to college part-time, but money's tight and the hours she's working right now make it next to impossible." Her brow creased in sympathy. "The best she can manage this term is a couple of night classes twice a week. At that rate it's going to take her a long time to earn a degree."

"Hmm." Shane stared into her cocoa. "Pat was a very bright girl as I remember."

"Bright and pretty as a picture."

Shane nodded. "Tell her to come see me."

"You?"

"After the shop's set up, I'm going to need some part-time help." She glanced over absently as the wind hurled rain at the windows. "I wouldn't be able to do anything for her for a month or so, but if she's still interested, we should be able to work something out."

"Shane, she'll be thrilled. But are you sure you can afford to hire someone?"

With a toss of her head, Shane lifted her drink. "I'll know within the first six months if I'm going to make it." As she considered, she twisted a curl around her finger—a gesture Donna recognized as nerves. She drew her brows together but said nothing. "I want to keep the place open seven days a week," Shane continued. "Weekends are bound to be the busiest time if I manage to lure in any tourists. Between sales and bookkeeping, inventory and the buying I have to do, I won't be able to manage alone. If I'm going down," she murmured, "I'm going down big."

"I've never known you to do anything halfway," Donna observed with a trace of admiration vying with concern. "I'd be scared to death."

"I am a little scared," Shane admitted. "Sometimes I imagine this place the way it's going to look, and I see customers coming in to handle merchandise. I see all the rooms and records I'm going to have to keep…" She rolled her eyes to the ceiling. "What makes me think I can handle all that?"

"As long as I can remember, you've handled everything that came your way." Donna paused a moment as she considered Shane carefully. "You're going to try this no matter how many pitfalls I point out?"

A grin had Shane's dimples deepening. "Yes."

"Then I won't point out any," Donna said with a wry smile. "What I will say is that if anyone can make it work, you can."

After frowning into her cocoa, Shane raised her eyes to Donna's. "Why?"

"Because you'll give it everything you've got."

The simplicity of the answer made Shane laugh. "You're sure that'll be enough?"

"Yes," Donna said so seriously that Shane sobered.

"I hope you're right," Shane murmured, then shook off the doubts. "It's a little late in the game to start worrying about it now. So," she continued in a lighter tone, "what's new besides Justine or Samuel?"

After a moment's hesitation, Donna plunged ahead. "Shane, I saw Cy the other day."

"Did you?" Shane lifted a brow as she sipped. "So did I."

Donna moistened her lips. "He seemed very…ah, concerned about your plans."

"Critical and concerned are entirely different things," Shane pointed out, then smiled as the color in Donna's cheeks deepened. "Oh, don't worry about it, Donna. Cy's never approved of any of my ideas. It doesn't bother me anymore. In fact, the less he approves," she continued slowly, "the more I'm sure it's the right thing to do. I don't think he's ever taken a chance in his entire life." Noting that Donna was busy gnawing on her bottom lip, Shane fixed her with a straight look. "Okay, what else?"

"Shane." Donna paused, then began running her fingertip around and around the rim of her cup. Shane recognized the stalling gesture and kept silent. "I think I should tell you before—well, before you hear it from someone else. Cy…"

Shane waited patiently for a few seconds. "Cy what?" she demanded. Miserably, Donna looked up.

"He's been seeing quite a lot of Laurie MacAfee." Seeing Shane's eyes widen, Donna continued in a rush. "I'm sorry, Shane, so sorry, but I did think you should know. And I figured it might be easier hearing it from me. I think…well, I'm afraid it's serious."

"Laurie…" Shane broke off and seemed to stare, fascinated, at the water dripping into the pot. *"Laurie MacAfee?"* she managed after a strangled moment.

"Yes," Donna said quietly, and she stared down at the table. "Rumor is they'll be married next summer." Donna waited, unhappily, for Shane's reaction. When she heard the burst of wild laughter, she looked up, fearing hysterics.

"Laurie MacAfee!" Shane pounded her palms on the

table and laughed until she thought she would burst. "Oh, it's wonderful, it's perfect! Oh God. Oh God, what an *admirable* couple!"

"Shane…" Concerned with the damp eyes and rollicking laughter, Donna searched for the right thing to say.

"Oh, I wish I had known before so I could have congratulated him." Almost beside herself with delight, Shane laid her forehead on the table. Taking this as a sign of a broken heart, Donna put a comforting hand on her hair.

"Shane, you mustn't take on so." Her own eyes filled as she gently stroked Shane's hair. "Cy isn't for you. You deserve better."

The statement sent Shane into a fresh peal of laughter. "*Oh, Donna!* Oh, Donna, do you remember how she always wore those neat little coordinates to school? And she got straight A's in home economics." Shane was forced to take deep breaths before she could continue. "She did a term paper on planning household budgets."

"Please, darling, don't think about it." Donna cast her eyes around the kitchen, wondering if there were any medicinal brandy in the house.

"She'll have her own shoe trees," Shane said weakly. "I just know it. And she'll label them so they don't get them mixed up. Oh, Cy!" On a new round of giggles, she pounded a fist on the table. "Laurie. Laurie MacAfee!"

Almost frantic with concern, Donna gently lifted

Shane's face. "Shane, I…" With a jolt she saw that rather than being devastated, her friend was simply overcome with amusement. For a moment, Donna stared into round dancing eyes. "Well," she said dryly, "I knew you'd be upset."

Shane howled with laughter. "I'm going to give them a Victorian whatnot as a wedding present. Donna," she added with grinning gratitude, "you've made my day. Absolutely made it."

"I knew you'd take it badly," Donna said with a baffled smile. "Just try not to weep in public."

"I'll keep my chin up," Shane promised, then smiled. "You're sweet. Did you really think I was carrying a torch for Cy?"

"I wasn't sure," Donna admitted. "You were…well, an item for so long, and I knew how crushed you were when the two of you broke up. You'd never talk about it after that."

"I needed some time to lick my wounds," Shane told her. "They've been healed over for a long while. I was in love with him, but I got over it. He put a large dent in my pride. I survived."

"I could have killed him at the time," Donna muttered darkly. "Two months before the wedding."

"Better than two months after," Shane pointed out logically. "We would never have made a go of it. But now, Cy and Laurie MacAfee…"

This time they both broke out into laughter.

"Shane." Donna gave her a sudden sober look. "A lot of people are going to be thinking you still care for Cy."

Shane shrugged it off. "You can't do anything about what people think."

"Or what they say," Donna murmured.

"They'll find something more interesting to talk about before long," Shane returned carelessly. "Besides, I have too much to do to be worried about it."

"So I noticed from the pile of stuff on the porch. What's under that tarp?"

"Lumber and materials."

"Just what are you going to do with it?"

"Nothing. Vance Banning's going to do it. Want some more cocoa?"

"Vance Banning!" Stunned, then fascinated, Donna leaned forward. "Tell me."

"There's not much to tell. You didn't answer me," Shane reminded her.

"What? No, no, I don't want any more." Impatiently, she brushed the offer away. "Shane, what is Vance Banning going to do with your lumber and materials?"

"The carpentry work."

"Why?"

"I hired him to do it."

Donna gritted her teeth. "Why?"

"Because he's a carpenter."

"Shane!"

Valiantly, Shane controlled a grin. "Look, he's out of work, he's talented, I needed someone who'd work under union scale, so…" She spread her hands.

"What have you found out about him?" Donna demanded the right to fresh news.

"Not much." Shane wrinkled her nose. "Nothing, really. He doesn't say much."

Donna gave her a knowing smirk. "I already knew that."

A quick grin was Shane's response. "Well, he can be downright rude when he wants to. He has a lot of pride and a marvelous smile that he doesn't use nearly enough. Strong hands," she murmured, then brought herself back. "And a streak of reluctant kindness. I think he can laugh at himself but he's forgotten how. I know he's a workhorse because when the wind's right I can hear him hammering and sawing at all hours." She glanced out the window in the direction of the path. "I'm in love with him."

"Yes, but what—" Donna caught her breath and choked on it. *"What!"*

"I'm in love with him," Shane repeated with an amused smile. "Would you like some water?"

For nearly a full minute, Donna only stared at her. *She's joking,* she told herself. But by Shane's expression, she saw her friend was perfectly serious. It was her duty, Donna decided, as a married woman starting on her second child, to point out the dangers of this kind of thinking.

"Shane," she began in a patient, maternal tone, "you only just met the man. Now—"

"I knew it the minute I set my eyes on him," Shane interrupted calmly. "I'm going to marry him."

"Marry him!" Beyond words, Donna could only come up with sputters. Indulgently, Shane rose to pour her some water. "He—he asked you to marry him?"

"No, of course not." Shane chuckled at the idea as she handed Donna a glass. "He only just met me."

In an attempt to understand Shane's logic, Donna closed her eyes and concentrated. "I'm confused," she said at length.

"I said I was going to marry him," Shane explained, taking her seat again. "He doesn't know it yet. First I have to wait for him to fall in love with me."

After setting the untouched water aside, Donna gave her a stern look. "Shane, I think you're under more strain than you realize."

"I've been giving this a lot of thought," Shane answered, ignoring Donna's comment. "Number one, why would I have fallen in love with him in the blink of an eye if it wasn't right? It must be right, so number two, sooner or later he's going to fall in love with me."

Donna followed the pattern of thought and found it

filled with snags. "And how are you going to make him do that?"

"Oh, I can't make him," Shane said reasonably. Her voice was both serene and confident. "He'll have to fall in love with me just as I am and in his own time—the same way I fell in love with him."

"Well, you've had some nutty ideas before, Shane Abbott, but this is the top." Donna folded her arms over her chest. "You're planning on marrying a man you've known barely a week who doesn't know he's going to marry you, and you're just going to sit patiently by until he gets the idea."

Shane thought for a moment, then nodded. "That's about it."

"It's the most ridiculous thing I've ever heard," Donna stated, then let out a surprised laugh. "And knowing you, it'll probably work."

"I'm counting on it."

Leaning forward, Donna took Shane's hands in hers. "Why do you love him, Shane?"

"I don't know," she answered immediately. "That's another reason I'm sure it's right. I know almost nothing about him except he's not a comfortable man. He'll hurt me and make me cry."

"Then why—"

"He'll make me laugh too," Shane interrupted. "And make me furious." She smiled a little, but her eyes were very serious. "I don't think he'll ever make me feel—inadequate. And when I'm near him, I *know*. That's enough for me."

"Yes." Donna nodded, giving Shane's hands a squeeze. "It would be. You're the most loving person I've ever known. And the most trusting. Those are wonderful traits, Shane, and—well, dangerous. I only wish we knew more about him," she added in a mutter.

"He has secrets," Shane murmured, and Donna's eyes sharpened. "They're his until he's ready to tell me about them."

"Shane…" Donna's fingers tightened on hers. "Be careful, please."

A little surprised by the tone, Shane smiled. "I will. Don't worry. Maybe I am more trusting than most, but I have my defenses. I'm not going to make a fool of my-self." Unconsciously, she glanced out the window again, seeing the path to his house in her mind's eye. "He's not a simple man, Donna, but he is a good one. That much I'm sure of."

"All right," Donna agreed. Silently, she vowed to keep a close eye on Vance Banning.

For a long time after Donna left, Shane sat in the kitchen. The rain continued to pound. The steady drip from the ceiling plopped musically into the pan. She was aware of how reckless her words to Donna had been, yet she felt better having said them out loud.

No, she wasn't as blindly confident as she appeared. Inside, she was terrified by the knowledge that she loved so irrationally. She was trusting, yes, but not naive. She understood there was a price to pay for trust, and that often it was a dear one. Yet she knew her choice had already been made—or perhaps she'd never had one.

Rising, Shane switched off the lights and began to wander through the darkened house. She knew its every twist and turn, every board that creaked. It was everything familiar and comforting to her. She loved it. She knew none of Vance's twists and turns, none of his secret corners. He was everything strange and disturbing. She loved him.

If it had been a quiet, gentle love, she could have accepted it easily. But there was nothing quiet in the storm churning inside her. For all her energy and love of adventure, Shane had grown up in a slow, peaceful world where excitement was a run through the woods or a ride on the back of a tractor at haymaking. To fall suddenly in love with a stranger might seem romantic and wonderful in a story, but when it happened in real life, it was simply terrifying.

Shane walked upstairs, habitually avoiding the steps that creaked or groaned. The rain was a hollow, drumming sound all around her, whipped up occasionally by the wind to fly at the windows. Her bare feet met bare wood with a quiet patter. A small bucket caught the drip in the center of the hall. Expertly, she skirted around it.

Who was she to think all she had to do was to sit patiently by until Vance fell in love with her? she asked herself. After flipping on the light in her room, she went to stare at herself in the mirror. Was she beautiful? Shane asked her reflection. Alluring? With a half laugh, she rested her elbows on the dresser to look closer.

She saw the dash of freckles, the large dark eyes and cap of hair. She didn't see the stunning vitality, the temptingly smooth skin, the surprisingly sensual mouth.

Was that a face to send a man into raptures? she asked herself. The thought amused her so, that the reflection grinned back with quick good humor. Hardly, Shane decided, but she wouldn't want a man who looked only for a perfect face. No, she hadn't the face or figure to lure a man into love had she wanted to. She had only herself and the love in her heart.

Shane flashed the mirror a smile before she turned away to prepare for bed. She'd always thought love the ultimate adventure.

Chapter 6

Weak sunlight filtered through the bad-tempered clouds. The creek was swollen from the rainfall so that it ran its course noisily, hissing and complaining as it rounded the bend at the side of Shane's house. Shane was doing some complaining of her own.

The day before, she had moved her car out of the narrow driveway so that the delivery truck could have easy access to the back porch. Not wanting to ruin the grass, she had parked in the small square of dirt her grandmother had used as a vegetable garden. Once the car had been moved, Shane had become involved with the unloading of lumber and had promptly forgotten it. Now, it was sunk deep in mud, firmly resisting all efforts to get it out.

She pressed the gas lightly, tried forward, then reverse. She gunned the engine and swore. Slamming out of the driver's side, Shane sloshed ankle-deep in mire as she stomped back to the rear tire. She gave it an accusing stare, then kicked it.

"That's not going to help," Vance commented. He had been watching her for the last few minutes, torn somewhere between amusement and exasperation. And pleasure. There was a simple pleasure in just seeing her. He'd stopped counting the times over the last few days that he'd thought of her.

Out of patience, Shane turned to him, hands on hips. Her predicament was annoying enough without the added benefit of an audience. "You might have let me know you were there."

"You were…involved," he said, glancing pointedly at her mired car.

She sent him a cool look. "You've got a better idea, I suppose."

"A few," he agreed, moving across the lawn to join her. Her eyes snapped with temper while her mouth pouted. Her boots were caked with mud past the ankle. Her jeans, rolled up to the calf, had fared little better. She looked ready to boil over at the first wrong word. A cautious man would have said nothing.

"Who the hell parked it in this mud hole?" Vance demanded.

"*I* parked it in this mud hole." Shane gave the tire another fierce kick. "And it wasn't a mud hole when I did."

He lifted a brow. "I suppose you noticed it rained all night."

"Oh, get out of my way." Incensed, Shane pushed him aside and stomped back to the driver's seat. She turned on the ignition, shoved the shift into first, then stepped heavily on the gas. Mud flew like rain. The car groaned and sank deeper.

For a moment, Shane could only pound on the steering wheel in enraged impotence. She would have dearly loved to tell Vance that she didn't require any assistance. There was nothing more infuriating than an amused, superior male...especially when you needed one. Forcing herself to take a deep breath, she climbed back out of the car to meet Vance's grin with icy composure. "What's the first of your few ideas?" she asked coolly.

"Got a couple of planks?"

Even more annoyed that she hadn't thought of it herself, Shane went to the shed and found two long, thin boards. Without fuss or conversation, Vance took them and secured them just under the front wheels. Shane folded her arms and tapped one muddy boot as she watched him.

"I'd have thought of that in a minute," she muttered.

"Maybe." Vance stood again to walk to the rear of the

car. "But you wouldn't get anywhere the way your back wheels are stuck."

Shane waited for him to make some comment on feminine stupidity. Then she would have an excuse to give him the full force of her temper. He merely studied her flushed face and furious eyes. "So?" she said at length.

Something suspiciously like a smile tugged at his mouth. Shane's eyes narrowed. "So, get back in and I'll push," he said, then put a restraining hand on her arm. "Gentle on the gas this time, hot rod. Just put it in Drive and easy does it."

"It's a four-speed," she told him with dignity.

"I beg your pardon." Vance waited until she had waded her way back to the front of the car. For the first time in months, perhaps years, he had to make a concentrated effort to control laughter. "Let the clutch out slow," he instructed after clearing his throat.

"I know how to drive," she snapped, and slammed the door smartly. Frowning into the rearview mirror, Shane watched him until he gave her a nod. With meticulous care, she engaged the clutch and gently pressed on the gas. The front wheels crept slowly onto the planks. The back tires slid, then stuck, then ponderously moved again. Shane kept the speed slow and even. It was humiliating, she thought, glaring straight ahead, absolutely humiliating that he was going to get her out without a hitch.

"Just a little more," Vance called to her, shifting his weight. "Keep it slow."

"What?" Shane rolled down the window, then stuck her head out to hear his answer. As she did, her foot slipped and fell heavily on the gas. The car shot out of the mud like a banana squeezed from its peel. With a gasp, Shane hit the brake, rocking to an abrupt halt.

Closing her eyes, she sat for a moment and considered making a run for it. She didn't dare glance in the rear-view mirror now. It wouldn't be difficult, she reflected, to make a U-turn, then keep right on going. But cowardice wasn't her way. She swallowed, bit her lip, then climbed out of the car to face the music.

Vance was kneeling in the mud. He was thoroughly splattered and hopping mad. *"You idiot!"* he shouted before Shane could say a word. Even as she started to agree with him, he continued. "What the hell did you think you were doing? Pea-brained little twit, I told you to take it *slow.*"

He didn't stop there. He swore at length, and fluently, but Shane lost track of the content. It was enough to know he was in a justifiable high rage, while she was fighting a desperate battle with laughter. She did her best, her very best, to keep her face composed and penitent. Feeling it would be unwise, as well as useless to interrupt with apologies, she folded her lips, bit the bottom one and swallowed repeatedly.

At first she concentrated on keeping her eyes directly on his, hoping the fury there would kill the urge to giggle. But the sight of his mud-splattered face had her sides aching with restrained mirth. She hung her head, ostensibly from shame.

"I'd like to know who the hell told you you could drive," Vance went on furiously. "And what person with a brain cell working would have parked the car in a swamp to begin with?"

"It was my grandmother's garden," Shane managed in a strangled voice. "But you're right. You're absolutely right. I'm so sorry, really…" She broke off here as a gurgle of laughter rose dangerously. Clearing her throat, she hurried on. "Sorry, Vance. It was very—" she had to look over his head in order to compose herself "—careless of me."

"Careless!"

"Stupid," she amended quickly, thinking that might placate him. "Absolutely stupid. I'm really sorry." Helplessly, she pressed both hands to her mouth, but the giggles came through. "I *am* sorry," she insisted, giving up as he glared at her. "I don't mean to laugh. It's terrible." Dizzy with the effort of trying to hold back, Shane bent over double. "Really awful," she added on a howl of laughter.

"Since you think it looks like fun…" he muttered

grimly, and grabbed her hand. Shane landed on her seat with a gentle splash and kept on laughing.

"I didn't—I didn't thank you," she said on a peal of giggles, "for getting my car out."

"Think nothing of it." Most women, he mused, would have been infuriated to find themselves sitting in a pile of mud. Shane was laughing just as hard at herself as she had at him. His grin was completely unexpected and spontaneous. "Brat," he accused, but Shane shook her head.

"Oh no, no, I'm not, really." She pressed the back of her hand to her mouth. "It's just this terrible habit of laughing at the wrong time. Because I really am sorry." The last word was drowned in a flood of laughter.

"I can see you are."

"Anyway, I didn't get it *all* over you." Scooping up some mud, she wiped it across his cheek. "I missed that part right there." She made a little choking sound in her throat. "That's much better," she approved.

"You aren't wearing nearly enough," Vance returned. He trailed both muddy palms down her face. Trying to avoid him, Shane slid, ending up flat on her back. Vance's boom of laughter broke into her shriek. "Much better," he agreed, then spotting the handful of mud she was about to heave, he made a grab for her arm. "Oh, no, you don't!"

As he laughed, she shifted. Vance landed half on his

chest, half on his side. With a muttered curse, he propped himself up, studying her out of narrowed eyes.

"City boy," she mocked on a whoop of appreciation. "Probably never been in a mud fight in your life." She was too pleased with her maneuver to see the next one coming.

In a flash, Vance had her by the shoulders. Rolling her over, he straddled her, holding a hand to the back of her head. Lying full length, Shane looked wide-eyed at the mud inches away from her face.

"Oh, Vance, you *wouldn't!*" The helpless laughter bubbled still as she struggled.

"The hell I wouldn't." He pushed her face an inch closer.

"Vance!" Though she was slippery as an eel by this time, Vance held her firmly, clamping his knees around her while his hand urged her down. As the distance between revenge and her nose lessened, Shane closed her eyes and held her breath.

"Give?" he demanded.

Cautiously, Shane opened one eye. She hesitated a moment, torn between the desire to win and the image of having her face pushed into the mud. She didn't doubt he'd do it. "Give," she said reluctantly.

Abruptly, Vance rolled her over so that she lay in his lap. "City boy, huh?"

"You wouldn't have won if I weren't out of practice," she told him. "It was just beginner's luck."

Her eyes were mocking him. Her face was streaked with mud from his own fingers. The hands pressed against his chest were slippery with it. The grip on the back of her neck lightened until it was a caress. The hand at her hip roamed absently down her thigh as he lowered his eyes to her mouth. Slowly, without any conscious thought of doing so, Vance began to draw her closer.

Shane saw the change in his eyes and was suddenly afraid. Did she really have the defenses she had bragged to Donna about? Now that she was certain she loved him, could there be any defense? It was too fast, she thought frantically. It was all happening too fast. Breathless from the race of her heart, she scrambled up.

"I'll beat you to the creek," she challenged, then was off in a flash.

Pondering on her abrupt retreat, Vance watched her run around the side of the house. Normally, he would have considered it a ploy, but he found it didn't fit this time. Nothing about her fit, he concluded as he rose. Oddly, he realized he didn't seem to fit either. He hadn't realized he could find anything amusing or enjoyable about wrestling in the mud. Nor had he realized he could find a woman like Shane Abbott both intriguing and desirable. Trying to organize his thoughts, Vance walked around the side of the house to find her.

She had stripped off her boots and was wading knee-deep in the rushing creek water. "It's freezing!" she called out, then lowered herself to her waist. At the shock of cold, she sucked in her breath. "If it was warmer, we could walk down to Molly's Hole and take a quick swim."

"Molly's Hole?" Watching her, Vance sat on the grass to pull off his own boots.

"Right around the bend." She pointed vaguely in the direction of the main road. "Great swimming hole. Fishing too." Shivering a bit, she rubbed at the front of her shirt to help the water take off the worst of the mud. "We're lucky it rained, or else the creek wouldn't be high enough to do any good."

"If it hadn't rained, your car wouldn't have been stuck in the mud."

Shane shot him a grin. "That's beside the point." She watched him step into the water. "Cold?" she said sweetly when he winced.

"I should have pushed your face in," he decided. Stripping off his shirt, Vance tossed it on the grassy bank before scrubbing at his hands and arms.

"You'd have felt really bad if you had." Shane rubbed her face with creek water.

"No, I wouldn't have."

Glancing up, Shane laughed. "I like you, Vance. Gran would have called you a scoundrel."

He lifted a brow. "Is that praise?"

"Her highest," Shane agreed, rising to rub at the thighs of her jeans. They were plastered against her, molding her legs while her shirt clung wetly to her breasts. The cold had her nipples taut, straining against the thin cotton. Involved with cleaning off her clothes, she chattered, sublimely unaware they left her as good as naked.

"She loved scoundrels," Shane continued. "I suppose that's why she put up with me. I was always getting into one scrape or another."

"What kind?" Vance's torso was wet, cleaned of mud now, but he stayed where he was. Her body was exquisitely formed. He wondered how he hadn't noted before how perfectly scaled it was—small round breasts, wasp-thin waist, narrow hips, lean thighs.

"I don't like to brag." Shane worked the mud from the slippery sleeves of her shirt. "But I can show you the best way into old man Trippet's orchard if you want to snitch a few green apples. And I used to have a great time riding Mr. Poffenburger's dairy cows." Shane sloshed over to him. "Here, you haven't got it all off your face." Cupping some water in her hand, she lifted it and began to clean his face herself. "I tore my britches on every farmer's fence for three miles," she went on. "Gran would patch them up saying she despaired of my being any more than a hooligan."

With one small, smooth hand, she methodically

scrubbed Vance's face. The other she held balanced against his naked chest. He made no protest, but stood still, watching her.

"'That Abbot girl,' they'd say," Shane told him, rubbing at a spot on his jawline. "Now I have to convince them I'm an upstanding citizen so they'll forget I filched their apples and buy my antiques. No one takes a hooligan very seriously. There, that's better." Satisfied, Shane started to lower her hand. Vance caught it in his. Her eyes didn't waver from his, but she became very still.

Without speaking, he began to wash the few lingering traces of mud from her face. He worked in very slow, very deliberate circles, his eyes fixed on hers. Though his palm was rough, his touch was gentle. Shane's lips trembled apart. With something like curiosity, Vance took a damp finger to trace their shape. He felt her quick, convulsive shudder. Still slow, still inquisitive, he ran his fingertip along the inside of her bottom lip. Under his thumb, the pulse in her wrist began to hammer. The sun broke briefly through the clouds, so that the light shifted and brightened before it dimmed again. He watched it play over her face.

"You won't run away this time, Shane," he murmured, as if to himself.

She said nothing, afraid to speak while his finger lingered on her lips. Slowly, he traced it down, over her chin, over the throbbing pulse in her throat. He paused there a moment, as if gauging and enjoying her response to him. Then he allowed his fingertip to sweep up over the swell of her breast and lie lightly on the erect peak covered only by the thin wet shirt.

Heat and cold shot through her; her skin was chilled from the water, her blood flamed at his touch. Vance watched the color drain from her face while her eyes grew impossibly large and dark. Yet she didn't draw away or protest the intimacy. He heard the sharp intake of her breath, then the slow, ragged expulsion.

"Are you afraid of me?" he asked, bringing his hand up to cup the back of her neck.

"No," she whispered. "Of me."

Puzzled, he drew his brows together. For a moment he looked hard and very fierce. Though his eyes weren't cold, they were piercing—full of questions, full of suspicion. Still Shane felt no fear of him, only of the needs and longing running through her. "An odd answer, Shane," he murmured thoughtfully. "You're an odd woman." With his fingers, he kneaded the back of her neck while he searched her face for answers. "Is that why you excite me?"

"I don't know," she said, struggling for breath. "I don't want to know. Just kiss me."

He lowered his lips, but only tested hers with the same lightness as his fingertip. "I wonder," he said softly against her mouth, "what it is about you I can't quite shake. Your taste?" He dug his teeth almost experimentally into her bottom lip. A low moan of pleasure was wrenched from her. "Fresh as rain one minute and honey soaked the next." Lightly, languidly, he traced her lips with his tongue. "Is it the way you feel? That skin of yours…like the underside of a rose petal." He ran his hands down her arms, then up again, gradually bringing her to him until she was caught close. The thud of her heart sounded like thunder in her ears.

"Why do you have to know?" The question was low and shaky. "Feeling's enough." They might have been naked, pressed body to body with only wet clinging clothes between them. "Kiss me, Vance, just kiss me. It's enough."

"You smell like rain now," he murmured, telling himself to resist her but knowing he wouldn't. "Pure and honest. When I look in your eyes, I'd swear there isn't a lie in you. Is there?" he demanded, but he crushed his mouth to hers before she could answer.

Shane reeled from the impact. Even as she gasped, his tongue was probing and exploring. The anger she had sensed in him before was now pure passion. Hunger, the rawness of his hunger, thrilled her. The water ran swiftly, grumbling as it hurried on its way to the river, but Shane heard only her own heartbeat. She no longer felt the stinging cold, only the warmth of his hand as it ran up her spine and down again.

He wasn't content with only her lips now, but took his own wild journey of her face. It was still wet, tasting of the cold freshness of the creek. But wherever his kisses wandered, he was drawn back again to the soft sweet taste of her mouth. It seemed always to be waiting for him, ready to open, invite, demand. Beneath the pliancy, beneath the willingness was a passion as great as his own and a strength he was just beginning to measure.

Vance told himself he needed a woman. That was why he was so desperate for Shane. He needed a woman's softness and flavor, and she was here. There was no exclusivity to it. How could there be? Yet there was something about her slight body, her fascinatingly different taste that drove every other woman to some dark corner of his mind, leaving only Shane in the light.

He could take her now, on the bank of the creek, in the dim daylight on the rain-damp grass. As her mouth moved, moist and warm under his, Vance could imagine how it would be to take full possession of her body. Her energy and hunger would match his own. There would be no false, foolish pretense of seduction, but an honest meeting of desires.

Her small round breasts pressed into his naked chest. Vance thought he could feel the aching need in them—or was it his own need? It raged in him, drove at him, until she was all he craved. Her mouth was small too, but avid, never retreating from the savageness of his. Instead, she matched it, propelling him further and further, pulling him closer and closer. All women or one woman, he was no longer certain, but she was overpowering him.

Somehow he knew that if he took her, he would never walk away easily. The reasons might not be fully clear yet, but she wasn't like the other women he had known and bedded. He was afraid her eager hands and mouth could hold him—and he wasn't yet ready to chance it.

Vance drew her away, but Shane dropped her head on his chest. There was something vulnerable in the gesture though the arms around his waist were strong. The contrast aroused him, as did the lightning fast beat of her heart. For a moment, he stood holding her while the water ran cold and fast around their legs and hazy sunlight drifted through the trees.

She'd once told him that a snowfall had made her feel a complete isolation. Vance felt it now. There might have been nothing, no one beyond the rushing creek and fringe of trees. And to his own confusion, he felt a need for none. He wanted only her. Perhaps they were alone… The thought both excited and disturbed him. Perhaps there was nothing beyond that forgotten little spot, and no reason not to take what he wanted.

Shane shivered, making him realize she must be chilled to the bone. It brought him back to reality in a rush. His arms dropped away from her.

"Come on," he muttered. "You should get inside." Vance pulled her up the slippery bank.

Shane bent over to pick up her boots. When she was certain she could do so calmly, she met his eyes. "You're not coming in." It wasn't a question. She had sensed all too well his change of attitude.

"No." His tone was cool again though his blood still throbbed for her. "I'll go change, then come back and get started on the porch."

Shane had known he would bring her pain, but she hadn't thought it would be so soon. The old wounds of rejection opened again. "All right. If I'm not here, just do whatever you have to do."

Vance could feel the hurt, yet she met his eyes and her voice was steady. Recriminations he could have dealt with easily. Anger he would have welcomed. For the first time in years, he was completely baffled by a woman.

"You know what would happen if I came in now." The words were rough with impatience. Vance found himself wanting to shake her.

"Yes."

"Is that what you want?"

Shane said nothing for a moment. When she smiled, the light didn't reach her eyes. "It's not what you want," she said quietly. Turning, she started back to the house, but Vance caught her arm, spinning her around. He was furious now, all the more furious when he saw the effort her composure was costing her.

"Damn it, Shane, you're a fool if you think I don't want you."

"You don't want to want me," she returned evenly. "That's more important to me."

"What difference does it make?" he ground out impatiently. Frustrated by the calmness of her answer, he did shake her. How could she look at him with those big quiet eyes when she'd driven him to the wall only moments before? "You know how close I came to taking you right here on the ground. Isn't it enough to know you can push me to that? What more do you want?"

She gave him a long searching look. "Push you to it," she repeated quietly. "Is that really how you see it?"

The conflict raged in him. He wanted badly to get away from her. "Yes," he said bitterly. "How else?"

"How else," she agreed with a shaky laugh that started a new ache moving in him. "I suppose for some that might be a compliment of sorts."

"If you like," he said curtly as he picked up his shirt.

"I don't," she murmured. "But then, you said I was odd." With a sigh, she stared into his eyes. "You've cut yourself off from your feelings, Vance, and it eats at you."

"You don't know a damn thing," he tossed back, only more enraged to hear her speak the truth.

As he glared at her, Shane heard a bird set up a strident song in the woods behind her. The high, piercing notes suited the air of tension and anger. "You're not nearly as hard or cold as you'd like to think," she said calmly.

"You don't know anything about me," he countered furiously, grabbing her arms again.

"And it infuriates you when the guard slips," Shane continued without breaking rhythm. "It infuriates you even more that you might actually feel something for me." His fingers loosened on her arms, and Shane drew away. "I don't push you, but something else certainly does. No, I don't know what it is, but you do." She took a long steadying breath as she studied him. "You've got to fight your own tug-of-war, Vance."

Turning, she walked to the house, leaving him staring after her.

Chapter 7

He couldn't stop thinking of her. In the weeks that passed, the mountains became a riot of color. The air took on the nip of fall. Twice, Vance spotted deer through his own kitchen window. And he couldn't stop thinking of her.

He split his time between the two houses. His own was taking shape slowly. Vance calculated he would be ready to start the more detailed inside work by winter.

Shane's was progressing more quickly. Between roofers and plumbers, the house had been bedlam for more than a week. The old kitchen had been gutted and stood waiting for new paint and trim. Shane had waited patiently for rain after the roof had been repaired. Then she had checked all the familiar spots for signs of leaks.

Oddly, she found herself a trifle sad that she didn't have to set out a single pan or bucket.

The museum area was completely finished. While Vance worked elsewhere, Shane busied herself arranging and filling the display cases that had been delivered.

At times she would be gone for hours, hunting up treasures at auctions and estate sales. He always knew the moment she returned because the house would spring to life again. In the basement, she'd set up a workroom where she refinished certain pieces or stored others. He saw her dash out, or dash in. He saw her carting tables, dragging packing boxes, climbing ladders. He never saw her idle.

Her attitude toward him was just as it had been from the first—friendly and open. Not once did she mention what had happened between them. It took all of his strength of will not to touch her. She laughed, brought him coffee and gave him amusing accounts of her adventures at auctions. He wanted her more every time he looked at her.

Now, as he finished up the trim on what had been the summer parlor, Vance knew she was downstairs. He went over his work critically, checking for flaws, while the simple awareness of her played havoc with his concentration. It might be wise, he thought, to take a trip back to Washington. So far, he had handled everything pertaining to his company by phone or mail. There was nothing urgent that required his attention, but he wondered if it wouldn't be wise to have a week of distance. She was haunting him. Plaguing him, Vance corrected. On a wave of frustration he packed his tools. The woman was trouble, he decided. Nothing but trouble.

Still, as he got ready to leave, Vance detoured to the basement steps. He hesitated, cursed himself, then started down.

Dressed in baggy cord jeans and a hip-length sweater, she was working on a tilt-top table. Vance had seen the table when Shane had first brought it in. It had been scarred and scratched and dull. Flushed with excitement, she had claimed to have bought it for a song, then had hustled it off to the basement. Now, the grain of mahogany gleamed through the thin coats of clear lacquer she had applied. She was industriously buffing it with paste wax. The basement smelled of tung oil and lemon.

Vance would have turned to go back upstairs, but Shane raised her head and saw him. "Hi!" Her smile welcomed him before she gestured him over. "Come take a look. You're the expert on wood." As he crossed the room, Shane stood back to survey her work. "The hardest thing now," she muttered as she twisted a curl around her finger, "is going to be parting with it. I'll make a nice profit. I only paid a fraction of its worth."

Vance ran a fingertip over the surface. It was baby

smooth and flawless. His mother had a similar piece in the drawing room of her Washington estate. Since he had purchased it for her himself, he knew the value. He also knew the difference between an amateur job of refinishing and an expert one. This hadn't been done haphazardly. "Your time's worth something," he commented. "And your talent. It would have cost a good deal to have this done."

"Yes, but I enjoy it, so it doesn't count."

Vance lifted his eyes. "You're in business to make money, aren't you?"

"Yes, of course." Shane snapped the lid back on the can of paste wax. "I love the smell of this stuff."

"You won't make a lot of money if you don't consider your own time and labor."

"I don't need to make a lot of money." She placed the can on a shelf, then examined the ladder-back chair, which needed recaning. "I need to pay bills and stock my shop and have a bit left over to play with." Turning the chair upside down, she frowned at the frayed hole in the center of the seat. "I wouldn't know what to do with a lot of money."

"You'd find something," Vance said dryly. "Clothes, furs."

Shane glanced up, saw he was serious, then burst out laughing. "Furs? Oh, yes, I can see myself waltzing into the general store to buy milk in a mink. Vance, you're a riot."

"I've never known a woman who didn't appreciate a mink," he countered.

"Then you've known the wrong women," she said lightly as she set the chair upright again. "I know this man in Boonsboro who does caning and rushing. I'll have to give him a call. Even if I had the time, I wouldn't know where to begin on this."

"What kind of woman are you?"

Shane's thoughts came back from her ladder-back chair. When she looked at him again, she noted that Vance's expression was cynical. She sighed. "Vance, why do you always look for complications?"

"Because they're always there," he returned.

She shook her head, keeping her hands on the top rung of the chair's back. "I'm exactly the kind of woman I seem to be. Perhaps that's too simple for you, but it's true."

"The kind who's content to work twelve hours a day just for enough money to get by on?" Vance demanded. "The kind who's willing to slave away hour after hour—"

"I don't slave," Shane interrupted testily.

"The hell you don't. I've watched you. Dragging furniture, lugging boxes, scrubbing on your hands and knees." Remembering only made him angrier. She was too small to labor the way he had seen over the past weeks. The fact that he wanted to insist she stop only infuriated him further. "Damn it, Shane, it's too much for you to handle by yourself."

"I know what I'm capable of," she tossed back, springing to her own defense. "I'm not a child."

"No, you're a woman who doesn't crave furs or all the niceties an attractive female can have if she plays her cards right." The words were cool with sarcasm.

Temper sprang into Shane's eyes. Struggling not to explode, she turned away from him. "Do you think everyone has a game to play, Vance?"

"And some play better than others" was his response.

"Oh, I feel sorry for you," she said tightly. "Really very sorry."

"Why?" he demanded. "Because I know that grabbing all they can get is what motivates people? Only a fool settles for less."

"I wonder if you really believe that," she murmured. "I wonder if you really could."

"I wonder why you pretend to believe otherwise," he retorted.

"I'm going to tell you a little story." When she turned back, her eyes were dark with anger. "A man like you will probably find it corny and a bit boring, but you'll just have to listen anyway." Stuffing her hands into her pockets, she paced the low-ceilinged room until she was certain she could continue.

"Do you see these?" Shane demanded, indicating a

row of shelves that held filled mason jars. "My grand-mother—technically, she was my great-grandmother—canned these. Putting by, she always called it. She'd dig and hoe and plant and weed, then spend hours in a hot, steamy kitchen canning. Putting by," Shane repeated more quietly as she studied the colorful glass jars. "When she was sixteen, she lived in a mansion in southern Maryland. Her family was very wealthy. They still are," Shane added with a shrug. "The Bristols. The Leonardtown Bristols. You might have heard of them."

He had, and though his eyes registered surprise, he said nothing. Bristols Department Stores were scattered strategically all over the country. It was a very old, very prestigious firm that catered to the wealthy and the prominent. Even now, Vance's firm was contracted to build another branch in Chicago.

"In any case," Shane continued, "she was a young, beautiful, pampered girl who could have had anything. She'd been educated in Europe, and there were plans for her to be finished in Paris before a London debut. If she had followed her parents' plans, she would have married well, had her own mansion and her own staff of servants. The closest she would have come to planting would have been watching her gardener prune a rosebush."

Shane gave a little laugh as though the thought both amused and baffled her. "She didn't follow the plan, though. She fell in love with William Abbott, an apprentice mason who had been hired to do some stone-work on the estate. Of course, her family would have none of it. They were already planning the groundwork for a marriage between Gran and the heir to some steel company. The moment they got wind of what was happening, they fired him. To keep it brief, Gran made her choice and married him. They disowned her. Very dramatic and Victorian. The I-have-no-daughter sort of thing you read in a standard Gothic."

Vance said nothing as she stared at him, almost daring him to comment. "They moved here, back with his family," Shane continued. "They had to share this house with his parents because there wasn't enough money for one of their own. When his father died, they cared for his mother. Gran never regretted giving up all the *niceties*. She had such tiny hands," she murmured, looking down at her own. "You wouldn't have thought they could be so strong." She shook off the mood and turned away. "They were poor by the standards she had grown up with. What horses they had were for pulling a plow. Some of your land was hers at one time, but with the taxes and no one to work it…" She trailed off, lifting down a mason jar, then setting it back. "The only gesture her parents ever made was when her mother left Gran the dining-room set and a few pieces of china. Even that was done through lawyers after her mother had died."

Shane plucked up her polishing cloth and began to run it through her hands.

"Gran had five children, lost two in childhood, another in the war. One daughter moved to Oklahoma and died childless about forty years ago. Her youngest son settled here, married and had one daughter. Both he and his wife were killed when the daughter was five." She paused a moment, brooding up at the small window set near the ceiling. Light poured through it to lie in a patch on the concrete floor. "I wonder if you can appreciate how a mother feels when she outlives every one of her children."

Vance said nothing, only continued to watch as Shane moved agitatedly around the room. "She raised her granddaughter, Anne. Gran loved her. Maybe part of the love was grief, I don't know. My mother was a beautiful child—there are pictures of her upstairs—but she was never content. The stories I've heard came mostly from people in town, though once or twice Gran talked to me. Anne hated living here, hated not having enough. She wanted to be an actress. When she was seventeen, she got pregnant."

Shane's voice altered subtly, but he heard the change. It was flat now, devoid of emotion. He'd never heard that tone from her before. "She didn't know—or wouldn't admit—who the father was," she said simply. "As soon as I was born, she took off and left me with Gran. From time to time, she came back, spent a few days and talked Gran out of more money. At last count she's been married three times. I've seen her in furs. They don't seem to make her happy. She's still beautiful, still selfish, still discontented."

Shane turned and looked at Vance for the first time since she had begun. "My grandmother only grabbed for one thing in her life, and that was love. She spoke French beautifully, read Shakespeare and tilled a garden. And she was happy. The only thing my mother ever taught me was that *things* meant nothing. Once you have a *thing,* you're too busy looking for the next one to be happy with it. You're too worried that someone might have a better one to be able to enjoy it. All the games my mother played never brought anything but pain to the people who loved her. I don't have the time or the skill for those games."

As she started to walk to the stairs, Vance stepped in front of her to bar her way. She lifted her chin to stare with eyes that glittered with anger and tears. "You should have told me to go to hell," he said quietly.

Shane swallowed. "Go to hell then," she muttered, and tried to move past him again.

Vance took her shoulders, holding her firmly at arm's length. "Are you angry with me, Shane, or with yourself for telling me something that was none of my business?" he asked.

After taking a deep breath, Shane stared at him, dry-eyed. "I'm angry because you're cynical, and I've never been able to understand cynicism."

"Any more than I understand an idealist."

"I'm not an idealist," she countered. "I simply don't automatically assume there's someone waiting to take advantage of me." She felt calmer suddenly, and sadder. "I think you miss a lot more by not trusting people than you risk by trusting them."

"What happens when the trust is violated?"

"Then you pick up and go on," she told him simply. "You're only a victim if you choose to be."

His brows drew together. Is that what he considered himself? A victim? Was he continuing to allow Amelia to blight his life two years after she'd died? And how much longer would he look over his shoulder for the next betrayal?

Shane felt his fingers relax, saw the puzzled consideration on his face. She lifted a hand to touch his shoulder. "Were you hurt very badly?" she asked him.

Vance focused on her again, then released her. "I was...disillusioned."

"That's the worst kind of hurt, I think." In compassion, she laid a hand on his arm. "When someone you love or care for turns out to be dishonest, or an ideal turns to glass, it's difficult to accept. I always set my ideals high. If they're going to crumble, I'd just as soon take the long fall." She smiled, slipping her hand down so it linked with his. "Let's go for a drive."

His thoughts were so bound up in her words, it took him a moment to understand the suggestion. "A drive?" he repeated.

"We've been cooped up for weeks," Shane stated as she pulled him toward the stairs. "I don't know about you, but I haven't done anything but work until I tumbled into bed. It's a beautiful day, maybe the last of Indian summer." She shut the basement door behind them. "And I bet you haven't had a tour of the battlefield yet. Certainly not with an expert guide."

"Are you," he asked with the beginnings of a smile, "an expert guide?"

"The best," she said without modesty. As she had hoped, the tension went out of the fingers that were laced with hers. "There's nothing about the battle I can't tell you, or as some of my critics would claim, won't tell you."

"As long as I don't have to take a quiz afterward," Vance agreed as she pulled him out the back door.

"I'm retired," she reminded him primly.

"The Battle of Antietam," Shane began as she drove down a narrow, winding road lined with monuments, "though claimed as a clear victory for neither side, resulted in the repulse of Lee's first effort to invade the

North." Vance gave a quick grin at her faintly lecturing tone, but didn't interrupt. "Near Antietam Creek here in Sharpsburg," she continued, "on September 17, 1862, Lee and McClellan engaged in the bloodiest single day of the Civil War. That's Dunker Church." Shane pointed to a tiny white building set off the road. "Some of the heaviest fighting went on there. I have some pretty good prints for the museum."

Vance glanced back at the peaceful little spot as Shane drove by. "Looks quiet enough now," he commented, and earned a mild look.

"Lee divided his forces," she went on, ignoring him, "sending Jackson to capture Harper's Ferry. A Union soldier picked up a copy of Lee's orders, giving McClellan an advantage, but he didn't move fast enough. Even when he engaged Lee's much smaller army in Sharpsburg, he failed to smash through the line before Jackson returned with support. Lee lost a quarter of his army and withdrew. McClellan still didn't capitalize on his advantage. Even so, twenty-six thousand men were lost."

"For a retired schoolteacher, you don't seem to have forgotten the facts," Vance remarked.

Shane laughed, taking a bend in the road competently. "My ancestors fought here. Gran didn't let me forget it."

"For which side?"

"Both." She gave a small shrug. "Wasn't that the worst of it really? The choosing sides, the disintegration of families. This is a border state. Though it went for the North, sympathies this far south leaned heavily toward the Confederacy as well. It isn't difficult to imagine a number of people from this area cheering secretly or openly for the Stars and Bars."

"And with this section being caught between Virginia and West Virginia—"

"Exactly," she said, very much like a teacher approving of a bright student. Vance chuckled but she didn't seem to notice. Shane pulled off the side of the road into a small parking area. "Come on, let's walk. It's beautiful here."

Around them mountains circled in the full glory of fall. A few leaves whipped by—orange, scarlet, amber—to be caught by the wind and carried off. There were rolling hills, gold in the slanting sunlight, and fields with dried, withering stalks of corn. The air was cooler now as the sun dropped toward the peaks of the western mountains. Without thinking, Vance linked his hand with hers.

"Bloody Lane," Shane said, bringing his attention to a long, narrow trench. "Gruesome name, but apt. They came at each other from across the fields. Rebs from the north. Yanks from the south. Artillery set up there—" she pointed "—and there. This trench is where most of them lay after it was over. Of course, there were engagements all around—at the Burnside Bridge, the Dunker Church—but this…"

Vance shot her a curious look. "War really fascinates you, doesn't it?"

Shane looked out over the field. "It's the only true obscenity. The only time killing's glorified rather than condemned. Men become statistics. I wonder if there's anything more dehumanizing." Her voice became more thoughtful. "Haven't you ever found it odd that to kill one to one is considered man's ultimate crime, but the more a man kills during war, the more he's honored? So many of these were farm boys," she continued before Vance could form an answer. "Children who'd never shot at anything more than a weasel in the henhouse. They put on a uniform, blue or gray, and marched into battle. I doubt if a fraction of them had any idea what it was really going to be like. I'll tell you what fascinates me." Shane looked back at Vance, too wrapped up in her own thoughts to note how intensely he watched her. "Who were they really? The sixteen-year-old Pennsylvania farm boy who rushed across this field to kill a sixteen-year-old boy from a Georgia plantation—did they start out looking for adventure? Were they on a quest? How many pictured themselves sitting around a campfire like men and raising some hell away from their mothers?"

"A great many, I imagine," Vance murmured. Affected by the image she projected, he slipped an arm around her shoulders as he looked out over the field. "Too many."

"Even the ones who got back whole would never be boys again."

"Then why history, Shane, when it's riddled with wars?"

"For the people." She tossed back her head to look at him. The lowering sun shining on her eyes seemed to accentuate the tiny gold flecks that he sometimes couldn't see at all. "For the boy I can imagine who came across that field in September more than a hundred and twenty years ago. He was seventeen." She turned back to the field as if she could indeed see him. "He'd had his first whiskey, but not his first woman. He came running across that field full of terror and glory. The bugles were blaring, the shells exploding, so that the noise was so huge, he never heard his own fear. He killed an enemy that was so obscure to him it had no face. And when the battle was over, when the war was over, he went home a man, tired and aching for his own land."

"What happened to him?" Vance murmured.

"He married his childhood sweetheart, raised ten kids and told his grandchildren about his charge to Bloody Lane in 1862."

Vance drew her closer, not in passion, but in camaraderie. "You must have been a hell of a teacher," he said quietly.

That made Shane laugh. "I was a hell of a storyteller," she corrected.

"Why do you do that?" he demanded. "Why do you underrate yourself?"

She shook her head. "No, I know my capabilities and my limitations. And," she added, "I'm willing to stretch them both a bit to get what I want. It's much smarter than thinking you're something you're not." Before he could speak, she laughed, giving him a friendly hug. "No, no more philosophizing. I've done my share for the day. Come on, let's go up in the tower. The view's wonderful from there." She was off in a sprint, pulling Vance with her. "You can see for miles," she told him as they climbed the narrow iron steps.

The light was dim though the sun shot through the small slits set in the sides of the stone tower. It grew brighter as they climbed, then poured through the opening at the top. "This is the part I like best," she told him, while a few annoyed pigeons fluttered away from their roost in the roof. She leaned over the wide stone, pleased to let the wind buffet her face. "Oh, it's beautiful, the perfect day for it. Look at those colors!" She drew Vance beside her, wanting to share. "Do you see? That's our mountain."

Our mountain. Vance smiled as he followed the direction of her hand. The way she said it, it might have belonged to the two of them exclusively. Beyond the tree-thick hills, the more distant mountains were cast in blue from the falling afternoon light. Farmhouses and barns were set here and there, with the more closely structured surrounding towns quiet in the early evening hush. Just barely, he could hear the whiz of a car on the highway. As he looked over a cornfield, he saw three enormous crows take flight. They argued, taunting each other as they glided across the sky. The air was very still after they passed, so quiet he could hear the breeze whisper in the dry stalks of corn.

Then he saw the buck. It stood poised no more than ten yards from where Shane had parked her car. It was still as a statue, head up, ears pricked. Vance turned to Shane and pointed.

In silence, hands linked, they watched. Vance felt something move inside him, a sudden sense of belonging. He wouldn't have been amused now if Shane had said "our mountain." Remnants of bitterness washed from him as he realized his answer had been staring him in the face. He'd kept himself a victim, just as Shane had said, because it was easier to be angry than to let go.

The buck moved quickly, bounding over the grassy hill, taking a low stone fence with a graceful leap before he darted out of sight. Vance felt rather than heard Shane's long, slow sigh.

"I never get used to it," she murmured. "Every time I see one, I'm struck dumb."

Shane turned her face up to his. It seemed natural to kiss her here, with the mountains and fields around them, with the feeling of something shared still on both of them. Above their heads a pigeon cooed softly, content now that the intruders were quiet.

Here was the tenderness Shane had sensed but had not been sure of. His mouth was firm but not demanding, his hands strong but not bruising. Her heart seemed to flutter to her throat. Everything warm and sweet poured through her until she was limp and pliant in his arms. She had been waiting for this—this final assurance of what she knew he held trapped inside him: a gentle goodness she would respect as much as his strength and confidence. Her sigh was not of surrender but of joy in knowing she could admire what she already loved.

Vance drew her closer, changing the angle of the kiss, reluctant to break the moment. Emotions seeped into him, through the cracks in the wall he had built so long ago. He felt the soft give of her mouth, tasted its moist generosity. With care, he let his fingertips reacquaint themselves with the texture of her skin.

Could she have been there all along, he wondered, waiting for him to stumble onto her through a curtain of bitterness and suspicion?

Vance drew her against his chest, holding her tightly with both arms as if she might vanish. Was it too late for him to fall in love? he wondered. Or to win a woman who already knew the worst of him and had no notion of his material advantages? Closing his eyes, he rested his cheek on her hair. If it wasn't too late, should he take the chance and tell her who and what he was? If he told her now, he might never be fully certain, if she came to him, that she came only to him. He needed that—to be taken for himself without the Riverton Banning fortune or power. He hesitated, torn and indecisive. That alone shook him. Vance was a man who ruled a multi-million-dollar company by being decisive. Now a slip of a woman whose hair curled chaotically under his cheek was changing the order of his life.

"Shane." Vance drew her away to kiss her brow.

"Vance." Laughing, she kissed him soundly, more like a friend than a lover. "You look so serious."

"Have dinner with me." It came out too swiftly and he cursed himself. What had become of his finesse with women?

Shane pushed at her windblown hair. "All right. I can fix us something at the house."

"No, I want to take you out."

"Out?" Shane frowned, thinking of the expense.

"Nothing fancy," he told her, thinking she was worried about her bulky sweater and jeans. "As you said, neither of us has done anything but work in weeks." He brushed his knuckles over the back of her cheek. "Come with me."

She smiled, pleasing him. "I know a nice little place just over the border in West Virginia."

Shane chose the tiny, out-of-the-way restaurant because it was inexpensive and she had some fond memories of an abbreviated career as a waitress there. She'd worked the summer after her high school graduation in order to earn extra money for college.

After they had settled into a cramped booth with a sputtering candle between them, she shot him a grin. "I knew you'd love it."

Vance glanced around at the painted landscapes in vivid colors and plastic frames. The air smelled ever so faintly of onion. "Next time, I choose."

"They used to serve a great spaghetti here. It was Thursday's special, all you can eat for—"

"It's not Thursday," Vance pointed out, dubiously opening the plastic-coated menu. "Wine?"

"I think they probably have it." Shane smiled at him when he peered over the top of the menu. "We could go next door and get a whole bottle for two ninety-seven."

"Good vintage?"

"Just last week," she assured him.

"We'll take our chances here." He decided next time he would take her somewhere he could buy her champagne.

"I'll have the chili," Shane announced, bringing his thoughts back.

"Chili?" Vance frowned at the menu again. "Is it any good?"

"Oh, no!"

"Then why are you—" He broke off as he lowered his menu and saw Shane buried behind her own. "Shane, what—"

"They just came in," she hissed, turning her menu toward the entrance and peeping around the side of it.

Curiously, he glanced over. Vance spotted Cy Trainer with a trim brunette in a severely tailored tan suit and sensible pumps. His first reaction was annoyance; then, looking the woman over again and noting the way her hand rested on Cy's arm, he turned back to Shane. She was fully hidden behind the menu.

"Shane, I know it must upset you, but you're bound to run into him from time to time and…" He heard a muffled sound from behind the plastic-coated cardboard. Instinctively, Vance reached for her hand. "We could go somewhere else, but we can't leave now without his seeing you."

"It's Laurie MacAfee." She squeezed Vance's fingers convulsively. He returned the pressure, furious that she still had feelings for the man who had hurt her.

"Shane, you've got to face this and not let him see you make a fool of yourself."

"I know, but it's so hard." Cautiously, she tilted the menu to the side. With a jolt, Vance saw she was convulsed not with tears but with laughter. "As soon as he sees us," she began confidentially, "he's going to come over and be polite."

"I can see that's going to cause you a lot of pain."

"Oh, it is," she agreed. "Because you've got to promise to kick me under the table or stomp on my foot the minute you see I'm going to laugh."

"My pleasure," he assured her.

"Laurie used to keep her dolls lined up according to height and she sewed little name tags on all their clothes," Shane explained, taking deep breaths to prepare herself.

"That certainly clears everything up."

"Okay, now I'm going to put the menu down." She swallowed, lowering her voice a bit more. "Whatever you do, don't look at them."

"I wouldn't dream of it."

After a final cleansing breath, Shane set the menu on the table. "Chili?" she said in a normal tone. "Yes, it's always been good here. I believe I'll have it too."

"You're an idiot."

"Oh yes, I agree." Smiling, she picked up her water glass. Out of the corner of her eye, she spotted Cy and Laurie crossing the room toward them. To kill the first bubble of laughter, she cleared her throat violently.

"Shane, how nice to see you."

Looking up, Shane managed to feign surprise. "Hello, Cy. Hello, Laurie. How've you been?"

"Very well," Laurie answered in her carefully modulated voice. She's really very pretty, Shane thought. Even if her eyes are just a fraction too close together.

"I don't think you know Vance," she continued. "Vance, this is Cy Trainer and Laurie MacAfee, old school friends of mine. Vance is my neighbor."

"Ah, of course, the old Farley place." Cy extended his hand. Vance found it soft. The grip was correctly firm and brief. "I hear you're fixing the place up."

"A bit." Vance allowed himself to study Cy's face. He was passable, Vance decided, considering he had a weak jaw.

"You must be the carpenter who's helping Shane set up her little shop," Laurie put in. Her glance slipped over his work clothes before it shifted to Shane's sweater. "I must say, I was surprised when Cy told me your plans."

Seeing Shane's lip quiver, Vance set his foot firmly on top of hers. "Were you?" Shane said as she reached for her water again. Her eyes danced with suppressed amusement as they met Vance's over the rim. "Well, I've always liked to surprise people."

"We couldn't imagine you with your own business, could we, Cy?" Laurie went on without giving him a chance to answer. "Of course, we wish you the very best of luck, Shane, and you can count on both of us to buy something to help you get started."

The laughter was a pain in her stomach. Shane had to press a hand against it while Vance increased the pressure on her foot. "Thank you, Laurie. I can't tell you what that means to me...I really can't."

"Anything for an old friend, right, Cy? You know we wish you every success, Shane. I'll be sure to tell everyone I know about your little shop. That should help bring a few people in. Though of course," she sighed apologetically, "the selling's up to you."

"Y-yes. Thank you."

"We'll just be running along now. We want to order before it gets too crowded. So nice meeting you." Laurie sent Vance a brief smile and drew Cy away.

"Oh, God, I think I'm going to burst!" Shane drank down the whole glass of water without a breath.

"Your boyfriend got just what he deserved," Vance murmured, glancing after them. "She'll regiment everything right down to their sex life." Thoughtfully, he looked after them. "Do you think they have one yet?"

"Oh, stop," Shane begged, savaging her lip in defense. "I'll be hysterical in a minute."

"Do you suppose she picked out that tie he's wearing?" Vance asked.

Giving up, Shane burst into laughter. "Oh, damn you,

Vance," she whispered when Laurie turned her head. "I was doing so well too."

"Want to give them something to talk about over dinner?" Before she could answer, Vance pulled her across the narrow booth and planted a long, lingering kiss on her lips. To keep Shane from ending it too soon, he caught her chin in his hand and held her still. He drew her away for only seconds, tilting her head, then pressing his mouth to hers again at a fresh angle. He heard her give a tiny moan of distress. Though she lifted a hand to his shoulder to push him away, when he deepened the kiss, she allowed it to lie unresisting until he took his lips from hers.

"Now you've done it," she said when she gathered her wits again. "By noon tomorrow it'll be all over Sharpsburg that we're lovers."

"Will it?" Smiling, he lifted her hand to his lips, then slowly kissed her fingers one by one. It satisfied him to feel the faint tremor of arousal.

"Yes," Shane answered breathlessly, "and I don't..." She trailed off when he turned her palm up to press another long kiss in its center.

"Don't what?" he asked softly, taking his lips to the inside of her wrist. Her pulse pounded against the light trace of his tongue.

"Think it's—it's wise," she managed, forgetting the restaurant and Cy and Laurie and everything else.

"That we're lovers or that it's all over Sharpsburg?" Vance enjoyed the confusion in her eyes and the knowledge that he had put it there.

Her pulse beat jerkily. He was different. Reckless? she thought, and felt a fresh thrill race down her spine. Smooth? How could he be both at once? Yet he was. The recklessness was in his eyes, but the romantic moves were smooth with experience.

She hadn't been afraid of the hard, angry man she had met, but she felt a skip of fear for the one who even now traced his thumb over the speeding pulse at her wrist.

"I'm going to have to give that some thought," she murmured.

"Do that," he said agreeably.

Chapter 8

Shane opened the doors of Antietam Antiques and Museum the first week of December. As she had expected, for the first few days the shop and museum were crowded, for the most part with people she knew. They had come to buy or browse out of curiosity or affection. Others came to see what "that Abbott girl" had up her sleeve this time. It amused Shane to hear her past crimes discussed as though they had taken place the day before. Cy's name was dropped a time or two, causing her to force back a chuckle and change the subject. Still, after the initial novelty had worn off, she had a steady trickle of customers. That was enough to satisfy her.

As planned, she hired Donna's sister-in-law, Pat, on a part-time basis. The girl was eager and willing, and not opposed to giving Shane weekend hours. Shane considered the additional expense well worth it when Pat, flushed with triumph, rang up her first sale. With her coaching, and Pat's own enthusiastic studying, Shane's assistant had learned enough to classify certain articles in the shop and to handle questions in the museum section.

Shane found herself busier than ever, managing the shop, watching for ads for estate sales and overseeing the remodeling still under way on the second floor. The long, chaotic hours stimulated her, and helped her deal with the slow but steady loss of her grandmother's treasures. It was business, Shane reminded herself again and again as she sold a corner cabinet or candle holder. It was necessary. The bills in her desk had mounted over the weeks of preparation, and they had to be paid.

She saw Vance almost daily as he came to hammer and saw and trim on the second floor. Though he wasn't as withdrawn as he once had been, the intimacy they had shared for an afternoon and evening had faded. He treated her as a casual friend, not a woman whose palm he would kiss in a restaurant.

Shane concluded that he had taken on a loverlike aspect for Cy's benefit, and now it was back to business as usual. She wasn't discouraged. In fact, the man she had dined with had made her nervous and uncertain. She was more confident with Vance's temper than with soft words and tender caresses. Knowing herself well, Shane was aware it would be difficult not to make a fool of herself over him if he continued to treat her with gentleness. She had little defense against romance.

Daily, her love for him grew. It only made her more certain than ever that he was the only man for her. It would only be a matter of time, she decided, before he realized she was the woman for him.

It was late afternoon when Shane carried her latest acquisition up the new front steps and into the shop. She was flushed with cold and highly pleased with herself. She was learning to be ruthless when bargaining. After pushing the door open with her bottom, she carried the table through the entrance sideways.

"Just look what I've got!" she said to Pat before she closed the door behind her. "It's a Sheridan. Not a scratch on it either."

Pat stopped washing the glass on the display case. "Shane, you were supposed to take the afternoon off." Automatically she polished off a lingering smear before giving Shane her full attention. "You've got to take some time for yourself," she reminded her with a hint of exasperation. "That's why you hired me."

"Yes, of course," Shane said distractedly. "There's a mantel clock in the car and a complete set of cut-glass saltcellars." Pat sighed, smart enough to know when she was being ignored, and followed Shane into the main showroom.

"Don't you ever quit?" she demanded.

"Uh-uh." After setting the table beside a Hitchcock chair, Shane stepped back to view the results. "I don't know," she said slowly. "It might look better in the front room, right under the window. Well, I want to polish it first anyway." She darted to the work counter, rummaging for the furniture polish. "How'd we do today?"

Pat shook her head. The first thing she had learned on the job was that Shane Abbott was a powerhouse. "I'll do that," she said, taking the polish and rag from Shane's hands. Shane grinned at Pat's weighty sigh but said nothing. "You had seven people come through the museum," Pat told her as she began to polish the Sheridan. "I sold some postcards and a print of the Burnside Bridge. A woman from Hagerstown bought the little table with the fluted edges."

Shane stopped unbuttoning her coat. "The rosewood piecrust?" It had sat in the summer parlor for as long as she could remember.

"Yes. And she was interested in the bentwood rocker." Pat tucked a strand of hair behind her ear while Shane struggled to be pleased. "I think she'll be back."

"Good."

"Oh, and you had a nibble on Uncle Festus."

"Really?" Shane grinned, thinking of the portrait of

a dour Victorian man she'd been unable to resist. She had bought it because it amused her, though she had had little hope of selling it. "Well, I'll be sorry to lose him. He gives the place dignity."

"He gives me the creeps," Pat said baldly as Shane headed for the front door to fetch the rest of her new stock. "Oh, I nearly forgot. You didn't tell me you'd sold the dining-room set."

"What?" Puzzled, Shane stopped with her hand on the knob.

"The dining-room set with the heart-shaped chairs," Pat explained. "The Hepplewhite," she added, pleased that she was beginning to remember makes and periods. "I nearly sold it again."

"Again?" Shane released the knob and faced Pat fully. "What are you talking about?"

"There were some people in here a few hours ago who wanted it. It seems their daughter's getting married, and they were going to buy it as a wedding gift. They must be rich," she added with feeling. "The reception's going to be at a Baltimore country club...with an orchestra." She began to daydream about this a bit, but then she noted Shane's hard look. "Anyway," she continued quickly, "I'd nearly finalized the sale when Vance came downstairs and explained it was taken already."

Shane's eyes narrowed. "Vance? Vance said it was already sold?"

"Well, yes," Pat agreed, puzzled by the tone. If she had known Shane better, she would have recognized the beginnings of rage. Innocently, she continued. "It was a lucky thing too, or else they'd have bought it and arranged for the shipping right then and there. I guess you'd have been in a fix."

"A fix," Shane repeated between set teeth. "Yeah, somebody's in a fix all right." Abruptly, she turned to stride toward the rear of the shop while Pat looked after her, wide-eyed.

"Shane? Shane, what's wrong?" Confused, she trotted after her. "Where are you going?"

"To settle some business," she said tightly. "Get the rest of the stuff out of my car, will you?" she called back without slackening her pace. "And lock up. This might take a while."

"Sure, but…" Pat trailed off when she heard the back door slam. She puzzled a moment, shrugged, then went to follow orders.

"A fix," Shane muttered as she crushed dead leaves underfoot. "Lucky thing he came down." Furiously, she kicked at a fallen branch and sent it skidding ahead of her, waiting to be kicked again. Grinding her teeth, she stormed purposefully down the path between denuded trees. "Already taken!" Enraged, she made a dangerous sound in her throat. A hapless squirrel started across the path, then dashed in the other direction.

Through the bare trees, she could see his house, with smoke puffing from the chimney to struggle up into a hard blue sky. Shane set her jaw and increased her pace. Into the quiet came a steady thump, pause, thump. Without hesitation, she skirted around to the back of the house.

Vance put another log on the tree stump he used as a chopping block, then bore down with his axe to split it neatly in two. Without a pause in rhythm, he set a new log. Shane took no time to admire the precision or grace of the movement.

"You!" she spat, and stuck her fists on her hips.

Vance checked his next swing. Glancing over, he saw Shane glaring at him with glittering eyes and a flushed face. He thought idly that she looked her best when in a temper, then followed through. The next log split to fall in two pieces on either side of the stump. The generous pile was evidence that he had been working for some time.

"Hello, Shane."

"Don't you 'hello Shane' me," she snapped, closing the distance between them in three quick strides. "How dare you?"

"Most people consider it an acceptable greeting," he countered as he bent down for another log. Shane knocked it off the stump with a sweep of her hand.

"You had no right to interfere, no right to cost me a

sale. An important sale," she added furiously. Her breath puffed out visibly in the frigid air. "Just who the hell do you think you are, telling my customers something's already taken? Even if it had been, which it wasn't, it's hardly your place to add your two cents."

Calmly, Vance picked up the log again. He had been expecting her—and her anger. He had acted on impulse but didn't regret it. Very clearly, he could recall the look on her face when she had first shown him her grandmother's pride and joy. There was no way he was going to stand by and do nothing while she watched it being carted out the door.

"You don't want to sell it, Shane."

Her eyes only became more furious. "It's none of your business what I want to do. I have to sell it. I'm *going* to sell it. If you hadn't opened your big mouth, I *would* have sold it."

"And spent several hours hating yourself and crying over the invoice," he tossed back, slamming the blade of the axe into the stump before he faced her. "The money isn't worth it."

"Don't you tell me what it's worth," she retorted, and poked a finger into his chest. "You don't know how I feel. You don't know what I have to do. *I* do. I need the money, damn it."

With strained calm, he curled his hand around the finger that dug into his chest, held it aloft a moment, then let it drop. "You don't need it enough to give up something that's important to you."

"Sentiment doesn't pay bills." The color in her cheeks heightened. "I've got a desk full of them."

"Sell something else," he shouted back at her. Her face was lifted to his, her eyes glowing with anger. He felt conflicting urges to protect her and to throttle her. "You've got the damn place packed with junk as it is."

"Junk!" He had just declared war. *"Junk!"* Her voice rose.

"Unload some of the other stuff you've got piled in there," he advised with a coolness that would have rattled his business associates. A dangerous hissing sound escaped through Shane's teeth.

"You don't know the first thing about it," she fumed, poking him again so that he stepped back. "I stock the very best pieces I can find, and *you*—" she poked again "—you don't know a Hepplewhite from a—a piece of pressboard. You keep your city nose out of my affairs, Vance Banning, and play with your planes and drill bits. I don't need some flatlander to hand out empty advice."

"That's it," he said grimly. In one swift move, he swept Shane off her feet and dumped her over his shoulder.

"What the hell do you think you're doing?" she screamed, thrashing and pounding him with her fists.

"I'm taking you inside to make love to you," he stated between his teeth. "I've had enough."

In absolute astonishment, Shane stopped thrashing. "You're *what?*"

"You heard me."

"You're crazy!" More furious than frantic, she renewed her efforts to inflict pain wherever she could land a hit. Vance continued through the back door. "You're not taking me inside," she raged, even as he carted her through the kitchen. "I'm not going with you."

"You're going exactly where I take you," he countered.

"Oh, you're going to pay for this, Vance," she promised as she pounded against his back.

"I don't doubt that," he muttered, starting up the stairs.

"You put me down this minute. I'm not putting up with this."

Weary of being kicked, he pulled off her shoes, tossed them over the banister, then tightened an arm around the back of her knees. "You're going to put up with a hell of a lot more in a few minutes."

With her legs effectively pinned, she wiggled uselessly as he continued up the stairs. "I'm telling you, you're in big trouble. I'll get you for this," she warned, beating furiously against him as he strode down the hall and into a bedroom. "If you don't put me down this minute, *right this minute,* you're fired!" Shane let out a shriek as she tumbled through the air, then a whoosh as she thudded heavily on the bed. Breathless and infuriated, she scrambled to her knees. "You idiot!" she raged, puffing a bit. "Just what do you think you're doing?"

"I told you what I was doing." Vance stripped off his jacket and tossed it aside.

"If you think for one minute you can toss me over your shoulder like a bale of hay and get away with it, you're sadly mistaken." Shane watched with mounting fury as he unbuttoned his shirt. "And you stop that right now. You can't *make* me make love with you."

"Watch me." Vance peeled off his shirt.

"Oh no, you don't." Though she stuck her hands on her hips, the indignant pose lost something as she knelt on the bed. "Just put that right back on."

Watching her coolly, Vance dropped it to the floor, then bent to pull off his boots.

Shane glared at him. "You think you can just dump me on the bed and that's all there is to it?"

"I haven't even started yet," he informed her as the second boot dropped with a clatter.

"You simpleminded clod," she returned, heaving a pillow at him. "I wouldn't let you touch me if—" She searched for something original and scathing but settled on the standby. "If you were the last man on earth!"

Vance sent her a long, glittering look before he unbuckled his belt.

"I told you to stop that." Shane pointed a warning finger. "I mean it. Don't you dare take another thing off.

Vance!" she added threateningly as he reached for the snap of his jeans. "I'm serious." The word ended on a giggle. His hands paused; his eyes narrowed. "Put your clothes back on this minute," she ordered, but pressed the back of her hand to her mouth. Over it, her eyes were wide and brilliant with amusement.

"What the hell's so funny?" he demanded.

"Nothing, not a thing." With this, Shane collapsed on her back, helpless with laughter. "Funny? No, no, this is a very grave situation." Convulsed with giggles, she pounded her fists on the bed. "The man is standing there, pulling off his clothes and looking fit for murder. Nothing could be more serious."

Shane glanced over at him, then covered her mouth with both hands. "*That* is the face of a man overcome by lust and desire." She laughed until tears came to her eyes.

Damn her, Vance thought as a grin tugged at his mouth. He crossed to the bed; then, sitting beside her, he planted his hands on either side of her head. The harder she tried to control her amusement, the more her eyes laughed at him. "Glad you're having a good time," he commented.

She swallowed a chuckle. "Oh no, I'm furious, absolutely furious, but it was *so* romantic."

"Was it?" His grin widened as he considered her.

"Oh yes, why you just swept me off my feet." Her

laughter rang through the room. "I don't know when I've been more *aroused,*" she managed.

"Is that so?" Vance murmured as Shane gave herself wholly to mirth. Very deliberately, he lowered his lips to brush her chin.

"Yes, unless it was when Billy Huffman pushed me into the briars in second grade. Obviously I inflame males into violent seizures of passion."

"Obviously," Vance agreed, tucking her hair behind her ear. "I've had several since I tangled with you." Her fit of giggles ceased abruptly when he caught her earlobe between his teeth. "I think I'm bound to have several more," he murmured, moving down to her neck.

"Vance—"

"Soon," he added against her throat. "Any minute."

"I have to get back," she began breathlessly. As she attempted to sit up, he pressed a hand to her shoulder to keep her still.

"I wonder what else might arouse you." He nibbled at the cord of her neck. "This?"

"No, I…"

"No?" He gave a deep, quiet laugh, feeling her pulse hammer against his lips. "Something else then." Her coat was unzipped, and deftly he loosened the range of buttons on her blouse. "This?" Very gently, he touched the tip of her breast with his tongue.

On a gasp, Shane arched against him. Vance drew her

nipple into his mouth to let her taste seep through him. He savored it a moment as Shane dug her nails into his bare shoulders. But when the heat shot into him, he knew he had to pull back before he took her too quickly. He'd been careful since the night they had dined together to keep some space between them. He hadn't wanted to rush her. Now that he had her in his bed, he intended to savor every moment.

Vance lifted his head and looked down at her. Her eyes were wide and fixed on his. For a moment, they both looked for answers. Very slowly, Shane smiled. "This," she whispered, and drew his mouth down to hers.

She hadn't been prepared for the sweetness of the kiss. His lips moved gently over hers. Their breath merged and matched rhythm. With light kisses he roamed her face, only to return over and over to her waiting mouth. To linger, to savor, to make each moment, each taste last; that was his only thought. The fiery needs were banked by the simple knowledge that she was his to touch, to kiss, to love. For the first time in his memory, he wanted to bring a woman pleasure much more than he wanted to take his own. He could give her that with the slow kisses that made his own blood thunder. Until he sensed she craved more, he used only his lips and tongue to arouse her.

Hardly touching her, Vance drew her jacket over her shoulders and arms, lifting her slightly to slip it from under her. His touch was so sure, so gentle, she remained unaware of his inner conflict between passion and tenderness. Without hurry, he drew off her shirt, following its progress over her shoulders with his lips. Shane sighed as his kisses ranged down her arm to nibble at the inside of her elbow. Fighting the growing need to rush, Vance trailed his lips down to her wrist.

If the wind still blew outside the windows, if leaves still rustled along the ground, Shane was unaware. There was only the play of Vance's fingertips, only the warm trace of his mouth. Content, almost sleepy, she ran her fingers through his thick mane of hair as his teeth tugged lightly at the cord of her neck. The lazy friction of his skin against hers had her pulse beating thickly. She felt she could stay forever, floating in a world halfway between passion and serenity.

He began the downward journey slowly, hardly seeming to move at all. With kisses and light love bites, he circled her breast, moving inward until he captured the peak. It grew hot and hard in his mouth while she began to move under him. He suckled, using his tongue to bring them both to the edge of delirium. Her breathing was as raspy as his. Now he could feel the energy flowing from her, pouring out in passion and urgency. Moaning his name, she pressed him closer to her.

But there was so much more to give, so much more to take. With deliberate care, Vance repeated the same aching journey around her other breast, feeling her shudders, listening to the storm of her heartbeat under his hungry, seeking lips.

"So soft," he murmured. "So beautiful." For a moment he merely buried his face against her breast, struggling to hang on to his control. On a moan of need, Shane reached for him as if to bring his mouth back to hers, but he slipped lower.

Taking her arching hips in his hands, Vance traced his tongue down her quivering skin. Shane felt her jeans loosen at the waist and shifted to help him. But he only pressed his mouth deep into the vee of exposed flesh. Again she shifted, curving her back to offer herself, but he lingered, tracing lazy circles with his tongue.

When he worked the jeans over her hips, she felt each searing brush of his fingers. Down her thighs he journeyed, pausing to caress their soft inner flesh, over her calves to nibble gently at the taut muscles, then to her ankles, sending a devastating flush of heat up her body with a quick flick of his tongue.

He found points of pleasure she had been unaware existed. Then he was at the core of her, his tongue stabbing inside her to catapult her beyond all bounds of reason. She moaned his name, moving with him, moving for him, with mind and body tormented by dark, pulsing delights.

Vance heard his name come huskily through her lips

and thrilled to it. Her energy, her wellspring of passion inflamed him, driving him to take her deeper before he took all. The sweet, sweet taste of her made him greedy. Somewhere in the back of his clouded mind he knew he was no longer gentle with her, but needs whipped at him.

Madness overcame him. His mouth roamed wildly over her body as his fingers took her from peak to staggering peak. Her breath was heaving when he found her breast. If she had been capable of words, Shane would have pleaded with him to take her. Her world was spinning at a terrifying speed, a speed far beyond the scope of her imagination. When his mouth crushed hers, she answered blindly. He thrust into her.

The flow of energy came from nowhere—a power, a strength that hurled her beyond the reasonable and into the impossible. One fed the other, driving higher and faster until they found the apex. Together, they clung to it, shuddering.

How long he lay still, Vance was unsure. Perhaps he even dozed. When his mind began to clear, he found his mouth nuzzled against Shane's throat, her arms wrapped around him. He was still inside her and could feel the light pulses of lingering passion deep within her. For a moment longer he kept his eyes closed, wondering how it was possible to be both sated and exhilarated. When he started to move, thinking of her comfort, Shane tightened her hold to keep him close.

"No," she murmured. "Just a little longer."

He laughed as his lips grazed her ear. "Can you breathe?"

"I'll breathe later."

Content, he snuggled back into the curve of her neck. "I like the way you taste. I've had a problem with that since the first time I kissed you."

"A problem?" she said lazily, running experimental fingers over the muscles of his back. "That doesn't sound much like a compliment to me."

"Would you like one?" He pressed his mouth to her skin. "You're the most exquisite creature I've ever seen."

Shane received this news with a snort of laughter. "Your first compliment was a bit more credible."

Vance lifted his head and looked down at her. Though her eyes were still sleepy with passion, they were amused. "You really don't see it, do you?" he said thoughtfully. Did she really have no notion what big velvet eyes and satin skin could do to a man when combined with her kind of vivacity? Didn't she realize the kind of power there was in striking innocence when it was offset by a sensual mouth and an open, honest sexuality? "You might lose it if you did," he said half to himself. "What if I said I liked your nose?"

She eyed him warily for a moment. "If you say I'm cute, I'll hit you."

He chuckled, then kissed both dimpled cheeks. "Do you know how long I've wanted you like this?"

"From the first moment in the general store." She smiled when he lifted his head to stare down at her. "I felt it too. It was as though I'd been expecting you."

Vance laid his forehead on hers. "I was furious."

"I was stunned. I forgot my coffee."

They laughed before their mouths met. "You were terribly rude that day," she remembered.

"I meant to be." He lured her lips back to his. "I wanted to get rid of you."

"Did you really think you could?" Chuckling, she nipped at his bottom lip. "Don't you know a determined woman when you see one?"

"I *would* have gotten rid of you if I'd been able to close my eyes at night without seeing you."

"Did you really? Poor Vance." She gave him a sympathetic kiss.

"I'm sure you're very sorry I lost sleep over you."

She made a suspicious sound. Vance lifted his head again to see her bottom lip caught firmly between her teeth. "I would be sorry," she assured him, "if I didn't think it was wonderful."

"I often wanted to strangle you at three o'clock in the morning."

"I'm sure you did," she returned soberly. "Why don't you kiss me instead?"

He did, roughly, as banked passions began to smolder again. "That day when you sat in the mud, laughing like a fool, I wanted you so badly I hurt. Damn you, Shane, I haven't been able to think straight for weeks." His mouth crushed down on hers again with a touch of the anger she remembered. She soothed the back of his neck with her fingers.

When he lifted his head, their eyes met in a long, deep look. Shane lifted her palm to his cheek.

So much turbulence, she thought. So many secrets.

So much sweetness, he thought. So much honesty.

"I love you," they said together, then stared at each other in amazement. For a moment, they neither moved nor spoke. It seemed even their breathing had halted at the same instant. Then, as one, they reached out, clinging heart to heart, mouth to mouth. What started as a desperate meeting of lips softened, then sweetened, then promised.

Vance closed his eyes on waves of relief and towering pleasure. When he felt Shane's shudders he drew his arms tighter around her. "You're trembling. Why?"

"It's too perfect," she said in a voice that shook. "It frightens me. If I were to lose you now—"

"Shh." He cut her off with a kiss. "It *is* perfect."

"Oh, Vance, I love you so much. I've been waiting all these weeks for you to love me back, and now..." She took his face in her hands and shook her head. "Now that you do, I'm scared."

Looking down at her, he felt a surge of passion and possession. She was his now; nothing was going to change it. No more mistakes, no more disillusionments. He heard her breath catch then shudder.

"I love you," he said fiercely. "I'm going to keep you, do you understand? We belong together. We both know it. Nothing, by God, nothing's going to interfere with that."

He took her on a wild surge of need and desperation, ignoring the shadow of trepidation that watched over his shoulder.

Chapter 9

It was dark when Shane woke. She had no idea of time or place, only of deep inner contentment and security. The weight of an arm around her waist meant love; the quiet breathing near her ear meant her lover slept beside her. She needed nothing more.

Idly, she wondered how long they had slept. The sun had been setting when she had closed her eyes. The moon was up now. Its cool white light filtered in through the windows to slant across the bed. Shifting slightly, Shane tilted her head back to look at Vance's face. In the dim light, she could make out the sweep of cheekbone and outline of jaw, the strong straight nose. With a fingertip, she traced his mouth gently, not wanting to wake him. As long as he slept, she could look her fill.

It was a strong face, even a hard one, she mused, with its sharp angles and dark coloring. His mouth could be cruel, his eyes cold. Even in his loving there was a ruthless sort of power in him. While a woman might feel safe in his arms, she would never be completely comfortable. A life with him would be full of constant demands, arguments, passion.

And he loves me, Shane thought in a kind of terrified wonder.

In sleep, Vance shifted, drawing her closer. As their naked bodies pressed intimately close, a dull throb of need moved through her. Her skin heated against his, tingling with the contact. Against the slow, steady beat of his heart, hers began to thud erratically. Desire had never seemed more demanding, yet he did nothing more than lie quietly beside her, deep in his own dreams.

It would always be like this, she realized as she settled her head in the crook of his shoulder. He would give her very little peace. Though she was a woman who had always taken peace for granted, Shane would now forfeit it cheerfully. He was her fate; she had known it from the first instant. Now, she felt as bound to him as if she had been his wife for decades.

For a long time she lay awake, listening to him sleep, feeling the steady rise and fall of his chest against her breasts. This would never change, she told herself. This need to hold each other. She burrowed against him for a moment, filling herself with his scent. As long as she lived, Shane knew she would remember every second, every word spoken during their first time together. She would need no diary to remind her of young, churning fires when she was old. No passage of time would dull her memory or her feelings.

With a sigh, she brushed a whisper of a kiss over his lips. He didn't stir, but she wondered if he dreamed of her. She wanted him to, and closing her eyes, she willed him to. Carefully, she drew away from him, then moving lightly, slipped from the bed. Their clothes were in scattered heaps. Finding Vance's shirt, Shane slipped it on before she left the room.

Her scent lingered on the pillowcase. It was the first thing to penetrate Vance's senses as he drifted awake. It suited her so, the fresh, clean fragrance with a suggestion of lemon. Lazily, he allowed it to seep into him. Even in sleep, his mind was full of her. There was a slight stiffness in his shoulder where her head had rested. Vance flexed it before reaching out to bring her back to him. He found himself alone. Opening his eyes, Vance whispered her name.

He experienced the same sense of time disorientation that Shane had. The room was dim with moonlight, so that for a moment he thought he must have dreamed it all. But the sheets were still warm from her, and her scent still lingered. No dream. The relief he felt overwhelmed him. Softly, he called her name. It was then he smelled the bacon. In the dark, he grinned foolishly and settled back. As he lay quietly, he could just hear Shane's voice as she sang some silly popular song.

She was in the kitchen, he thought. Vance stayed where he was, listening. She was rooting through the cupboards, clattering something. Water was running. The scent of bacon grew stronger. How long, he wondered, had he waited to feel this way? *Complete.* He hadn't known he had been waiting, but he did know what he had found. She filled the emptiness that had nagged at him for years, healed an old, festering wound. She was all the answers to all the questions.

And what would he bring her? his conscience demanded. Vance closed his eyes. He knew himself too well to pretend he would give her a smooth, serene life. His temper was too volatile, his responsibilities too intrusive. Even with adjustments to both, he could paint her no soft pastoral scene. His life, past, present and future, had too many complications. Even this, their first night together, would have to be marred by one of his ghosts. He had to tell her about Amelia. There was a burst of rage followed by a prickle of fear.

No, he wouldn't accept the fear, he told himself as he rose quickly from the bed. Nothing, no one was going to interfere with him. No shadow of a dead wife or demands of a hungry business were going to take her from him. She was strong, he reminded himself, trying to override the apprehension. He could make her see his past as it was—something that had happened before her. It might shock her to learn he was president of a multi-million-dollar firm, but she could hardly be displeased once it was out in the open. He would tell Shane everything and wipe the slate clean. When it was done, he could ask her to marry him. If he had to make professional adjustments, he'd make them. He had sacrificed his own youthful dream for the good of the company, but he wouldn't sacrifice Shane.

As he pulled on his jeans, Vance tried to work out the best way to tell her and, perhaps more important, to explain why he had yet to tell her.

Shane added a dash of thyme to the canned soup she was heating. She rose on her bare toes to reach for a bowl on the shelf, the hem of Vance's shirt skimming her naked thighs. Her hair was tousled, her cheeks flushed. Vance stood for a moment in the doorway watching her.

Then in three strides, he was behind her, wrapping his arms around her waist and burying his face in the curve of her neck. "I love you," he murmured in a low, fierce whisper. "God, how I love you."

Before she could answer, he spun her around to take her mouth with his. Both stunned and aroused, Shane clung to him as her knees buckled. But she met the kiss with equal passion with soft, willing lips until he slowly drew her away. As the flame mellowed to a glow, Vance looked down at her and smiled.

"Any time you want to drive me crazy, just put on one of my shirts."

"If I'd known the kind of results I'd get, I'd have done it weeks ago." Returning his smile, Shane clasped her hands around his neck. "I thought you'd be hungry. It's after eight."

"I smelled food," he said with a grin. "That's why I came down."

"Oh." Shane lifted a brow. "Is that the only reason?"

"What else?"

Her retort ended on a laugh as he nuzzled her neck. "You could make something up," she suggested.

"If it makes you feel better, I could pretend it was because I couldn't keep away from you." He kissed her until she was limp and breathless. "That I woke up reaching for you, then lay listening to your clattering in the kitchen and knew I'd never been happier in my life. Will that do?"

"Yes, I…" She sighed as his hands slid down to caress beneath the loose shirt. Behind her, bacon popped and hissed. "If you don't stop, the food's going to burn."

"What food?" He chuckled, pleased that she was flushed and breathing unsteadily when she struggled away from him.

"My own specially doctored tomato soup and prize-winning BLTs."

He pulled her back to nuzzle her neck another moment. "Mmm, it does smell pretty good. So do you."

"It's your shirt," she claimed as she wiggled out of his arms again. "It smells like wood chips." Deftly, Shane took the sizzling bacon from the frying pan to let it drain. "If you want coffee, the water's still hot."

Vance watched her finish preparing the simple meal. She did more than fill the kitchen with the scents and sounds of cooking. He'd done that himself often enough in the past weeks. Shane filled it with life. He may have repaired and renovated and remodeled, but the house had always been empty. Vance realized now that without her, it would have always been unfinished.

There would be no living there without her—no living anywhere. Fleetingly, he thought of the large white house in an exclusive Washington suburb—the house he had bought for Amelia. There was an oval swimming pool sheltered by a white brick wall, a formal rose garden with flagstone paths, a clay tennis court. Two maids, a gardener and a cook. When Amelia had been alive there had been yet another maid to tend to her personally. Her dressing room alone had been larger than the kitchen where Shane was now fixing soup and sandwiches. There was a parlor with a rosewood cabinet Shane would adore, and heavy damask drapes she would detest.

No, Vance thought, he wouldn't go back there now, nor would he ask Shane to share his ghosts. He had no right to ask her to cope with something he was only beginning to resolve himself. But he would have to tell her something of his former marriage, and of his work, before yesterday could be buried.

"Shane..."

"Sit down," she ordered, busily pouring soup into bowls. "I'm starving. I skipped lunch this afternoon bargaining for this wonderful Sheridan table. I paid a bit more for the clock than I should have, but made it up on the table and the saltcellars."

"Shane, I have to talk to you."

Deftly, she sliced a sandwich in half. "Okay, I can talk and eat at the same time. I'm going to have some milk. Even I can tell that instant coffee's dreadful."

She was bustling here and there, putting bowls and plates on the table, poking into the refrigerator. Vance was suddenly struck with the picture of his life before she had come into it—the rush, the demands, the work that had ultimately added up to nothing. If he lost her... He couldn't bear thinking about it.

"Shane." He stopped her abruptly, taking both of her arms in a strong grip. Looking up, she was surprised by the fierceness in his eyes. "I love you. Do you believe it?" His grip tightened painfully on the question, but she made no protest.

"Yes, I believe it."

"Will you take me just as I am?" he demanded.

"Yes." There was no hesitation in her, no wavering. Vance pulled her toward him.

A few hours, he thought, squeezing his eyes tight. Just a few hours with no questions, no past. It's not too much to ask.

"There are things I have to tell you, Shane, but not tonight." As the tension drained, he loosened his hold to a caress. "Tonight, I only want to tell you that I love you."

Sensing turmoil and wanting to soothe it, Shane tilted her face back to his. "Tonight it's all I need to know. I love you, Vance. Nothing you tell me will change that." She pressed her lips to his cheek and felt some of the tightness in his body loosen. Part of her wanted to coax him to tell her what caused the storm inside him, but she was conscious of the same need for isolation that Vance had. This was their night. Problems were for the practical, for the daytime. "Come on," she said lightly, "the food's getting cold." The fierce hug she gave him made him laugh. "When I fix a gourmet meal, I expect it to be properly appreciated."

"I do," he assured her, kissing her nose.

"Do what?"

"Appreciate it. And you." He dropped a second kiss on her mouth. "Let's go into the living room."

"Living room?" Her brow creased, then cleared. "Oh, I suppose it would be warmer."

"Exactly what I had in mind," he murmured.

"I tossed a couple of logs onto the fire when I came downstairs."

"You're a clever soul, Shane," Vance said admiringly as he took her arm and steered her from the room.

"Vance, we have to take the food."

"What food?"

Shane laughed and started to turn back, but he propelled her into the sparsely furnished, firelit room. "Vance, the soup'll have to be reheated in a minute."

"It'll be terrific," he told her as he began to unbutton the oversize shirt she wore.

"Vance!" Shane brushed his fingers away. "Be serious."

"I am," he said reasonably, even as he pulled her down on the oval braided rug. "Deadly."

"Well, *I'm* not going to reheat it," she promised huffily while he leaned on an elbow to undo the rest of the buttons.

"No one would blame you," he told her as he parted the shirt. "It'll be fine cold."

She gave a snort. "It'll be dreadful cold."

"Hungry?" he asked lightly, cupping her breast.

Shane looked up at him. He saw the dimples flash.

"Yes!" In a quick move, she was lying across his chest, her mouth fixed greedily on his.

The verve and speed of her passion stunned him. He had meant to tease her, to stoke her desires slowly, but she was suddenly and completely in command. Her mouth was avid, demanding, with her small teeth nibbling, her quick tongue arousing him so quickly he would have rolled her over and taken her at once had his limbs not been so strangely weak. Her weight was nothing, yet he couldn't move her when she shifted to do clever, torturous things to his ear. Her hands were busy too, stroking through his hair, skimming over his shoulders and chest to find and exploit small, devastating points of pleasure.

He reached to pull off her shirt, too dazed to realize his fingers shook, but he fumbled, dragging at it. High on her own power, Shane gave a quick, almost nervous laugh. "Too soon," she whispered into his ear. "Much too soon."

He swore, but the curse ended on a groan when she pressed her lips to his throat. She burned even as he did, but she was driven to heighten his pleasure to the fullest. It spun through her mind until she was giddy that her touch, her kisses were enough to make him weak and vulnerable. Under her roaming mouth, his skin grew hot and damp. He stroked her where he could reach, but there was something dreamlike in the touch, as though he had passed the first feeling of desperation. For all his strength and power, he had surrendered to hers.

The light shifted and jumped with the crackling of the fire. A log broke apart, crumbling in a shower of sparks. The wind picked up, pushing a sluggish puff of smoke back down the chimney so that it struggled half-heartedly into the room to vie with the lingering scent of fried bacon. Neither of them was aware.

Shane heard the thunderous beat of his heart under her ear, the shallow, ragged sound of his breathing. Taking his mouth again, she kissed him deeply, filling herself on him, knowing she drained him. She luxuriated in him, experimenting with angles, allowing her tongue to twine with his. Then she began the journey down his throat.

Once, he murmured her name as though he were dreaming. She grew bolder. With firm, quick kisses, she ranged down his chest to the taut flat stomach. Vance jolted as though he had been scorched. Shane pressed her lips to the heated skin, wrenching a moan from him, then circled almost lazily with her tongue.

Her excitement was almost unbearable. He was hers, and she was learning his secrets. Her body felt weight-less and capable of anything. The gnawing hunger in the pit of her stomach was growing, but the need to learn, to explore was greater. With a kind of greedy wonder, she took her hands and lips over him, reveling in a man's taste—*her* man's taste. The hair on his chest tapered down. Shane followed it.

Slowly, with a light touch, she loosened his jeans and began to draw them over his hips. Curious, Shane moved her lips over his hipbone and down to his thigh.

She heard him call out to her, hoarse, desperate, but she found the corded muscles of his thighs fascinating. So strong, she thought as her heart began to thud painfully. She ran fingers down his leg, aroused by the lean firmness and straining sinews. Testing, she replaced her fingers with her tongue, then her teeth. Vance shifted under her, murmuring something between his short, ragged breaths. His taste was everything male and mysterious. Shane felt she would never get her fill of him.

But he was on the point of madness. Her slender fingers, her curious tongue had him plunging down and rocketing up so that each breath he drew was an agony of effort. His body was alive with pleasure and pain, his blood swimming with passion that was both tantalized and frustrated. He wanted her to go on touching him, driving him mad. He wanted to take her quickly before he lost his mind. Then slowly, her small avid mouth roamed back up over his stomach, so that his skin quivered with fresh dampness. The heat was unbearable and more wonderful than anything he had ever known. Her breasts with their hard, erect points brushed over him, making him long to taste them. She gave him her mouth instead. Lying full length on his, her body was furnace hot and agile.

"Shane, in the name of God," he breathed, groping for her. Then she slid down, taking him inside her with a shuddering sigh of triumph.

His sanity shattered. Not knowing what he did, Vance seized her shoulders, rolling her over roughly, driving inside her with all the fierce, desperate strength that was pent up in him. Passion hammered through his core. Need was delirium.

She cried out as her hips arched to meet him, but he was far beyond any control. Harder and faster he took her, never feeling the bite of her nails on his flesh, barely hearing her harsh, quick breathing. She dragged him closer when he could get no closer. He drove her, drove himself to a crest that was dangerously high. Even the plummet was a shattering thrill.

She was shuddering beneath him, dazed, weak, powerful. Experimentally, Vance ran a hand over her arm, then linked his fingers around it. His thumb and forefinger met. "You're so small," he murmured. "I didn't mean to be rough."

Shane brushed a hand through his hair. "Were you?"

His sigh ended on a chuckle. "Shane, you make me crazy. I don't usually toss women around."

"I don't think this is a good time to go into that," she said dryly.

Shifting, he supported himself on his elbow so he could look down at her. "Would it be better to tell you that you inflame me into violent seizures of passion?"

"Infinitely."

"It appears to be true," he murmured.

She smiled at him, running her hand down his shoulder to the arm taut with muscle. "Would you rather I didn't?"

"No," he said definitely, then covered her laughing lips with his.

"Actually," she began in a considering tone, "since you do the same to me, it's only fair."

He liked seeing her with the sleepy, just-loved look on her face. Her eyes were soft and heavy, her mouth slightly swollen. With shifting shadows and a red glow, firelight danced over her skin. "I like your logic." Gently, he traced the shape of her face with a fingertip, imagining what it would be like to wake beside her every morning. Shane captured his hand, pressing his palm to her lips.

"I love you," she said softly. "Will you get tired of hearing that?"

"No." He kissed her brow, then her temple. Slipping an arm under her, he drew her close. "No," he said again on a sigh.

Shane snuggled, running a casual hand over his chest. "The fire's getting low," she murmured.

"Mmm."

"We should put some more wood on."

"Mmm-hmm."

"Vance." She tilted her face to look up at him. His eyes were closed. "Don't you dare go to sleep. I'm hungry."

"God, the woman's insatiable." After a long sigh, he cupped her breast. "I might find the energy with the right incentive."

"I want my dinner," she said firmly, but made no move to stop his caressing hand. *"You're* going to re-heat the soup."

"Oh." Vance considered that a moment, running a lazy finger over the peak of her breast. "Aren't you afraid I might interfere with that special touch you have?"

"No," she told him flatly. "I have every confidence in you."

"I thought you might," he said as he sat up to tug on his jeans. Leaning over, he planted a quick kiss on her mouth. *"You* can toss some logs in the fire."

But after he had gone to the kitchen, Shane lay dreaming a moment. The hiss of the fire was comforting. She drew the soft flannel of Vance's shirt closer around her, smiling as his scent stayed with her. Could it really be true that he needed her so much? she wondered sleepily. Love, yes, and desire, but she had a deep, innate knowledge that he very simply needed her. Not just for love-making, for holding, but to *be* there. Though she was unsure what it was, Shane knew there was something she had—or something she was—that Vance needed. Whatever she brought to him, it was enough to balance his anger, his mistrust. Fleetingly, she wondered again what had caused him to retreat behind cynicism. Disillusioned, he had said. Who or what had disillusioned him? A woman, a friend, an ideal?

Shane watched the sizzling red coals in the fire and wondered. The anger was still there. She had sensed it when he had demanded to know if she would take him just as he was. Patience, she told herself. She had to be patient until he was ready to share his secrets with her. But it was difficult for Shane to love and not try to help. Shaking her head, she sat up to rebutton her shirt. She'd promised him that love was enough for tonight; she had to abide by it. Tomorrow would be soon enough for problems. Expertly, she arranged more wood on the coals before she went to the kitchen.

"About time," Vance said coolly as she walked in. "There's nothing I hate more than having food get cold."

Shane shot him a look. "How inconsiderate of me."

After setting the bowls back on the table, Vance shrugged. "Well, no harm done," he told her in a forgiving tone. His eyes brimmed with amusement as Shane sat. "Coffee?"

"Not yours," she said witheringly. "It's terrible."

"I suppose if someone really cared, they'd see to it that I had decent coffee in the morning."

"You're right." Shane lifted her spoon. "I'll buy you a percolater." Grinning, she began to eat. The soup was hot and tangy, causing her to close her eyes in appreciation. "Good grief, I'm starving!"

"You should know better than to miss meals," Vance commented before applying himself to the meal. He quickly discovered he was famished.

"It was worth it." Shane shot him another grin. "The Sheridan I bought is fabulous." When he only lifted a brow, she chuckled. "Then I had intended to have an early dinner…but I was distracted."

Vance reached over to take her hand. Gently, he lifted it to his lips, then bit her knuckle. "Ow!" Shane snatched her hand away as she picked up his sandwich. "I didn't say it wasn't an enjoyable distraction," she added after a moment. "Even if you did make me furious."

"The feeling was mutual," he assured her mildly.

"At least I control my temper," she said primly. She eyed him coolly as he choked over his soup. "I *wanted* to punch you," she explained. "Hard."

"Again the feeling was mutual."

"You're not a gentleman," she accused with her mouth full.

"Good God, no," he agreed. For a moment, he hesitated, wanting to choose his words carefully. "Shane, will you hold off for a little while on that dining-room set?"

"Vance," she began, but he took her hand again.

"Don't tell me I shouldn't have interfered. I love you."

Shane stirred her soup, frowning down at it. She didn't want to tell him how pressing her bills were. In the first place, she had every confidence that between her current stock and the small amount of capital she had left, she could straighten out her finances. And more, she simply didn't want to heap her problems on him.

"I know you did what you did because you cared," she began slowly. "I appreciate that, really. But it's important to me to make the shop work." She lifted her eyes now to meet the frown in his. "I didn't fail as a teacher, but I didn't succeed either. I have to make a go of this."

"By selling the one tangible thing you have left of your grandmother's?" Immediately, he saw he had hit a nerve. He tightened his fingers around hers. "Shane..."

"No. It is hard for me, I won't pretend it isn't." Wearily, she let out a long breath. "I'm not basically a practical person, but in this case I have to be. I have no place to keep that set and it's very valuable. The money it'll bring into the shop will keep me going for quite a while. And more than that..." She broke off with a little shake of her head. "If you can understand, it's more difficult for me having it there, knowing it has to be sold, than if it were already done."

"Let me buy it. I could—"

"No!"

"Shane, listen to me."

"No!" Pulling her hand from his, she rose to lean against the sink. For a moment she stared hard out the window at the trees splattered with moonlight. "Please, it's very sweet of you, but I couldn't allow it."

Frustrated, Vance rose. Taking her shoulders, he drew Shane back against him. And how, he wondered, was he going to begin to explain? "Shane, you don't understand. I can't bear watching you hurting, watching you work so hard when I could—"

"Please, Vance." Shane turned to him. Though her eyes were dry, they were eloquent. "I'm doing what I have to do, and what I want." She took his hands tightly in hers. "It's not that I don't love you even more for wanting to help. I do."

"Then let me help," he began. "If it's just a matter of the money right now—"

"It wouldn't make any difference if you were a millionaire," she said, giving him a little shake. "I'd still say no."

Not knowing whether to laugh or swear, Vance pulled her against him. "Stubborn little twit, I could make it easier for you. Let me try to explain."

"I don't want anyone, not even you, to make it easier." She gave him a fierce squeeze. "Please understand. All of my life I've been cute little Shane Abbott, Faye's sweet, slightly odd granddaughter. I need to prove something."

Remembering how frustrating it had been to be known as Miriam Riverton Banning's son, Vance sighed. Yes, he understood. And the understanding made him keep his silence on how simple it would be for him to help. "Well," he said, wanting to hear her laugh, "you are kind of cute."

"Oh, Vance," she moaned.

"And sweet," he added, tilting her face up for a kiss. "And slightly odd."

"That's no way to endear yourself to me," she warned. "I'll wash, you dry."

"Wash what?"

"The dishes."

He pulled her closer, wrapping his arms firmly around her waist. "I don't see any dishes. You have wonderful eyes, just like a cocker spaniel."

"Watch it, Vance," she said threateningly.

"I like your freckles." He placed a light kiss on the bridge of her nose. "I've always thought that Becky Thatcher had freckles."

"You're heading for trouble," she told him, narrowing her eyes.

"And your dimples," he continued blithely. "She probably had dimples too, don't you think?"

Shane bit her lips to hold back a smile. "Shut up, Vance."

"Yes," he continued, beaming down at her, "I'd say that's definitely a cute little face."

"Okay, that does it." Putting a good deal of effort into it, Shane tried to wiggle out of his hold.

"Going somewhere?"

"Home," she told him grandly. "You can do your own dishes."

He sighed. "I guess I have to get tough again."

Anticipating him, Shane began to struggle in earnest. "If you throw me over your shoulder again, you really are fired!"

Hooking an arm behind her knees, Vance swept her up. "How's this?"

She circled his neck. "Better," she said grudgingly. The smile was becoming impossible to control.

"And this?" Softly, he placed his lips on hers, letting the kiss deepen until he heard her sigh.

"Much better," she murmured as he carried her from the room. "Where are we going?"

"Upstairs," he told her. "I want my shirt back."

Chapter 10

"Yes, of course you could convert it," Shane agreed, passing her fingertip over the porcelain base of a delicate oil lamp.

"That's just what I thought." Mrs. Trip, her potential customer, nodded her carefully groomed white head. "And my husband's very handy with electrical things too."

Shane managed a smile for Mr. Trip's prowess. It broke her heart to think that the sweet little lamp would be tampered with. "You know," she began, trying another tactic, "an oil lamp is a smart thing to have around in case of power failure. I keep a couple myself."

"Well yes, dear," Mrs. Trip said placidly, "but I have candles for that. This lamp's going to go right next to my rocker. That's where I do my crocheting."

Though she knew the value of a sale, Shane couldn't stop herself from adding, "If you really want an electric lamp, Mrs. Trip, you could buy a good reproduction much cheaper."

Mrs. Trip sent her a vague smile. "But it wouldn't be a real antique then, would it? Do you have a box I can carry it in?"

"Yes, of course," Shane murmured, seeing it was useless to repeat that converting the lamp would decrease both its value and its charm. Resigned, she wrote out the sales slip, comforting herself with the thought that the profit from the lamp would help pay her own electric bill.

"Oh my, I didn't see this!"

Glancing up, Shane noted that Mrs. Trip was admiring a tea set in cobalt blue. The sun slanting in the windows fell generously on the dark, rich glass. There was a contrast of delicate gold leaf painted around the rim of each cup and the edge of each saucer.

"It's lovely, isn't it," Shane agreed, though she bit the underside of her lip as the lady began to handle the sugar bowl. When she found the discreet price tag, she lifted a brow. "It goes as a complete set," Shane began, knowing the price would seem staggering to someone unacquainted with valuable glass. "It's late nineteenth century and..."

"I must have it," Mrs. Trip said decisively, cutting off Shane's explanation. "It's just the thing for my corner cabinet." She sent a surprised Shane a grin. "I'll tell my husband he's just bought me a Christmas present."

"I'll wrap it for you," Shane decided, as pleased as Mrs. Trip with the idea.

"You have a lovely shop," the woman told her as Shane began to box the glass. "I must say, I only stopped in because the sign at the bottom of the hill intrigued me. I wondered what in the world I would find. But it wasn't a big barn of a place with nonsense packed around like a yard sale." She pursed her lips, glancing around again. "You've done very well." Shane laughed at the description and thanked her. "And it's so nice to have the little museum too," she went on. "A very clever idea, and so tidy. I believe I'll bring my nephew by the next time I'm in the area. Are you married, dear?"

Shane sent her a look of wary amusement. "No, ma'am."

"He's a doctor," Mrs. Trip disclosed. "Internal medicine."

Clearing her throat, Shane sealed the box. "That's very nice."

"A good boy," Mrs. Trip assured her as Shane adjusted the sales ticket to include the tea set. "Dedicated." She dug out her checkbook, pulling her wallet along with it. "I have a picture of him right here."

Politely, Shane examined the snapshot of a young, attractive man with serious eyes. "He's very good-look-ing," she told his aunt. "You must be proud of him."

"Yes," she said wistfully, tucking the wallet back into her purse. "Such a pity he hasn't found the right girl yet. I'm going to be sure to bring him by." Without a blink for the amount, Mrs. Trip wrote out a check.

It wasn't easy, but Shane maintained her composure until the door shut behind her customer. With a shout of laughter, she dropped into a button-back chair. Though she was uncertain if the nephew should be congratulated or pitied for having such a dedicated aunt, she did know what appealed to her sense of humor. Her next thought was how Vance would try not to grin when she told him of the lady's matchmaking attempts.

He'd lift a brow, Shane thought, and make some dry comment about her charming the old ladies so that they'd dangle their nephews under her nose. She was begin-ning to know him very well. Most of him, Shane cor-rected with a considering smile. The rest would come.

She checked her watch, finding herself impatient that two hours remained before he would be with her. She'd promised him dinner—a more elaborate dinner than the soup and sandwiches they had eaten the night be-fore. Even now, the small rib roast was cooking gently in the oven upstairs. She considered closing early, calcu-lating she had just about enough time to whip up some outrageous, elaborate dessert before he arrived. As the thought passed through her head, the door opened again.

Laurie MacAfee stepped in, buttoned to the neck in a long tan coat. "Shane," she said, observing her casual posture in the chair. "Not busy I see."

Though she smiled in greeting, some demon kept her seated. "Not at the moment. How are you, Laurie?"

"Just fine. I took off work early to go to the dentist, so I thought I'd drop by afterward."

Shane waited, half expecting Laurie to comment on her good checkup. "I'm glad you did," she said at length. "Would you like a tour?"

"I'd love to browse," Laurie told her, glancing around. "What sweet things you have."

Shane swallowed a retort and rose. "Thank you," she said with a humility Laurie never noticed. Shane thought again how well suited she was to Cy.

"I must say, the place looks so much different." In her slow, measured step, Laurie began to wander the old summer parlor. Though she hadn't expected to approve, she could find nothing to condemn in Shane's taste. The room was small, but light and airy with its ivory-toned walls, and the gleaming natural wood floor was scattered with hand-hooked rugs. Furniture was set to advantage, with accessories carefully arranged to give the appearance of a tidy, rather comfortable room instead of a store. Loosening the first few buttons of her coat, she roamed to the main showroom, then stood perusing it from the doorway.

"Why, you've hardly changed this at all?" she exclaimed. "Not even the wallpaper."

"No," Shane agreed, unable to keep her eyes from skimming over the dining-room set. "I didn't want to. Of course, I had to set more stock in here, and widen the doorways, but I loved the room as it was."

"Well, I'll confess I'm surprised," Laurie commented as she wandered through to what had been the kitchen. "It's so organized, not jumbled up at all. Your bedroom was always a disaster."

"It still is," Shane replied dryly.

Laurie gave what passed for a laugh before continuing into the museum. "Yes, this I might have expected." She gave a quick nod. "You always were a whiz at this sort of thing. I could never understand it."

"Because I wasn't a whiz at anything else?"

"Oh, Shane." Laurie flushed, revealing how close Shane's words had been to her thoughts.

"I'm sorry." Immediately contrite, Shane patted her arm. "I was only teasing you. I'd show you the upstairs, Laurie, but it's not quite finished, and I shouldn't leave the shop in any case. Pat has classes this afternoon."

Mollified, Laurie strolled back into the shop. "I'd heard she was working for you. It was very kind of you to give her the job."

"She's been a big help. I couldn't manage it seven days a week all alone." Shane felt a twinge of impatience as Laurie began to browse again. There wasn't going to be time to whip up anything more than instant chocolate pudding at this rate.

"Oh well, this is very nice." Laurie's voice held the first true ring of admiration as she studied the Sheridan table Shane had bought the day before. "It doesn't look old at all."

That was too much for Shane. She gave a burst of appreciative laughter. "No, I'm sorry," she assured Laurie when she turned to frown at her. "You'd be surprised how many people think antiques should look moldy or dented. It's quite old, really, and it is lovely."

"And expensive," Laurie added, squinting at the price. "Still, it would look rather nice with the chair Cy and I just bought. Oh…" Turning, she gave Shane a quick, guilty look. "I wonder if you'd heard—that is, I'd been meaning to have a talk with you."

"About Cy?" Shane controlled the smile, noting Laurie was truly uncomfortable. "I know you're seeing quite a lot of each other."

"Yes." Hesitating, Laurie brushed some fictitious lint from her coat. "It's a bit more than that really. You see, we're—actually…" She cleared her throat. "Shane, we're planning to be married next June."

"Congratulations," Shane said so simply that Laurie's eyes widened.

"I hope you're not upset." Laurie began to twist the strap of her purse. "I know that you and Cy…well, it was quite a few years ago, but still, you were…"

"Very young," Shane said kindly. "I really do wish you the best, Laurie." But a demon of mischief had her adding, "You suit him much better than I ever could."

"I appreciate your saying that, Shane. I was afraid you might…" She flushed again. "Well, Cy's such a wonderful man."

She means it, Shane noted with some surprise. She really loves him. She felt simultaneous tugs of shame and amusement. "I hope you're happy, Laurie, both of you."

"We will be." Laurie gave her a beaming smile. "And I'm going to buy this table," she added recklessly.

"No," Shane corrected her. "You're going to take the table as an early wedding present."

Comically, Laurie's mouth dropped open. "Oh, I couldn't! It's so expensive."

"Laurie, we've known each other a long time, and Cy was a very important part of my—" she searched for the proper phrase "—growing up years. I'd like to give it to both of you."

"Well, I—thank you." Such uncomplicated generosity baffled her. "Cy will be so pleased."

"You're welcome." Laurie's flustered appreciation made her smile. "Can I help you out to the car with it?"

"No, no, I can manage." Laurie lifted the small table, then paused. "Shane, I really hope you have a tremendous success here. I really do." She stood awkwardly at the door a moment. "Goodbye."

"Bye, Laurie."

Shane closed the door with a smile, then immediately put Laurie and Cy out of her mind. After a glance at her watch, she noted that she had barely more than an hour now before Vance would be there. She hurried around to lock up the museum entrance. If she moved fast, she would have time to... The sound of an approaching car had her swearing.

Business is business, she reminded herself, and unlocked the door again. If Vance wanted dessert, he'd have to settle for a bag of store-bought cookies. Hearing the sound of footsteps on the porch, she opened the door with a ready smile. It faded instantly, as did her color.

"Anne," she managed in a voice unlike her own.

"Darling!" Anne bent down for a quick brush of cheeks. "What a greeting. Anyone would think you weren't glad to see me."

It took only a few seconds to see that her mother was as lovely as ever. Her pale, heart-shaped face was unlined, her eyes the same deep china blue, her hair a glorious sweeping blond. She wore a casual, expensive blue fox stroller belted at the waist with black leather, and silk slacks unsuitable for an Eastern winter. Her beauty, as always, sent the same surges of love and resentment through her daughter.

"You look lovely, Anne."

"Oh, thank you, though I know I must look a wreck after that dreadful drive from the airport. This place is in the middle of nowhere. Shane, dear, when are you going to do something about your hair?" She cast a critical eye over it before breezing past. "I'll never understand why… Oh, my Lord, what *have* you done!"

Stunned, she gazed around the room, taking in the display cases, the shelves, the racks of postcards. With a trill of laughter, she set down her exquisite leather bag. "Don't tell me you've opened a Civil War museum right in the living room. I don't believe it!"

Shane folded her hands in front of her, feeling foolish. "Didn't you see the sign?"

"Sign? No—or perhaps I did but didn't pay any attention." Her eyes slid, sharp and amused around the room. "Shane, what *have* you been up to?"

Determined not to be intimidated, she straightened her shoulders. "I've started a business," she said boldly.

"You?" Delighted, Anne laughed again. "But, darling, surely you're joking."

Stabbed by the utter incredulity in Anne's voice, Shane angled her chin. "No."

"Well, for heaven's sake." She gave a pretty chuckle and eyed Shane's dented bugle. "But what happened to your teaching job?"

"I resigned."

"Well, I can hardly blame you for that. It must have been a terrible bore." She brushed away Shane's former career as a matter of indifference. "But why in God's name did you come back here and bury yourself in Hicksville?"

"It's my home."

With a mild *hmm* for the temper in Shane's eyes, Anne spun the rack of postcards. "Everyone to his own taste. Well, what have you done with the rest of the place?" Before Shane could answer, Anne swept through the doorway and into the shop. "Oh, no, don't tell me, an antique shop! Very quaint and tasteful. Shane, how clever of you." Her eye was sharp enough to recognize a few very good pieces. She began to wonder if her daughter wasn't quite the fool she'd always considered her. "Well…" Anne unbelted her fur and dropped it carelessly over a chair. "How long has this been going on?"

"Not long." Shane stood rigid, knowing part of herself was drawn, as it always was, to the strange, beautiful woman who was her mother. Knowing too that Anne was deadly.

"And?" Anne prompted.

"And what?"

"Shane, don't be difficult." Masking quick annoyance, Anne gave her a charming smile. She was an actress. Though she had never made the splash she had hoped for, she wrangled a bit part now and again. She felt she knew her trade well enough to handle Shane with a friendly smile. "Naturally I'm concerned, darling. I only want to know how you're doing?"

Uncomfortable with her own manners, Shane unbent. "Well enough, though I haven't been open long. I wasn't happy with teaching. Not bored," she explained, "just not suited for it. I am happy with this."

"Darling, that's wonderful." She crossed her nylon-clad legs and looked around again. It occurred to her that Shane might be useful after all. It had taken brains and determination to set up this kind of establishment. Perhaps it was time she started to take a little more interest in the daughter she had always thought of as a mild annoyance. "It helps to know you're settling your life, especially since mine's such a mess at the moment." Noting the wariness in Shane's eyes, she sent her a sad smile. If memory served her, the girl was very susceptible to an unhappy story. "I divorced Leslie."

"Oh?" Shane only lifted a brow.

Momentarily set back by Shane's coolness, Anne continued. "I can't tell you how mistaken I was in him, how foolish it feels to know I was deceived into thinking he was a kind, charming man." She didn't add that he had failed, again and again, to get her the kind of parts that would lead to the fame she craved—or that she'd already begun to cultivate a certain producer she felt would be more successful. In any event, Leslie had begun to bore her to distraction. "There's nothing more devastating than to have failed in love."

You've had practice, Shane thought, but held her tongue.

"These past few months," Anne added on a sigh, "haven't been easy."

"For any of us," Shane agreed, understanding Anne too well. "Gran died six months ago. You didn't even bother to come to the funeral."

She'd been ready for this. With a tiny sigh, she dropped her eyes to her soft, pampered hands. "You must know how badly I felt, Shane. I was finishing a film. I couldn't be spared."

"You couldn't find the time for a card, a phone call?" Shane asked. "You never even bothered to answer my letter."

As if on cue, Anne's lovely eyes filled with tears. "Darling, don't be cruel. I couldn't—I just couldn't put the words down on a piece of paper." She drew a delicate swatch of silk from her breast pocket. "Even though she was old, somehow I felt she would just live forever, always be here." Mindful of her mascara, she dabbed at the tears. "When I got your letter telling me she was…I was so devastated." She lifted beautifully drenched eyes to Shane's, waiting while a single tear trickled gently down her cheek. "You of all people must know how I feel. She raised me." A little sob caught in her throat. "I still can't believe she's not in the kitchen, fussing over the stove."

Because the image tore at her own grief, Shane knelt at her mother's feet. She'd had no family to mourn with her, no one to help her through the wrenching, aching hours after the numbness had passed. If she had been unable to share anything else with her mother through-out her life, perhaps they could share this. "I know," she managed in a thick voice. "I still miss her terribly."

Anne began to think the little scene had a great deal of possibility. "Shane, please forgive me." Anne gripped her hands, concentrating on adding a tremor to her voice. "I know it was wrong of me not to come, wrong to make excuses. I just wasn't strong enough to face it. Even now, when I thought I could..." She trailed off, bring-ing Shane's hand to her damp cheek.

"I understand. Gran would have understood too."

"She was so good to me always. If I could only see her one more time."

"You mustn't dwell on it." Those very thoughts had haunted Shane's mind a dozen times after the funeral. "I felt the same way, but it's better to remember all the good times. She was so happy here in this house, doing her gardening, her canning."

"She did love the house," Anne murmured, casting a nostalgic eye around the old summer parlor. "And I imagine she'd have been pleased with what you're doing here."

"Do you think so?" Earnestly, Shane looked up into her mother's damp eyes. "I was so sure, but still sometimes…" Trailing off, she glanced at the freshly painted walls.

"Of course she would," Anne said briskly. "I suppose she left the house to you?"

"Yes." Shane was looking around the room, remembering how it had been.

"There was a will then?"

"A will?" Distracted, Shane glanced back at her. "Yes, Gran had a will drawn up years ago. She had Floyd Arnette's son do it after he passed the bar. She was his first client." Shane smiled, thinking how proud Gran had been of the fancy legal terms that "sassy Arnette boy" had come up with.

"And the rest of the estate?" Anne prompted, attempting to curb her impatience.

"There was the house and land of course," Shane answered, still looking back. "Some stocks I sold to pay the taxes and the funeral expenses."

"She left everything to you?"

The tightness in Anne's voice didn't penetrate. "Yes.

There was enough cash in her savings to handle most of the repairs on the place, and—"

"You're lying!" Anne shoved at her as she sprung to her feet. Shane grabbed the arm of the chair to keep from toppling; then, too stunned to move, she stayed on the floor. "She wouldn't have cut me off without a penny!" Anne exploded, glaring down at her.

The blue eyes were hard and glittery now, the lovely face white with fury. Once or twice before, Shane had seen her mother in this sort of rage—when her grandmother hadn't given her precisely what she had wanted. Slowly, she rose to face her. Anne's tantrums, she knew, had to be handled carefully before they turned violent.

"Gran would never have thought of it as cutting you off, Anne," Shane said with a calm she was far from feeling. "She knew you'd have no interest in the house or land, and there weren't that many extra pennies after taxes."

"What kind of fool do you think I am?" Anne demanded in a harsh, bitter voice. It was her temper more than a lack of talent that had snagged her career. Too often, she had let it rake over directors and other actors. Even now, when patience and the right words would have ensured success, she lashed out. "I know damn well she had money socked away, moldering in some bank. I had to pry every penny I got out of her when she was alive. I'm going to have my share."

"She gave you what she could," Shane began.

"What the hell do you know? Do you think I'm so stupid I don't know this property is worth a tidy sum on the market?" She glanced around once in disgust. "You want the place, keep it. Just give me the cash."

"There isn't any to give. She didn't—"

"Don't hand me that." Anne shoved her aside and strode toward the stairs.

For a moment, Shane stood still, caught in a turmoil of disbelief. How was it possible anyone could be so unfeeling? And how, she asked herself, was it possible for her to be taken in again and again? Well, she would end it this time, once and for all. On her own wave of fury, she raced after her mother.

She found Anne in her bedroom, pulling papers out of her desk. Without hesitation, Shane dashed across the room and slammed the desk lid shut. "Don't you touch my things," she said in a dangerous voice. "Don't you ever touch what belongs to me."

"I want to see the bankbooks, and this so-called will." Anne turned to leave the room, but Shane grabbed her arm in a surprisingly strong grip.

"You'll see nothing in this house. This is mine."

"There *is* money," Anne said furiously, then jerked away. "You're trying to hide it."

"I don't have to hide anything from you." Rage raced through Shane, fed by years of cast-aside love. "If you want to see the will and the status of the estate, get yourself a lawyer. But I own this house, and everything in it. I won't have you going through my papers."

"Well…" Anne's blue eyes became slits. "Not such a sweet simpleton after all, are you?"

"You've never known what I am," Shane said evenly. "You've never cared enough to find out. It didn't matter, because I had Gran. I don't need you." Though saying the words was a relief, they didn't bank her fury. "There were times I thought I did, when you came sweeping in, so beautiful I hardly believed you were real. That was closer to the truth than I knew, because there's nothing real about you. You never cared about her. She knew that and she loved you anyway. But I don't." Her breathing was coming quickly, but she was unaware of how close it was to sobbing. "I can't even work up a hate. I just want to be rid of you."

Turning, she pulled open the desk and drew out her checkbook. Quickly, she wrote out a check for half of the capital she had left. "Here." She held it out to Anne. "Take it; consider it from Gran. You'll never get anything from me."

After snatching the check, Anne scanned the amount with a smirk. "If you think I'll be satisfied with this, you're wrong." Still, she folded the check neatly, then slipped it into her pocket. She knew better than to press her luck, and her own financial status was far from solid.

"I'll get that lawyer," she promised, though she had no intention of wasting her money on the slim chance of getting more. "And I'll contest the will. We'll just see how much I get from you, Shane."

"Do what you like," Shane said wearily. "Just stay away from me."

Anne tossed back her hair with a harsh laugh. "Don't think I'll spend any more time in this ridiculous house than I have to. I've always wondered how the hell you could possibly be my daughter."

Shane pressed a hand to her throbbing temple. "So have I," she murmured.

"You'll hear from my lawyer," Anne told her. Turning on her heel, she glided from the room, exiting gracefully.

Shane stood beside the desk until she heard the slam of the front door. Bursting into tears, she crumpled into a chair.

Chapter 11

Vance sat in the one decent chair he had in the living room. Impatiently, he checked his watch. He should have been with Shane ten minutes ago. And would have been, he thought with a glance at the front door, if the phone hadn't caught him as he'd been leaving the house. Resigned, he listened to the problems listed by the manager of his Washington branch. Though it wasn't said in words, Vance was aware there was some grumbling in the ranks that the boss had taken a sabbatical.

"...and with the union dispute, the construction on the Wolfe project is three weeks behind schedule," the manager continued. "I've been informed that there will be a delay in delivery of the steel on the Rheinstone site—possibly a lengthy one. I'm sorry to bother you with this, Mr. Banning, but as these two projects are of paramount importance to the firm, particularly with the bids going out on the shopping mall Rheinstone is planning, I felt..."

"Yes, I understand." Vance cut off what promised to be a detailed explanation. "Put a double shift on the Wolfe project until we're back on schedule."

"A double shift? But—"

"We contracted for completion by April first," Vance said mildly. "The increase in payroll will be less than the payment of the penalty clause, or the damage to the firm's reputation."

"Yes, sir."

"And have Liebewitz check into the steel delivery. If it's not taken care of satisfactorily by Monday, I'll handle it from here." Picking up a pencil, Vance made a scrawled note on a pad. "As to the Rheinstone bid, I looked it over myself last week. I see no problem." He scowled at the floor a moment. "Set up a meeting with the department heads for the end of next week. I'll be in. In the meantime," he added slowly, "send someone... Masterson," he decided, "up here to scout out locations for a new branch."

"New branch? Up there, Mr. Banning?"

The tone had a smile tugging at his mouth. "Have him concentrate on the Hagerstown area and give me a

report. I want a list of viable locations in two weeks."
He checked his watch again. "Is there anything else?"

"No, sir."

"Good. I'll be in next week." Without waiting for a reply, Vance broke the connection.

His last orders, he thought ruefully, would put them into quite a stir. Well, he reflected, Riverton had expanded before; it was going to expand again. For the first time in years, the company was going to bring him some personal happiness. He would be able to settle down with the woman he loved, where he chose to settle down, and still keep a firm rein on his business. If he had to justify the new branch to the board, which he would certainly have to do, he would point out that Hagerstown was the largest city in Maryland. There was also its proximity to Pennsylvania to consider...and to West Virginia. Yes, he mused, the expansion could be justified to the board easily enough. His track record would go a long way toward swaying them.

Rising, Vance shrugged back into his coat. All he had left to do now was to talk to Shane. Not for the first time, he speculated on her reaction. She was bound to be a bit stunned when he told her he wasn't precisely the unemployed carpenter she had taken him for. And he hadn't discounted the possibility that she might be angry with him for allowing her to go on believing him to be one.

Vance felt a slight tug of apprehension as he stepped out
into the cold, clear night.

There was a stiff breeze whipping in from the west.
It sent stiff, dead leaves scattering and smelled faintly
of snow. With his mind fully occupied, Vance never noticed the old stag fifty yards to his right, scenting the
air and watching him.

He'd never set out to deceive her, he reminded himself.
When they had first met, it had been none of Shane's
business who he was. More, he added thoughtfully, he
had simply wanted to shake loose of his company title
for a while and be exactly what she had perceived him
to be. Had there been any way of knowing she would
become more important to him than anything else in his
life? Could he have guessed that weeks after he met her
he would be planning to ask her to marry him, finding
himself ready to toss his company into a frenzy of rush
and preparation so that she wouldn't have to give up her
home or the life she had chosen for herself?

Once he'd explained the circumstances, Vance told
himself as he crunched through frosted leaves, she'd
understand. One of Shane's most endearing qualities
was understanding. And she loved him. If he was sure
of nothing else, he was sure of that. She loved him without questions, without demands. No one had ever given
him so much for so little. He intended to spend the rest
of his life showing her just what that meant to him.

He imagined that once the surprise of what he had to tell her had worn off, she would laugh. The money, the position he could offer her would mean nothing. She would probably find it funny that the president of Riverton had cut and hammered the trim in her kitchen.

Telling her about Amelia would be more difficult, but it would be done—completely. He wouldn't pass over his first marriage, but would tell her everything and rely on her to understand. He wanted to tell her that she had been responsible for softening his guilt, lightening his bitterness. Loving her was the only genuine emotion he'd felt in years. Tonight, he would open up his past long enough to let the air in; then he would ask Shane to share his future.

Still, Vance felt a twinge of apprehension as he approached her house. He might have ignored it if it hadn't been for the sudden realization that all the windows were dark. It was odd, he thought, unconsciously increasing his pace. She was certainly home, not only because her car was there, but because he knew she was expecting him. But why in God's name, he wondered, wasn't there a single light on? Vance tried to push away a flood of pure anxiety as he reached the back door.

It was unlocked. Though he entered without knocking, he called her name immediately. The house remained dark and silent. Hitting a switch, Vance flooded the rear showroom with light. A quick glance showed him nothing amiss before he continued through the first floor.

"Shane?"

The quiet was beginning to disturb him even more than the darkness. After making a quick circle of the lower floor, he went upstairs. At once he caught the scent of cooking. But the kitchen was empty. Absently turning off the oven, Vance went back into the hall. The thought struck him that she might have lain down after closing the shop and had simply fallen asleep. Amused more than concerned now, he walked quietly into her bedroom. All the amusement fled when he saw her curled up in the chair.

Though the room was in darkness, there was enough moonlight to make her out clearly. She wasn't asleep, but was curled up tightly with her head resting on the arm of the chair. He'd never seen her like that. His first thought was that she looked lost; then he corrected himself. Stricken. There was no innate vivacity in her eyes, and her face glowed palely in the silvery light of the moon. He might have thought her ill, but something told him that even in illness Shane wouldn't lose all of her spark. The thought ran through his mind in only seconds before he crossed the room to her. She made no sign that she saw him, nor was there any response when he spoke her name again. Vance knelt in front of her and took her chilled hands.

"Shane."

For a moment, she stared at him blankly. Then, as though a dam had burst, desperate emotion flooded her eyes. "Vance," she said brokenly, throwing her arms around his neck. "Oh, Vance."

She trembled violently, but didn't weep. The tears were dry as stone inside her. With her face pressed into his shoulder, she clung to him, breaking out of the numbed shock which had followed her earlier bout of tears. It was the warmth of him that made her realize how cold she had been. Without questions, with both strength and sweetness he held her to him.

"Vance, I'm so glad you're here. I need you."

The words struck him more forcibly than even her declaration of love. Up to that moment he had been almost uncomfortably aware that his needs far outweighed hers. Now it seemed there was something he could do for her, if it was only to listen.

"What happened, Shane?" Gently he drew her away only far enough to look into her eyes. "Can you tell me?"

She drew a raw breath, making him eloquently aware of the effort it cost her to speak. "My mother."

With his fingertips, he brushed the tousled hair from her cheeks. "Is she ill?"

"No!" It was a quick, furious explosion. The violence of the denial surprised him, but he took her agitated hands in his.

"Tell me what happened."

"She came," Shane managed, then fought to compose herself.

"Your mother came here?" he prompted.

"Near closing time. I didn't expect… She didn't come for the funeral or answer my letter." Her hands twisted in his, but Vance kept them in a gentle grip.

"This is the first time you've seen her since your grandmother died?" he asked. His voice was calm and quiet. Shane's eyes were still for a moment as she met his eyes directly.

"I haven't seen Anne in over two years," she said flatly. "Since she married her publicity agent. They're divorced now, so she came back." Shaking her head, Shane drew in a breath. "She almost made me believe she cared. I thought we could talk to each other. Really talk." She squeezed her eyes shut. "It was all an act, all the tears and grief. She sat there begging me to understand, and I believed—" Breaking off again, she shuddered with the effort of continuing. "She didn't come because of Gran or because of me." When she opened her eyes again Vance saw they were dull with pain. With a savage effort he kept his voice calm.

"Why did she come, Shane?"

Because her breathing was jerky again, she took a moment to answer. "Money," she said flatly. "She thought there would be money. She was furious that Gran left everything to me, and she wouldn't believe me when I told her how little there had been. I should have known!" she said in a quick rage, which then almost immediately subsided. "I did know." Her shoulders slumped as though she bore an intolerable weight. "I've always known. She's never cared about anyone. I'd hoped there might be some feeling in her for Gran, but... When she came running up here to paw through my papers, I said horrible things. I can't be sorry that I did." Tears sprang to her eyes, only to be swiftly controlled. "I gave her half of what's left and made her leave."

"You gave her money?" Vance demanded, incredulous enough to interrupt.

Shane gave him a weary look. "Gran would have given it to her. She's still my mother."

Disgust and rage rose in his throat. It took all the willpower he had not to give in to it. His anger wouldn't help Shane. "She's not your mother, Shane," he said matter-of-factly. When she opened her mouth to speak, he shook his head and continued. "Biologically, yes, but you're too smart to think that means anything. Cats have kittens too, Shane." He tightened his grip when he saw the flicker of pain on her face. "I'm sorry, I don't want to hurt you."

"No. No, you're right." Her hands went limp again as she let out a sigh. "The truth is, I very rarely think of her. Whatever feelings I have for her are mostly because Gran loved her. And yet..."

"And yet," he finished, "you make yourself sick with guilt."

"How can it be natural to want her to stay away?" Shane demanded in a rush. "Gran—"

"Your grandmother might have felt differently, might have given her money out of a sense of obligation. But think, who did she leave everything to? Everything important to her?"

"Yes, yes, I know, but..."

"When you think of the meaning of 'mother,' Shane, who comes to your mind?"

She stared at him. This time when the tears gathered, they brimmed over. Without a word, she dropped her head back onto his shoulder. "I told her I didn't love her. I meant it, but..."

"You don't owe her anything." He drew her closer. "I know something about guilt, Shane, about letting it tear at you. I won't let you do that to yourself."

"I told her to stay away from me." She gave a long, weary sigh. "I don't think she will."

Vance remained silent for a moment. "Is that what you want?"

"Oh God, yes."

He pressed his lips to her temple before lifting her

into his arms. "Come on, you're exhausted. Lie down for a while and sleep."

"No, I'm not tired," she lied as her lids fluttered down. "I just have a headache. And dinner's—"

"I turned off the oven," he told her as he carried her to the bed. "We'll eat later." After flipping down the quilt, he bent to lay Shane between the cool sheets. "I'll go get you some aspirin." He slipped off her shoes, but as he started to pull the quilt over her, Shane took his hand.

"Vance, would you just...stay with me?"

Touching the back of his hand to her cheek, he smiled at her. "Sure." As soon as he had pulled off his boots, he slipped into bed beside her. "Try to sleep," he murmured, gathering her close. "I'll be right here."

He heard her long, quiet sigh, then felt the feather-brush of her lashes against his shoulder as her eyes shut.

How long they lay still, he had no idea. Though the grandfather clock which stood in Shane's sitting room struck the hour once, Vance paid no attention. She wasn't trembling anymore, nor was her skin chilled. Her breathing was slow and even. The fingers that absently soothed at her temple were gentle, but his thoughts were not.

No one, nothing, was ever going to put that look on Shane's face again. He would see to it. He lay staring at the ceiling as he thought out the best way to deal with Anne Abbott. He'd let the money go, because that's the way Shane wanted it. But he couldn't resign himself to allowing her to deal with a constant emotional drain. Nothing had ever wrenched at him like the sight of her pale, shocked face or pain-filled eyes.

He should have known that anyone with as open a heart as Shane's could be hurt just as deeply as she could be made happy. And how, he wondered, could anyone who had dealt with that kind of pain since childhood be so generous and full of joy? The trial of a careless mother, the embarrassment and hurt of a broken engagement, the loss of the one constant family member she had known—none of it had broken her spirit, or her simple kindness.

But tonight she needed an arm around her. It would be his tonight—and whenever she needed him. Unconsciously he drew her closer as if to shield her from anything and everything that could hurt.

"Vance."

He thought she spoke his name in sleep and brushed a light kiss over her hair.

"Vance," Shane said again, so that he looked down to see the glint of her eyes against the darkness. "Make love with me."

It was a quiet, simple request that asked for comfort rather than passion. The love he already thought infinite tripled. So did his concern that he might not be gentle enough. Very softly, cupping the shape of her face in one hand, he touched his lips to hers.

Shane let herself float. She was too physically and emotionally drained to feel stinging desire, but he seemed to know what she asked for. Never had she felt such tenderness from him. His mouth was warm, and softer than she had thought possible. Minute after minute, he kissed her—and only kissed her. His fingers stroked soothingly over her face, then moved to the base of her neck as if he knew the dull, throbbing ache that centered there. Lovingly, patiently, he drew the quiet response from her, never asking for more than she could give. She relaxed and let him guide her.

With slow care, he roamed her face with kisses, touching his lips lightly to her closed lids as he shifted the gentle massage to her shoulders. There was a concentrated sweetness in his touch that was more kind than loverlike. When his mouth came back to hers, he used only the softest pressure, taking the kiss deep without fire or fury. With a sigh, she answered it, letting her needs pour out.

Passively, she let him undress her. His hands were deft and slow and undemanding. With a sensitivity neither of them had been aware he possessed, he made no attempt to arouse. Even when they were naked, he did nothing more than kiss her and hold her close. She knew she was taking without giving anything in return, and murmuring, reached for him.

"Shh." He kissed her palm before turning her gently

onto her stomach. With his fingertips only at first, he stroked and soothed, running them down her back, over her shoulders. She hadn't known love could be so compassionate or unselfish. With a sigh, she closed her eyes again and let her mind empty.

He was drawing out the pain, bringing back the warmth. As she lay quietly, Shane felt herself settle and balance. There was no need to think, and no need to feel anything but Vance's strong, sure hands. All of her trust was his. Knowing this, he took even more care not to abuse it.

The old bed swayed slightly as he bent to kiss the back of her neck. Shane felt the first stir of desire. It was mild and wonderfully easy. Content, she remained still to allow herself the full enjoyment of being treasured. He was treating her like something fragile and precious. She wallowed in the new experience as he ranged soft kisses down her spine. Tension and tears were a world away from the Jenny Lind bed with a sagging mattress and worn linen sheets. The only reality now was Vance's sweet loving and the growing response of her pampered body.

He heard the subtle change in her breathing, the faint quickening, which meant relaxation was becoming desire. Still, he kept his hands easy, not wanting to rush her. The clock in the sitting room struck the hour again with low, ponderous bongs. Creakily the house settled around them with moans and groans. Vance heard little but Shane's deepening breathing.

The moonlight shivered over her skin, seeming to chase after his roaming hands. It only made him see more clearly how slender her back was, how slight the flare of her hips. Pressing his lips to her shoulder, he could smell the familiar lemon tang of her hair mixed with the lavender sachet lingering on the sheets. The room was washed in shadows.

Her cheek rested on the pillow, giving him a clear view of her profile. She might have been sleeping had it not been for the breath hurrying between her lips and the subtle movements her body was beginning to make. Still gentle, he turned her onto her back to press his mouth to hers.

Shane moaned, so lost in him she noticed no sound, no scent that didn't come from him. But his pace never altered, remaining slow and unhurried. He wanted her, God, yes, but felt no fierce, consuming drive. Love, much more than desire, pulled him to her. When he lowered his mouth to her breast, it was with such infinite tenderness that she felt a warmth, half glow, half ache, pour into her. His tongue began to turn the warmth into heat. She rose up, but seemed to take the journey on a cloud.

With the same infinite care, he took his lips and hands over her. Her skin hummed at his touch, but softly. There was no sweet pain in the passion he brought her, but such pleasure, such comfort, she desired him all the more. Her thoughts became wholly centered on her own body and the quiet delights he had awakened.

Though his lips might stray from hers to taste her neck or her cheek, they returned again and again. Her mindless answer, the husky breath that trembled into his mouth, had the fires roaring inside him. But he banked them. Tonight, she was porcelain. She was as fragile as the moonlight. He wouldn't allow his own passion and needs to overtake him, then find he had treated her roughly. Tonight he would forget her energy and strength and only think of her frailty.

And when he took her, the tenderness made her weep.

Chapter 12

In a thick, steady curtain, the snow fell. Already the road surface was slick. Trees had been quickly transformed from dark and stark to glittery. Vance's windshield wipers swept back and forth with the monotonous swish of rubber on glass. The snow brought him neither annoyance nor pleasure. He barely noticed it.

With a few phone calls and casual inquiries, he had learned enough about Anne Abbott—or Anna Cross, as she called herself professionally—to make his anger of the night before intensify. Shane's description had been too kind.

Anne had been through three turbulent marriages. Each had been a contact in the film industry. She had coolly bled each husband for as much as she could get before jumping into the next relationship. Her latest, Leslie Stuart, had proven a bit too clever for her—or his attorney had. She'd come out of her last marriage with nothing more than she had going into it. And, as she had a penchant for the finer things, she was already badly in debt.

She worked sporadically—bit parts, walk-ons, an occasional commercial. Her talent was nominal, but her face had earned her a few lines in a couple of legitimate films. It might have earned her more had her temper and self-importance not interfered. She was tolerated more than liked by Hollywood society. Even the tolerance, it seemed, was due more to her various husbands and intermittent lovers than to herself. Vance's contacts had painted a picture of a beautiful, scheming woman with a streak of viciousness. He felt he already knew her.

As he drove through the rapidly falling snow, his thoughts centered on Shane. He'd held her through the night, soothing her when she became restless, listening when she needed to talk. The shattered expression in her eyes would remain with him for a long time to come. Even that morning, though she had tried to be cheerful, there'd been an underlying listlessness. And he sensed her unspoken fear that Anne would come back and put her through another emotional storm. Vance couldn't change what had happened, but he could take steps to protect her in the future. That was precisely what he intended to do.

Vance turned into the lot of the roadside motel and parked. For a moment, he only sat, watching the snow accumulate on the windshield. He had considered telling Shane he intended to see her mother, then had rejected the idea. She'd been so pale that morning. In any case, he didn't doubt she would have been against it—even violently opposed to it. She was a woman who insisted on solving her own problems. Vance respected that, even admired it, but in this instance he was going to ignore it.

Stepping out of the car, he walked across the slippery parking lot to find the office and the information he needed. Ten minutes later, he knocked on Anne Abbott's door.

The crease of annoyance between her brows altered into an expression of consideration when she saw Vance. He was certainly a very pleasant surprise. Vance eyed her coolly, discovering that Shane's description hadn't been exaggerated. She was lovely. Her face had a delicacy of bone and complexion complemented by the very deep blue eyes and mane of blond hair. Her body, clad in a clinging pink dressing gown, was ripe and rounded. Though her glittery fairness was the direct opposite of Amelia's sultry beauty, Vance knew instantly they were women of the same mold.

"Well, hello." Her voice was languid and sulky, her

eyes amused and appraising. Though he looked for it, Vance found not the slightest resemblance to her daughter. Overcoming a wave of disgust, he smiled in return. He had to get in the door.

"Hello, Ms. Cross."

He saw instantly that the use of her stage name had been a wise move. She flashed him the full-power smile that was one of her best tools. "Do I know you?" She touched the pink tip of her tongue to her top lip. "There is something familiar about you, but I can't believe I'd forget your face."

"Vance Banning, Ms. Cross," he said, keeping his eyes on hers. "We have some mutual friends, the Hourbacks."

"Oh, Tod and Sheila!" Though she couldn't abide them, Anne infused her voice with rich pleasure. "Isn't that marvelous! Oh, but you must come in. It's freezing out there. Appalling Eastern weather." She closed the door behind him, then stood leaning back against it a moment. Perhaps, she mused, the hometown visit wouldn't be so boring after all. This was the best-looking thing to knock at her door for quite some time. And, if he knew the stuffy Hourbacks, chances were he'd have a few dollars as well. "Well, well, isn't it a small world," she murmured, gently tucking a strand of delicate blond hair behind her ear. "How are Tod and Sheila? I haven't seen them for an age."

"Fine when I last spoke to them." Well aware where

her thoughts were traveling, Vance smiled again, this time with cold amusement. "They mentioned that you were in town. I couldn't resist looking you up, Ms. Cross."

"Oh, Anna, please," she said graciously. With a sigh, she gave the room a despairing glance. "I must apologize for my accommodations, but I have some business nearby, and…" She gave a tiny shrug. "I'm forced to make do. I can offer you a drink, however, if you'll take bourbon."

It was barely eleven, but Vance answered smoothly, "If it's not too much trouble."

"None at all." Anne glided to a small table. She felt particularly grateful that she had packed the silk dressing gown and hadn't yet drummed up the energy to change. It was, she knew, both becoming and alluring. A quick glance in the mirror as she poured assured her she looked perfect. Thank God she'd just finished putting on her makeup. "But tell me, Vance," she continued, "what in the world are you doing in this dull little place? You're not a hometown boy, are you?"

"Business," he said simply, nodding his thanks as she handed him a neat bourbon.

Anne's eyes narrowed a moment, then widened. "Oh, of course. How could I be so foolish!" She beamed at him as the wheels began to spin in her head. "I've heard Tod speak of you. Riverton Construction, right?"

"Right."

"My, my, I am impressed." Her tongue ran lightly over her teeth as she considered. "It's about the biggest in the country."

"So I'm told," he answered mildly, watching her eye him over the rim of her glass. Without much interest, he wondered how much bait she would toss out before she tried to reel him in. If it hadn't been for Shane, he might have enjoyed letting her make a fool of herself.

With her carefully languid grace, Anne sat on the edge of the bed. As she sipped again, she wondered how soon he would try to sleep with her and how much resistance she should feign before she obliged him. "Well, Vance, what can I do for you?"

Vance swirled the bourbon without drinking. He sent her a cool, direct stare. "Leave Shane alone."

The change in her expression might have been comical under any other circumstances. She forgot herself long enough to gape at him. "What are you talking about?"

"Shane," he repeated. "Your daughter."

"I know who Shane is," Anne said sharply. "What has she to do with you?"

"I'm going to marry her."

Shock covered her face, then dissolved with her burst of laughter. "Little Shane? Oh, that's too funny. Don't tell me my cute little daughter caught herself a live one! I've underestimated her." Tossing her head, she sent Vance a shrewed glance. "Or I overestimated you."

Though his fingers tightened on the glass, he controlled his temper. When he spoke, his voice was dangerously mild. "Be careful, Anne."

The look in his eye checked her laughter. "Well," she continued with an unconcerned shrug, "so you want to marry Shane. What's that to me?"

"Not a damn thing."

Masking both apprehension and irritation, Anne rose gracefully. "I suppose I should go congratulate my little girl on her luck."

Vance took her arm. Though he applied no pressure, the meaning was very clear. "You'll do nothing of the kind. What you're going to do is pack your bags and get out."

Enraged, Anne jerked away from him. "Who the hell do you think you are? You can't order me to leave."

"Advise," Vance corrected. "You'd be wise to take the suggestion."

"I don't like the tone of your suggestion," she retorted. "I intend to see my daughter—"

"Why?" Vance stopped her cold without raising his voice. "You won't get another dime, I promise you."

"I haven't any idea what you're talking about," Anne claimed with frigid dignity. "I don't know what nonsense Shane's been telling you, but—"

"You'd be wise to think carefully before you say any more," Vance warned quietly. "I saw Shane shortly after you left her last night. She had to tell me very little before I got the picture." He gave her a long, hard look. "I know you, Anne, every bit as well as you know yourself. There'll be no more money," he continued when Anne fell silent. "You'd be smarter to cut your losses and go back to California. It would be a simple matter to stop payment on the check she's already given you."

That annoyed her. Anne cursed herself for not getting up early and cashing the check before Shane thought better of it. "I have every intention of seeing my daughter." She gave him a glittering smile. "And when I do, I'll have a few words to say to her about her choice of lovers."

His eyes neither heated nor chilled, but became faintly bored. Nothing could have infuriated her more. "You won't see Shane again," he corrected.

Under the silk, her lovely bust heaved. "You can't keep me from seeing my own daughter."

"I can," Vance countered, "and I will. If you contact her, if you try to wheedle another dollar out of her or hurt her in any way, I'll deal with you myself."

Anne felt the first prickle of physical fear. Warily, she stepped back from him. "You wouldn't dare touch me."

Vance gave a mirthless laugh. "Don't be too sure. I don't think it'll come to that though." Casually, he set down the glass of liquor. "I have a number of contacts in the movie industry, Anne. Old friends, business associates, clients. A few words in the right ears, and what little career you have is out the window."

"How dare you threaten me," she began, both furious and afraid.

"Not a threat," he assured her. "A promise. Hurt Shane again and you'll pay for it. You're getting the best of the deal, Anne," he added. "She doesn't have anything you want."

Smoldering, she took a step toward him. "I have a right to my share. Whatever my grandmother had should be split fifty-fifty between Shane and me."

He lifted a brow in speculation. "Fifty-fifty," he said thoughtfully. "You must be desperate if you're willing to settle for that." Without pity, he shrugged off her problems. "I won't waste my time arguing legalities with you, much less morals or ethics. Just accept that what Shane gave you yesterday is all you'll ever get." With this he turned toward the door. In a last-ditch effort, Anne sank down on the bed and began to weep.

"Oh, Vance, you can't be so cruel." She lifted an already tear-drenched face to his. "You can't mean to keep me from seeing my own daughter, my only child."

He studied the beautiful tragic face, then gave a slight nod of approval. "Very good," he commented. "You're a better actress than they give you credit for." As he pulled the door to behind him, he heard the sound of smashing glass on the wood.

Springing up, Anne grabbed the second glass, then hurled it as well. No one, *no one,* she determined, was going to threaten her. Or mock her, she fumed, remembering the cool amusement in his eyes. She'd see he paid for it. Sitting back on the bed, she clenched her fists until she could bring her temper to order. She had to think. There had to be a way to get to Vance Banning. *Riverton Construction,* she reflected, closing her eyes as she concentrated. Had there been any scandal connected with the firm? Frustrated, she hurled her pillow across the room. She could think of nothing. What did she know about a stupid firm that built shopping centers and hospitals? It was all so boring, she thought furiously.

Grabbing the second pillow, she started to toss it as well when a sudden glimmer of memory arrested her. Scandal, she repeated. But not about the firm. There had been something…something a few years back. Just a few whispers at a party or two. *Damn!* she swore silently when her recollection took her no further. Sheila Hourback, Anne thought, tightening her lips. Maybe the stuffy old bird could be useful. Scrambling over the unmade bed, Anne reached for the phone.

Shane was busy detailing a skirmish of the Battle of Antietam for three eager boys when Vance walked in.

She smiled at him, and he heard enthusiasm in her voice as she spoke, but she was still pale. That alone brushed away any doubts that he had done the right thing. She'd bounce back, he told himself as he wandered into the antique shop, because it was her nature to do so. But even someone as intrinsically strong as Shane could take only so much. Spotting Pat dusting glassware, he went over to her.

"Hi, Vance." She sent him a quick, friendly grin. "How're you doing?"

"I'm fine." He cast a look over his shoulder to be certain Shane was still occupied. "Listen, Pat, I wanted to talk to you about that dining-room set."

"Oh yeah. There was some mix-up about that. I still haven't gotten it straight. Shane said—"

"I'm going to buy it."

"You?" Her initial surprise turned into embarrassment. Vance grinned at her, however, and her cheeks cooled.

"For Shane," he explained. "For Christmas."

"Oh, that's so sweet!" The romance of it appealed to her immediately. "It was her grandmother's, you know. She just loves it."

"I know, and she's determined to sell it." Idly, he picked up a china demitasse cup. "I'm just as determined to buy it for her. She won't let me." He gave Pat a conspirator's wink. "But she can hardly turn down a Christmas present, can she?"

"No." Appreciating his cleverness, Pat beamed at him. So the rumors were true, she thought, pleased and interested. There was something going on between them. "She sure couldn't. It'll mean so much to her, Vance. It just about kills her to have to sell some of these things, but that's the hardest. It's...ah, it's awfully expensive though."

"That's all right. I'm going to give you a check for it today." It occurred to him that it would soon be all over town that he had a great deal of money to spend. He would have to talk to Shane very soon. "Put a Sold sign on it." He glanced back again, seeing Shane's three visitors were preparing to leave. "Just don't say anything to her unless she asks."

"I won't," Pat promised, pleased to be in on the surprise. "And if she does, I'll just say the person who bought it wants it held until Christmas."

"Clever girl," he complimented. "Thanks."

"Vance." She lowered her voice to a whisper. "She looks kind of down today. Maybe you could take her out for a while and cheer her up. Oh, Shane," she continued quickly in a normal tone, "how did you manage to keep those little monsters quiet for twenty minutes? Those are Clint Drummond's boys," she explained to Vance with a shudder. "I nearly ran out the back door when they came in."

"They were thrilled that school was called off because

of the snow." Instinctively, she reached for Vance's hand as she came in. "What they wanted was to work out the fine details of a few engagements so they could have their own Battle of Antietam with snowballs."

"Get your coat," Vance told her, planting a kiss on her brow.

"What?"

"And a hat. It's cold outside."

Laughing, Shane gave his hand a squeeze. "I know it's cold outside, fool. There's already six inches of snow."

"Then we'd better get started." He gave her a friendly swat on the seat. "You'll need boots too, I suppose. Just don't take all day."

"Vance, it's the middle of the day. I can't leave."

"It's business," he told her gravely. "You have to get your Christmas tree."

"Christmas tree?" With a chuckle, she picked up the duster Pat had set down. "It's too early in the season."

"Early?" Vance sent Pat a grin. "You've got just over two weeks until Christmas, and no tree. Most self-respecting stores are decked out by Thanksgiving."

"Well, I know, but—"

"But nothing," he interrupted, taking the duster from her and handing it back to Pat. "Where's your holiday spirit? Not to mention your sales strategy. According to the most recent poll, people spend an additional twelve and a half percent in a store decorated for the holidays."

Shane gave him a narrow glance. "What poll?"

"The Retail Sale and Seasonal Atmosphere Survey," he said glibly.

The first genuine laugh in nearly twenty-four hours burst from her. "That's a terrible lie."

"Certainly not," he disagreed. "It's a very good one. Now go get your coat."

"But, Vance—"

"Oh, don't be silly, Shane," Pat interrupted, giving her a push toward the stairs. "I can handle the shop. We're not likely to have customers pouring in with all this snow. Besides," she added, shrewd enough to know her employer, "I'd really love a tree. I'll make a place for it right in front of this window." Without waiting for a reply, Pat began to rearrange furniture.

"Gloves too," Vance added as Shane hesitated.

"All right," she said, surrendering. "I'll be back in a minute."

In little more than ten, she was sitting beside Vance in the cab of his small pickup. "Oh, it's beautiful out here!" she exclaimed, trying to look everywhere at once. "I love the first snow. Look, there're the Drummond boys."

Vance glanced in the direction she indicated and saw three boys pelting each other violently with snow.

"The battle's under way," he murmured.

"General Burnside's having his problems," Shane observed, then turned back to Vance. "By the way, what did you and Pat have your heads together about when I went upstairs to get my things?"

Vance lifted a brow. "Oh," he said complacently, "I was trying to make a date with her. She's cute."

"Really?" Shane drew out the word as she eyed him. "It would be a shame for her to be fired this close to Christmas."

"I was only trying to develop good employee relations," he explained, pulling up at a stop sign. Taking her by surprise, he pulled her into his arms and kissed her thoroughly. "I love that little choking sound you make when you try not to laugh. Do it again."

Breathless, she pulled away from him. "Firing a trusted employee is no laughing matter," she told him primly, and adjusted her ski hat. "Turn right here." Instead of obeying, he kissed her again. The rude blast of a horn had her struggling out of his arms a second time. "Now you've done it." She ruined the severity of the lecture with a smothered chuckle. "The sheriff's going to arrest you for obstructing traffic."

"One disgruntled man in a Buick isn't traffic," Vance disagreed as he made a right turn. "Do you know where you're going?"

"Certainly. There's a place a few miles down where you can dig your own tree."

"Dig?" Vance repeated, shooting her a look. Shane met it placidly.

"Dig," she repeated. "According to the latest conservation poll—"

"Dig," he agreed, cutting her off.

Laughing, Shane leaned over to kiss his shoulder. "I love you, Vance."

By the time they arrived at the tree farm, the snow had slowed to a gentle mist. Shane dragged him from tree to tree, examining each one minutely before rejecting it. Though he knew the color in her face was a result of the cold, the spark was back. Even if he sensed some of the energy was a product of nerves, he was satisfied that she was bouncing back. The simple pleasure of choosing a Christmas tree was enough to put the laughter back in her eyes.

"This one!" Shane exclaimed, stopping in front of a short-needle pine. "It's exactly right."

"It doesn't look much different from the other five hundred trees we've looked at," Vance grumbled, slicing the point of his shovel into the snow.

"That's because you don't have a connoisseur's eye," she said condescendingly. He scooped up a handful of snow and rubbed it into her face. "Be that as it may," Shane continued with remarkable aplomb, "this is the one. Dig," she instructed, and stepping back, folded her arms.

"Yes, ma'am," he said meekly, bending to the task. "You know," he said a few moments later, "it suddenly occurs to me that you're going to expect me to dig a hole to put this thing in after Christmas."

Shane sent him a guileless smile. "What a good idea. I know just the place too. You'll probably need a pick though. There are an awful lot of rocks." Ignoring Vance's rude rejoinder, she waved over an attendant. With the roots carefully wrapped in burlap and the tree itself paid for—by Shane over Vance's objection—they headed home.

"Damn it, Shane," he said in exasperation. "I wanted to buy the tree for you." The truck rumbled over the narrow wooden bridge.

"The tree's for the shop," she pointed out logically as they pulled in front of the house. "So the shop bought the tree. Just as it buys the stock and pays the electric bill." Noting that he was annoyed, Shane walked around the truck to kiss him. "You're sweet, Vance, and I do appreciate it. Buy me something else."

He gave her a long, considering look. "What?"

"Oh, I don't know. I've always had a fancy for something frivolous and extravagant…like chinchilla earmuffs."

With difficulty, he maintained his gravity. "It would serve you right if I did buy you some. Then you'd have to wear them."

She rose on her toes, inviting another kiss. As he bent down, Shane slipped the handful of snow she'd been holding down his back. When he swore pungently, she made a dash for safety. Shane fully expected the snowball that bashed into the back of her head, but she didn't expect to be agilely tackled so that she landed facedown in the snow.

"Oh! You really aren't a gentleman," she muttered, hampered by a mouthful of snow. Vance sat back, roaring with laughter while she struggled to sit up, wiping at her face.

"Snow looks even better on you than mud," he told her.

Shane lunged at him, catching him off-balance so that he toppled onto his back. She landed with a soft thud on his chest. Before she could deposit the snow she held in his face, he rolled her over and pinned her. Resigned, she closed her eyes and waited. Instead of the cold shock of snow, she felt his lips crush down on hers. In immediate response, she pulled him closer, answering hungrily.

"Give?" he demanded.

"No," she said firmly, and dragged him back again.

The urgency of her response made him forget they were lying in the snow in the middle of the afternoon. He no longer felt the wet flakes that drifted down the back of his neck, though he could taste others on her skin. He fretted against the bulky clothes that kept the shape of her from him, against the gloves that prevented him from feeling the softness of her skin. But he could taste, and he did so greedily.

"God, I want you," he murmured, savaging her small, avid mouth again and again. "Right here, right now." Lifting his head, he looked down on her, but whatever he would have said was cut off by the sound of an approaching car. "If I'd had any sense I'd have taken you to my house," he mumbled, then helped her to her feet.

Hugging him, she whispered in his ear, "I close in two hours."

While Shane dealt with a straggle of customers who touched everything and bought nothing, Vance made himself useful by setting up the tree. Pat's lighthearted chatter helped cool the blood Shane had so quickly heated. Following Shane's instructions, he found the boxes of ornaments in the dusty attic.

Dusk was falling before they were alone again. Because she was still looking pale, Vance bullied her into a quick meal before they began to sort through the ornaments. They made do with cold meat from the rib roast neither of them had touched the night before.

But as well as alleviating her hunger, the meal reminded her forcibly of her mother's visit. She struggled to push away the depression, or at least to conceal it. Her chatter was bright and mindless and entirely too strained.

Vance caught her hand, stopping her in midsentence. "Not with me, Shane," he said quietly.

Not bothering to pretend she didn't understand, Shane squeezed his hand. "I'm not dwelling on it, Vance. It just sneaks up on me sometimes."

"And when it does, I'm here. Lean on me, Shane, when you need to." He lifted her hand to his lips. "God knows, I'll lean on you."

"Now," she said shakily. "Just hold me a minute."

He drew her into his arms, pressing her head to his heart. "As long as you want."

She sighed, relaxing again. "I hate being a fool," she murmured. "I suppose I hate that worse than anything."

"You're not being a fool," he said, then drew her away as he came to a decision. "Shane, I went to see your mother this morning."

"What?" The word came out in a whisper.

"You can be angry if you like, but I won't stand by and watch you be hurt again. I made it very clear that if she bothered you again, she'd have me to deal with."

Shaken, she turned away from him. "You shouldn't—"

"Don't tell me what I shouldn't have done," he interrupted angrily. "I love you, damn it. You can't expect me to do nothing while she puts you through the wringer."

"I can deal with it, Vance."

"No." Taking her shoulders, he turned her around. "With an amazing number of things, yes, but not with this. She turns you inside out." His grip lightened to a caress. "Shane, if it had been me hurting, what would you have done?"

She opened her mouth to speak, but only released a pent-up breath. Taking his face in her hands, she pulled it down to hers. "I hope I'd have done the same thing. Thank you," she said, kissing him gently. "I don't want to know what was said," she added with more firmness. "No more problems tonight, Vance."

He shook his head, acknowledging another delay in making everything known to her. "All right, no more problems."

"We'll trim the tree," she stated decisively. "Then you're going to make love to me under it."

He grinned. "I suppose I could do that." He allowed her to pull him down the stairs. "What if I make love to you under it, then we trim it?"

"There's nothing festive in that," she said gravely as she began unpacking ornaments.

"Wanna bet?"

She laughed, but shook her head. "Absolutely not. There's an order to these things, you know. Lights first," she announced, pulling out a neatly coiled string.

It took well over an hour as Shane shared her memories about nearly every ornament she unpacked. As she took out a red felt star, she recalled the year she had made it for her grandmother. It brought both a sting and a warmth. She'd been dreading Christmas. It hadn't seemed possible to celebrate the holiday in that house without the woman who had always shared it with her. Gran would have reminded her that there was a cycle, but Shane knew she would have found a tree and tinsel unbearable had she been alone.

She watched Vance carefully arranging a garland. How Gran would have loved him, she thought with a smile. And he her. Somehow she found it didn't matter that the two people she loved most in the world had never met. She knew both of them, and the link was formed. Shane was ready to give herself to him completely.

If he doesn't ask me to marry him soon, she mused, I'll just have to ask him. When he glanced over, she sent him a saucy smile.

"What are you thinking?" he demanded.

"Oh, nothing," she said innocently, stepping back to view the results. "It's perfect, just as I knew it would be." She gave a satisfied nod before taking out the old silver star that would adorn the top.

Vance accepted it from her, then eyed the top branch. "I'm not going to be able to get this on there without knocking half of everything else off. We need a ladder."

"Oh no, that's okay. Let me up on your shoulders."

"There's a stepladder upstairs," he began.

"Oh, don't be so fussy." Shane jumped nimbly onto his back, hooking her legs around his waist for balance. "I'll be able to reach it without any trouble," she assured him, then began scooting up to his shoulders. Vance felt every line of her body as if he'd run his hands over it. "There," she said, settled. "Hand it to me and I'll stick it on."

He obliged, then gripped her knees as she leaned forward. "Damn it, Shane, not so far; you're going to fall into the tree."

"Don't be silly," she said lightly as she secured the star. "I have terrific balance. There!" Putting her hands on her hips, she surveyed the results. "Step back a bit so I can see the whole thing." When he had, Shane gave a long sigh, then kissed the top of his head. "It's beautiful, isn't it? Just smell the pine." Carelessly, she linked her ankles against his chest.

"It'll look better with the overhead lights off." Still carrying her, he moved to flick the wall switch. In the dark, the colored lights on the tree seemed to jump into life. They shimmered against garland and tinsel, glowed warmly against pine.

"Oh yes," Shane breathed. "Just perfect."

"Not quite yet," Vance disagreed.

With a deft move, he pulled her around into his arms as she slid down from his shoulders. "This," he told her as he laid her on the rug, "is perfect."

The lights danced on her face as she smiled up at him. "It certainly is."

His hands weren't patient tonight, but neither were

hers. They undressed each other quickly, laughing and swearing a bit at buttons or snaps. But when they were naked, the urgency only intensified. Their hands sought to touch, their mouths hurried to taste—everywhere. She marveled again at his taut, corded muscles. He filled himself again on the flavor and fragrance of her skin. They paid no more notice to the warmth of the lights or the tang of pine than they had to the chill of the snow. They were alone. They were together.

Chapter 13

It wasn't easy for Shane to keep her mind on her work the next day. Though she made several sales, among them the tilt-top table she had so painstakingly refinished, she was distracted throughout the morning. Distracted enough that she never noticed the discreet Sold sign Pat had attached to the Hepplewhite set in lieu of a price tag. She could think of little else but Vance. Once or twice during the morning, she caught herself glancing at the Christmas tree and remembering. In all of her dreams, in all of her wishes, she had never imagined it could be this way. Each time they made love it was different, a new adventure. Yet somehow it was as though they had been together for years.

Every time she touched him it was like making a

fresh discovery, and still Shane felt she had known him for a lifetime rather than a matter of three short months. When he kissed her, it was just as thrilling and novel as the first time. The recognition she had felt the instant she had seen him had deepened into something much more abiding. Faith.

Without doubt, she was certain that the excitement and the learning would go on time after time over the comfortable core of honest love. There was no need to romanticize what was real. She had only to look at him to know what they shared was special and enduring. With another glance at the tree, she realized she'd never been happier in her life.

"Miss!" The customer considering the newly caned ladder-back chair called impatiently for Shane's attention.

"Yes, ma'am, I'm sorry." If the smile Shane gave her was a bit dreamy, the woman didn't seem to notice. "It's a lovely piece, isn't it? The seat's just been redone." Calling herself to order, Shane turned the chair over to show off the workmanship.

"Yes, I'm interested." The woman poked at the caning a moment. "But the price…"

Recognizing the tone, Shane settled down to bargain.

It was just past noon when things began to quiet down. The morning's profits weren't extraordinary, but solid enough to help Shane stop worrying over the large chunk of her capital that she had given to her mother. The wolf wasn't at the door yet, she told herself optimistically. And with luck—and the Christmas rush—she could hold him off for quite some time. Two or three good sales would keep her books from dipping too deeply into the red. Professionally, she wanted little more at the moment than to calmly tread water. Personally, she knew precisely what she wanted, and she had every intention of seeing to it quickly.

She was going to marry Vance, and it was time she told him so. If he was too proud to ask her because he didn't yet have a steady job, she would simply have to persuade him to see things differently. Shane had made up her mind to take a firm stand that very day. There was an excitement bubbling inside her, a sense of purpose. Today, she thought, almost giddy from it, nothing could hurt her. She was going to propose to the man she loved. And she wasn't going to take no for an answer.

"Pat, can you handle things if I go out for an hour?"

"Sure, it's slow now anyway." Pat glanced up from the table she was polishing. "Are you going to another auction?"

"No," Shane told her blithely. "I'm going on a picnic."

Leaving Pat staring behind her, Shane raced upstairs.

It took her less than ten minutes to fill the wicker basket. There was a cold bottle of Chablis inside it, which she had splurged on madly. It might be a bit rich for the peanut butter sandwiches, but Shane's mind wasn't on proprieties. As she raced out the back door, she was already picturing spreading the checked tablecloth in front of Vance's living-room fire.

Wet, slushy snow sloshed over her boots as she stepped off the porch onto the lawn. The perfect day for a picnic, she decided, letting the hamper swing. The air was absolutely still. Melted snow dripped from the roof with a musical patter. The fast water in the creek broke through thin sheets of ice with an excited hissing and bubbling. Shane paused to listen a moment, enjoying the mixture of sounds. The feeling of euphoria built. She found it the most exquisite of days, with the sky coldly blue, the snow-laced mountains rising and the naked trees slick with wet.

Then the low purr of an engine intruded. She looked back, then stopped as she recognized Anne pulling up in the drive. All of her joy in the afternoon slipped quietly away. She hardly noticed the fingers of tension that crept up to the base of her neck.

With her faultless grace, Anne picked her way over the melting snow in calfskin boots. She wore a trim fox-fur hat now to match her coat, and a small, smug smile. There were ruby studs, or clever imitations, glinting at her ears. Though her daughter stood rigid as a stone, she glided up to greet her with the customary brush of cheeks. Without speaking, Shane set the hamper down on the bottom step of the porch.

"Darling, I had to drop by before I left." Anne beamed at her with a cold gleam in her eye.

"Going back to California?" Shane asked flatly.

"Yes, of course, I have the most marvelous script. Of course, I'll probably be weeks on location, but..." She gave a gay shrug. "But that's not why I dropped by."

Shane studied her, marveling. It was as though the ugly scene between them had never taken place. She has no feelings, she realized abruptly. It meant less than nothing to her. "Why did you come by, Anne?"

"Why, to congratulate you, of course!"

"Congratulate me?" Shane lifted a brow. It was easier somehow knowing that the woman in front of her was simply a stranger. A few shared genes didn't make a bond. It was love that did that, or affection. Or at the very least, respect.

"I admit I didn't think you had it in you, Shane, but I'm pleasantly surprised."

Shane then surprised both of them by giving an impatient sigh. "Will you get to the point, Anne? I was on my way out."

"Oh, now, don't be cross," she said placatingly. "I'm really thrilled for you, catching yourself a man like that."

Shane's eyes chilled. "I beg your pardon?"

"Vance Banning, darling." She gave a slow, appreciative smile. "What a catch!"

"Strange, I never thought about it quite that way." Bending, Shane prepared to pick up the hamper again.

"The president of Riverton Construction isn't just a mild triumph, sweetheart, it's a downright *coup*."

Shane's fingers froze on the handle. Straightening, she looked Anne dead in the eye. "What are you talking about?"

"Only your fantastic luck, Shane. After all, the man's *rolling* in it. I imagine you'll be able to turn this little shop of yours into an antique palace if you want a hobby." She gave a quick, brittle laugh. "Leave it to cute little Shane to land herself a millionaire the first time around. If I had a bit more time, darling, I'd insist on hearing the details of how you managed it."

"I don't know what you're talking about." Cold panic was beginning to rush through her. She wanted to turn and run away, but her legs were stiff and unyielding.

"God knows why he decided to dump himself in this town," Anne went on mildly. "But it's your good fortune he did, and right next door too. I suppose he means to keep it for a little hideaway once the two of you move to D.C." *A fabulous house,* she thought on a flash of envy. *Servants, parties.* Carefully, she kept her tone gay. "I can't tell you how thrilled I was to learn you'd hooked up with the man who owns virtually the biggest construction firm in the country."

"Riverton," Shane repeated numbly.

"Very prestigious, darling Shane. It does give me
cause to wonder how you'll fit in, but…" She shrugged
this off and aimed her coup de grâce. "It's a shame about
that nasty scandal though." Shane merely shook her head
and stared at Anne blankly. "His first wife, you know.
A terrible tangle."

"Wife?" Shane repeated faintly. She felt the nausea
rising in her stomach. "Vance's wife?"

"Oh, Shane, don't tell me he didn't mention it!" It was
exactly what she'd hoped for. Anne shook her head and
sighed. "That's disgraceful of him, really. Isn't it just
like a man to expect some wide-eyed girl to take everything on face value." She clucked her tongue in disapproval, thinking with inner appreciation that Vance
Banning was going to take his knocks on this one. She
didn't think of Shane at all.

"Well, the very least he might have done was tell you
he was married before," she continued primly. "Even if
he didn't go into the nasty business."

"I don't…" Shane managed to swallow the sickness
and continue. "I don't understand."

"A spicy little scandal," Anne told her. "His wife
was a raving beauty, you know. Perhaps too much so."
Anne paused delicately. "One of her lovers put a bullet

in her heart. At least that's what the Bannings would have everyone believe." The shock in Shane's eyes gave Anne another surge of gratification. Oh yes, she thought grimly, Vance Banning was going to get back some of his now. "Hushed it up rather quickly too," she added, then brushed the matter away with the back of an elegantly gloved hand. "An odd business. Well, I must run, don't want to miss my plane. *Ciao,* darling, and don't let that handsome gold mine slip away from you. There are plenty of women just dying to catch him." Pausing, she touched Shane's cap of curls with a finger. "For God's sake, Shane, find a decent hairdresser. I suppose he thinks you're…refreshing. Get the ring on your finger before he gets bored." She brushed Shane's cold cheek with hers, then dashed off, satisfied she'd paid Vance back for his threats.

Shane stood perfectly still, staring after her. But she didn't see her. She saw nothing. Trapped in the ice of shock, the pain was dormant. That would have surprised Anne had she given it any thought. As a woman who knew nothing of emotional pain, she would assume Shane would feel only fury. But the fury was surrounded by pain, and the pain lay waiting to spring out.

The sun bounced glaringly off the melting snow. A breeze, chill and sharp, whipped through her carelessly unbuttoned coat. In a flash of scarlet, a cardinal swooped over the ground to roost comfortably on a low branch.

Shane stood absolutely still, noticing nothing. Sluggishly, her mind began to work.

It wasn't true, she told herself. Anne had made it up for some unexplainable purpose of her own. *President of Riverton?* No, he said he was a carpenter. He *was,* she thought desperately. She'd seen his work herself… He'd…he'd worked for her. Taken the job she had offered. Why would he—how could he—if he was everything Anne had said? *His first wife.*

Shane felt the first stab of pain. No, it couldn't be, he would have told her. Vance loved her. He wouldn't lie or pretend. He wouldn't make a fool of her by letting her think he was out of work when he was the head of one of the biggest construction firms in the country. He wouldn't have said he loved her without telling her who he really was. *His first wife.* Shane heard a soft, despairing moan without realizing it was hers.

When she saw him coming down the path, she stared blankly. As she watched him, her whirling thoughts came to a sudden halt. She knew then she'd been a fool.

Spotting her, Vance smiled in greeting and increased his pace. He was still several yards away when he recognized the expression on her face. It was the same stricken look he'd seen in the moonlight only a few nights before.

"Shane?" He came to her quickly, reaching for her. Shane stepped back.

"Liar," she said in a broken whisper. "All lies." Her eyes both accused and pleaded. "Everything you said."

"Shane—"

"No, don't!" The panic in her voice was enough to halt the hand he held out to her. He knew that somehow she had learned everything before he could tell her himself.

"Shane, let me explain."

"Explain?" She dragged shaking fingers through her hair. "Explain? How? How can you explain why you let me think you were something you're not? How can you explain why you didn't bother to tell me you were president of Riverton, that you—that you'd been married before? I *trusted* you," she whispered. "God, how could I have been such a fool!"

Anger he could have met and handled. Vance faced despair without any notion of how to cope with it. Impotently he thrust his hands into his pockets to keep from touching her. "I would have told you, Shane. I intended—"

"Would have?" She gave a quick, shaky laugh. "When? After you'd gotten bored with the joke?"

"There was never any joke," he said furiously, then clamped down on his panic. "I wanted to tell you, but every time—"

"No joke?" Her eyes glittered now with the beginnings of anger, the beginnings of tears. "You let me give you a job. You let me pay you six dollars an hour, and you don't think that's funny?"

"I didn't want your money, Shane. I tried to tell you. You wouldn't listen." Frustrated, he turned away until he had himself under control. "I banked the checks in an account under your name."

"How dare you!" Wild with pain, she shouted at him, blind and deaf to everything but the sense of betrayal. "How dare you play games with me! *I believed you.* I believed everything. I thought—I thought I was helping you, and all the time you were laughing at me."

"Damn it, Shane, I never laughed at you." Pushed beyond endurance, he grabbed her shoulders. "You know I never laughed at you."

"I wonder how you managed not to laugh in my face. God, you're clever, Vance." She choked on a sob, then swallowed it.

"Shane, if you'd try to understand why I came, why I didn't want to be connected with the company for a little while..." None of the words he needed would come to him. "It had nothing to do with you," he told her fiercely. "I didn't expect to get involved."

"Did it keep you from being bored?" she demanded, struggling against his hold. "Amusing yourself with a stupid little country girl who was so gullible she'd believe anything you said? You could play the poor working man and be entertained."

"It was never like that." Enraged by the words, he shook her. "You don't really believe that."

The tears gushed out passionately, strangling her voice. "And I was so willing to fall into bed with you. You knew it!" She sobbed, pushing desperately at him. "Right from the first I had no secrets from you."

"I had them," he admitted in a tight voice. "I had reasons for them."

"You knew how much I loved you, how much I wanted you. You *used* me!" On a moan, she covered her face with her hands. "Oh God, I left myself wide open."

She wept with the same honest abandon he'd seen when she laughed. Unable to do otherwise, he crushed her against him. He thought if he could only calm her down, he could make her understand. "Shane, please, you have to listen to me."

"No, no, I don't." She pulled in breath after jerky breath as she struggled for release. "I'll never forgive you. I'll never believe anything you say again. Damn you, let me go."

"Not until you stop this and hear what I have to say."

"No! I won't listen to any more lies. I won't let you make a fool of me again. All this time, all this time when I was giving you everything, you were lying and laughing at me. I was just something to keep the nights from being dull while you were on vacation."

He jerked her back, his face rigid with fury. "Damn it, Shane, you know better than that."

Her struggles ceased abruptly. As he watched, the tears seemed to turn to ice. Without expression, she stared up at him. Nothing she had said so far had struck him to the core like that one cool look.

"I don't know you," she said quietly.

"Shane—"

"Take your hands off me." The command was devoid of passion. Vance felt his stiff fingers loosen. Freed, Shane stepped back until they were no longer touching. "I want you to go away and leave me alone. Stay away from me," she added flatly, still looking directly into his eyes. "I don't want to see you again."

Turning, she walked up the steps and to the door. After its final click came absolute silence.

Far beneath the window, the streets were packed with traffic. The steady fall of snow increased the confusion. Beneath the overhang of the department store across the street, a red-cheeked Santa rang his bell, ho-hoing when someone dropped a coin into his bucket. The scene below was played in pantomime. The thick glass of the window and well-constructed walls allowed no street sounds to intrude. Vance kept his back to his plush, spacious office and continued to watch.

He'd made his obligatory appearance at the company

Christmas party. It was still going on, with enthusiasm, in a large conference room on the third floor. When it broke up, everyone would go home to spend Christmas Eve with their families or friends. He'd refused more than a dozen invitations for the evening since his return to Washington. It was one thing to do his duty as the head of the company, and another to put himself through hours of small talk and celebrating. *She wouldn't be there,* he thought, staring down at the snowy sidewalk.

Two weeks. In two weeks, Vance had managed to straighten out a few annoying contractual tangles, plot out a bid for a new wing to a hospital in Virginia and head a heated board meeting. He'd dealt with paperwork, and some minor corporate intrigue he might have found amusing if he'd been sleeping properly. But he wasn't sleeping properly any more than he was forgetting. Work wasn't an elixir this time. As she had from the very first moment, Shane haunted him.

Turning from the window, Vance took his place behind the massive oak desk. It was clear of papers. In a fury of frustrated energy, he'd taken care of every letter, memo and contract, putting his secretary and assistants through an orgy of work over the last two weeks. Now, he had nothing but an empty desk and a clear calendar. He considered the possibility of flying to Des Moines to supervise the progress of a condominium development. That would throw the Iowa branch into a panic, he thought with a quick laugh. Hardly fair to upset their applecart because he was restless. He brooded at the far wall, wondering what Shane was doing.

He hadn't left in anger. It would have been easier for Vance if that had been the case. He had left because Shane had wanted it. He didn't blame her, and that too made it impossibly frustrating. Why should she listen to him, or understand? There had been enough truth in what she had flung at him to make the rest difficult to overturn. He had lied, or at the very least, he hadn't been honest. To Shane, one was the same as the other.

He'd hurt her. He had put that look of helpless despair on her face. That was unforgivable. Vance pushed away from the desk to pace over the thick stone-colored carpet. But damn it, if she'd just listened to him! If she'd only given him a moment. Going to the window again, he scowled out. Laughed at her? Made fun of her? No, he thought with the first true fury he'd felt in two weeks. No, by God, he'd be damned if he'd stand quietly aside while she turned the most important thing in his life into a joke.

She'd had her say, Vance told himself as he headed for the door. Now he was going to have his.

"Shane, don't be stubborn." Donna followed her through the doorway from the museum into the shop.

"I'm not being stubborn, Donna, I really have a lot to

do." To prove her point, Shane leafed through a catalog to price and date her latest stock. "With the Christmas rush, I've really fallen behind on the paperwork. I've got invoices to file, and if I don't get the books caught up before the quarter, I'm going to be in a jam."

"Baloney," Donna said precisely, flipping the catalog closed.

"Donna, please."

"No, I don't please." She stuck her hands on her hips. "And it's two against one," she added, indicating Pat with a jerk of her head. "We're not having you spend Christmas Eve alone in this house, and that's all there is to it."

"Come on, Shane." Pat joined ranks with her sister-in-law. "You should see Donna and Dave chase after Benji when he heads for the tree. And as Donna's putting on a little weight," she added, grinning at the expectant mother, "she isn't as fast as she used to be."

Shane laughed, but shook her head. "I promise I'll come by tomorrow. I've got a very noisy present for Benji. You'll probably never speak to me again."

"Shane." Firmly, Donna took her by the shoulders. "Pat's told me how you've been moping around. And," she continued, ignoring the annoyed glance Shane shot over her shoulder at the informant, "anyone can take one look at you and see you're worn-out and miserable."

"I'm not worn-out," Shane corrected.

"Just miserable?"

"I didn't say—"

Donna gave her a quick affectionate shake. "Look, I don't know what happened between you and Vance—"

"Donna..."

"And I'm not asking," she added. "But you can't expect me to stand by while my best friend is unhappy. How much fun can I have, thinking about you here all alone?"

"Donna." Shane gave her a fierce hug then drew away. "I appreciate it, really I do, but I'm lousy company now."

"I know," Donna agreed mercilessly.

That made Shane laugh and hug her again. "Please, take Pat and go back to your family."

"So speaks the martyr."

"I'm not—" Shane began furiously, then broke off, seeing the gleam in Donna's eyes. "That won't work," she told her. "If you think you can make me mad so I'll come just to prove you wrong—"

"All right." Donna settled herself in a rocker. "Then I'll just sit here. Of course, poor Dave will spend Christmas Eve without me, and my little boy won't understand where his mother could be, but..." She sighed and folded her hands.

"Oh, Donna, really." Shane dragged her hand through her hair, caught between laughter and tears. "Talk about martyrs."

"I'm not complaining for myself," she said in a long-suffering tone. "Pat, run along and tell Dave I won't be home. Dry little Benji's tears for me."

Pat gave a snort of laughter, but Shane rolled her eyes. "I'll be sick in a minute," she promised. "Donna, go home!" she insisted. "I'm closing the shop."

"Good, go get your coat. I'll drive."

"Donna, I'm not..." She trailed off as the shop door opened. Seeing her friend pale, Donna turned her head to watch Vance walk in.

"Well, we have to run," she stated, springing quickly to her feet. "Come on, Pat, Dave's probably at his wit's end keeping Benji from pulling over the tree. Merry Christmas, Shane." She gave Shane a quick kiss before grabbing her coat.

"Donna, wait..."

"No, we just can't stay," she claimed, making the reversal without blinking an eye. "I've got a million things to do. Hi, Vance, nice to see you. Let's go, Pat." They were out the door before Shane could fit in another word.

Vance lifted a brow at the hasty exit but made no comment. Instead, he studied Shane as the silence grew long and thick. The anger that had driven him there melted. "Shane," he murmured.

"I—I'm closing."

"Fine." Vance turned and flicked the lock on the door. "Then we won't be disturbed."

"I'm busy, Vance. I have..." She searched desperately

for something important. "Things to do," she finished lamely. When he neither spoke nor moved, she sent him a look of entreaty. "Please go away."

Vance shook his head. "I tried that, Shane. I can't." He slipped off his coat and dropped it on the chair Donna had vacated. Shane stared at him, thrown off-balance by his appearance in a trimly tailored suit and silk tie. It brought it home to her again that she didn't know him. And, God help her, she loved him anyway. Turning, she began to fiddle with an arrangement of cut glass.

"I'm sorry, Vance, but I have a few things to finish up here before I leave. I'm supposed to go to Donna's tonight."

"She didn't seem to expect you," he commented as he walked to her. Gently, he laid his hands on her shoulders. "Shane—"

She stiffened immediately. "Don't!"

Very slowly, he took his hands from her, then dropped them to his sides. "All right, damn it, I won't touch you." The words came out savagely as he whirled away.

"Vance, I told you I'm busy."

"You said that you loved me."

Shane spun around, white with anger. "How can you throw that in my face?"

"Was it a lie?" he demanded.

She opened her mouth, but closed it again before any impetuous words could be spoken. Lifting her chin, she looked at him steadily. "I loved the man you pretended to be."

He winced, but he didn't back away. "Direct hit, Shane," he said quietly. "You surprise me."

"Why, because I'm not as stupid as you thought I was?"

Anger flashed into his eyes, then dulled. "Don't."

Shaken by the pain in the single word, she turned away. "I'm sorry, Vance. I don't want to say spiteful things. It would be better for both of us if you just went away."

"The hell it would, if you've been half as miserable as I've been. Have you been able to sleep, Shane? I haven't."

"Please," she whispered.

He took a deep breath as his hands clenched into fists. He'd come prepared to fight with her, to bully her, to plead with her. Now, it seemed he could do nothing but try to fumble through an explanation. "All right, I'll go, but only if you listen to me first."

"Vance," she said wearily, "what difference will it make?"

The finality of her tone had fear twisting in his stomach. With a strong effort, he kept his voice calm. "If that's true, it won't hurt you to listen."

"All right." Shane turned back to face him. "All right, I'll listen."

He was quiet for a moment, then began to pace as

though whatever ran through him wouldn't allow him to keep still. "I came here because I had to get away, maybe even hide. I'm not sure anymore. I was still very young when I took over the company. It wasn't what I wanted." He stopped for a moment to send her a direct look. "I'm a carpenter, Shane, that was the truth. I'm president of Riverton because I have to be. *Why* doesn't really matter at this point, but a title, a position, doesn't change who I am." When she said nothing, he began to pace again.

"I was married to a woman you'd recognize very quickly. She was beautiful, charming and pure plastic. She was totally self-consumed, emotionless, even vicious." Shane's brows drew together as she thought of Anne. "Unfortunately, I didn't recognize the last of those qualities until it was too late." He stopped because the next words were difficult. "I married the woman she pretended to be." Because his back was to her, Vance didn't see the sudden change in Shane's expression. Pain rushed into her eyes, but it wasn't for herself. It was all for him.

"For all intents and purposes, the marriage was over very soon after it had begun. I couldn't make a legal break at first because too many things were involved. So, we lived together in mutual distaste for several years. I involved myself in the company to the point of obsession, while she began to take lovers. I wanted her out of my life more than I wanted anything. Then, when she was dead, I had to live with the knowledge that I'd wished her dead countless times."

"Oh, Vance," Shane murmured.

"That was over two years ago," he continued. "I buried myself in work...and bitterness. I'd come to a point where I didn't even recognize myself anymore. That's why I bought the house and took a leave of absence. I needed to separate myself from what I'd become, try to find out if that was all there was to me." He dragged an agitated hand through his hair. "I brought the bitterness with me, so that when you popped up and started haunting my mind, I wanted nothing more than to be rid of you. I looked...I searched," he corrected, turning to her again, "for flaws in you. I was afraid to believe you could really be so...generous. The truth was, I didn't want you to be because I'd never be able to resist the woman you are." His eyes were suddenly very dark, and very direct on hers. "I didn't want you, Shane, and I wanted you so badly I ached. I loved you, I think, from the very first minute."

On a long breath, he moved away again to stare at the flickering lights of the tree. "I could have told you— should have—but at first I had a need for you to love me without knowing. Unforgivably selfish."

She remembered the secrets she had seen in his eyes. Remembered too, telling herself they were his until he shared them with her. Still, she felt the hurt of not being trusted. "Did you really think any of it would have mattered to me?"

Vance shook his head. "No."

"Then why did you hide it all from me?" Confused, she lifted her hands palms up.

"I never intended to. Circumstances—" He broke off, no longer sure he could make her understand. "The first night we were together, I was going to tell you, but I didn't want any past that night. I told myself it wasn't too much to ask, and that I'd explain things to you the next day. God, Shane, I swear to you I would have." He took a step toward her, then stopped himself. "You were so lost, so vulnerable after Anne had left, I couldn't. How could I have dumped all this on you when you already had that to deal with?"

She remained silent, but he knew she listened very carefully. He didn't know she was remembering very clearly the things he had said to her their first night together, the tension in him, the hints of things yet to be told. And she remembered too his compassion the next evening.

"You needed my support that night, not my problems," Vance went on. "From the very first, you gave everything to me. You brought me back, Shane, and I knew that I took much more than I gave. Until that night, you'd never asked me for anything."

She gave him a puzzled look. "I never gave you anything."

"Nothing?" he countered with a baffled shake of his head. "Trust, understanding. You made me laugh at myself again. Maybe you don't see just how important that is because you've never lost it. If I could give you nothing else, I thought that for a few days I could give you some peace of mind. I tried to tell you again when we argued about that damned dining-room set." Pausing, he sent her a narrowed look. "I bought it anyway."

"You—"

"There's not a thing you can do about it," he stated, cutting off her astonished exclamation. "It's done."

She met the angry challenge in his eyes. "I see."

"Do you?" He let out a quick, rough laugh. "Do you really? The only thing you see when you lift your chin up like that is your own pride." He watched her mouth open, then close again. "It's just as well," he murmured. "It would be difficult if you were perfect." He moved to her then but was careful not to touch her. "I never set out to deceive you, but I deceived you nonetheless. And now I have to ask you to forgive me, even if you can't accept who and what I am."

Shane lowered her eyes to her hands a moment. "It's not accepting so much as understanding," she said quietly. "I don't know anything about the president of Riverton. I knew the man who bought the old Farley place, you see." She lifted her eyes again. "He was rude, and nasty, with a streak of kindness he did his best to overcome. I loved him."

"God knows why," Vance replied, thinking over her description. "If that's who you want, I can promise I'm still rude and nasty."

With a small laugh, she turned away. "Vance, it's all hit me, you see. Maybe if I had time to get used to it, to think it through...I don't know. When I thought you were just..." She made an uncharacteristically helpless gesture with her hands. "It all seemed so easy."

"Did you only love me because you thought I was out of work?"

"No!" Frustrated, she tried to explain herself. "I haven't changed though," she added thoughtfully. "I'm still exactly what I seem. What would the president of Riverton do with me? I can't even drink martinis."

"Don't be absurd."

"It's not absurd," she corrected. "Be honest. I don't fit in. I'd never be elegant if I had years to practice."

"What the hell's wrong with you?" Suddenly angry, he spun her around. "*Elegant!* In the name of God, Shane, what kind of nonsense is that? I had my share of elegance the way you mean. I'll be damned if you're going to put me off because you've got some twisted view of the life I lead. If you can't accept it, fine. I'll resign."

"W-what?"

"I said I'll resign."

She studied him with wide, astonished eyes. "You mean it," she said wonderingly. "You really do."

He gave her an impatient shake. "Yes, I mean it. Can you really believe the company means more to me than you do? God, you're an idiot!" Furious, he gave her an unloverlike shove and strode away. "You don't yell at me for anything I've done. You don't demand to hear all the filthy details of my first marriage. You don't make me crawl as I was damn well ready to do. You start spouting nonsense about martinis and elegance." After swearing rudely, he stared out the window.

Shane swallowed a sudden urge to laugh. "Vance, I—"

"Shut up," he ordered. "You drive me crazy." With a quick jerk, he pulled his coat from the chair. Shane opened her mouth, afraid he was about to storm out, but he only pulled an envelope out of the pocket before he flung the coat down again. "Here." He stuck it out to her.

"Vance," she tried again, but he took her hand and slapped the envelope into her palm.

"Open it."

Deciding a temporary retreat was advisable, Shane obeyed. She stared in silent astonishment at two round-trip tickets to Fiji.

"Someone told me it was a good place for a honeymoon," Vance stated with a bit more control. "I thought she might still think so."

Shane looked up at him with her heart in her eyes. Vance needed nothing more to pull her into his arms, crushing the envelope and its contents between them as he found her mouth.

Shane's answer was wild and unrestricted. She clung to him even as she demanded, yielded even as she aroused. She couldn't get enough of him, so that the desperate kisses incited only more urgent needs. "Oh, I've missed you," she murmured. "Make love to me, Vance. Come upstairs and make love to me."

He buried his face against her neck. "Uh-uh. You haven't said you're taking me to Fiji yet." But his hands were already searching under her sweater. As his fingers skimmed over her warm, soft skin, he groaned, pulling her to the floor.

"Oh, Vance, your suit!" Laughing breathlessly, Shane struggled against him. "Wait until we go upstairs."

"Shut up," he suggested, then assured himself of her obedience by crushing his mouth on hers. It only took a moment to realize her trembling came from laughter, not from passion. Lifting his head, Vance studied her amused eyes. "Damn you, Shane," he said in exasperation. "I'm trying to make love to you."

"Well, then at least take off that tie," she suggested, then buried her face against his shoulder and laughed helplessly. "I'm sorry, Vance, but it just seems so funny. I mean, there you are asking if I'll take you to Fiji before I've even gotten around to asking you to marry me, and—"

"*You* asking *me?*" he demanded, eyeing her closely.

"Yes," she continued blithely. "I've been meaning to, though I thought I'd have to overcome some silly ego thing. You know, I thought you were out of work."

"Ego thing," he repeated.

"Yes, and of course, now that I know you're such an important person… Oh, this tie is *silk!*" she exclaimed after she had begun to struggle with the knot.

"Yes." He allowed her to finger it curiously. "And now that you know I'm such an important person?" he prompted.

"I'd better snap you up quick."

"Snap me up?" He bit her ear painfully.

Shane only giggled and linked her arms around his neck. "And even if I refuse to drink martinis or be elegant, I'll make an extremely good wife for a…" She paused a moment, lifting a brow. "What are you?"

"Insane."

"A corporate president," Shane decided with a nod. "No, I don't suppose you could do any better. You're making a pretty good deal now that I think about it." She gave him a noisy kiss. "When do we leave for Fiji?"

"Day after tomorrow," he informed her before he rose and dumped her over his shoulder.

"Vance, what are you doing?"

"I'm taking you upstairs to make love with you."

"Vance," she began with a half laugh. "I told you before I won't be carted around this way. This is no way for the fiancée of the president of Riverton to be treated."

"You haven't seen anything yet," he promised her.

Exasperated, Shane gave him a hearty thump on the back. "Vance, I mean it, put me down!"

"Am I fired?"

He heard the telltale choke of laughter. "Yes!"

"Good." He tucked his arm firmly around her knees and carried her up the stairs.

* * * * *

Song of the West

Chapter 1

The land in southeast Wyoming is a magnificent paradox. Spreading plains and rolling hills coexist with rocky mountains and thick velvet pines. From the kitchen window, the view was astounding, and Samantha Evans halted in her duties for a moment to drink it in.

The Rockies dominated the vast curtain of sky, their peaks laced with snow, though it was late March.

Samantha wondered if she would still be in Wyoming the following winter. She dreamed of long walks with the air biting and sharp on her cheeks, or wild rides on a spirited mount with hooves kicking up a flurry of white. But none of that could happen until her sister was well enough to be left alone.

A frown creased her smooth brow. Sabrina was her

reason for being in Wyoming, with its majestic mountains and quiet plains, rather than in the more familiar surroundings of Philadelphia's tall buildings and traffic-choked streets.

The two sisters had always been close, with that special, magical intimacy that twins share. They were not identical. Though they were the same in height and build, Samantha's eyes were a dark cornflower blue, widely set, with thick, spiky lashes, while Sabrina's eyes were a light gray. Both faces were oval set with small, straight noses and well-shaped mouths, but while Samantha's rich brown hair, with its highlights of gold, was shoulder length with a fringe of bangs, Sabrina's ash blond was short, framing her face with delicate curls. The bond between them was strong and enduring. Even when Sabrina had married Dan Lomax and moved so many miles away to settle on his ranch in the Laramie Basin, their devotion had remained constant and unwavering.

They kept in touch by phone and letter, which helped to mitigate Samantha's aching loneliness. And she was happy in her sister's delight in the coming baby. The two women had laughed and planned together over the phone. But that was before Dan's call. Samantha had been aroused from a deep predawn sleep by the shrill ringing of the phone. She reached groggily for it, but was instantly alerted by the anxious tone of her brother-in-law's voice. "Sam," he said without any preamble,

"Bree's been very ill. We did manage to save the baby, but she has to be very careful for a while now. She will have to stay in bed and have constant round-the-clock care. We are trying to find someone to—"

Samantha had only one thought—her sister, the person she loved best in the world. "Don't worry, Dan, I will come immediately."

She was on the plane to Wyoming less than twenty-four hours later....

The whistle of the kettle brought Samantha back to the present. She began to brew the herbal tea, placing delicate floral cups on a silver tray.

"Teatime," she called as she entered the living room. Sabrina was propped up with pillows and comforters on the long wood-edged sofa. Though her smile was warm, her cheeks still retained a delicate pallor.

"Just like the movies," Sabrina commented as her sister set a tray on the pine table. "But the role of Camille is getting to be a bore."

"I imagine so." Samantha poured the fragrant tea into cups. "But you may as well get used to it, Bree, you've got the part for a month's run." She transferred a large gray-striped cat from Sabrina's lap to her own, offered Sabrina a steaming cup and sat on the rug. "Has Shylock been keeping you company?"

"He's a terrible snob." With a wry smile, Sabrina sipped at her tea. "He did graciously allow me to scratch his ears. I have to admit, I'm glad you brought him with you, he's my biggest entertainment." She sighed and lay back against the pillows, regarding her sister seriously. "I'm ashamed to be lying here feeling sorry for myself. I'm lucky." She rested her hand on her stomach in a protective gesture. "I shall have my baby, and I sit here moaning about your waiting on me."

"You're entitled to moan a bit, Bree," said Samantha, immediately sympathetic. "You're used to being active and busy."

"I've no right to complain. You gave up your job and left home to come out here and take care of me." Another deep sigh escaped, and her gray eyes were dangerously moist. "If Dan had told me what you were planning to do, I would never have allowed it."

"You couldn't have stopped me." Samantha attempted to lighten the mood. "That's what older sisters are for."

"You never forget those seven minutes, do you?" Sabrina's eyes cleared, and a reluctant smile curved her generous mouth.

"Nope, it gives me seniority."

"But your job, Sam."

"Don't worry." Samantha made another dismissive gesture. "I'll get another job in the fall. There's more than one high school in the country, and they all have gym teachers. Besides, I needed a vacation."

"Vacation!" Sabrina exclaimed. "Cleaning, cooking, caring for an invalid. You call that a vacation?"

"My dear Sabrina, have you ever tried to teach an overweight, totally uncoordinated teenager the intricacies of the parallel bars? Well, the stories I could tell you about vacations."

"Sam, what a pair we are. You with your teenagers and me with my preadolescent Mozarts. Lord knows how many times I cleaned peanut butter off the keys of that old Wurlitzer before Dan came along and took me away from scales and infant prodigies. Do you think Mom expected us to come to this when she dragged us to all those lessons?"

"Ah, but we're well-rounded." Samantha's grin was faintly wicked. "Aren't you grateful? She always told us we'd be grateful one day for the ballet and the piano lessons."

"The voice lessons and the riding lessons," Sabrina continued, ticking them off on her fingers.

"Gymnastics and swimming lessons," Sabrina concluded with a giggle.

"Poor Mom." Samantha shifted Shylock to a more comfortable position. "I think she expected one of us to marry the president, and she wanted us to be prepared."

"We shouldn't make fun." Sabrina wiped her eyes with a tissue. "The lessons did give us our living."

"True. And I can still whip up a mean spinach soufflé."

"Ugh." Sabrina grimaced, and Samantha lifted her brows.

"Exactly."

"You have your medals," Sabrina reminded her. Her smile warmed with pride and a trace of awe.

"Yes, I have the medals and the memories. Sometimes, it feels like yesterday instead of nearly ten years ago."

Sabrina smiled. "I can still remember my terrified excitement when you first swung onto the uneven bars. Even though I'd watched the routine countless times, I couldn't quite believe it was you. When they put that first Olympic medal around your neck, it was one of the happiest moments of my life."

"I remember thinking just before that competition, after I'd botched the balance beam so badly, that I couldn't do it. My legs felt like petroleum jelly, and I was mortally afraid I was going to be sick and disgrace myself. Then I saw Mom in the stands, and it ran through my mind how much she'd sacrificed. Not the money. The bending of those rather strange values of hers to allow me those years of training and those few heady moments of competition. I had to prove it was justified, I had to pay her back with something, even though I knew she'd never be able to say she was proud of me."

"You proved it was justified." Sabrina gave her twin a soft smile. "Even if you hadn't won on the bars and the floor exercises, you'd proved it by just being there. And she was proud of you, even if she didn't say it."

"You've always understood. So get over the idea I'm doing you a favor coming here. I want to be here. I *belong* here."

"Sam." Sabrina held out a hand. "I don't know what I'd do without you. I don't know what I *ever* would have done without you."

"You'd manage," Samantha returned, giving the frail hand a squeeze. "You have Dan."

"Yeah, I do." The smile became soft. "This is the time of day that I miss him most. He should be home soon." Her gaze wandered to the glass-domed anniversary clock on the mantel above the fire.

"He said something about checking fences today. I can't quite get away from the image of him chasing rustlers or fighting off renegade Indians."

With a light laugh, Sabrina settled back among the cushions. "City slicker. You know, Sam, sometimes I can't even remember what Philadelphia looks like. Jake Tanner was riding along with Dan today to make sure the boundary fences were in good repair."

"Jake Tanner?" Samantha's question was idle.

"Oh, that's right, you haven't met him yet. The northwest corner of the ranch borders his. Of course, the Lazy L would fit into one corner of his ranch. He owns half the county."

"Ah, a land baron," Samantha concluded.

"A very apt description," Sabrina agreed. "The Double T, his ranch, is the most impressive I've seen. He runs it like clockwork, super efficient. Dan says he's not only an incredible rancher, but a very crafty businessman."

"Sounds like a bore," Samantha commented, wrinkling her nose. "Steel-gray hair around a leathered face, a handlebar mustache drooping over his mouth and a generous belly hanging over his belt..."

Sabrina's laughter rang out, high and sweet.

"You're about as far off the mark as you can get. Jake Tanner is anything but a bore, and speaking from the safety of marital bliss, he's a fascinating man to look at. And, being rich, successful and unattached, all the females under forty buzz around him like bees around honey."

"Sounds like a good catch," Samantha said dryly. "Mom would love him."

"Absolutely," Sabrina agreed. "But Jake has eluded capture so far. Though from what Dan says, he does enjoy the chase."

"Now he sounds like a conceited bore." Samantha tickled Shylock's smooth belly.

"You can hardly blame him for taking what's offered." Sabrina defended the absent Jake Tanner with a vague movement of her shoulders. "I imagine he'll settle down soon. Lesley Marshall—her father's ranch borders the other side of the Double T—has her sights set on him. She's a very determined woman, as well as being more than a little spoiled, and dreadfully rich."

"Sounds like a perfect match."

"Mmm, maybe," Sabrina murmured. Her face creased in a small frown. "Lesley's nice enough when it suits her, and it's about time Jake had a wife and family. I'm fond of Jake. I'd like to see him set up with someone with more warmth."

"Listen to the old married woman." Samantha addressed a dozing and unconcerned Shylock. "A year of nuptial bliss, and she can't stand to see anyone unattached."

"True. I'm going to start on you next."

"Thanks for the warning."

"Wyoming's full of good-looking cowboys and handsome ranchers." Sabrina continued to smile as her sister grimaced. "You could find a worse place to settle down."

"I have no objection to settling here, Bree. I've become quite attached to the wide open spaces. But—" she paused significantly "—cowboys and ranchers are not among my immediate plans for the future." She rose from the floor in a fluid motion. "I've got to check on that roast. Here." She handed her sister the novel that rested on the table. "Read your love stories, you incurable romantic."

"You won't be so cynical when you fall in love," Sabrina predicted with the wisdom of experience.

"Sure." Samantha's grin was indulgent.

"There'll be bells ringing and fireworks shooting and trumpets blaring." She patted her sister's hand and strolled from the room, calling over her shoulder. "Angels singing, flames leaping..."

"Just you wait," Sabrina shouted after her.

Samantha busied herself preparing vegetables for the evening meal, clucking her tongue at her sister's nonsense. *Love,* she sniffed derisively. Her only experience with that complex emotion had been fending off unwanted attentions from eager males. Not once had any man lit an answering spark in her. But whatever this love was, it worked for Bree. The younger twin had always been more delicate, softer and more dependent. And though Sabrina was trying to be brave and strong, her sister knew the fear of miscarriage still lurked in the back of her mind. She needed Dan's support and love, and right now, she needed to feel his arms around her.

Like the answer to a prayer, Samantha spotted two figures on horseback approaching from the lower pasture. Grabbing her heavy jacket from the hook by the back door, she scurried out of the kitchen and into the cold March air.

As Dan and his companion drew closer, Samantha

greeted him with a smile and a wave. She had noticed, even at a distance, Dan's expression of concern. But a smile relaxed his features when he spotted Samantha.

"Sabrina's all right?" he asked as he reined in next to her.

"She's fine," Samantha assured him. "Just a trifle rest-less, and tremendously lonely for her husband."

"Did she eat better today?"

Samantha's smile warmed, lighting her face with a quick flash of astonishing beauty.

"Her appetite was much better. She's trying very hard." Samantha lifted a hand to stroke the smooth flank of the gelding he rode. "What she needs now is you."

"I'll be in as soon as I stable my horse."

"Oh, Dan, for heaven's sake. Let your hand do it, or I'll do it myself. Bree needs you."

"But…"

"'S all right, boss," the other horseman interrupted, and Samantha spared him a brief glance. "I'll tend to your horse. You go on and see the missus."

Dan flashed his companion a wide grin and dis-mounted. "Thanks," he said simply as he handed over the reins and turned to Samantha. "Coming in?"

"No." She shook her head and hunched her shoulders in the confines of her jacket. "You two could use some time alone, and I'd like some air."

"Thanks, Sam." He pinched her cheek with brotherly affection and moved off toward the house.

Waiting until the door closed behind him, Samantha walked over and dropped wearily onto the stump used for splitting wood. Resting her back against the fence, she breathed deeply, devouring the brisk, cold air. The strain of caring for her sister in addition to running the house and cooking the meals, including, over his objection, Dan's predawn breakfast, had taken its toll.

"A few more days," she whispered as she closed her eyes. "A few more days and I'll have adjusted to the routine and feel more like myself." The heavy corded jacket insulated her from the bite of the cold, and she tilted back her head, allowing the air to play on her cheeks as her mind drifted on the edge of exhaustion.

"Funny place to take a nap."

Samantha sat up with a jerk, confused and disoriented by sleep. Her eyes traveled up to the speaker's face. It was a lean face, skin bronzed by the sun and stretched tightly over cheekbones, all lines and shadows, hollows and angles. The eyes were arresting, deep-set and heavily lashed. But it was their color, a deep, pure jade that caught and held her attention. His dusky gold hair curled from under a well-battered Stetson.

"Evening, ma'am." Though he touched the brim of

his hat with due respect, his extraordinary eyes were faintly mocking.

"Good evening," she returned, struggling for dignity.

"Person could catch a bad chill sitting out too long after the sun's low. Wind's picking up, too." His speech was slow and thickly drawled. His weight was distributed evenly on both legs, hands deep in pockets. "Oughtn't to be out without a hat." His comment was accompanied by a fractional movement of his head toward her unadorned one. "Hat helps keep the heat in."

"I'm not cold." She feared for a moment her teeth would chatter and betray her. "I was...I was just getting some air."

"Yes, ma'am." He nodded in agreement, glancing behind her at the last, dying brilliance of sun as it slipped behind circling peaks. "Fine evening for setting out and watching the sunset."

Her eyes flashed at the teasing. She was embarrassed to have been caught sleeping. He smiled a slow, careless smile that crept unhurried across his face. The movement of his lips caused the hollows to deepen, the shadows to shift. Unable to resist, Samantha's lips curved in response.

"All right, I confess. You caught me napping. I don't suppose you'd believe I was just resting my eyes."

"No, ma'am." His answer was grave, with just a hint of apology.

"Well." She rose from her seat and was dismayed at how far she still had to look up to meet his eyes. "If you keep quiet about it, I'll see to it that you get a piece of the apple pie I baked for dinner."

"That's a mighty tempting offer." He considered it with a long-fingered hand reaching up to stroke his chin. "I'm partial to apple pie. Only one or two things I'm more partial to." His eyes roamed over her in a thorough and intense study that caused her heart to pound with unaccustomed speed.

There was something different about this man, she thought swiftly, something unique, a vitality at odds with lazy words and careless smiles. He pushed his hat back farther on his head, revealing more disorderly curls. "You've got yourself a deal." He held out his hand to confirm the agreement, and she placed her small hand in his.

"Thanks." The single word was breathless, as she found her speech hampered by the currents running up her arm. Abruptly, she pulled her hand away, wondering what it was about him that disturbed her equilibrium. "I'm sorry if I was short before, about Dan's horse." She spoke now in a rush, to conceal a reaction she could not understand.

"No need to apologize," he assured her, and the new soft texture in his tone both warmed and unnerved her. "We're all fond of Mrs. Lomax."

"Yes, well, I…" she stammered, suddenly needing to put a safe distance between herself and this slow-talking man. "I'd better go inside. Dan must be hungry." She looked past him and spotted his horse, still saddled, waiting patiently. "You didn't stable your horse. Aren't you finished for the day?" Hearing the concern in her own voice, she marveled at it. Really, she thought, annoyed, why should I care?

"Oh, yes, ma'am, I'm finished." There was laughter in his voice now, but Samantha failed to notice. She began to study the mount with care.

It was a magnificent animal, dark, gleaming chestnut, at least sixteen hands, she estimated, classic lines, fully flowing mane and proud, dished face. Arabian. Samantha knew horses and she recognized a full-blooded Arabian stallion when she saw one. What in the world…? "That's an Arabian." Her words interrupted her thoughts.

"Yes, ma'am," he agreed easily, entirely too easily. Her eyes narrowed with suspicion as she turned to him.

"No ranch hand is going to be riding around on a horse that's worth six months' pay." She stared at him and he returned the steady survey with a bland, poker face. "Who are you?"

"Jake Tanner, ma'am." The slow grin appeared again, widening, deepening, then settling as he lifted the brim of his hat at the introduction. "Pleased to meet you."

The land baron with the women at his feet, Samantha's brain flashed. Anger darkened her eyes.

"Why didn't you say so?"

"Just did," he pointed out.

"Oh." She tossed back her thick fall of hair. "You know very well what I mean. I thought you were one of Dan's men."

"Yes, ma'am." He nodded.

"Stop *ma'aming* me," she commanded. "What a mean trick! All you had to do was open your mouth and say who you were. I would have stabled Dan's horse myself."

"I didn't mind." His expression became annoyingly agreeable. "It wasn't any trouble, and you had a nice rest."

"Well, Mr. Tanner, you had a fine laugh at my expense. I hope you enjoyed it," she said coldly.

"Yes, ma'am." The grin widened without seeming to move at all. "I did."

"I told you to stop…" She halted, biting her lip with frustration. "Oh, forget it." Tossing her head, she took a few steps toward the house, then turned back crossly. "I notice your accent has modified quite a bit, Mr. Tanner."

He did not reply, but continued to stand negligently, his hands in his pockets, his face darkened by the late-afternoon shadows. Samantha spun back around and stomped toward the house.

"Hey," he called out, and she turned toward him before she could halt the reflex. "Do I still get that pie?"

She answered his question with a glare. His laughter, deep and rich, followed her into the house.

Chapter 2

The sound of the slamming door reverberated through the ranch house as Samantha struggled out of her jacket and marched into the living room. At the sight of her sister's face Sabrina slipped down into the pillows, picked up the novel lying on her lap and buried her nose in its pages. Dan, however, did not recognize the storm warning in his sister-in-law's blue eyes and flushed cheeks. He greeted her with a friendly, ingenuous smile.

"Where's Jake?" His gaze slid past her. "Don't tell me he went home without a cup of coffee?"

"He can go straight to the devil without his coffee."

"I expect he wanted to get home before dark," Dan concluded. His nod was sober, but his eyes were brilliant with merriment.

"Don't play innocent with me, Dan Lomax." Samantha advanced on him. "That was a rotten trick, letting me think he was one of your hands, and…" A giggle escaped from behind the paperback. "I'm glad you think it's amusing that your sister's been made a fool of."

"Oh, Sam, I'm sorry." Warily, Sabrina lowered the book. "It's just hard to believe anyone could mistake Jake Tanner for a ranch hand." She burst out laughing, and Samantha was torn between the pleasure of seeing her sister laugh and irritation at being the brunt of the joke.

"Well, really, what makes him so special?" she demanded. "He dresses like every other cowboy I've seen around here, and that hat of his has certainly seen better days." But, she remembered, there *had* been something special about him that she had not quite been able to define. She firmly dismissed this disquieting thought. "The nerve of him." She rounded on Don again. "Calling you boss, and ma'aming me in that exaggerated drawl."

"Reckon he was just being polite," Dan suggested. His smile was amiable and pure. Samantha sent him the look that terrified her students.

"Men." Raising her eyes, she searched the ceiling in hopes of finding the answer there. "You're all alike, and you all stick together." She bent and scooped up the sleeping Shylock and marched into the kitchen.

Time at the ranch passed quickly. Though her days were full and busy, Samantha fretted for some of the physical outlet that had so long been part of her life. At times, the confinement of the house was suffocating. Years of training and discipline had left her with an inherent need for activity.

Unconsciously, she separated her life into three categories: the pre-Olympic years, the Olympic years and the post-Olympic years.

The pre-Olympic years were a blur of lessons, piano teachers, dance instructors, her mother's gentle but inescapable admonishments to "be a lady." Then, the first time she had gripped the lower bar of the unevens, the new chapter had begun.

By the time she was twelve years old, she had remarkable promise. The gymnastics instructor had informed her mother, who was more distressed than pleased at the praise. Though her mother had objected to more intense training, Samantha had ultimately prevailed.

The hours of training became months, county meets became state meets, and national competitions became international competitions. When Samantha was picked for the Olympic team, it was just another step down a road she was determined to follow. Weariness and aching muscles were accepted without hesitation.

Then it was over, and at fifteen she had found it necessary to alter what had become a way of life. College had to be considered, and earning a living. The years passed into the post-Olympic period, and she remem-

bered her days of athletic competitions as a dream. Now
her life was shifting again, though she was unsure as to
the direction. The mountains and plains were calling to
her, inviting her to explore, but she buried her desires,
remaining indoors to see to her sister's needs. Dan is a
busy man, she thought as she prepared lunch, and Bree
needs someone within calling distance during this critical period. When she's better, there will be plenty of
time to see the country.

She arched her back and rubbed a small spot of tension at the base of her neck. The kitchen door opened and
Dan burst in, accompanied by Jake Tanner. Samantha
met the amused green eyes levelly, though once more
she felt treacherously at a disadvantage.

Her hair had been carelessly scooped on the top of her
head that morning, and now, with their usual abandon-
ment, stray locks were beginning to escape confinement.
She was dressed in a black ribbed sweater that had seen
too many washings and ancient jeans, splattered, faded,
patched and too tight. She resisted the urge to raise her
hand to her tumbling hair, forced a smile and turned to
her brother-in-law.

"Hello, Dan. What are you doing home this time of
day?" Purposefully, she ignored the tall figure beside
him.

"Wasn't too far out," Dan explained. Slipping off his
jacket and hat, he tossed both over the hooks provided.

"Jake was giving me a hand, so I figured it was only neighborly to bring him back for lunch."

"Hope I'm not imposing, ma'am." The slow smile spread, once more rearranging the angles of his face.

"No imposition, Mr. Tanner. But you'll have to settle for potluck."

"My favorite dish—" he paused, giving her a cheeky wink "—next to apple pie."

Samantha sent him a withering glance and turned away to warm the previous evening's stew.

"I'll just go tell Sabrina I'm home," Dan announced to the room in general, and strode away. Samantha did her best to ignore Jake's disturbing presence. She stirred the stew busily.

"Smells good." Jake moved over to the stove and lounged against it. Samantha went to the cupboard to get the bowls.

When she turned back to place them on the round kitchen table, she noticed that he had shed his outdoor clothing. The slim-fitting jeans, snug and low on narrow hips, accentuated his leanness. His flannel shirt fitted over his broad shoulders and hard chest before tapering down to a narrow waist. The athlete in her immediately responded to the firm, well-proportioned body; there was not an ounce of spare flesh on him.

"Don't talk much, do you?" The drawl was there again, the exaggerated twang of the previous evening.

Samantha turned her head, prepared to freeze him with her eyes.

His face was barely inches from hers as he slouched by the stove. For a moment, her mind ceased to function.

"I really have nothing to say to you, Mr. Tanner." She struggled to keep her voice cold and detached, but she could feel the blood rush to her face.

"Well, now, we'll have to see if we can change that." He spoke with easy confidence as he straightened to his full height. "We're not much on formalities around here. Just make it Jake." Though his words were spoken with his usual lazy delivery, there was an undertone of command. Samantha's chin rose in defense.

"Maybe I prefer to keep things formal between us, Mr. Tanner."

His lips were curved in his careless smile, but in his eyes she now recognized that special something that separated him from an ordinary ranch hand. *Power.* She wondered how she had missed it at their first meeting.

"I don't think there's much chance of that." He paused and tugged at a loose lock of his hair before adding with irritating emphasis, "Ma'am. Nope, I don't think there's much chance of that at all."

Samantha was saved from coming up with a suitable rebuttal by Dan's reappearance. She began to spoon the stew into ceramic bowls, noting to her dismay that her hands were not altogether steady. This man was infuriating her with his arrogantly lazy confidence. I have never met a more irritating male, she thought. He thinks he can switch on that rugged cowboy charm and women will drop in droves at his feet. Well, maybe some do, but not this one.

"Okay, Sam?" Dan's voice shattered the electric silence.

"What? I'm sorry, I wasn't listening."

"You'll keep Jake company over lunch, won't you? I'll have mine in the living room with Sabrina."

She swore silently. "Of course," she answered with an impersonal smile.

Within a short time, Samantha found herself sitting across from the man she wanted most to avoid.

"You've a fine hand with dumplings, Sam." Her brows rose involuntarily at his easy use of her nickname, but she kept her voice even.

"Thank you, Mr. Tanner. It's just one of my many talents."

"I'm sure it is," he agreed with an inclination of his head.

"You haven't changed much from the girl in the picture in Sabrina's parlor." Samantha was astonished.

"You'd have been about fifteen," he continued. "A bit skinnier than you are now, but your hair was the same, not quite willing to stay bundled on top of your head."

Samantha's blank expression had turned to a frown at the word skinnier. She remembered the photo clearly.

"You'd just finished winning your second medal." She had indeed been fifteen. The picture had been snapped at the moment she had completed her floor routine. It had captured the look of stunned triumph, for she had known in that instant that a medal was hers.

"Sabrina's just about as proud of you as you are worried about her." Samantha said nothing, only staring into the lean, handsome features. His brows rose ever so slightly, a movement that would have gone unnoticed had she not been so intent on his face. For a moment, she forgot the thread of the conversation, caught up suddenly in a series of small, irrelevant details: the curling gold which spilled over his brow, the tiny white scar on his jawline, the thickness of his long lashes. Confused, she dropped her eyes to her bowl and struggled to bring her thoughts to order.

"I'd forgotten Bree had that picture," she said. "It was a long time ago."

"So now you teach. You don't look like any gym teacher I ever knew."

"Oh, really?"

"No, ma'am." He shook his head slowly and considered her through another mouthful of stew. "Don't look strong enough or old enough."

"I assure you, Jake, I'm both strong enough and old enough for my profession."

"What made you become a gym teacher?" His sudden question caught her off balance, and she stared at him.

"Well, I…" Her shoulders moved restlessly. "Our mother was a fanatic on lessons when Bree and I were growing up." She smiled in spite of herself. "We took lessons in everything, Mom's theory on being well-rounded. Anyway, Bree found her talent in music and I developed a knack for the physical. For a while, I focused on gymnastics, then, when the time came to work, it seemed natural. Bree taught little people to play the classics, and I teach bigger people to tumble."

"Do you like your work? Are you happy with it?"

"As a matter of fact, I do," she retorted. "I like the activity, I like being involved in a physical type of work. It can be frustrating at times, of course. Some of the girls I teach would rather be flirting with their boyfriends than learning gymnastics, I suspect."

"And you yourself are more interested in calisthenics than men?" The question was delivered with a broad masculine smile.

"That's hardly relevant," she snapped, annoyed that she had lowered her guard.

"You don't think so?"

Samantha scraped back her chair and moved to the stove. "Coffee?"

"Yes, ma'am, black." It was unnecessary to turn around; she felt the slow grin crease his face as clearly as if she had witnessed it with her eyes. She set the cup down on the table with a bang. Before she could spin back to pour her own, her hand was captured in a firm grip. There was nothing soft about the hand. It was hard and masculine.

Completely outmatched in the short battle that ensued, Samantha discovered that under the lean, lanky exterior lay an amazing strength. Deciding that it was undignified to grapple in her sister's kitchen, she allowed her hand to rest quietly in his, meeting his laughing eyes with a resentful glare. Her heart began to pound uncomfortably against her ribs.

"What do you want?" Her voice came out in a husky whisper. His eyes left hers to travel slowly down to the generous curve of her mouth, lingering until she could taste the heat on her lips, as real as a kiss. Taking his time, he moved his gaze back to her eyes.

"You're jumpy." His observation was laconic, as if none of the heat had touched him, though she herself was beginning to suffocate. "Powerful strong for such a little bit of a thing."

"I'm not little," she retorted. "You're just so big." She began to tug at her hand again, feeling a near desperate urgency to shake off the contact that was infusing her with an unexplained weakness around the knees.

"Your eyes are fabulous when you're angry, Sam." His tone was conversational. "Temper agrees with you. You grow beautiful with it." He laughed and pulled her closer.

"You're insufferable," she said, still struggling to escape his grasp.

"For telling you you're beautiful? I was just stating the obvious. I'm sure it's been mentioned to you once or twice before."

"You men are all the same." She ceased her struggles long enough to aim a lethal glare. "Always grabbing and groping."

"I don't grope, Samantha." His drawl was feathersoft. For an instant, the cocky cowboy vanished, and she glimpsed the man, shrewd and ruthless, beneath. Here was a man who not only expected to have his own way, but would. "And the next time I grab you, it won't only be to hold your hand." Releasing her, he leaned back in his chair. "You have been warned."

Later, as Sabrina napped and the house grew still around her, Samantha found herself staring blankly at the pages of a novel. Scowling, she tossed it aside and rose from the sofa to pace to the window. What an infuriating man. Obviously, he considers himself irresistible. She began to wander the room, attempting to block out the effect his blatant virility had had on her.

It was too bad, she decided on her fourth circle, that

all those good looks, all that strength and appeal, had to belong to such a rude, arrogant man.

Deciding that a brisk walk was just what she needed to get Jake Tanner out of her mind, she stopped her pacing and grabbed a warm jacket. Moments later she was out the door, gazing around her in delight at the beauty of the starlit Wyoming night. Her breath puffed out in thin white mists as she moved. The air, tinged with frost, carried the aroma of pine, and she drank it in greedily, enjoying the mixed scent of hay and horses and aged wood. She could hear the lonely sound of a coyote calling to the full silver moon. And suddenly she realized that she had fallen in love with Wyoming. The spell of the mountains and plains was on her, and she was inexplicably glad she had come.

"Goodness, you were out a long time," her sister commented as Samantha plopped down in a wing-backed chair in front of the fire a few minutes later. "You must be frozen."

"No." Samantha stretched out her legs and sighed. "I love it out there. It's fantastic! I never realized how big the sky was before, and I don't think I'll ever get used to the space, the openness."

She turned her attention to the powerfully built man sitting next to her sister on the sofa. "I wonder if you appreciate it, Dan, living here all of your life. Even your

letters, Bree, didn't do justice to that world out there."
Running her fingers through her hair, she made a small
sound of pleasure. "To someone used to traffic-choked
streets and huge buildings, all this…" Her hands moved
in an inadequate gesture.

"You haven't had much of a chance to see anything
since you've been here," Dan observed. "You've been
with us a month and you haven't gone a quarter mile
away from the house. And that's been mostly to fetch
the mail in the mornings."

"I'll have plenty of time to explore later. I'll be around
through the summer."

"Just the same, we're not having you tied to the house
while you're here, Sam," Dan announced, and sat back
against the cushions. "Even the most devoted sister is
entitled to a day off."

"Don't be silly. You make it sound as though I were
slaving from dawn to dusk. Half the time I'm not doing
anything."

"We know how hard you're working, Sam," Sabrina
said quietly, glancing up at Dan before returning her
gaze to her twin. "And I know the lack of activity is
harder on you than the work. I also know how you dis-
rupted your life to come out here and take care of me."

"Oh, Bree, for heaven's sake," Samantha began, shifting uncomfortably. "I never would have found out how
much I love Wyoming if I hadn't come."

"Don't try to shrug if off, Sam." Dan grinned at the embarrassed motion of her shoulders. "We're grateful, and you'll just have to get used to us telling you so. But tomorrow, we're going to show we're grateful instead of just talking about it. We're kicking you out for the day."

"Huh?" Blankly, Sam blinked at the bland smile before shifting her gaze to Sabrina's serene one.

"That's right." His grin widened as she drew her brows together. "Tomorrow's Sunday, and I'm staying home with my wife. And you..." He pointed a warning finger at his sister-in-law. "You're going to have your pick of the horses and take off."

Samantha sprung up from her slouched position. "Do you mean it?" Her face was glowing with pleasure, and Dan's smile warmed with affection.

"Yes, little sister, I mean it. It should be more."

"The dapple-gray gelding," she began in a rush, ignoring the last part of his comment. "Can I take him?"

"Already inspected the stock, and it appears you know your horses." Dan chuckled and shook his head. "Spook's a good mount. A little frisky, but from what Sabrina's told me, you can handle him."

"Oh, I can, and I promise I'll be careful with him." She sprang from her chair and crossed the room, flinging her arms around his neck. "Thanks, Dan. You are absolutely my favorite brother-in-law, bar none."

"I think she likes the idea, Sabrina," Dan commented

as he met his wife's eyes over Samantha's head. "In fact, I'd say she's downright pleased about it."

"And I thought I hid my emotions so effectively." She gave his cheek a loud, smacking kiss.

"You be ready to start out about nine." He patted Samantha's slim shoulder. "Jake'll be around, then."

"Jake?" Samantha repeated. Her smile froze.

"Yeah, he'll be riding out with you. Actually," Dan continued, "he suggested the idea this afternoon. He thought it would do you good to get out of the house for a while." He sighed and scratched his dark head, managing to appear sheepish, for all his size. "I'm ashamed I didn't think of it first. I guess I've been a bit preoccupied and didn't notice you were looking a littled tired and hemmed in."

"I'm not tired," she denied automatically.

"Hemmed in?" Sabrina offered with a knowing smile.

"A little, maybe, but I'm hardly in the last stages of cabin fever. I'm sure it's very kind of Mr. Tanner to be so concerned about my welfare." She managed to say his name in a normal voice. "But there's certainly no need for him to go with me. I know he has hundreds of more important things to do with his Sunday."

"Well, now, he didn't seem to think so," Dan said. "It was his suggestion, and he seemed keen on the idea, too."

"I don't know why he would be," she muttered. "Besides, I don't want to impose on him. We're practically strangers. I can just go by myself."

"Nonsense." Dan's refusal was good-natured but firm. "I couldn't possibly let you ride out by yourself just yet, no matter how good you are on a horse. You don't know the country, and it's easy to get lost. There's always the possibility of an accident. Besides," he added, and his grin was expansive, "you're part of the family, and I grew up with Jake, so you're not strangers. If anyone knows his way around this part of Wyoming, he does." He shrugged and rested his back against the cushions. "He owns half of it, anyway." Samantha glanced at her sister for help. Sabrina, however, appeared to be engrossed in her needlepoint.

Frowning at the lack of support, Samantha stewed over her predicament. If she refused Jake's company, she would not only forfeit the opportunity to ride the Wyoming countryside, but she would spoil Sabrina's and Dan's plans for a day alone together. She shrugged in resignation and offered a smile.

"I'll be ready at nine." She added to herself, If Jake Tanner can stand a day in my company, I guess I can stand a day in his.

Chapter 3

Sunday dawned with a sky as cold and clear as sapphire. The sun offered thin light and little warmth. To her annoyance, Samantha had overslept. Hurriedly, she showered and dressed in forest-green cords and a chunky beige pullover.

Her riding boots clattered on the parquet floor as she hurried from her room and down the hall to the kitchen. She frowned as she reached the doorway. Jake was sitting at the table, enjoying a cup of coffee with the air of one very much at home.

He was, she noted with illogical irritation, every bit as attractive as she remembered.

"Oh, you're here." Her greeting was hardly welcoming, but he returned it with his slow smile.

"Morning, ma'am."

"Don't start ma'aming me again," she said.

He remained silent as she clattered the cups in the cupboard and filled one with the steaming liquid from the pot on the stove.

"Sorry." She popped a piece of bread in the toaster and turned to offer a peace-offering smile. "My! I overslept. I hope you haven't been waiting long."

"I've got all day," he answered, leaning back in his chair as if to emphasize his words.

She drew a slab of bacon and a carton of eggs from the refrigerator. "Have you eaten?" she asked in invitation.

"Yeah, thanks." He rose, poured himself another cup of coffee and resumed his position at the table. "Dan's already seen to breakfast for himself and Sabrina. They're having it in their room."

"Oh." She replaced the items and pulled out the butter. "Aren't you going to eat?"

"Toast and coffee. I'm not much on breakfast."

"If you always eat like that," he observed over the rim of his cup, "it's no wonder you never grew any bigger."

"For goodness' sake." She whirled around, brandishing the butter knife. "I'm hardly a midget. I'm five-four, that's tall enough for anybody."

He held up his hands in mock surrender. "I never argue with an armed woman.

"Ready?" He rose when she had finished both the toast and another cup of coffee.

When she mumbled her assent, he plucked her jacket from its hook, holding it out so that she had no choice but to allow him to help her into it. She stiffened as his hands touched her shoulders and turned her to face him. Her pulses responded immediately. As if he were aware of her reaction, he began to do up her leather buttons with slow care. She jerked back, but his hold on the front of her coat prevented her from a clean escape.

"You're a pretty little thing," he drawled, completing his task with his eyes directly on hers. "Can't have you catching cold." He reached out and plucked Sabrina's dark wide-brimmed hat from a peg and placed it neatly on her head. "This'll keep your head warm."

"Thanks." She pushed the hat firmly in place.

"Anytime, Sam." His face was unperturbed as he pulled his own sheepskin jacket over his flannel shirt and jeans.

On the way to the stables, Samantha increased her pace to a trot to keep up with Jake's long, careless stride. Despite herself, she admired the confident, loose-limbed grace of his movement. He took his time, she noted, deciding he probably did nothing quickly, and more than likely still finished ahead of everyone else.

The dapple gray had been saddled and led outside by a smiling ranch hand.

"Howdy, ma'am. Dan said to have Spook ready for you."

"Thanks." She returned his friendly smile and patted

the gelding's neck. "But I could have done it. I don't like to give you extra work."

"No trouble, ma'am. Dan said you weren't to do a lick of work today. You just go and have yourself a good time, and I'll rub old Spook down when you get back."

Samantha vaulted easily onto the horse's back, happy to feel a mount beneath her again. Riding was an old pleasure, to be enjoyed only when finances allowed.

"Now, you take good care of Miss Evans, Jake," the cowboy admonished with a conspirator's wink Samantha failed to catch. "Dan sets great store by this little lady."

Little again, Samantha thought.

"Don't you worry about Miss Evans, Lon." Jake mounted his stallion with a fluid motion. Again Samantha noticed that he wasted no time on superfluous movement. "I intend to keep a close eye on her."

Samantha acknowledged Jake's statement with a wrinkled nose, then, following the direction his hand indicated, set off in a brisk canter.

As the neat cluster of ranch buildings was left behind, her irritation vanished. The rushing air was exciting, filling her lungs and whipping roses into her cheeks. She had almost forgotten the sense of liberation riding gave her. It was the same sensation that she had experienced many times when flying from top to bottom or springing high in a double twist.

They rode in silence for a quarter of an hour. Jake allowed her to fill her being with the thrill of movement and the beauty of the countryside. Wild peaks jutted arrogantly into the sky. The rolling plains below were yellow-green with winter. They rode by Herefords, white-faced and sleek, who noted their passing with a lazy turn of the head before resuming their grazing.

A shape darted across an open field, and Samantha slowed her horse to a walk and pointed. "What's that?"

"Antelope," Jake answered, narrowing his eyes against the sun.

"Oh!" She halted her mount and watched the animal's graceful, bounding progress until it streaked over a hill and out of her view. "It must be marvelous to run like that, graceful and free." She turned her unguarded face to the man beside her and found him regarding her intently. His eyes held an expression she did not understand. A strange tingling raced along her spine, like warm fingers on cold skin. The tingling increased, the sensation spreading to settle somewhere in her stomach. Suddenly, his expression changed. The shadows of his face shifted as his lips moved into a smile.

"Someday you will be caught, little antelope."

She blinked at him, totally disoriented, trying to remember what they had been talking about. His grin increased. He pointed to a large, bare-limbed tree a quarter of a mile away.

"Race you." There was challenge under the lazy dare.

Her eyes brightened with excitement. "Fine chance I'd have against a horse like that. What handicap do I get?"

Jake pushed his hat back as if to view her more completely. "From the look of you, I'd say you've got a good fifty-pound advantage. That should balance the odds some."

"No head start?"

"No, ma'am."

She pouted for a moment, then grinned. "All right, Jake Tanner, I'll give you a run for your money."

"Whenever you say, Sam." He pulled the brim of his hat low over his forehead.

"Now!"

She met the gelding's sides with her heels and spurted forward in a gallop. The quiet morning air vibrated with the thunder of hooves. Samantha, her hair flowing behind her, gave herself over to the thrill of the race. She reached the finish just ahead of her competitor and reined in, filling the morning with dusty, breathless laughter.

"Oh, that was wonderful, absolutely wonderful."

"Any time you want to give up teaching, Sam, you can work for me. I can use a hand who rides like you."

"I'll keep that in mind, even though I know you let me beat you."

"Now what makes you think that?" He leaned his arm on the horn of his saddle and watched her thoughtfully.

"I'm not stupid." Her grin was good-natured and

friendly. "I couldn't beat that Arabian in a million years. You, maybe," she added with a touch of arrogance, "but not that horse."

"Pretty sharp, aren't you?" he returned, answering her grin.

"As a tack," she agreed. "And," she continued, brushing her hair from her shoulders, "I am not a weak female who needs to be placated. With my background, I know how to compete, I know how to lose, and—" she grinned and lifted her brows "—I know how to win."

"Point taken." He tilted his head as if to view her from a different angle. "From now on, Sam, we play head-to-head." He smiled, and she was no longer sure they were talking about the same thing. "I know how to win, too," he added slowly. They continued at a leisurely pace for a time, crossing a narrow branch of the Medicine Bow River. They paused there for the horses to quench their thirst in the icy water that forced its way over shining rocks with hisses and whispers. At Samantha's request, Jake began to identify the surrounding mountains.

Pointing to the long fingers of peaks at the south, the Laramie Range, he told her they extended from eastern Colorado. The middle section was the Medicine Bow Range, and the Sierra Madre loomed to the west. The vast ranges were separated by broad tongues of the Wyoming Basin. Silver-blue, they gleamed in the sunlight, lacings of snow trembling from their summits.

She had reined in without being aware of her action. "I can never look at them long enough. I suppose you're used to them."

"No." There was no laughter or mockery in his tone. "You never get used to them."

She smiled a bit uncertainly, not at all sure she could deal with this side of him.

"Are there bears up there?" she asked.

He glanced up at the mountains, smiled, then looked back at her. "Black bear and grizzly," he informed her. "Elk, coyotes, mountain lions…"

"Mountain lions?" she repeated, a little nervously.

"You're not likely to run into one down here," he returned with an indulgent smile.

She ignored the mockery in his voice and looked around her, again awed by the miles of open space. "I wonder if this looked the same a century ago."

"Some of it. Those don't change much." He indicated the Rockies with an inclination of his head. "The Indians are gone," he continued, as if thinking aloud. "There were Arapaho, Sioux, Cheyenne, Crow, Shoshone, all roaming free over the state before the first white man set foot here. Then trappers came, trading with Indians, dressing like them, living like them, and the beaver was nearly driven into extinction." He turned back to her, as if suddenly remembering she was there. "You're the teacher." His smile appeared. "You should be telling me."

Samantha shook her head in mock despair. "My knowledge of Wyoming's history is limited to late-night westerns." They were walking their horses slowly, side by side. She had completely forgotten her aversion to the man beside her. "It's impossible to believe the killing and cruelty that must have gone on here. It's so serene, and so vast. It seems there would have been room enough for everyone."

This time it was Jake who shook his head. "In 1841 more than a hundred and fifty thousand people crossed the South Pass going west, and a few years later, fifty thousand more came through on their way to California looking for gold. This was Indian land, had been Indian land for generations. Game disappeared, and when people get hungry, they fight. Treaties were signed, promises made by both sides, broken by both sides." He shrugged.

"In the 1860s, they tried to open the Bozeman Pass from Fort Laramie to Montana, and open war broke out. The trail ran through the Sioux hunting ground. The fighting was of the worst kind, massacres, indiscriminate killing of women and children, butcheries by both white and Indian. More treaties were signed, more misunderstandings, more killing, until the whites outnumbered the Indians, drove them away or put them on reservations."

"It doesn't seem fair," Samantha whispered, feeling a wave of sadness wash over her.

"No, it doesn't." He heard the wistful note in her voice and turned to regard her. "Life isn't always fair, though, is it, Samantha?"

"I suppose not." She sighed. "You seem to know quite a bit about what happened here. You must have had a good history teacher."

"I did." He held her curious look with a teasing half-smile on his lips. "My great-grandmother lived to be ninety-eight. She was Sioux."

Samantha lifted her brows in surprised interest. "Oh, I'd love to have met her. The things she must have seen, the changes in nearly a century of living."

"She was quite a woman." His smile faded a moment. "She taught me a lot. Among other things, she told me that the land goes on no matter who walks on it, that life moves on whether you fight against it or flow with it, that when you want something, you go after it until it's yours."

Suddenly, she felt he was leading her out of her depth, reaching for something she was not sure she possessed. She turned from the directness of his eyes to search the land.

"I'd like to have seen all this before there were any fences, before there was any fighting."

Jake pointed skyward. Glancing up, Samantha watched the graceful flight of an eagle. For a timeless moment, it soared overhead, the undisputed sovereign of the skies. They moved off again, in companionable silence. "I hope you're getting some fun out of this trip, some compensation for taking care of your sister," Jake said at last.

"I don't need any compensation for taking care of Bree, she's my sister, my…"

"Responsibility?"

"Well…yes. I've always looked out for Bree, she's more delicate, more…dependent than I am." She shrugged and felt uncomfortable without knowing why. "Dad always joked that I took my share of strength and half of Bree's while we were still in the womb. She needs me," she added, feeling compelled to defend what she had always taken for granted.

"She has Dan," Jake reminded her. "And she's a grown woman now—just as you are. Did it ever occur to you that you have your own life to lead now that Sabrina has a husband to care for her?"

"I'm not trying to take over for Dan," she said quickly. "Perhaps you can figure out how he could see to her needs and tend to the house and the ranch all at the same time, but I can't." She glared at him, half in anger, half in exasperation. "What do you expect me to do? Sit up in Philadelphia teaching kids to jump on a tramp while my sister needs help?"

"No, Samantha." He met her eyes with a quiet patience that was more disturbing than angry words and shouts. "What you're doing is very kind and unselfish."

"There's nothing kind or unselfish about it," she interrupted, shrugging the words away. "We're sisters. More than that, we're twins. We shared life from its beginning. You can't understand the kind of bond that creates. I'd give up a hundred jobs to help Bree if she needed me."

"No one's condemning your loyalty, Samantha. It's an admirable trait." He gave her a long, level look. "Just a word of advice. Don't become so involved that you forget who Samantha Evans is, and that she just might have the right to her own woman's life."

Samantha drew herself up to her full height in the saddle. "I hardly need your advice on how to run my life. I've been managing nicely for some time now."

His face creased in a lazy smile. "Yes, ma'am, I'm sure you have."

Chapter 4

Samantha had been riding the dapple gray in stubborn silence for nearly thirty minutes when she noticed more cattle. Her guide seemed unperturbed by her silence and slowed his Arabian's gait to the gelding's meandering walk. She would never have admitted to the man at her side that his words had disturbed her peace of mind.

What business was it of his how she chose to run her life? What gave Jake Tanner the right to question her relationship with Sabrina? No one asked him for his advice. And why in heaven's name should anything he said matter in the first place?

They were approaching a large ranch house. A red-wood porch skirted the building's front, graced by ever-green shrubs. A gray wisp of smoke rose in a welcoming spire from the chimney. Ranch buildings sat neat and unobtrusive in the background.

"Welcome to the Double T, ma'am."

Jake drew her eyes with the uncharacteristic formality in his tone. She turned to see him smile and touch the brim of his well-worn Stetson.

"Thank you, Mr. Tanner. I can honestly say your ranch is spectacular. But what, may I ask, are we doing here?"

"Well, now…" Jake shifted in the saddle to face her directly. "I don't know about you, but nearly three hours in the saddle gives me a powerful appetite. I figured here we might do a bit better than beef jerky."

"Three hours?" Samantha repeated, and pushed Sabrina's hat from her head so it lay against her back. "Has it really been that long?"

The angles of his face moved slowly with his grin, and she found herself once more intrigued by the process. "I'll take that to mean you were so delighted with my company, time stood still."

She answered with a toss of her head. "I hate to tread on your ego, Jake, but the credit goes to Wyoming."

"Close enough for now." Reaching over, he plopped the brimmed hat back in place on Samantha's head and urged his mount into a canter.

Samantha stared after him in exasperation, watching the confidence with which he rode the Arabian. They moved like one form rather than horse and man. Scowling, she pressed her heels to the gelding's side and raced forward to join him.

As she reached his side, he skirted the ranch house and rode toward the buildings in the rear, following the left fork on a long, hard-packed road. A large, sleepy-eyed Saint Bernard rose from his siesta and romped forward to greet them. A deep, hoarse bark emitted from his throat. Jake halted in front of the stables. He slid off the Arabian's back, running his hand through the dog's thick fur as he hit the ground.

"Wolfgang's harmless." He acknowledged the loving, wet kisses with another brief caress and moved to the gelding's side. "He's just a puppy."

"A puppy," Samantha repeated. "You don't see many hundred-and-fifty-pound puppies." Tilting her head, she gave the overgrown baby a thorough examination before she brought her leg over the saddle to dismount.

Jake gripped her waist as she made her descent, holding her off the ground a moment as if she were weightless. As her boots touched earth, she was turned around and drawn against a hard chest. She tilted her head to inform him that his assistance was unnecessary, but saw only a brief blur of his face before his lips captured hers.

Her mind whirled with the touch and scent of him. She felt as though she were falling into a deep well and her heart began to beat a mad tempo against her ribs. She clutched at his jacket in defense. Perhaps the kiss was brief. It could have lasted no more than a portion of a minute, but it felt like forever. She knew his mouth was warm and sure on hers while decades flew into centuries.

The strange sensations of timelessness and loss of control frightened her. She stiffened and began to struggle against his grasp. He released her immediately, staring down at her clouded blue eyes with a satisfied smile. The smile transformed terror into fury.

"How dare you?"

"Just testing, ma'am." His answer was complacent, as though the kiss had been no more than that, a traditional touching of lips.

"Testing?" she repeated, running an agitated hand through her hair. "Testing what?"

"I've always wanted to kiss a teacher." Grinning, he gave her a friendly pat on the cheek. "I think there're some holes in your education."

"I'll show you holes, you conceited, high-handed—" her mind searched for something appropriately derogatory and settled on a generality " *–man*. If I didn't consider that kiss so insignificant, you'd be lying on your back checking out the sky."

He surveyed her as she trembled with a mixture of fury and wounded pride. He rubbed his chin thoughtfully. "You know, Sam, I almost believe you could do it."

"You can bank on it," she confirmed with an arrogant

toss of her head. "And the next time you…" Feeling her arm sharply pulled, she glanced down to see the sleeve of her jacket captured in the awesome jaws of the Saint Bernard. "What'd you do, teach him to eat unwilling females?"

"He just wants to make your acquaintance," Jake laughed, as he led the horses to the stable to turn them over to one of his men.

Samantha was not normally timid, and her pride refused to allow her to call Jake to untangle her from the teeth of his puppy. She swallowed and spoke to her canine captor.

"Hello…Wolfgang, wasn't it?" she muttered. "I'm Sam. You, ah, wouldn't consider letting go of my jacket, would you?" The dog continued to stare with droopy, innocent eyes. "Well, that's all right," she said, trying out magnanimity. "It's just an old one, anyway. I'm very fond of dogs, you know." Tentatively, she brought her free hand up to touch the fur on his huge head. "Well, actually, I have a cat," she admitted in apology, "but I have absolutely no prejudices."

Though his expression did not alter, she decided it was prudent to give him time for consideration. Her patience was rewarded when he released her sleeve and bathed her hand with his enormous tongue.

"Well, I see you two have made friends," Jake drawled, coming up behind her.

"No thanks to you," she said. "He might have eaten me alive."

"Not you, Sam," Jake disagreed, taking her hand and striding toward the house. "Too tough for Wolfgang's taste."

Jake led her to the back entrance through a paneled, tiled-floor mudroom and into the kitchen. A large square room, it was bright and cheery with tangerine curtains framing the wide windows. The pleasant-looking woman who stood by the sink smiled at Samantha. "Jake, you scoundrel, have you had this poor little lady out in the cold all this time?" Samantha met the warm brown eyes with a returning smile.

Jake grinned, unabashed. "Samantha Evans, meet Annie Holloway, my cook, housekeeper and best girl."

"Don't you try soft soaping me, you young devil." She brushed off his words with indulgent affection, but pleased color rose to her pudgy cheeks. "Thinks he can get around me with sweet talk. Pleased to meet you, Miss Evans." Samantha found her hand enclosed in a firm grip.

"Hello, Miss Holloway, I hope I'm not putting you out."

"Putting me out?" Annie let out a rich, full laugh, her ample bust heaving with the sound. "Isn't she the sweet one? Don't you be silly, now, and you just call me Annie like everyone else."

"Thank you, Annie." Samantha's smile warmed. "Everyone calls me Sam."

"Now that's a pretty thing," Annie commented, peering candidly into Samantha's face. "Yes, sir, a right pretty thing. You two run along," she commanded with an attempt at sternness. "Out of my kitchen. Lunch will be along, and I'll bring you in some tea to warm you up. Not you," she said with a scowl as Jake grimaced. "For the little lady. You don't need any warming up."

"Annie runs things," Jake explained as he led Samantha down a wide hall into the living room.

"I can see she does, even when she's securely wrapped around your little finger."

For a moment, his smile was so boyish and full of mischief, she nearly gave in to the urge to brush the curls from his forehead.

The paneling in the living room was light. The expanse of wood was broken by a large stone fireplace and wide windows framed with cinnamon-colored sheers. The dark gleaming furniture had been upholstered in gold, burnt sienna and rich browns. There was a comfortable hodgepodge of Hepplewhites and Chippendales with piecrust tilt-top tables and Pembrokes, ladder-back chairs and candlestands. In the center of the hardwood floor lay a wide rug of Indian design, so obviously old and handworked, that Samantha wondered if it had been his great-grandmother's fingers that had hooked it perhaps nearly a century ago. The room reflected a quiet, understated wealth, a wealth she somehow did not associate with the rangy, brash cowboy side of Jake.

A Charles Russell painting caught her eye. She turned to study it, attempting to sort out her new impressions of this complex man. Turning back, she found him watching her reaction with unconcealed amusement.

"I have a feeling you were expecting bearskins and oilcloth."

Samantha focused her attention on the inviting fire. "I never know what to expect from you," she muttered.

"No?" He dropped his lanky form into a wing-backed chair and pulled out a long, thin cigar. "I thought you were pretty bright."

Samantha seated herself in the chair across from him, keeping the warmth and hiss of the fire between them. "This is a lovely room, very appealing and very warm."

"I'm glad you like it." If he noticed her blatant change of subject, he gave no sign. Lighting his cigar, he stretched out his legs and looked totally relaxed and content.

"I have a weakness for antiques," she continued, deciding the topic was safe and impersonal.

He smiled, the smoke curling lazily above his head. "There's a piece in one of the bedrooms you might like to see. A blanket chest in walnut that was brought over from the East in the 1860s."

"I'd like that very much." She returned his smile and settled back as Annie wheeled a small tea cart into the room.

"I brought you coffee," she said to Jake, and passed him a cup. "I know you won't take tea unless you douse it with bourbon. Something not quite decent about doing that to a good cup of tea."

"Tea is an old ladies' drink," he stated, ignoring her rapidly clucking tongue.

"How do you think Sabrina looks?" Samantha asked him when Annie had bustled back to the kitchen.

"I think you worry too much about her."

She bristled instinctively before replying. "Perhaps you're right," she surprised herself by admitting. "Our mother always said Bree and I were mirror images, meaning, I discovered after a while, opposites."

"Right down to Sabrina being right-handed, and you being left."

"Why, yes." She looked at him in faint surprise. "You don't miss much, do you?" He merely shook his head and gave her an enigmatic smile. "Well," she plunged on, not sure she liked his expression, a bit like a cat who already had the mouse between his paws. "I suppose the summary of my discrepancies was that I could never keep the hem in my white organdy party dress. You'd have to know my mother to understand that. She would have Bree and me all decked out in these frilly white organdy dresses and send us off to a party. Brec would come back spotless, pure and angelic. I'd come back with dirt on my frills, bloody knees and a trailing hem."

During her story, Jake's smile had widened. The coffee in his cup cooled, unattended as he watched her. "There're doers and there're watchers, Samantha. I imagine you had fun scraping up your knees."

As ridiculous as it seemed, she felt she'd just been complimented, and was both pleased and faintly embarrassed.

"I suppose you're a doer, too." She dropped her eyes. "You couldn't run a ranch like this and not be. Cattle ranching sounds romantic, but I imagine it's long hours, hot summers and cold winters. I don't suppose it's really all that different from the way it used to be a hundred years ago."

"The range isn't open anymore," he corrected. "You don't find cowboys going off to Texas to punch cattle with a ten-dollar horse and a forty-dollar saddle." He shrugged and set his empty cup on the table beside him. "But some change slow, and I'm one who likes to take my time."

She was frowning into his smile when Annie announced lunch. It was not until they were settled in the dining room that she spoke directly to him again, pressing him for more details on how the ranch was run.

He explained how roundups, which had once been accomplished on the vast open range with only men and horses, were now aided by fences and technology. But it was still men and ponies who moved the cattle into corrals. Over a few states there were still strongholds of riders and ropers, men who cultivated the old technique and blended it with the new. On the Double T, Jake employed the best of both.

"If roundups aren't what they once were, they still accomplish the same end. Getting the cattle together and branding them."

"Branding?" Samantha interrupted, and shuddered.

"Your Philadelphia's showing, Sam." He grinned. "Take my word for it, branding is a good deal more unpleasant for the branders than the brandees."

She decided to ignore his comments and changed the subject abruptly. "Bree told me your ranch borders Dan's. This place must be huge for it to have taken us three hours to get here."

Jake's deep, rich laughter filled the room, and she decided unwillingly that she liked the sound very much. "It's a pretty big spread, Sam, but if you take the straight road north for the Lazy L, you can be here in twenty minutes on horseback. I took you on a big circle today," he explained. "Just a small taste of our part of the Laramie Basin."

They lingered over coffee, relaxed in each other's company.

"We'd better get started back," Jake said after a while. He rose and extended his hand. Her own slipped without hesitation into it as he pulled her to her feet. When she looked up at him, her smile was warm and spontaneous.

"Annie was right, that's a pretty thing." He lifted his hand and traced his fingers over the curve of her mouth. She started. "Now don't go skittish on me, Sam, I'm not going to use spurs and a whip."

His mouth lowered, gentle and persuasive. One hand held hers while the other circled the back of her neck to soothe with coaxing fingers. She had only to sway forward to feel his body against hers, had only to lift her hand to bring his mouth firmer and warmer on hers. Before the choice could be made, he drew her away and the decision was taken out of her hands.

"Sam." He shook his head as if exasperated and lightly amused. "You're enough to try a man's patience."

With this, he pulled her through to the kitchen.

"Well, so you're off again." Annie wiped one hand on her apron and wagged the other at Jake. "And don't be keeping her out in that cold too long."

"No, ma'am," Jake returned with suspicious respect.

"Thank you, Annie," Samantha broke in. "Lunch was wonderful."

"Well, now, that's fine, then." She gave Samantha a friendly pat on the cheek. "You just come back real soon, and you say hi to Sabrina for me, and that young rascal Dan, too. As soon as she's fit again, I'll be coming by to see her. Oh, Jake, I clean forgot." Annie turned to him and sighed at her absentmindedness. "Lesley Marshall called earlier, something about dinner tonight. I told her you'd give her a call, then it went straight out of my mind."

"No problem," Jake said easily. "I'll get back to her later. Ready, Sam?"

"Yes, I'm ready." She kept her smile in place, though a large black cloud seemed to have suddenly smothered the sunshine.

Lesley Marshall, she mused, automatically going through the motions of securing her hat and coat. That was the woman Bree had predicted would marry Jake when he decided to settle down. Why should it matter to me? She straightened her spine and accompanied Jake to the waiting horses. I have absolutely no interest in Jake Tanner's affairs.

He's probably had dozens of girlfriends. Well, it's no concern of mine. Vaulting into the saddle, she followed as he set off down the hard-packed road.

They spoke little on the return journey. Samantha pretended an engrossment with the scenery that she was far from feeling. Unhappily, she realized Wyoming's magic was not quite enough to lift her flagging spirits. Snow-capped peaks glistened just as brightly in the late afternoon sun, and the land still spread and beckoned, but as she surveyed them now she felt strangely depressed.

It had been an unusual day, she concluded. Jake had annoyed her, charmed her, angered her and delighted her, all in a handful of hours. His kiss had aroused excitement and a deeper feeling she could not explain.

The knowledge that he was dining with another woman that evening depressed her beyond belief. She stole a sidelong look at his lean, tanned features.

He was undeniably attractive, she admitted, pulling her eyes away from him before he could sense her study. There was a powerful aura of virility about him, which alternately intrigued her and made her wary. Perhaps it would be wise to avoid his company. He confused her, and Samantha liked to know precisely where she stood with a man. She wanted to call the shots, and she realized that this man would never allow anyone to call the shots but himself.

She would keep her distance from now on. Let him spread his charm over this Lesley Marshall, or any of the other women who were undoubtedly thirsting for his attention. Samantha Evans could get along very easily without him. As the Lazy L grew closer, she resolved to be polite and casually friendly to her escort. After all, she reflected, there was no reason to be rude. He was perfectly free to dine with whomever he chose; his life was most assuredly his own. Besides, she added to herself, if she had anything to say about it, they would be seeing very little of each other in the future.

When they reached the ranch, she dismounted, handing Spook's reins to a waiting cowboy. "I had a wonderful time, Jake." Samantha's smile was faultless in its social politeness as he walked her toward the ranch house, leading his stallion behind him. "I appreciate your time and hospitality."

Jake's mouth lifted at one corner. "It was my pleasure, ma'am."

If there was a mockery in his tone, Samantha chose to ignore it. Reaching the back door, she turned to smile at him again as he stood, tall and lean, beside the gleaming chestnut.

"Would you like some coffee before you go?" she invited, determined to be polite.

"No, thanks, Sam." He continued to watch her, his eyes shaded by the brim of his hat. "I'd best be getting along."

"Well." She breathed a small sigh of relief when her hand touched the doorknob and safety was in easy reach. "Thanks again."

"Sure." He nodded briefly and turned to his horse, paused and turned back to look at her with a penetrating intensity that turned her legs to water. When he spoke, it was soft and final. "I mean to have you, you know."

Several moments of silence passed before she could summon up an answer.

"D-Do you?" Her voice was a shaky whisper, unlike the coolly flippant tone she would have wished for.

"Yes, ma'am." He vaulted onto the chestnut's back and pushed the Stetson back on his head so that she had a disturbingly clear view of his eyes. "I do," he confirmed, turning his mount and galloping away.

Chapter 5

Often over the next few days, Samantha told herself that her reaction to Jake's kiss had been merely a passing physical attraction. She was a normal woman, wasn't she? So why feel guilty about it?

Jake Tanner *was* a very attractive man. *Too attractive,* she added to herself. And he knew too much about charming women. The fact that Jake was abrasive, smug and irritating had nothing to do with the way she had acted. It had just been a passing fancy. *And would certainly not occur again.*

Finally Sabrina was allowed up from the confinement of her bed. Samantha decided it was safe to leave her sister for a few hours. With a light heart, she saddled Spook and set off from the ranch at a brisk canter. For a while she enjoyed the feeling of Spook's hooves pounding the hard road. The sky hung low above her, and heavy, leaden gray clouds draped the distant mountains in mysterious gloom. There was a stillness, a waiting in the air, unnoticed by Samantha in her eagerness to escape the close confines of the house.

She rode swiftly past the bored, white-faced cattle and the stretches of barbed wire, eager to explore new territory, tasting the joy of motion and freedom. The mountains, grim sentinels above her, stood stone-gray under the unbroken sky. Remembering Dan's instructions, Samantha took care to mark her route, choosing a clump of rocks, a cottonwood tree with a broken limb, and a gnarled stump as landmarks for her return trip.

She led her mount to a crest of a hill, watching as a jackrabbit, startled by her intrusion, darted across the road and out of sight.

Nearly an hour passed before the first flakes began to drift lazily from sky to earth. She stopped and watched their progress in fascination. The snow fell slowly. Lifting her face, she let it caress her cheeks and closed lids. The air was moist, coming to life around her, and she stirred herself out of her dream.

"Well, Spook, this is my first Wyoming snow. I'd like to stay here all day and watch it fall, but duty calls. We'd better head back." Patting the horse's neck, she turned back toward the ranch.

They rode slowly. Samantha was enchanted with the fairyland that was forming around her. Cottonwoods and aspens were draped in white, their branches a stark contrast to the brilliant etchings of snow. The ground was cloaked quickly. Though the beauty was breathtaking, Samantha began to feel uncomfortably alone.

She took Spook into a canter. The sound of his hooves was soft and muffled. The quiet surrounding her was unearthly, almost as though the world had ceased to breathe. She shivered, suddenly cold in the warm confines of her jacket. To her annoyance, she saw that in her preoccupation with the landscape she had taken a wrong turn, and she began to backtrack, berating herself for carelessness.

The snow increased, plunging down from a sky she could no longer see. She cursed herself for having come so far, fighting down a sudden surge of panic. "Don't be silly, Sam," she spoke aloud, wanting the reassurance of her own voice. "A little snow won't hurt you."

The cold became more intense, piercing the layers of her skin. Samantha tried to concentrate on steaming coffee and a blazing fire as she looked around for a familiar landmark. Nothing was the same as it had been. She clamped her lips tight to still the chattering of her teeth, telling herself that it was impossible that she could be lost. But it was a lie. The trees and hills around her were strangers blanketed in white.

The snow fell thickly, a blinding white wall blocking her vision. A wind had sprung up, breaking the silence with its moans and tossing snow, hard and bitter, into her face. She was forced to slow the gelding to a walk, afraid of tangling with the sharp teeth of barbed wire she was unable to see. Her teeth savaged her lips in an effort to control a growing terror.

It's so cold, she thought as she began to shiver convulsively, so unbelievably cold.

The snow had soaked through the wool of her slacks and slipped mercilessly down the neck of her coat. She hunched her shoulders against the driving wind. Snow was everywhere, blocking her in and seeping into her clothing.

She let the reins hang limp, praying that the horse's instinct would guide him back to the warm shelter of his stables. They trudged on, the vortex of white that had begun so innocently now whirling around her. Time and direction had lost all meaning, and though she tried calling out, her voice was soundless against the fierce breath of the wind.

Now she felt the cold. Her body was numbed into submission. Her mind was following suit. The swirling snow was hypnotic, and a growing lethargy was creeping over her. In a small part of her mind, she knew her survival depended on remaining alert.

Horse and rider plodded on. There was no time, no world beyond the unbroken curtain of white. Samantha felt her eyelids growing heavy, but she willed them open with all her strength. The snow piled onto her back, weighing her down until she slumped onto the gelding's mane and clung to him. Staring down at the gelding's front hoof, she began to count each drudging step that Spook took as he continued his slow progress through the blinding storm.

Samantha's concentration on the horse's halting steps began to fade.

If I close my eyes, she thought dimly, I won't see all that white and I can sleep. Oh, how I want to sleep….

The snow was talking, she mused deliriously. Well, why not? It's alive. Why should it sound like Jake? Helplessly, she began to giggle. Well, why shouldn't it? *They both play to win.*

"Samantha!" The snow was shouting at her. "Open your eyes. Stop that insane laughing and open your eyes!"

Wearily, she forced herself to obey the command. Dimly she saw the blur of Jake's features through the flurries of snow. "You would be the last thing I see before I die." With a moan, she closed her eyes again and sought the silence.

"Tell Dan we've found her," Jake shouted against the howl of the wind. "I'm taking her back to the Double T."

The darkness was comforting. Samantha gave herself over to it, feeling herself falling slowly into a hole with no bottom. She burrowed deeper into it. Her consciousness swam to the surface.

Bemused, she looked around a dimly lit room. The snow that pooled around her was not snow at all, but a bed with a thick, warm quilt. She allowed her heavy lids to close again.

"Oh, no, you don't." The lids opened fractionally, and Samantha saw Jake standing in the open doorway.

"Hello."

His mouth thinned as he advanced to the bed to tower over her. It seeped through the misty reaches of her brain that he was angry. She stared at him with lazy fascination.

"What in heaven's name were you doing out in such a storm? I've seen some dumb stunts, but taking a joyride in the middle of a blizzard tops them all."

She wanted to ask him to stop shouting at her, but lacked the energy. "Where am I?" was all she could find to say.

Sitting on the edge of the bed, he drew her head from the pillow, then held a cup to her lips. "Here, drink this first, then we'll talk."

The brandy was warm and strong, and she sputtered and gasped as he poured it down her throat. Its power spread through her, pushing back the mists of unconsciousness.

"Now, to answer your question, you're at the Double T." Jake set the empty cup aside, and laid her head back on the mound of pillows.

"Oh."

"Is that all you can say?" He was shouting again. He took her shoulders as if to shake her. "Just 'Oh'? What in heaven's name were you doing out there?"

"It seems so long ago." She frowned in concentration, closing her eyes with the effort. "It wasn't snowing when I left," she said in weak defense.

"Wasn't snowing?" Jake repeated, incredulous. "Samantha, didn't you see the sky? Where are your brains?"

"There's no excuse for insults," she retorted with a small flash of spirit.

"No excuse for insults? Are you stark raving mad? Do you realize what nearly happened to you?" His hands retreated to his pockets, as though he could barely prevent them from throttling her. "Out here in the middle of a blizzard, half-frozen and helplessly lost! It was a miracle we found you. A little longer, and you'd be lying somewhere buried in it, and no one would have found what was left until spring. Dan was half out of his mind when he got through to me and told me you'd gone out in this."

"Bree?"

"Knew nothing." He whirled to face her again. "She was taking a nap. It never occurred to her that you had gone out with a storm brewing." He laughed harshly.

The memory of the snow and the terror washed over her, and she began to shake. "I'm sorry," she managed through the tears that threatened to flow. With a brief oath, Jake ran a hand through his hair. He closed the distance between them and gathered her in his arms. "Samantha," he murmured against her hair. "What hell you put us all through."

"I'm sorry," she repeated, and she began to sob in earnest. "I was so scared, so cold."

He rocked and murmured words she could not understand, his lips brushing through her hair and over her damp cheeks until they met hers. The kiss mingled with the salt of her tears. "I've gotten your shirt all wet," she murmured after a while.

He let out a deep breath. She saw his smile begin to spread before he rested his brow against hers. "That is without doubt the worst calamity of the day."

"It's dark," she said with sudden realization. "How long...?"

"Too long. What you need now is rest."

"Spook?" she began as he lay her down on the pillows.

"Is sleeping off his adventure in the stables. He looks a lot better than you, I might add."

"I want to thank you for everything." Samantha reached for his hand. In that instant, she discovered there was nothing covering her save sheets and blankets. "M-My clothes," she stammered, drawing the quilt higher in a purely feminine gesture that caused Jake's mouth to twitch.

"Soaked through, Sam." Rising, he stood, rocking gently on his heels. "It was necessary to get you warm and dry."

"Did Annie?" she managed a smile at the thought of the matronly presence of Jake's housekeeper. "I seem to have put everyone to a lot of trouble. Will you thank her for me?"

"Well, Sam, I'd like to oblige you, but Annie left yesterday for Colorado to spend a week with her nephew." Jake's grin broadened.

"Then who—?" The question caught in her throat, and her eyes became round and impossibly dark. "Oh, no," she whispered, closing her eyes in humiliation.

"No need to be embarrassed, Sam, you have a beautiful body."

"Oh, no." With a moan, she squeezed her eyes tighter.

"Now, don't you fret." His tone took on the light insolence of the cowboy she'd met a month before in the cold March sunset. "When I took off your clothes and rubbed you down, it was strictly medical. I'd do as much for any stray." He patted her hand, and her eyes opened warily at his touch.

"Yes, of course." Moistening her lips, she attempted to see the practical side. "I, well...thank you."

"'S all right, don't give it a thought." He moved toward the door, then paused and turned back. "Now, the next time I get your clothes off, my purpose'll be completely different."

He strolled casually from the room, leaving a speechless Samantha.

Chapter 6

Samantha looked around her. She remembered with a shock that she was in Jake's house—and, worse yet, *naked* in bed. She was debating the wisdom of wrapping the quilt around her and searching for more appropriate attire when footsteps sounded down the hall outside her room. She pulled the covers to her chin as Jake strode through the open door.

"So, you're awake. How do you feel?"

"Fine." Her respiratory system behaved erratically as he continued toward her and dropped onto the bed. "I'm just fine," she repeated, then added unnecessarily, "It's still snowing."

"So it is," he agreed without taking his eyes from her face. "Slowing down, though."

"Is it?" She forced herself to look out the window.

"The worst'll be over by midday." He reached up and pried one of her hands loose from the death grip on the blankets. "Calm down, Sam, I'm not going to ravish you, I'm going to check your pulse."

"I'm fine," she repeated again.

"Far from fine, Samantha," he corrected. His fingers brushed against her cheek, as if to test its substance. "The first thing is to get some food into you." Rising, he held out a large flannel robe that he had dropped at the foot of the bed. "You'd probably feel better if you had something on." His smile was gently mocking. "Can you manage to get into this by yourself?"

"Of course." Plucking it from him, she kept a cautious grip on the blankets. "I'm not an invalid."

"You best think like one. Put that on, then get back in bed. I'll bring you some breakfast."

"I don't..."

"Don't argue." The two words were swift and final. He was gone before she could say another word.

He had shut the door, however, and grateful for the concession, Samantha tossed back the covers and slipped her arm into the robe. When she stood, the room swayed and spun around her. She sank back onto the bed and slipped her other arm into its sleeve, pulling the robe around her before attempting to stand again. Her limbs felt heavy and weak, and she noted with puzzlement that her ankle was throbbing lightly. Gripping one poster of the bed until the room steadied, she rolled up the sleeves of the robe several times until her hands became visible, then moved to the bathroom to study herself in the mirror.

The sight of her own face caught at her breath. Her skin seemed nearly transparent, her eyes darker and larger in contrast. The breath of color that resulted when she pinched her cheeks faded instantly. She ran a hand through her hair falling on the shoulders of the dark green robe.

It must be his, she realized, looking down at the sleeves, which swallowed her arms, and the hem, which fell nearly to her ankles. A strange sensation flowed over her as she felt the material on her skin. Turning away from the mirror, she studied the bed.

"I'm not getting in there again," she muttered, and with a small gesture of defiance belted the robe more securely. "I can eat at the table like a normal person."

After a moment, her progress down the hall seemed more of a crawl than a walk. Her legs were heavy with a weakness which infuriated her. The stillness of the house vibrated around her, playing havoc with her nerves, and the need to hear the natural, everyday movements of another human being became increasingly important. She cursed the waves of giddiness that swam around in her head, forcing her to stop time after time to rest her hand against the wall.

"This is ridiculous."

"You're right."

The harsh agreement came from behind as Jake's hands gripped her shoulders.

"What are you doing out of bed?"

"I'm all right." She swayed against his chest. He gripped her waist to support her, and she rested her hands on his arms.

"I'm just a bit wobbly, and I'm having some trouble with my ankle."

He let his gaze travel down to rest on her bare feet. "Probably turned it when you fell off the horse."

"I fell off Spook?" Her expression was incredulous.

"You were unconscious at the time. Now, get back in bed and stay there." Effortlessly, he swept her into his arms, and she laid her head against his shoulder.

"Jake, don't make me go back to bed. It's so quiet in there, and I don't feel like being alone now."

He bent and brushed lips that parted in confusion. "If you think you can sit in a chair without sliding on your face, you can come in the kitchen."

She nodded, sighed and closed her eyes. "I hate being so much trouble."

She felt him shift her in his arms before he began the

journey down the hall. "I knew you were trouble the minute I set eyes on you."

"Don't tease, Jake, I'm trying to thank you."

"What for?"

She lifted a hand to his cheek, turning his face so that he would look at her. "For my life."

"Then take better care of it in the future," he suggested.

"Jake, please, I'm serious. I owe you…"

"Nothing, you owe me nothing." His voice had hardened with annoyance. "I don't want your gratitude." They had reached the kitchen, and he placed her in a chair at the table. "Which ankle did you hurt?" He crouched down by her feet.

"The left one. Jake, I— Ouch!"

"Sorry." He grinned up at her, then rested his hand with friendly ease on her knee. "It's not swollen."

"It still hurts," she said stubbornly.

"Keep off it, then," he advised with simple logic, and turned away to finish breakfast.

"You've got some bedside manners, Dr. Tanner," she observed sharply.

"Yes, ma'am, so I've been told." When he turned to face her, his smile was bland. "Tell me, Sam, does Sabrina have a mole on her left hip, too?"

Color flooded her face. "You…you…" she faltered, and clutched the robe tight at her throat.

"Around here, we call that locking the barn door after the cow's got loose. Have some coffee," he invited with sudden graciousness, pouring a cup and setting it on the table. "Start on this bacon," he ordered, sliding a plate in front of her. "That color didn't last long, you're pale as a ghost again. When did you eat last?"

"I…at breakfast yesterday, I guess."

"Toast and coffee, I imagine," he said disgustedly. "It's a wonder you can manage to sit up at all. Eat." He plucked a piece of bacon from the plate and held it out to her. "I'll have some eggs ready in a minute."

Obediently, she accepted the bacon and took a bite. "Are you going to have something?"

"In a minute," he answered absently, involved with breaking and beating eggs in a bowl.

With the first bite of bacon, Samantha realized she was ravenous. Through her preoccupation with food, she watched Jake cook with a deftness that amused and surprised her.

In a moment, he sat across from her, his plate piled high. She wondered how he could eat with such abandon and remain hard and lean.

She watched him under the cover of her lashes, and the thought came unbidden into her mind that never before had she shared the breakfast table with a man. The intimacy of their situation washed over her; the scent of bacon and coffee drifting through the air, the house quiet and empty around them, the soft flannel of his robe against her skin, the faint masculine scent of him clinging to it. It was as if they were lovers, she thought suddenly, as if they had shared the night, and now they were sharing the morning. Her face grew warm.

"I don't know what thought put roses back in those cheeks, Sam, but keep it up."

Her eyes lifted to his, and she had the uncomfortable feeling that he knew very well what road her thoughts had taken. She dropped her eyes to her plate. "I should call Bree and let her know I'm all right."

"Phones are out," he said simply, and her eyes flew back to his.

"The phones are out?" she repeated.

No telephone, her mind said again. Without a telephone, they might as well be on an island a thousand miles from anyone. Their isolation was complete, and the snow was still falling as though it would never stop.

"With a storm like this, it's not surprising to lose the phones. Power's out, too. We're on generator. Don't worry about Sabrina, she knows you're with me." His words did nothing to erase her tension.

"When…when do you think I'll be able to get back?"

"Couple of days," he returned with an easy shrug, and sipped his coffee. "The roads'll have to be cleared after the storm lets up, and you're not in any shape to travel through a mess like that yet. In a day or two, you'll be more up to it."

"A couple of days?"

He leaned back comfortably in his chair, his voice smooth as a quiet river. "Of course, by then you'll be hopelessly compromised, not a scrap of your sterling reputation left. Alone with me for two or three days, without Annie to add a thread of decency to the situation." His eyes traveled down her slim figure. "Wearing my bathrobe, too." He shook his head. "Not too many years back, I'd have had to marry you."

"Thank goodness for progress," she retorted smartly.

"Oh, I don't know, Sam." His sigh was convincing. "I'm an old-fashioned sort of man."

"It's only a matter of circumstance that we're alone here in the first place." With great dignity, she folded her arms. "And I've hardly been compromised, as you so quaintly put it."

"No?" He watched her through lazily narrowed eyes. "So far, I've undressed you, tucked you in and fixed your breakfast. Who knows what that might lead to?"

His smile might have been lazy, but it was full of meaning. Suddenly Samantha found it difficult to swallow.

"Relax, Sam." His laugh was full of arrogant enjoyment. "I told you I mean to have you, but it's not in my plans to take on a pale child who barely has the strength to stand." He paused, lit one of his long, thin cigars and blew smoke at the ceiling. "When I make love to you, I want you to have your wits about you. I don't want you passing out in my arms."

The man's arrogance was amazing! "You conceited mule," she began. "How dare you sit there and tell me you're going to make love to me? You seem to think you're irresistible! Well, you have another think coming—"

"I'm going to remind you of that one day, Sam," Jake said mildly as he crushed out his cigar. "Now, I think you better lie down again. You're not quite up to sparring with me yet."

"I do not have to lie down. And I certainly don't need you carting me around. I can manage." She stood up, then was forced to grasp the table as the room revolved around her.

"You don't look ready to turn cartwheels, teacher," Jake observed as he took her arm.

"I'm all right." Her hand, which she had lifted to push him away, lay weakly on his chest for support. He tilted her chin, and he was no longer smiling. "Samantha, sometimes you have to be strong enough to let someone else take care of things. You're going to have to hand over the reins to me for a couple of days. If you fight it, you're only going to make it harder on yourself."

With a sigh, she allowed her head to fall against his

chest, not protesting as his arms encircled her. "Do I have to like it?"

"Not necessarily." He gave a short laugh and lifted her easily and carried her back to bed.

Her small spurt of energy deserted her. With an odd feeling of contentment, she settled down under the covers. She was asleep even before his lips had lightly touched her forehead in a farewell kiss...

"I was beginning to think you'd sleep through the night."

She turned her head quickly. Jake was sitting across the room, the smoke of his cigar spiraling upward, the flickering lights from the fire shooting specks of gold into his eyes. Samantha brushed the tousled hair from her face and struggled into a sitting position.

"It's dark," she said. "What time is it?"

He glanced at the gold watch on his wrist and took a slow drag from his cigar. "It's a bit past six."

"Six? I've slept for hours. I feel as if I've slept for weeks."

"You needed it." Tossing the stub of his cigar into the mouth of the fire, Jake rose and moved toward her. His concerned eyes roamed over her sleep-flushed cheeks and heavy eyes. Gradually, his expression lightened, the angles of his face moving into a satisfied smile. "Your color's coming back." He took her wrist, and her eyes dropped from his to study the dancing flames of the fire. "Pulse's a bit jumpy." The smile reflected in his voice. "Strong though. Hungry?"

"I shouldn't be." She forced her eyes to meet his. "I've done nothing but lie around all day, but I'm starved."

He smiled again, lifting her without comment. She felt small and vulnerable in his arms, a sensation that was both pleasant and disturbing. She found it difficult to resist the impulse to rest her head against the strong curve of his shoulder. Instead, she concentrated on the sharp, clean lines of his profile.

"I'm sure I can walk. I really feel fine."

"I doubt it." She could feel his warm breath on her face. "Besides, you seem to fit in my arms pretty well."

Finding no quick comeback to this comment, she took the journey to the kitchen in silence.

Leaning back in her chair, replete and content, Samantha sipped the cool white wine in her glass and gave Jake a nod of approval.

"You're going to make some woman a terrific husband. You're an outstanding cook."

"I think so." He nodded smugly. "My wife wouldn't have to be a gourmet cook," he added with casual consideration. "I'd demand other qualities."

"Adoration," Samantha suggested. "Obedience, unswerving loyalty, solicitude."

"That's all right for a start."

"Poor woman."

"Of course, I don't want her to be a doormat. Let's say I like a woman who knows how to think, one who doesn't pretend to be anything but who she is. Of course," he added, finishing off his wine, "I'm also partial to good looks."

"Well, so far it doesn't sound as though you're asking for much," Samantha giggled. "Just perfection."

"The woman I have in mind can handle it." He smiled broadly as he rose to pour coffee. Samantha stared at his back, feeling as though her heart had been dropped into a deep hole. *Lesley Marshall.* Her mind flashed the name like a neon sign in bright red letters.

Jake squelched her offer to do the dishes and swooped her from her chair and deposited her on the living room sofa.

"I feel useless," she muttered, helplessly cocooned by blankets and pillows. "I'm not made for lying around. I'm never sick." She gave Jake a sulky glare as if the entire matter was his fault. "I don't know how Bree coped with this sort of thing for a month."

"Could be you got her share of strength, and she got your share of patience," he considered, then shrugged. "Of course, I could be wrong." She heard his chuckle and the quiet click of his lighter as he lit a cigar.

Well, Samantha, she chided herself, you've really done

it this time. Not only are you isolated with a man who constantly confuses you, but you can't even stand on your own feet. They say people learn about each other quickly when they live together, but I think it's going to take much more than one day to learn what this man is all about. *Living together,* she repeated, finding herself more amused than embarrassed. If Momma could see me now, we'd need a gallon of smelling salts.

Chapter 7

Dawn was breaking. Pink and gold streaks split the hazy blue of the sky, and light tumbled through to rest on Samantha's closed lids.

Morning? Sitting up with a start, she shook her head vigorously to dispel the last remnants of sleep. Pulling on the borrowed robe, she set her feet on the floor, took three deep breaths and stood. When both the room and her head remained stable, she let out a long sigh of relief. Her legs were weak, but they no longer felt as if they would melt from under her, and the stiffness in her ankle had disappeared.

Mobility, she thought with arrogant glee. I've never truly appreciated it until now. Coffee. One thought followed swiftly on the trail of the other, and she deserted the room with the intention of making fantasy fact. A door opened as she passed it, and with a cry of surprise, she fell against the opposite wall.

Jake stood in the doorway, rubbing a towel briskly through his damp hair, a terry-cloth robe tied loosely around his waist. "Morning, ma'am."

"You startled me." She swallowed, over-powered by the lean, bronzed maleness that the terry cloth did little to hide. He took a step toward her, and her breath caught instinctively. "I—I'm much better." She began to babble, unconsciously cowering against the smooth paneling. "I can actually walk a straight line."

Her voice died to a whisper as he stood directly in front of her. Her eyes were on a line with the tanned column of throat revealed by the open neck of the robe. His hand lifted her chin, and she trembled.

"Relax, Sam." His laughter sounded deep in his throat. "I just want to look you over. You must have the constitution of an elephant," he concluded with unflattering candor. "You look as though you've been on vacation instead of battling blizzards. One day's rest after nearly freezing to death. Most women would have been stretched out for a week."

"I'm not most women." She pushed his hand away from her face. "I'm not fragile and delicate, and I'm not going back to bed. I'm going to fix breakfast." She nudged him out of her path and started down the hall.

"Coffee's already on," he called after her.

Samantha had breakfast under way by the time Jake joined her. Clad in the less disturbing attire of corded jeans and flannel shirt, he watched her prepare the meal as he silently sipped at his coffee at the kitchen table.

"I'm getting used to having a pretty face across from me at breakfast," he commented when she sat down to join him.

"I'm sure I'm not the first," she commented with studied indifference. Nor, she added to herself, will I be the last.

"Nope," he agreed easily, "but there's something to be said for big blue eyes first thing in the morning."

"Blue eyes are common enough," she muttered, and lowered them to the contents of her plate. "Besides, this is hardly a long-term arrangement." He did not speak for a moment, and her fork moved restlessly among her eggs.

"We should have the road clear enough sometime tomorrow."

"Tomorrow?" she repeated. A hollow feeling spread through her stomach.

"There's a lot of snow out there, some of the drifts are small mountains. It's going to take a little time to move it."

"I see."

"Do you think you could manage on your own for a while today?"

"What? Oh, sure, I'll be fine."

"There's a lot I should see to. My foreman was in charge yesterday, but the men need all the help they can get." He was frowning. "Cattle need hay brought out to them. They haven't the sense to dig through to the grass. They'll just stand there and starve to death."

"I suppose the storm did a lot of damage."

"It's only minor from the reports I've gotten. We were hit worse a couple years ago."

"Reports?"

"One of my men came by yesterday afternoon to fill me in." Pouring more coffee in his cup, he reached for the cream. "You were asleep."

"Oh." Strange, she thought, there had been a ripple in their isolation and she had been totally unaware of it.

Lifting his cup, he studied her over the rim. "I don't like leaving you alone, especially with the phones out."

Her shoulders moved. "Don't worry about me, I'll be fine." Glancing up, she met his speculative gaze.

"I don't know how long I'll be gone."

"Jake, stop fussing. I feel fine."

He tilted his head to the side, his eyes still narrowed. "Stand up. I want to see how you feel for myself."

Before she realized his intent, his arms were around her, and his mouth was on hers. Her legs buckled.

His mouth was light, teasing, his teeth nibbling at the fullness of her bottom lip until she moaned from the exquisite agony. She gripped his shoulders as a dim light of control seeped into the darkness. Pulling away she shook her head in refusal.

"Now, Sam…" His voice was soft and persuasive, but the hands that descended to her hips were firm. "You wouldn't send a man out in the cold without something warm to remember, would you?"

Insistently, he brought her closer, molding her hips, exploring the soft roundness until she was pressed against him with exciting intimacy. His mouth closed over her protest, his tongue moving with slow devastation to tease hers until she felt the room spinning as wildly as it had the day before. Slowly, his hands ascended, his thumbs circling the side of her breasts while his mouth and tongue destroyed all resistance. She was straining against him, moving against him, reason forgotten. Her body heated urgently at his touch. Her sigh was a moan as his mouth descended to her throat. His lips tasted, lingered, traveled to new territories, the tip of his tongue moist and warm against her skin, erotic and devastating against her ear, until her mouth was desperate for its return to hers.

Her mouth was to go unsatisfied. He pulled her away with the same arrogance as he had pulled her to him. Dazed and limp, she could do no more than stare up at him as her body throbbed with a myriad of newly discovered desires.

"You're learning fast, Sam. That was enough to keep any man moving through a six-foot snowdrift."

Furious, and humiliated by her own response, she drew back her hand.

"Now, Sam." He caught her wrist easily, holding it aloft, ignoring her efforts to escape. "You're not strong enough yet for wrestling. Give yourself a couple more days." Turning her hand over, his lips brushed her palm, causing her struggles to cease abruptly. "I'm going to bring in Wolfgang to keep an eye on you. Take it easy today, and try to remember, you're not as tough as you'd like to think."

Ruffling her hair as though she were a child, he disappeared into the adjoing mudroom.

Later Samantha indulged in a hot, steaming shower, attempting to forget, as she soaped her skin, the feel of Jake's hands running over her. In the bedroom, she noticed her clothes piled neatly on the spoon-back chair. She slipped them on and wandered through the house in aimless exploration, the Saint Bernard lumbering at her heels.

The house abounded in small, delightful treasures, an oak rolltop desk, a wall box with Friesian carving, a Windsor cradle. With a small sigh, she wondered if the latter had rocked the baby Jake. Opening yet another door, she found Jake's library.

It smelled of leather and age, and her fingers ran over volume after volume. She pulled out a small volume of love poetry and opened the cover. Light, feminine handwriting adorned the top corner, and her mouth turned down at the inscription.

Darling Jake... To remind you.

Love, Lesley

Shutting the book with a snap, Samantha held it for one heat-blinded movement over the wastebasket, then, grinding her teeth, stuck it firmly back in place.

"It makes no difference to me," she informed Wolfgang. "She can give him a hundred books of poetry, she can give him a thousand books of poetry. It's her privilege."

She nudged the big dog with her toe. "Come on, Wolfgang, let's get moving."

She returned to the living room and built up the fire, which had burned down to a hissing pile of embers. She curled up beside it.

One hour slipped into two, two slipped into three. Surely, Jake should be home by now, she told the silent clock as the hands crept past six. It was getting dark. Rising, Samantha stared out into the diminishing light.

What if something had happened to Jake? Her throat

went dry, fear creeping along her skin. Nothing could happen to him, she told herself, running her hands over her arms to combat the sudden chill. He's strong and self-reliant.

But why am I so worried about him?

"Because," she said aloud, slowly, *"I love him. I've lost my mind and fallen in love with him."* Her hands lifted to cover her eyes as the weight of the knowledge crushed down on her. "Oh, how could I be so stupid? Of all the men in the world, I had to fall in love with this one."

A man, she remembered, *who had chosen Lesley Marshall to be his wife.* Is that why I've felt pulled in two? Is that why I responded to him when I've never responded to anyone else? Looking out into the darkness, she shuddered. I might as well admit that I don't care about anything except his getting home….

When finally the sound of the outside door slamming reached her ears, she ran into the mudroom and threw herself at an astonished, snow-covered Jake.

"Sam, what's going on?" He tried to pull her away from his cold, wet jacket.

"I was afraid something had happened to you." Her voice was muffled against his chest, her cheek oblivious to the frigid dampness.

"Nothing's happened, except I'm half-frozen and soaked to the skin." Firmly now, he took her shoulders, disentangling himself from her arms. "You're getting covered with snow." His grip was gentle. She stared up at him with huge, swimming eyes. "I'm sorry I was gone so long, but things were piled up, and it's slow working in a mess like this."

Embarrassed by her outburst, she backed away. "You must be exhausted. I'm sorry, it was stupid to go on like that. It must come from being alone in the house all day." As she babbled, she was backing purposefully toward the door. "You probably want a shower and something hot to drink. I—I've got dinner on."

"Something smells good," he commented. His eyes roamed over her flushed face, and a smile spread over his features.

"S-Spaghetti," she stammered and despised herself. "I'll go finish it up."

Retreating into the kitchen, Samantha kept her back toward him when he emerged and announced casually that he would have a hot shower before dinner. She mumbled a vague reply, pretending a complete involvement with her dinner preparation. Listening to his receding footsteps, she let out a long, pent-up breath.

"Oh, idiot that I am," she sighed, and pushed her hair from her face in an angry gesture. The type of behavior she had displayed in the mudroom would only lead to trouble. She took a solemn oath to keep her emotions on a tight leash as long as Jake Tanner was around.

Tomorrow, she remembered, with a mixture of relief

and disappointment, she would be back with her sister, and avoiding Jake would be a great deal easier. She had only to get through one more evening without making a fool of herself, and then she would sort out her thinking.

She was setting the table when Jake returned.

"If that tastes as good as it smells, I'll die a happy man." He lifted the lid on the pot and gave a sigh of approval. Grinning, he disappeared for a moment, then returned with a bottle of wine just as she was placing the pot on the table.

"A nice burgundy," he said, opening the bottle and setting out two glasses.

"Samantha, this is fantastic." He broke off eating long enough to give her a smile. "Where'd you learn to cook like this?"

"More of my mother's famous lessons."

"What else can you do?"

"Well, let's see. I do a rather superb swan dive, a very graceful arabesque, I can walk on my hands as easily as some walk on their feet, whip up an incredible quiche, and waltz without counting the time."

"I am suitably impressed. How did a woman of your talents spend the day?"

She sighed and grimaced and began to toy with her spaghetti. "Sleeping, mostly."

"Hmm." His cough did not quite cover his laugh.

After dinner, Samantha insisted on seeing to the

washing up herself. She wanted to avoid the intimacy of working side by side with him in the confines of the kitchen.

When the last signs of the man had vanished, she walked down the hall to the living room. Jake was adding another log to the low, shifting blaze. As she entered, he turned to smile at her. "Want some brandy?"

"No, no, thank you." She took a deep breath and willed her legs to carry her to the sofa.

"Not in training, are you?" He moved from the hearth to join her on the sofa.

Smiling, she shook her head. "The fire's wonderful." Grasping the first topic that came to mind, she riveted her eyes on the flames. "I always wanted one in my apartment. We had one at home, and Bree and I used to pop corn over it. We'd always burn it, and…"

The rest of her rush of words was lost as Jake placed his finger under her chin and turned her face to his. His face moved closer, and when she jerked back in defense, his brow lifted in amusement. He bent toward her again, and again she started.

"I'm only going to kiss you, Samantha." His grip tightened on her chin. Sliding from her chin, his hand framed her face as his lips moved over hers, soft as a whisper. In spite of herself, she relaxed against him. Her lips parted, inviting him to explore, begging him to take.

"Samantha." Her name was a sigh.

"Kiss me again," she whispered slowly as she lifted her mouth to his.

With a low groan, he brought his lips down on hers. She clung to him, her body throbbing with heat, her heart desperate against his, while a part of her looked on, aghast, as she answered his kiss.

Her mouth clung, avid and sweet, to his. Dormant passion exploded into life until there remained only man and woman and the need, older than time, to love and be loved, to possess and be possessed.

He opened her shirt and claimed her breast. The first desperation mellowed into slow exploration as his fingers trailed lightly, drugging her with a new, delirious languor. His mouth moved to sample the taste of her neck, his face buried in the spreading lushness of her hair. She pressed against the rippling muscles of his back as his mouth and tongue and hands raged fire over her.

She felt rather than heard him say her name against her mouth, sensed rather than felt the tension enter his body before her lips were set free. Dimly, she heard the strident insistence of bells ringing as she groped to bring heaven back within reach.

"Hell of a time for them to fix the phones." She opened her eyes, dark as sapphires, and stared without comprehension. "There's nothing I'd like more than to ignore it, Samantha, but it might be important." Her lids fluttered in confusion. She could feel the warm raggedness of his breath against her cheek. "The phones have been out for two days, and there's a lot of damage out there."

His body left hers and took the warmth with it. She struggled to sit up, pulling her shirt closed. The hands that worked at the buttons were unsteady and, rising on weak legs, she sought the warmth of the fire. Pushing at tumbled hair, she wrapped her arms around her body and closed her eyes.

What had she done, losing herself that way? Tossing away pride like damaged goods! What if the phone hadn't rung? Her arms closed tighter. Does love always hurt? Does it always make a fool of you?

"Samantha." She whirled at the sound of her name, her arms still tight in protection. "It's Sabrina." Dropping her eyes from his, she moved into the hall.

Samantha picked up the phone and swallowed. "Hi, Bree." Her voice sounded strangely high-pitched to her ears, and her fingers gripped hard on the receiver.

"Sam, how are you?"

Taking a deep breath, she answered. "Fine. How *you* are is more important."

"Stronger every minute. I'm so glad you had the sense to head for the Double T when the snow started. The thought of you getting caught in that blizzard makes my blood turn cold."

"That's me, a steady head in a crisis." Samantha nearly choked on a gurgle of hysterical laughter.

"Are you sure you're all right? You sound strange. You aren't coming down with a cold, are you?"

"It's probably the connection."

"I thought they'd never get the phones fixed! I guess I just couldn't really relax until I'd talked to you and made sure you were safe! Of course, I know Jake would take care of you, but it's not the same as hearing your voice. I won't keep you, Sam, we'll see you tomorrow. By the way, I think Shylock misses you."

"Probably indigestion. Tell him I'll see him tomorrow." After replacing the receiver, she stared at it for a full minute.

"Samantha." She whirled again at Jake's voice, finding him watching her from the living room archway.

"I…ah…Bree seems fine." She avoided his eyes and toyed with the ink pot by the phone. She took a step backward as Jake advanced. "She said she thought Shylock misses me. That's quite an accomplishment, he's so self-sufficient and aloof."

"Samantha. Come, sit down." He held out his hand for hers. She knew if he touched her, she would be lost.

"No, no, I think I'll go to bed, I'm still not quite myself." Her color had ebbed again, leaving pale cheeks and darkened eyes.

"Still running, Sam?" The anger in his tone was well controlled.

"No, no, I…"

"All right, then, for the moment we seem to be at a stalemate." He captured her chin before she could avoid the gesture. "But we haven't finished by a long shot. Do you understand?"

She nodded, then broke away to flee to the sanctuary of her room.

Chapter 8

As each day passed, Sabrina became more cheerful. Her features took on a roundness that gave her a contented appearance. And as Samantha watched her, she wondered if Sabrina possessed more strength than she had ever given her credit for. It was a sobering experience to see her usually dreamy sister grabbing life with determination and purpose while she herself couldn't seem to stop day-dreaming. Jake Tanner, she had to admit, was disturbing her days and sneaking into her dreams.

Stuffing her hands in her pockets, she scowled and continued her morning trudge to the mailbox. He meant to have her, did he? Well, Samantha Evans had no intention of being had by anyone, especially some annoying cowboy with too much charm for his own good... and fascinating green eyes, and that beautiful mouth.....

Now the days began to lengthen. The sun grew in strength. Spring began to drift over the basin, greening the grass and teasing the crocuses to push their heads from the earth.

Scurrying down the hall as the doorbell interrupted her latest project—painting the nursery—Samantha wiped a few streaks of canary yellow on her jeans and opened the door.

The woman in the doorway smiled, her almond-shaped dark eyes making a thorough survey. "Hello, you must be Samantha. I'm Lesley Marshall."

The introduction was unnecessary, for with an instinct she had been unaware of possessing, Samantha had recognized the woman instantly. "Please, come in. It's still rather cold, isn't it?" She smiled, refusing to acknowledge the effort it cost her, and shut the nippy May air outside.

"I'm so glad to meet you at last." The dark eyes swept down, then up Samantha briefly. "I've heard so much about you." There was light amusement in her voice.

"Oh, really? I'm afraid I can't say the same." Her smile was faintly apologetic. "But, of course, I've been rather busy."

"I would have been by sooner, but I wanted to wait until Sabrina was more up to company."

"Bree's feeling much better these days. I'm sure she'll be glad to see you. Let me take your coat." Samantha hung the soft fur in the hall closet. Turning back to her visitor, she needed all her willpower to keep the social smile in place. The oatmeal slacks accentuated Lesley's sleekness; the trim cerise blouse set off her delicately feathered ebony hair and the perfect ivory of her skin. Desperately, Samantha wished a miracle would transform her navy sweatshirt with its Wilson High School banner and her paint-streaked jeans into something smart and sophisticated. As usual, her hair was escaping from its pins. She resisted the urge to bring her hand up to it and jam them in tightly.

"Bree's in the living room," she announced, knowing the pale gray eyes had studied her and found her wanting. "I was just about to make some tea."

Sabrina appeared at that moment, and Samantha gladly relinquished the role of hostess and escaped to the kitchen.

"So, she's beautiful," she grumbled to an unconcerned Shylock as she set the kettle on to boil. "So, she's smooth and sophisticated and makes me feel like a pile of dirty laundry." Turning, she lowered her face to his and scowled. "Who cares?" Shylock scowled back and went to sleep. Her thoughts wandered on. "I don't imagine he's ever laughed at her and patted her head as though she were a slow-witted child," she muttered as she gathered up the tea tray.

"Sabrina, you look wonderful," Lesley commented sometime later, sipping from a dainty china cup. "I'm sure having your sister with you must be very good for you. I don't have to tell you how concerned everyone has been."

"No, and I appreciate it. Sam's made everything so easy. I didn't have anything to do but sit and heal." She shot her sister an affectionate glance. "I don't know what we would have done without her these past two months."

Lesley followed her gaze. "Jake was telling me that you're a gym teacher, Samantha," she purred, managing to make this sound faintly disgusting.

"Physical education instructor," Samantha corrected, slipping into a vague southern drawl.

"And you were in the Olympics, as well. I'm sure it must have been fascinating. You don't look the sturdy, athletic type." The shrug of her shoulders was elegant, as was the small gesture of her hand. "I suppose one can never tell." Samantha gritted her teeth against a biting retort and was vastly relieved when, glancing at a slender gold watch, Lesley suddenly rose from her chair. "I must run now, Sabrina, I have a dinner engagement." Turning to Samantha, she offered a small smile. "So happy to have met you. I'm sure we'll be seeing each other again soon."

She left amidst a swirl of fur and the drifting scent of roses. Samantha sat back in the cushioned chair, relaxing for the first time in more than an hour.

"Well, what did you think of Lesley?" Sabrina questioned, shifting into a more comfortable position on the sofa.

"Very sophisticated."

"Come on, Sam." Sabrina grinned, her hands folding across the mound of her belly. "This is Bree."

"I don't know why I should have to comment, since you seem to be reading me so well. But—" her mouth curved into a rueful smile "—I suppose she's a bit smooth for my taste, and I didn't much care for the way she looked down that aristocratic nose at me."

"Actually, you really don't appear very sturdy." The observation was made with wide-eyed innocence. Samantha grimaced, pulling pins from her hair with a sharp tug until a cascade of golden brown tumbled in confusion about her shoulders.

"She'd have gotten her own back on that one if you hadn't sent me that 'Don't make a scene' look."

"Oh, well, Lesley can be nice enough when it suits her. Her father spoils her dreadfully. Her mother died when she was barely into her teens, and he transferred all his attention to Lesley. An overabundance of clothes, the best horses, and, as she grew older, cars and European tours and so on. Whatever Lesley wants, Lesley gets."

"Poor thing." The sarcasm caused her to feel spiteful and unjust. She sighed. "I suppose too much is as bad as too little. It was nice of her to come and see how you were getting along."

Sabrina's laughter floated through the room. "Sam, darling, I've never known you to be so slow." At her sister's puzzled expression, she continued. "Lesley didn't come to see me, she came to get a look at you."

"At me?" Finely etched brows disappeared under a fringe of bangs. "What for? I wouldn't think a lowly gym teacher from Philadelphia would interest Lesley Marshall."

"Any teacher who caught Jake Tanner's attention the way you have would interest Lesley. He wouldn't have gone out of his way to show just anyone around the ranch, you know."

A light color rose in Samantha's cheeks. "I think Miss Marshall's mind was put to rest after she got a good look." Her hand moved expressively down her sweatshirt and jeans. "She'd hardly see any danger here."

"Don't underestimate yourself, Sam."

"No false modesty." Samantha's sigh came from nowhere. "If a man's attracted to silk and champagne, cotton and beer are no competition. I'm cotton and beer,

Bree," she murmured. Her voice trailed away with her thoughts. "I couldn't be anything else if I wanted to."

The following day, Samantha's continuing battle with her paints and brushes was interrupted by a more welcome visitor. Annie Holloway arrived at the ranch's kitchen door with a beaming smile and a chocolate cake.

"Hi." Samantha opened the door wide in welcome. "It's nice to see you again, and bearing gifts, too."

"Never like to come empty-handed," Annie announced, handing the thickly frosted cake to Samantha. "Dan always had a partiality for chocolate cake."

"Me, too." She eyed the cake hungrily. "He's not here right now, and I was just going to make some coffee. Do you suppose we could start without him?"

"Good idea." Setting herself comfortably in a chair, Annie waved a wide-palmed hand. "I reckon it wouldn't hurt for us to have a slice or two."

"Bree's taking a nap," Samantha explained as she put down the mugs of steaming coffee. "The doctor says she still has to lie down every day, but she's beginning to grumble about it a bit. Very quietly, of course."

"You're keeping an eye on her." Annie nodded and added two generous spoons of sugar to her coffee. "Dan says she's up to company now."

"Oh, yes, people have been dropping by now and

again. Ah…" Samantha added cream to her own cup. "Lesley Marshall was by yesterday."

"I wondered how long it would be before Lesley hauled herself over to get a look at you."

"You sound like Bree." Sipping her coffee, Samantha shook her head. "I don't know why Lesley Marshall would want to meet me."

"Easy. Lesley's a mite stingy with her possessions, and she'd like to group Jake among them. She hasn't figured out yet that Jake is his own man, and all her daddy's money can't buy him for her. When my Jake picks his woman, he'll decide the time and place. He's always been an independent rascal. He was barely twenty when he lost his folks, you know." Samantha lifted her eyes to the warm brown ones. "It wasn't an easy time for him, they'd been close. They were a pair, Jake's folks, always squabbling and loving. You're a bit like her when she was a young thing." Annie smiled, her head tilting with it as Samantha remained silent. "Nobody's going to ride roughshod over you, at least not for long. I saw that straight off. She was stubborn as a mule with two heads, and there's times, though it's been better than ten years, I still miss her."

"It must have been hard on Jake, losing his parents and having all the responsibility of the ranch when he was still so young," Samantha murmured.

"Seemed to change from boy to man overnight, just

out of college and still green. 'Course," she continued, "he'd been in the saddle since childhood and what he hadn't learned about ranching from his father and that fancy college, he learned from doing. He picked up the reins of that ranch with both hands. There's not a man who works for him wouldn't wrestle a long-horned bull if he asked them to. He can fool you with that easygoing way of his, but nobody gets the better of Jake Tanner. He runs the ranch like his life, and Lesley's going to find him a hard steer to rope and brand."

"Maybe it's more the other way around," Samantha suggested. Annie's response was prevented by the appearance at the kitchen door of the man in question.

He entered with the easy familiarity of an old friend.

"Howdy, ma'am." He broke the silence with a cocky smile, removed his battered Stetson and glanced at her attire. "Been painting?"

"Obvious, isn't it?" Samantha said sharply.

"Nice colors." He helped himself to a cup of coffee. "Are you going to part with another piece of that cake?"

"Jake Tanner!" Annie exclaimed in disgust. "You should be ashamed, gobbling Dan's cake when you've got a perfectly good one of your own at home."

"Somebody else's always tastes better, Annie." He slipped off his jacket, tossing it over a hook, and grinned boyishly. "He won't miss it, anyway. I brought you and the cake over, didn't I? You're not going to begrudge me one little piece?"

"Don't waste those eyes on me, you young devil." Annie attempted to sniff and look indignant. "I'm not one of your fillies."

Jake's appearance had successfully shattered Samantha's peace of mind. After a reasonable period of politeness, she excused herself to Annie and Jake and went back to her job in the nursery.

Samantha's artistic talent was decidedly impressionistic. The floor, protected by plastic, was splotched and splattered, but the walls were coming to life with a joy of brilliant colors. Of the four walls, two were yellow and two were white, and each was trimmed with its opposite's color. On the one wall that was unbroken by door or windows, she had begun the construction of a wide, arching rainbow, carefully merging blues into pinks into greens.

Time passed, and in the quiet concentration of her work she forgot her preoccupation with Jake. Sitting on the ladder's top step, she paused, brushing the back of her hand across her cheek absently as she viewed the results.

"That's a mighty pretty sight."

She jolted, dropping the brush with a clatter, and

would have fallen from the ladder had Jake's arms not gripped her waist and prevented the tumble.

"Sure spook easy," Jake commented, removing the dangerously sloshing paint bucket from her hand.

"You shouldn't come up behind a person like that," she complained. "I might have broken my neck." She wiped her hands on the legs of her jeans. "Where's Annie?"

"With your sister. She wanted to show Annie some things she's made for the baby." He set the bucket on the floor and straightened. "I didn't think they needed me."

"No, I'm sure they didn't. I need that paint, though, and the brush you made me drop." She glanced down, but his eyes remained on hers.

"I like the blue, especially that spot on your cheek," Jake said.

She rubbed at the offending area in annoyance. "If you'd just hand those things back to me, I could finish up."

"Green's nice, too," he said conversationally, and ran a finger over a long streak on her thigh. "Wilson High." His eyes lowered to the letters on her shirt. "Is that where you taught back east?"

"Yes." She shifted, uncomfortable that the name was prominent over her breasts. "Are you going to hand me my things?"

"What are your plans for tonight?" he countered easily, ignoring her request. She stared, completely thrown off balance by his unexpected question.

"I, ah, I have a lot of things to do." She searched her mind for something vital in her schedule.

"Things?" he prompted. His smile grew as his finger began to twist through a stray curl that had escaped its confines.

"Yes, things," she retorted, abandoning the attempt to elaborate. "I'm going to be very busy, and I really want to finish this room."

"I suppose I could let you get by with that, even though we both know better. Well." He smiled and shrugged. "Come down and kiss me goodbye, then. I've got to get back to work."

"I will not kiss you goodbye...." she began, the words trailing off as he gripped her waist. Her hands automatically went to his arms, and he plucked her from her perch.

He lowered her slowly, his eyes never leaving hers, and her mouth was roughly claimed before her feet could reach the floor. His hands slipped under her shirt to roam the smooth skin of her back, pressing her closer as her body betrayed her and dissolved against his. Slowly he explored her soft, firm breasts, subtly rounded hips, lean thighs.

Every time, every time, her mind murmured. Every time he kisses me, I go under deeper, and one day I'll never find my way back. His teeth moved to nip at her ear and neck, searching and finding new vulnerabilities before returning to ravage her mouth again. Without will, without choice, she rested in his arms, surrendering to forces she could never defeat.

He drew her away, breaking the intimacy, but his mouth returned to hers to linger briefly before he spoke. "About tonight, Samantha."

"What?" she murmured as his tongue traced the softness of her lips.

"I want to see you tonight."

Jerking herself back into reality, she pressed her hands against his chest, but did not manage to break away. "No, no, I'm busy. I told you."

"So you did," he acknowledged, and his eyes narrowed in speculation.

His words were cut off by the sound of Sabrina's laughter drifting down the hall. Samantha wiggled against Jake's hold. "Let me go, will you?"

"Why?" He was grinning now, enjoying the flood of color in her cheeks.

"Because…"

"Don't ever play poker, Sam." The warning was curt. "You'd lose your shirt."

"I…I…"

"Sabrina's due in September, right?"

The sudden question caused her to blink in confusion. "Well, yes, she…"

"That gives you a little breathing space, Samantha." He leaned down, and his kiss was hard and brief and to the point. "After that, don't expect to get away so lightly."

"I don't know what…"

"You know exactly what I mean," he said interrupting. "I told you I meant to have you, and I always get what I want."

Her eyes flashed. "If you think I'm going to let you make love to me just because you say so, then you…"

The suggestion she would have made died as his mouth took hers again. She went rigid telling herself she would not amuse him with a response this time. As she told herself she would not, her arms circled his neck. Her body became pliant, her lips parted with the hunger she had lived with all through the past month. As he took, she offered more; as he demanded, she gave. Her own mouth was mobile, her own hands seeking, until it seemed the month of fasting had never been.

"I want you, I don't have to tell you that, do I?"

She shook her head, trying to steady her breathing as his eyes alone caused her pulse to triple its rate.

"We'll settle this in September, unless you decide to come to me sooner." She began to shake her head again, but the fingers on the back of her neck halted the movement. "If you don't come to me, I'll wait until after the baby's born and you've got that much off your mind. I'm a patient man, Sam, but..." He stopped talking as Annie and Sabrina stepped into the room.

"Well." Annie shook her head at the two of them. "I can see he's been giving you a hard time." She turned to Sabrina with a half-exasperated shrug. "He's always been fresh as a new-laid egg. This is going to be a beautiful room, Sam." She glanced around at Samantha's handiwork, nodding in approval. "Let go of the little lady now, Jake, and take me back home, I've got dinner to fix."

"Sure. I've already said what I came to say." He released Samantha with a last, penetrating look and strode from the room, calling a goodbye over his shoulder.

"Fresh as a new-laid egg," Annie reiterated, and echoing his goodbye, followed him.

When the guests had departed, Samantha began to gather up paint buckets and brushes.

"Sam." Walking over, Sabrina placed a hand on her sister's arm. "I had no idea."

"No idea about what?" Bending, she banged the lid securely on rose pink.

"That you were in love with Jake." The truth she had avoided for so long was out in the open now: She had fallen hopelessly, irrevocably in love with Jake Tanner! Standing, Samantha searched in vain for words of denial.

"We know each other too well, Sam," Sabrina said before she could answer. "How bad is it?"

Samantha lifted her hands and let them fall to her sides. "Terminal."

"Well, what are you going to do about it?"

"Do about it?" Samantha repeated. "What can I do about it? After the baby comes, I'll go back east and try to forget about him."

"I've never known you to give up without a fight," Sabrina spoke sharply. At the unexpected tone, Samantha's brows rose.

"I'd fight for something that belonged to me, Bree, but I don't move in on someone else's territory."

"Jake's not engaged to Lesley Marshall. Nothing's official."

"I'm not interested in semantics." Samantha began to fiddle with the paint cans. "Jake wants an affair with me, but he'll marry Lesley Marshall."

"Are you afraid to compete with Lesley?" Bree asked.

Samantha whirled around, eyes flashing. "I'm not afraid of anyone," she stormed. Sabrina's lips curved in a smug smile. "Don't try your psychology on me, Sabrina! Lesley Marshall and I don't belong in the same league, but I'm not afraid of her. I *am* afraid of getting hurt, though." Her voice wavered and Sabrina's arm slipped over her shoulders.

"All right, Sam, we won't talk about it any more right

now. Leave those brushes, I'll wash them out. Go take a ride. You know the only way to clear your head is to go off by yourself."

"I'm beginning to think you know me too well." With a wry smile, Samantha wiped her hands on her jeans.

"I know you, all right, Samantha." Sabrina patted her cheek and urged her from the room. "I just haven't always known what to do about you."

Chapter 9

During the months since their first meeting, Samantha had grown to know Jake Tanner, and to realize that when he wanted something, he made certain he got it. And she knew he wanted her.

If, when she rode out on horseback, she kept closer to the ranch than had been her habit, she told herself it was not fear of encountering Jake that prompted the action, but simply her desire to spend more of her free time with Sabrina. Now Sabrina was growing cumbersome in her pregnancy, there was a grain of truth to this, so Samantha found it easy to accept the half-truth.

Every day she fell more under the spell of Wyoming. Bare branches were now fully cloaked in green. The cattle grew sleek and fat. The land was fully awakened and rich.

"I think you may just have twins in there, Bree," Samantha commented as the two sisters took advantage of golden sun and fragrant warmth. Sabrina glanced down to where Samantha sat cross-legged on the wide front porch. "Dr. Gates thinks not." She patted the mound in question. "He says there's only one, and I'm just getting fat. One of us should have twins, though."

"I'm afraid that's going to be up to you, Bree. I think I'll revive the tradition of old-maid schoolteachers."

Sabrina was sensitive to the wistfulness in the words. "Oh, no, you'll have to get married, Sam. You can't let all those lessons go to waste."

This brought the light laugh it had intended. "I'm perfectly serious. Remember what Madame Dubois always said, 'Von must reach for ze stars.'"

"Oh, yes, Madame Dubois." Samantha smiled at the memory of their former ballet teacher. "You know, of course, that accent was a phony. She came from New Jersey."

"I'm suitably crushed. She did think she had a genuine protégé in you."

"Yes, I was magnificent." Samantha sighed with exaggerated pride.

"Let's see a few of your famous leaps now, Sam."

"Not on your life!"

"Come on, cutoffs are as good as a tutu any day. I'd join you in a pas de deux, but it would actually be a pas de trois."

Samantha rose reluctantly from her seat on the porch. "All right, I don't mind showing off a little."

With quiet dignity, Sabrina began to hum a movement from *Swan Lake,* and Samantha lowered into a purposefully dramatic body sweep before exploding with an energetic series of grand jetés, stage leaps and cabrioles. She concluded the performance with a group of pirouettes, ended by dropping in a dizzy heap on the grass.

"That's what you get," she said, closing her eyes and shaking her head at the giddiness, "when you forget to spot focus."

"Is this show open to the public?"

Samantha glanced sharply toward the sound of the all-too-familiar voice.

"Dan!" Sabrina exclaimed. "I didn't expect you back so early."

"Ran into Lesley and Jake out on the north boundary," he explained, striding over and planting a firm kiss. "I thought you and Sam might like some company."

"Hello, Lesley, Jake." Sabrina included them both in her smile. "Have a seat, I'll bring out something cool."

Samantha had been sitting, praying without result for the ground to open up and swallow her. "I'll do it, Bree." She jumped at the opportunity to escape. "Don't get up."

"I'm up," Sabrina pointed out, disappearing inside before Samantha could argue.

"Do you teach ballet, as well, Samantha?" Lesley asked. She surveyed Samantha's outfit of semiragged cutoffs and T-shirt with dark, mocking eyes.

"No, no," Samantha muttered, feeling once more desperately at a disadvantage next to the slim woman in elegantly tailored breeches and silk shirt.

"I thought it was real nice," Dan commented, innocently turning the knife.

"Samantha's just full of surprises," Jake said.

Now that he had spoken again, Samantha was forced to give Jake a portion of her attention. He looked devastatingly male, the denim shirt rolled past his elbows to expose bronzed, corded arms, the low-slung belt in his jeans accentuating his leanness. She concentrated on a spot approximately six inches to the left of his face, in order to avoid the smile that had already mastered his face.

"Yeah," she returned. "I'm just a bushel of surprises."

"Anything you can't do, Sam?"

"A few things." She attempted a cool sophistication.

"You're so energetic," Lesley commented, slipping her hand through Jake's arm. "You must be horribly strong and full of bulging muscles."

For one heady moment, Samantha considered flight.

She was opening her mouth to make her excuses when Dan effectively cut off all hope.

"Sit down, Sam, I want to talk over a little idea with you and Sabrina." Sinking down on the porch steps, Samantha avoided any glimpse of Jake's face. "Do you think Sabrina's up to a little party?" Samantha looked up at Dan's question and attempted to marshal her thoughts.

"A party?" she repeated, drawing her brows together in concentration. "I suppose so. Dr. Gates says she's doing very well, but you could always ask to be sure. Did you want to go to a party?"

"I was thinking of having one," he corrected with a grin. "There're these twins I know who have this birthday in a couple of weeks." Bending over, he tugged at Samantha's loosened locks. "Seems like a good excuse for having a party."

"Oh, our birthday." Samantha's response was vague. The impending anniversary had slipped her mind.

"Did I hear someone say party?" Sabrina emerged through the screen door with a tray of iced tea.

Samantha sipped the cool, sweet tea her sister handed her and watched Sabrina's face light up with anticipation.

"A birthday party, Sam." She turned to her sister, eyes shining with excitement. "When's the last time we had one?"

"When we were twelve and Billy Darcy got sick all

over Mom's new carpet." Leaning back against the porch rail, Samantha unwittingly lifted her face to Jake's.

"Well, then, it's high time for another," Dan said. "What do you say, Sam? I know it means extra work for you."

"Huh." Tearing her eyes from Jake's smile, she endeavored to pick up the threads of the conversation. "What? Oh, no, it's no trouble. It'll be fun." Concentrating on Dan's face, she blocked out the sight of Lesley lounging intimately against Jake. "How many people did you have in mind?"

"Just neighbors and friends." He reached up to rub his chin. "About thirty or forty, I'd say. What do you think, Lesley?"

The full mouth pouted a moment in thought. "If you want to keep it small, Dan," she agreed after a short deliberation. Samantha's eyes grew wide. These people definitely had a different idea of small than she did.

"Oh, Lesley, come take a look at this punch bowl I've got, see if you think we should use it." Rising, Sabrina took Dan's hand. "Come, get it down for me, Dan." Throwing her sister an innocent smile, Sabrina disappeared inside and left her alone with Jake.

"How's the painting coming?" Jake stretched both arms over the back of the swing.

"Painting? Oh, the nursery. It's finished."

That, she recalled with a frown, was just one of many

times he had come upon her in a ridiculous situation. Sleeping on stumps, covered with paint, and now leaping across the lawn like some crazed ballerina. Samantha, she told herself, you have class.

"What do you want for your birthday, Sam?" He prodded her with the toe of his boot and earned a scowl.

Blowing a wisp of hair from her eyes, she moved her shoulders. "Fur, diamonds."

"No, you're not the type for furs." Taking out a cigar, he lit it and blew a lazy stream of smoke. "You'd be thinking about all the little minks that were scalped to make it. And diamonds wouldn't suit you."

"I suppose I'm more the quartz type." She rose, irritated.

"No, I was thinking more of sapphires." He caught her wrist. "To go with your eyes, or maybe rubies to go with your temper."

"I'll be sure to put both on my list. Now, if you'll excuse me." She glanced at her captured hand, then back at him. "I've got to go feed my cat." She gestured to where Shylock lay on the far side of the porch.

"He doesn't look very hungry."

"He's pretending to be dead," she muttered. "Shylock, let's eat."

Amber eyes opened and blinked. Then, to her pleasure, Shylock rose and padded toward her. However, upon reaching his mistress, he gave her a disinterested stare, leaped into Jake's lap and began to purr with wicked enjoyment.

"No, ma'am." Jake glanced down at the contented cat. "He doesn't look hungry at all."

With a final glare, Samantha turned, stalked to the door and slammed the screen smartly behind her.

The sun shone warm and friendly on the morning of the twins' birthday. Samantha carried a large parcel into the kitchen. Dumping her burden on the table where her sister was enjoying a cup of tea, she nudged Shylock away with her foot. She had not yet decided to forgive him for his treacherous advances to Jake.

"This just came, it's from the folks."

"Open it, Sam." Sabrina poked an experimental finger at the package. "Dan refuses to give me my present yet, and I've searched everywhere I can think of."

"I bet it's six books on child rearing for you, and six on etiquette for me."

"A present's a present," Sabrina stated, and tore the mailing paper from the box.

"Here's a note." After breaking the seal, Samantha produced a sheet of paper and read aloud.

"To Samantha and Sabrina:

A very happy birthday and our love to you both. Sabrina, I do hope you are taking good care of yourself. As you know, proper diet and rest are essential. I'm sure having Samantha with you during the last weeks of your confinement is a great comfort. Samantha, do look after your sister and see that she takes the necessary precautions. However, I hope you're not overlooking your own social life. As your mother, it is my duty to remind you that you are long past the marriageable age. Your father and I are looking forward to seeing you and our first grandchild in a few weeks. We will be in Wyoming the first part of September, if Dad's schedule holds true.

With love,
Mom and Dad

"There's a postscript for you, Bree.

"Sabrina, doesn't Daniel know any suitable men for your sister?"

With a sigh, Samantha folded the letter and dropped it on the table. "She never changes." Dipping into the box, Samantha plucked out a smaller one with Sabrina's name on it and handed it to her. "Marriageable age," she muttered, and shook her head.

"Did you peek in here before?" Sabrina accused, dumping out volumes on infant and child care.

"No," Samantha denied with a superior smirk. "I just know Mom." Drawing out her own package, she ripped off the concealing paper. "Good grief." She let the box drop to the table and held up a brief black lace negligee.

"I thought I knew Mom." Both sisters burst into laughter. "She must be getting desperate," Samantha concluded, holding the negligee in front of her.

"Now that's a pretty thing," Jake observed as he and Dan entered the kitchen. "But it's even prettier with something in it." Samantha bundled the garment behind her and flushed scarlet.

"Presents from Mom and Dad," Sabrina explained, indicating her stack of books.

"Very suitable." Dan grinned as he glanced through the volumes.

"Doesn't look like Sam feels the same about hers." Jake smiled. Samantha felt her already alarming color deepen. "Let's see it again."

"Don't tease, Jake." Sabrina turned to her husband. "Mom says they'll be here the first part of September."

"I'll put this stuff away." Samantha tossed the gown into the box and began to bury it under books.

"Leave that till later." Dan took her hand and pulled her away. "I need you outside for a minute."

She went willingly. Escape was escape. Imagining it had something to do with Sabrina's gift, she was surprised when Dan slowed his pace and allowed his wife to join them in their walk toward the ranch buildings. He kept her involved in a running conversation about the party until they came to a halt at the paddock fence.

"Happy birthday, Sam." Sabrina kissed her sister's cheek as Samantha's eyes focused on the golden Arabian mare.

"Oh." She could manage no more.

"She's from a good line," Dan informed her, his arm slipping around Sabrina's shoulders. "She's out of the Double T stock, no finer in Wyoming."

"But I…" Words faltered, and she swallowed and tried to begin again.

"What do you give someone who packs their own life away for six months without hesitation, without asking for anything in return?" Dan's free arm slipped around Samantha and pulled her to his side.

"We figured if you insisted on going back east, we'd always have a hold on you. You'd have to come visit us to ride your mare."

"I don't know how to thank you."

"Then don't," Dan ordered. "Go try her out."

"Now?"

"Now's as good a time as any." Not needing a second urging, Samantha was over the fence, stroking the mare and murmuring.

"We may convince her to stay yet," Dan commented,

watching as she slipped into the saddle and took the mare around the paddock. "I could have a word with Jake."

Sabrina shook her head. "No, Sam would be furious if we interfered. She'd bolt back to Philadelphia before we could take a breath. For now, we'd better keep out of it." She lowered her voice as a beaming Samantha trotted around to them and slipped off the little mare.

"She's a real beauty," she sighed. "I don't know how I can ever bear to leave her..."

Sabrina's eyes met her husband's in silent satisfaction. Perhaps it will not be necessary, their unspoken message said.

"Come, little sister," Dan said. "If you can tear yourself away from your new friend, I sure could use a cup of coffee now."

As the trio trooped back toward the house, Jake swung through the back door. "Delivery just came. It's in the living room."

"Oh," Dan murmured, looking entirely too innocent. "Come on, Sabrina, we'd best see what it is."

"Is it the piano?" Sam asked Jake, as Dan and Sabrina disappeared inside.

"Looked like one to me. I guess that's another present that'll go over big. Walk to the truck with me," Jake commanded, and captured her hand before she could protest.

"Really, Jake, I have a million things to do." She trotted to keep pace with his loose, lanky stride.

"I know, you're indispensable." Stopping by his truck, he reached in the cab and produced a package. "But this seems to be the time for gift giving. I thought I'd let you have your present now."

"You didn't have to get me anything."

"Samantha." His drawl was lazy, but his eyes narrowed in annoyance. "I never do anything unless I want to." Taking her hand from behind her back, he placed the box in it. "Open it."

Lifting the statue from its tissue bedding, she examined it in silent amazement. The alabaster was smooth and cool in her hands, carved into the shape of a horse and rider in full gallop. The artist had captured the fluid grace, the freedom of motion. She ran a hesitant finger over the delicate features.

"It looks like me." She lifted her eyes to Jake's.

"And so it should," he answered easily. "It's supposed to be you."

"But how?" She shook her head, torn between pleasure and confusion.

"A man I know does this kind of thing. I described you to him."

For the second time that day, Samantha found herself at a loss for words.

"Why?" The question was out before she could swallow it.

Slowly, a smile drifted across his face. He pushed

back his hat. "Because it suits you better than furs and diamonds."

She braced herself to meet his eyes again. "Thank you."

He nodded, his face solemn. He took the box from her hands and placed it on the hood of the truck. "I think a birthday kiss is traditional."

Swallowing, she took an instinctive step in retreat, but he gripped her arms and held her still. She offered her cheek, and his laughter broke out, full and rich on the summer air. "Sam," he turned her face to his, and his eyes sparkled with humor, "you're incredible."

His lips met hers. His hands moved from her arms to her hips, drawing her firmly against the hard lines of his body. She submitted to the embrace, as long as his arms held her, as long as they were mouth to mouth, as long as the heat from his body infused hers, he owned her, and she could not run.

Finally he drew her away, bringing his hands to her shoulders while hers rested on his chest for support.

"Happy birthday, Sam."

"Thank you," she managed, still breathless from the impact of his embrace.

He lifted the box from the hood of the truck and placed it in her hands before sliding into the cab. "See you tonight." With a salute, he started the engine. The truck moved down the road, leaving her staring after it.

Chapter 10

Party sounds filled the house. Laughter and voices and music mingled and drifted through open windows to float on the night air.

On this evening, the twins were dramatically different in their appearance. Sabrina's pale blue gown floated around her, cunningly disguising her pregnancy. Her hair was a glinting halo around rose-tinted cheeks. Samantha's black-striped satin clung to her body, her halter neckline plunging deep to a wide, gathered waist. Her hair was free and thick around her shoulders.

As she moved and mingled with the crowd, Samantha searched for a tall, lanky form, noting with increasing despair and a gnawing jealousy that a slim, dark woman had also as yet failed to put in an appearance.

Cornered by an enthusiastic young cowboy, Samantha was feeling her attention begin to wander from a detailed account of horse breeding when her eyes met dark jade across the room.

He was standing with two men she did not recognize, and Lesley Marshall stood beside him. She was elegant in an oyster-white gown. Her fine-boned ivory hand was placed from time to time on Jake's arm, as if, Samantha thought grimly, she were flaunting her possession.

Furious with the sudden feeling of inadequacy, Samantha turned to her companion with a dazzling smile. He stammered over his lecture, his words grinding to a halt. She tucked her arm in his and used her eyes without shame.

"Howdy, Tim." Jake appeared from nowhere and placed a hand on the young man's shoulder. "I'm going to steal this little lady for a moment." He paused and smiled easily into Samantha's mutinous face. "There's a couple of people she hasn't met yet."

Without waiting for an assent, he had her unwilling hand in his, propelling her through the crowd. "Tim won't be the same for weeks," he whispered close to her ear. "A woman could get run out of town for using her eyes that way on susceptible young boys," he warned, pulling her through the sea of people.

"You don't have to drag me."

"I know a stubborn mule when I see one," he countered, without bothering to lower his voice. Her furious retort was swallowed as Jake presented her to the two men who flanked Lesley.

"Sam, I'd like you to meet George Marshall, Lesley's father." Samantha's hand was enveloped in a hearty grip. "And Jim Bailey," he continued, nodding toward the second man.

"Jim only works with cattle on paper. He's a lawyer."

"My, this is a mighty pretty girl!" George Marshall boomed. Giving Jake a sly wink, he patted his daughter's shoulder.

"You always manage to rope in the pick of the herd, don't you, Jake?"

Jake slipped his hands easily into his pockets. "I do my best. But then, roping them's one thing, getting them's another."

"Well, now, little lady," George's genial voice continued, "Les tells me you're a gym teacher."

"That's right, Mr. Marshall."

"Now, you just call me George," he instructed, squeezing her shoulder with a genial affection. "Tell me, why isn't a pretty little thing like you married and settled down instead of running around some gymnasium?"

Jake was grinning with obvious enjoyment. Samantha tossed her hair behind her back, but before she could think of a suitable answer, George's laughter boomed through the room.

"I like this girl," George announced to the group. "Looks like she has spirit. You come over to our ranch any time, little lady, any time at all."

In spite of herself, Samantha found herself liking his expansive hospitality. "If you'll excuse me now, I've got…got to get a tray out of the kitchen." She gave the group an all-encompassing smile and melted into the crowd.

In the kitchen, she pulled a tray from the refrigerator to give her excuse credibility and was glad she had when Jake followed her in a moment later.

"George is a good man. He has the right ideas when it comes to women." Smiling knowingly at her, he leaned against the door watching her every move.

"That's your opinion," she returned tartly, bustling around the kitchen in an attempt to ignore him.

"Sit down a minute, Sam."

She glanced up, immediately wary, then lifted the tray as a defense. "No, I've got to get back."

"Please."

Despite herself, she lowered the tray to the table and herself into a chair.

"I ran into Jack Abbot, the school principal, the other day."

"Oh?"

"He told me the girls' phys ed instructor isn't coming

back next term." Leaning back in his chair, Jake studied her. "He's going to offer you the job."

"Oh," she repeated before she could stop herself.

"He wants you pretty bad. He really needs someone this fall. I told him I'd be seeing you, and that I'd mention it. He's going to call you officially, of course."

How simple, Samantha thought.

How simple it would all be if I didn't love this man. I could stay where I want to stay, work where I want to work. But now, I've got to refuse, I've got to go away.

"I appreciate your telling me, and I appreciate Mr. Abbot wanting me, but…"

"Don't appreciate it, Samantha, think about it."

"You don't know what you're asking me to do."

He rose to pace the room, his hands seeking the depths of his pockets. "I'm just asking you to think about it. You like it here. You've made friends. You like being near your sister. You'd still have the satisfaction of doing what you feel you're suited for. Is it so much to ask that you consider it?"

"Yes, it's quite a lot. Jake, I don't want to argue with you. There are things I have to do, the same way there are things you have to do."

"All right." He nodded, then repeated slowly, as if coming to a decision. "All right, there *are* things I have to do." Moving over, he captured her chin between his thumb and fingers.

His arms slipped around her waist to bring her close, his mouth lowering to brush her cheeks and the corners of her lips. "Come home with me now, Samantha. We can be alone there." His voice had become low and seductive, as his fingers trailed over the bare skin of her back.

"No, please don't." She turned her face away.

"I want to make love to you. I want to feel your skin under my hands, all of you. I want to hear you sigh when I touch you."

"Jake, please." She dropped her head to his chest. "It's unfair, here, like this."

"Then come home with me."

"No, I can't." She shook her head without raising it. "I won't."

"All right, Samantha." He framed her face and brought it up to his. "I said I'd give you until the baby was born. We'll stick to that. We won't argue tonight. Let's call it a truce for your birthday. Agreed?"

He kissed her once, briefly, and turned to lift the tray. "Then we'll both do what we have to do when the time comes."

Leaving her confused, Jake moved through the doorway.

Rejoining the festivities, Samantha moved from group to group, but her thoughts were only about Jake. Why was he so interested in her career choices? Why did he want her to take the job in Wyoming? *Maybe he cared for her.* For a brief moment, she allowed hope to shimmer. Her eyes swept the room to find him. Finally she spotted him. He was dancing with Lesley. The shining cap of her raven hair brushing his cheek, the ivory of her hand entwined with the bronze of his. Samantha winced as he threw back his head and laughed at something Lesley had said for his ears alone.

Care for me? her mind repeated in a scathing whisper. Grow up, Samantha, *caring* and *wanting* don't always mean the same thing. In a few weeks, she comforted herself, she would no longer be subjected to this constant pain. When the ache had eased, she could visit Bree again. Jake would probably be too busy with his wife to spare time for visits to the Lazy L. Samantha felt her heart contract with pain.

She turned away and bumped solidly into Jim Bailey.

"Sorry." He took her shoulders to steady her. "I didn't see you."

"It's all right," she returned, offering a smile. "Besides, I think I ran into you."

"Well, no harm done either way." She watched his eyes slide past her and focus on Jake and Lesley. "They look nice together, don't they?"

Embarrassed that he must have seen her staring at them, Samantha nodded, and looked down at her empty glass. "Come on, we better get you a refill."

A few moments later, they joined the group around the piano as Sabrina played.

"So, you're a lawyer." She smiled at Jim. "I don't think I've ever met a lawyer before."

Jim returned her smile. "And you're a gymnast."

"No, actually, I'm a gym teacher now."

He lifted his glass in a toast and drank. "I remember you. I've always been an avid fan of the Olympics. I thought you were fabulous."

"Well, that's nice to hear after a decade."

He tapped his glass to hers. "Well, Olympic star, would you like to dance?"

"I'd love to."

Samantha enjoyed Jim Bailey's easy conversation. She learned during their two dances that he was interested in getting into politics. His dark good looks and ready wit would certainly be assets, she decided.

"Sam." Sabrina motioned to her as they moved back toward the piano. "It's your turn. Union rules."

"Okay," Samantha agreed, sliding onto the bench.

She played with practiced ease, moving from one song to the next. Time slipped through her fingers. As in a dream, she was aware of the voices behind her, the faint, drifting breeze of Wyoming through the open windows.

Someone sat beside her. Recognizing the lean fingers that lifted to turn the page of her sheet music, she faltered and missed a note.

"You and Jim seem to have hit it off." Samantha heard the click of his lighter over the sounds of the party.

"He's a very nice man. Have you known him long?"

"Oh, only since we were about eight and I gave him a black eye and he loosened a few of my teeth."

"Sounds like a loving friendship."

Jake again turned the page before she could do so herself. "Well, after that we sort of stuck together." He pushed the curtain of hair behind her shoulder, and Samantha struggled not to break the thread of the melody. "The two of you seemed to have a lot to talk about."

"He's very charming, and we have a few mutual interests."

"Hmm." Jake shifted slightly in his seat. His thigh brushed hers, and her fingers responded by hitting three wrong notes.

"You play very well."

Was he being ironic? She turned to look at him, but found no mockery in his jade eyes.

"Pleasantly," she corrected. "I get the general melody, but the details are a bit fuzzy."

"I've noticed that you have a tendency to shrug off your own capabilities. Are you aware of that?"

"That's not true. I just know what I do well and what I don't."

"You're a very tough critic, and you're inclined to underestimate."

"Honesty," she countered, finishing the song with a flourish. "I am a totally honest person."

"Are you, Samantha?" he said softly. "That's what I plan to find out."

Chapter 11

The days grew hot and sultry. The skies were improbably blue, rarely softened by clouds.

Long hours in the sun had deepened the honey of Samantha's skin, teasing out the gold in her hair. As long as she was occupied, she had no time for soul searching. She could enjoy the long summer days without thinking of the fall. As Sabrina wilted like a thirsty rose in the searing heat, Samantha confined her own activities to the early-morning hours. In the long, hot haze of the afternoon, Sabrina moved slowly through the house, her body clumsy. Samantha did not dare leave her. The baby was due in two weeks, and Samantha wanted to remain within calling distance of her sister as much as possible.

One particularly humid afternoon, the two women

were sitting idly in the living room. Sabrina got up heavily from her chair to look out the window. "Sam," she said, "before Dan left for town, he said a storm was brewing. From the looks of the sky, I'd say he was right."

Before Samantha could answer, there was a sudden flash of lightning. A blast of thunder rolled in on the wind, and the rain began to fall in sheets.

"It's coming down fast," Samantha agreed. "It should cool us off a bit." She looked sympathetically at her sister's bulky form.

The storm built in power. Jagged flashes of lightning illuminated the room and an angry wind hurled the rain against the windows. The two women watched in fascination as the storm exhausted itself. Soon rain dripped tentatively from the eaves and the thunder was a mere grumble in the distance.

The sun struggled to reappear, breaking through the gloom with a hazy promise of light.

"That," Sabrina commented with an enormous sigh, "was a mean one."

Samantha turned from her place by the window and again slumped into a chair. "Remember when you used to hide in the closet whenever we had a thunderstorm?"

"All too well." She gave her sister a pained smile. "And you used to stand on the porch, loving every minute of it, until Mom dragged you in, soaking wet. On that note from the past," Sabrina announced, "I'm going to take a nap, Sam." She turned at the doorway and studied the woman slouched in the chair, bare legs and feet stretched out in unconscious grace. "I love you."

With a rather puzzled smile, Samantha watched her walk away.

Wandering out to the porch, Samantha drank in the rain-fresh air. Everything sparkled. Raindrops clung like jewels to blossoms and leaves. Though the flowers had drooped with the weight of the storm, their colors had been washed into brilliant life. A bird, flying by on a shaft of light, trilled above her. She could hear the steady dripping of the rain off the eaves above the whisper of the dying wind. Satisfied, she curled up on a porch rocker and instantly fell asleep.

She had no idea how long she had drifted in the soft twilight world when, with reluctance, she woke at the touch of a hand on her shoulder. She looked up drowsily and yawned. "Oh, Bree, I must have fallen asleep. It's so wonderfully cool out here."

"Sam, I think the baby's decided to put in an unscheduled appearance."

"Huh? Oh!" Springing to her feet, she was instantly awake. "Right now? Dan's not here, and it's not time yet. Sit down, sit," she ordered, running agitated fingers through her hair.

"I think the first thing to do is to calm down," Sabrina suggested.

"You're right. I'm not going to fall apart, it was just a shock. I wasn't expecting this for another week or two."

"Neither was I." Sabrina's smile was half amused, half apologetic.

"All right, how long have you been having contractions, and how far apart are they?"

"Only for an hour or so."

"That should give us plenty of time." Samantha patted Sabrina's hand.

"But they've been getting awfully strong, and..." Breaking off, she closed her eyes and began to breathe in a deep, methodical rhythm. "And," she continued, after a final long breath, "awfully close together."

"How close?" Samantha asked, feeling new tension at the base of her neck.

"Ten minutes."

"Ten minutes," Samantha repeated. "I'd better get you to the hospital. I'll bring the car around. Stay put," she told her sister, and raced to the garage.

Upon reaching Sabrina's compact and sliding behind the wheel, Samantha was horrified to find the engine unresponsive to the turn of the key. The little car sputtered, emitted an apologetic groan and died.

"You can't," she insisted, and smacked the steering wheel. "We just had you fixed."

There was no use wasting more time trying to figure out what was wrong with the car. It was clearly not going to start, and Samantha hadn't the first idea of where to look for the problem.

Rushing back to the house, she picked up the phone in the kitchen. At least she could call Dr. Gates. A groan of despair was wrenched from her when she heard the dead silence on the line. Oh, no, the storm must have knocked out the phones!

Forcing herself to appear calm, she returned to the living room where Sabrina was waiting for her.

Reaching her sister again, Samantha knelt down so their eyes were level. "Bree, the car won't start. All the trucks and jeeps are out with the men, and the storm must have knocked down the phone lines."

"Looks like we've got a few problems." Sabrina took a deep breath.

"It's going to be all right." Samantha took her hand in reassurance. "I'll help you get into bed, and then I'll take a horse and ride toward the Double T. If I don't see any of the men on the way, I'll get a truck there and bring it back. Most of them have radios, and I can call ahead to the doctor."

"Sam, it's going to take time for you to get there, and to get back. I don't think I'll make it in time to get to the hospital after that. You'll have to have the doctor come here."

"Here?" Samantha repeated. Her throat closed on the word. Sabrina nodded. "All right. Don't worry, I won't be long. I'll be back as soon as I can." Samantha raced off to the stables, and without wasting the time for a saddle, she leaped on her mare's back.

The familiar landscape was a blur, as she urged more speed out of the powerful horse. The sound of her own breath was masked by the sound of thudding hooves. Every minute she took was a minute longer that Sabrina was alone. She crouched lower on the horse and dug in bare heels.

When Samantha spotted the men on horseback, she spurred the Arabian over the fence in a fluid leap. As her hooves touched earth, she met the horse's sides again. They streaked across the field, scattering annoyed cattle.

When she reached the group, she reined in sharply. The mare reared, nearly unseating her. Her breath came in gasps as she struggled to keep her seat.

"What are you trying to do, break your neck?" Furiously Jake snatched the reins from her hands. "If you're stupid enough not to care about yourself, think of your horse. What do you mean riding like a fool and jumping fences? Where's your saddle? Have you lost your mind?"

"Bree," she managed at last between giant gulps of air. "The baby's coming, and the phone's out. The car wouldn't start, and there's nobody around. Dan's in town. Bree says there's no time to get her to the hospital now, and I have to call the doctor." She felt tears of fear burning at her eyes and bit her lip.

"All right, take it easy." Twisting in the saddle, Jake called out to one of his men. "Get back to the ranch and get hold of Dr. Gates on the CB radio. Tell him Sabrina Lomax is in labor and to get to the Lazy L in a hurry." Turning back, he handed the reins to Samantha. "Let's go."

"Are you coming back with me?" Flooded with relief, she gripped tight on the leather.

"What do you think?"

Together, they sprang forward in a gallop.

Speed and thundering hooves were all Samantha ever remembered of the ride back. There was no time for conversation, no time for thought. She was sliding to the ground before she came to a full stop and Jake once more secured her reins.

"Keep your head, Samantha," he ordered, watching her bound up the steps and through the front door.

The house was silent. Her stomach tightened as she rushed to the master bedroom. Sabrina sat up in bed, propped by a mound of pillows and greeted her with a cheerful smile.

"That was quick, did you fly?"

"Just about," Samantha returned, faint with relief.

"We've sent for the doctor. Everything's under control." She sat down on the bed, taking her sister's hand. "How are you doing?"

"Not too bad." Her hand closed over Samantha's,

as much to reassure as seeking reassurance. "I'm glad you're back. Here comes another one."

Samantha looked on with unfamiliar helplessness. Her fingers grew tighter over her twin's, as if to steal some of her pain.

"We can thank Mom for that book on natural childbirth." Sabrina gave a long, shaky sigh and relaxed against the pillows.

"Don't look so worried, I'm doing fine. Oh, hello, Jake." Glancing at the doorway, Sabrina greeted him with friendly cheerfulness. "I didn't know you were here. Come in. It's not contagious."

He advanced into the room, looking tall, male and out of place. His hands retreated to his pockets. "How're you doing?"

"Oh, well, you've seen a cow in labor before, I don't imagine there's much difference." The small hand tightened on Samantha's. "Here we go again."

Samantha lifted the hand to her cheek. *Where was the doctor?* Sabrina should be in the hospital, surrounded by experts.

"This baby's in a big hurry," Sabrina announced with a small moan. "I'm sorry, Sam, it's not going to wait much longer."

I don't know anything about childbirth, Samantha thought in a moment of terror. *What am I going to do? What do I do first?*

Standing, she turned to Jake. "Go sterilize some towels, lots of them, and some string and scissors."

"All right." His hand rested on her shoulder a moment. "If you need me, give a call."

Nodding, she moved into the adjoining bath and scrubbed her hands and arms until they hurt.

"You're going to be fine," she stated as she reentered the bedroom.

"Yes, I am." Sabrina lay back on the pillows and closed her eyes. "I'm going to have this baby, Sam, and I'm going to do a good job of it. You can't do this for me, I have to be strong."

"You are strong." Brushing away the hair from Sabrina's cheeks, she realized with a sudden jolt that it was true. "You're stronger than I ever knew."

Her calm had returned, and she took over the duties of midwifery with an instinct as old as time. She wiped moisture from her sister's face, working with her, breathing with her, uttering soothing encouragements. Sabrina had not gone through all she had to lose now, and Samantha would not allow anything to go wrong.

"All right." Wiping beads of sweat from her own brow, Samantha straightened. "I think she's going to come this time, it's almost over. You have to help."

Sabrina nodded, her face pale and composed. Her hair had darkened with dampness. She shuddered and moaned with the final pang of childbirth. A thin, shrill cry pierced the stillness of the room. Samantha held new life in her hands.

"Oh, Bree." She stared down at the tiny, wriggling form.

Dan burst into the room two steps ahead of the doctor.

Suddenly, it was all so simple, Dan standing by Sabrina's side, his large hand clutching hers, the small, fresh form swaddled in the curve of her mother's arms.

"Only one." Sabrina sighed, her eyes luminous. "You'll have to handle the twins, Sam. One at a time is enough for me."

Sometime later, Samantha shut the door behind her and walked toward the kitchen. Jake looked up at her approach.

"A girl." She lowered herself into a chair. "The doctor says she's perfect, almost seven pounds. Bree's fine." She pushed at her tumbled hair and ran a hand across her brow. "I want to thank you."

"I didn't do anything."

"You were here." She lifted her eyes, and they were young and vulnerable. "I needed to know you were here."

"Samantha." He smiled and shook his head. "You sure find a man's weak points. I'll get you a drink."

He was back in a moment with a decanter of brandy and two snifters. Sitting across from her, he filled both generously. "It's not champagne, but it'll do." Lifting his glass, he touched it solemnly to hers. "To mother and child, and to Samantha Evans." He paused, his smile fading into seriousness. "She's one hell of a woman."

Samantha folded her arms on the table, laid her head on them and burst into tears.

"I was so scared." She found her voice muffled against his shoulder as he brought her against him. "I've never been so scared. I thought I would lose them both."

He tilted her chin as one hand rubbed the small of her back. "You're a survivor, Sam, and too stubborn to let anything happen to Sabrina or the baby."

Her forehead dropped to his chest as she struggled to stem the flow of tears.

"I always seem to fall apart in front of you."

"Don't much care for that, do you?" She felt his lips descend to her hair and allowed herself the joy of being cradled in his arms. "Most people don't look for perfection, Sam, they find it boring. You," he said, framing her face with his hands, "are never boring."

She sniffed and smiled. "I guess that was a compliment." Giving in to impulse, she leaned over and rested her cheek against his. "I don't think you're boring, either."

"Well." He stroked her hair a moment, and his voice was curiously soft. "That's about the nicest thing you've ever said to me.

"Now drink some of that." He pushed her gently away and handed her the brandy.

Obeying, she allowed the warm strength to seep into her veins and relaxed with a sigh. "Bree certainly came through this better than I did." She drank again. Jake straddled a chair, leaning his arms on the back. "When I left her, she was lying there with the baby, looking like she'd just finished having a picnic. Dan looked like he was about to keel over, I was ready for someone to cart me away. Yet Bree lies there, glowing like a rose."

"Your sister's quite a woman."

"I know." Her eyes dropped to the surface of the table. "She said she has someone to depend on her now. I guess the time's come to stop playing big sister. She doesn't need that anymore."

"So, what will you do now?" His voice was casual.

"I'll stay around a couple of weeks, then I'll go on." She struggled, seeing only a void.

"To what?"

Her fingers tightened on her glass. "To my work, to my life." She drank, and the brandy was bitter.

"Still set on leaving?" He lifted his own glass, swirling the liquid. Amber danced under the kitchen light. "You haven't seen Wyoming in the autumn."

"No, I haven't," she answered, evading his prior question. "Maybe I'll come back next year." She stared down at her hands, knowing she never would.

"She's hungry!" Dan charged into the kitchen, his grin threatening to split his face. "Just had a baby, and she says she's hungry. Sam, I love you." Plucking her from her chair, Dan tossed her into the air. Her laughter ended on a shriek as she clutched at him on her journey down. The shriek was strangled as she was smothered by a bear hug. "I swear, if bigamy wasn't against the law, I'd marry you."

"If I was still all in one piece," she managed, turning her face and gulping for air.

"I ask you, Jake." He consulted the other man as his arms threatened to destroy the alignment of Samantha's rib cage. "Have you ever known another like this one?"

"Can't say that I have." She heard the smile in his voice, though it was impossible in her position to see his face. "I'd say Samantha is unique. One of a kind."

Rising, he lifted his brandy and toasted them both.

Chapter 12

"Sam, you're going to spoil her."

"Impossible." Sitting in the front porch rocker with the week-old Jennifer, Samantha smiled at her sister. "She's much too intelligent to be spoiled. Anyway, it's an aunt's privilege."

As she continued to rock, her lips strayed to Jennifer's soft tuft of dark hair. I won't be able to do this much longer. She looked to the massive peaks gleaming silver-blue in the afternoon sun. A light breeze stirred the air, bringing the sweet scent of freshly mowed grass. She breathed it in, and the soft scent of Jennifer's talc mingled with it. A sigh escaped.

She had not realized such a small creature could wrap her way around the heart so completely. Another love to leave behind. In just a week, I'll have to say goodbye to all the things that matter: Bree, Dan, Wyoming, and now Jennifer.

Dents and bruises, she thought again, but not the open wound that comes from leaving the man. Arrogant and gentle, demanding and kind, hot-tempered and easy; the parts that made up Jake Tanner were complicated and many, but to Samantha, it was a simple equation of love.

Blast you, Jake Tanner, if it weren't for you, I could stay. I belong here. I felt it from the first time I saw the mountains. There's nothing for me in Philadelphia. You've left me without anything to go back to.

"Looks like Lesley's coming to pay a visit," Sabrina observed. Samantha jerked back to the present with a snap.

She watched the late-model compact winding down the drive. Ignoring the flare of impossible jealousy, she set her features in casual lines.

"Sabrina, how well you look." Lesley's greeting was obviously tinged by surprise. "It's only been a week, and you look positively..." She hesitated, searching for a word.

"Radiant?" Sabrina suggested, and laughed. "I just had a baby, Lesley, not open-heart surgery."

"But to go through all that here, and without a doctor." She turned to Samantha. "I heard from Jake that you were marvelous and handled everything."

Samantha shrugged, uncomfortable at hearing Jake's praise from Lesley's lips. "It was nice of him to say so, but Sabrina did all the work."

"Well, having a baby is not a prospect I look forward to." Lesley shivered delicately. "I certainly intend to put it off as long as possible." Gliding over, she bent her head over the sleeping infant. "She is quite lovely, Sabrina. Very sweet."

"Would you like to hold her?" Samantha offered.

"Oh, no." Lesley stepped back. "I'm afraid I'm not very good with babies."

As she moved, Samantha caught the glint of the large square-cut diamond on her left hand. Lesley followed her gaze, and held out her hand. "You didn't know I was engaged, did you, Sabrina?"

"No." Sabrina cast a quick glance at her sister. "We hadn't heard."

"Well, you have been rather busy." She moved her fingers, enjoying the changing lights. "And we haven't made any formal announcement yet. We're planning a bit of a party for next week. As a matter of fact, I'm just on my way into town to begin shopping for my trousseau. Of course, I'll have to make a trip into New York for some proper clothes, but I'll just have to make do locally for the time being. We've set the wedding for the end of September." She smoothed her perfectly groomed hair with a well-manicured hand. "I could have done with a bit more time, but men have no idea how diffi-cult things are to arrange properly." She smiled again. "Well, I must fly. I have so much to do. I do hope you'll be able to make it to the wedding, Samantha."

Sabrina glanced again at her sister. "Sam won't be here in September, Lesley."

"Oh, too bad." The regret in Lesley's voice was mild. Her mind had already run ahead to her wardrobe. She opened the door of the compact and slid behind the wheel. Lifting a slim arm in farewell, she drove away.

Rising, Sabrina took the sleeping Jennifer from her sister's arms and went into the house. When she re-turned, she sat on the arm of the rocker and laid her hand on Samantha's shoulder.

"I knew it was going to happen," Samantha mur-mured. "I just didn't want to be here when it did. I didn't think it would hurt this much. Oh, Bree." She looked up at her twin with helpless, swimming eyes. "What am I going to do?"

For the first time in their relationship, their situations were reversed, and Samantha was vulnerable, seeking comfort and advice.

"Sam, you can't go on like this. Why don't you talk to him?" Sabrina stroked the thick fall of her sister's hair. "Something is wrong here, and the two of you have to talk things out."

"No. I won't give him the opportunity to feel sorry for me."

"Pride can be a very cold companion," Sabrina murmured.

Samantha stood up. "I'm going back early, Bree. I can have everything arranged by the day after tomorrow, maybe even by tomorrow night."

"Sam, you can't run away from this."

"Just watch me."

"Mom and Dad won't be here for a few more days. They'll be disappointed."

"I'm sorry, I hate to miss them, but I can't handle this." Pausing, she repeated, the admission surprising her, "I *really* can't handle this."

"But, Sam…" Sabrina joined her at the porch rail. "You should at least talk to Jake. Don't you want to know how he feels? You can't just go flying off without speaking to him, without saying goodbye. Something's not right about all this. I've thought about the two of you. I've seen the way he looks at you."

Shaking her head, Samantha moved toward the door. "No, he hasn't shown his face since the baby was born, and Lesley Marshall has his ring on her finger. A diamond. He has what he wants."

Samantha spent the evening packing, while Shylock watched her in silent accusation from his habitual place in the center of her bed.

Once in bed, she spent most of the night staring at a

moon-washed ceiling. When the first pale light of dawn crept into the room, she rose. The mauve shadows under her eyes were a sad tribute to the restless hours.

The house slept on, and she deserted it, making her way to the stables. She saddled her mount with quick, deft movements, then galloped over the faint mist of morning.

As the sky lightened, the air came to life with the sweet song of birds. Sadly, she listened to the song of the west, for she knew that the melody would linger forever in her heart. She watched the mountains transformed by the dawn. Ribbons of rose and gold melted into blue until the peaks were no longer silhouettes, but stood proud in the full glory of the sun. She stayed for a last look at the white-faced Herefords grazing on the short, coarse grass. She knew now that her love for this wild, free country was forever bound up with her love for Jake. In saying goodbye to one, she was saying good-bye to the other. Straightening her shoulders, she turned the little mare back to the Lazy L.

When she returned to the house, she greeted her sister with bright chatter, the meaningless words no disguise for sleep-starved eyes. Sabrina made no comment, and shortly disappeared into the bedroom to tend to the baby.

Alone, Samantha wandered aimlessly from window to window. Tonight, she thought, slipping her hands into the pockets of her jeans, I'll be on a plane. And tomorrow morning, all this will just be a dream.

"Morning, ma'am."

She whirled, nearly upsetting a vase of roses with the movement. Jake leaned against the door frame, legs crossed at the ankles, as if he had been watching for some time.

"What are you doing here?"

He took a few strides into the room. "Well, now, I came to fetch you." This information was imparted in an irritatingly slow drawl.

"Fetch me? What are you talking about? I'm not a dog or a maverick calf to be fetched."

"Maverick calf sounds pretty close. You're always running off in the wrong direction." Reaching out, he took her arm. "Come on, we're going for a ride." His voice was pleasant, but the steel was there. She jerked away, angry with his arrogance, wary of his tone.

"I have no intention of going anywhere with you. Why don't you just go away and leave me alone?"

"Now, I can't do that, Sam," he returned in a reasonable tone. "We have some unfinished business to attend to. Your time's up."

The fire in her eyes flickered and died. "You can't be serious."

"I'm dead serious."

"What...what about Lesley?"

"She's not invited," he returned simply.

"I'm not going with you," she said, somewhere between terror and fury. "You can't make me."

Stopping, he looked down at her from his overpowering height. "Sure I can," he corrected with easy confidence. With a swift movement, he swung her over his shoulder. "See?" He walked effortlessly down the hall. "Nothing to it."

"Let me down!" Furious fists beat against his back. "This is crazy, it's illegal. I'll have you thrown in jail!"

"No kidding? Sam, you're scaring me to death."

He continued easily down the hall, as if he carried an empty sack, rather than an irate woman who was thumping against his back. Pausing, he touched the brim of his hat as Sabrina appeared in the bedroom doorway, the baby in her arms.

"Morning, Sabrina." His greeting was genial, and he cocked his head to get a better view of Jennifer. "She's a real beauty."

"Thank you, Jake. We certainly think so." She shifted the baby and smiled. "Are you two going out?"

"Thought we'd go for a little ride," Jake informed her. "We may be gone some time."

"It's a fine day for it, hardly a cloud in the sky."

"Bree." Samantha's voice was desperate. "Don't just stand there, *do* something." She pushed at the hair that hung over her face. "Don't you see what he's doing? He's kidnapping me. Call the police, call Dan." She continued to plead as Jake touched the brim of his hat once more and moved down the hall. "Bree, say something."

"Have a good time" was her sister's surprising response.

Samantha's mouth fell open in dumb astonishment. A stream of imaginative curses was hurled on Jake's unperturbed head as he took the reins of his mount from a grinning cowboy.

"Looks like you got yourself a real handful there, Jake."

"No more than I can handle," he countered, swinging into the saddle with Samantha still held over his shoulder. With a speed that defied his easygoing manner, he had her in front of him in the saddle, spurring the horse into a gallop, before she could think of escape.

"You're going to pay for this," Samantha promised, clutching the saddle horn to keep her balance. "You can't just run off with me this way!"

"I didn't see anybody try to stop me," Jake pointed out.

He followed the road for some time without decreasing his pace, then cut across an open field. At a small grove of trees, he reined in, gripping Samantha around the waist when she attempted to wiggle down.

"Now, don't do that, Sam," he warned in a friendly

voice. "I'd just have to catch you, and I throw a mean lasso."

He slid from the chestnut, and before her feet could touch the ground, she was back over his shoulder. Without ceremony, she was dumped under the fragile, bending leaves of a willow while he towered over her, grinning with obvious enjoyment.

"You're going to be sorry," she predicted, smoldering with fury. "I'm going to…" The rest of her words slipped back down her throat as he dropped down next to her. "You—you can't do this, Jake. You're not the kind of man who forces himself on a woman."

"Who says?" Pushing her back on the soft grass, he covered her body with his.

Her body betrayed her with instant response. Her skin tingled as his mouth brushed over it. "You're not really going to do this."

"I told you once —" his mouth moved to her ear, and his words were warm and soft against it "—not to forget your own words. There are some things you just have to do."

His kiss was long and lingering.

When her mouth was free, she drew in a deep breath and spit out with all her strength, "What kind of man are you, to make love to one woman and plan to marry another?"

His eyes lazily narrowed. He propped himself on one

elbow, his other arm pinning her down. Lifting his head from his elbow, he undid the top button of her blouse. "Suppose," he continued, moving down to the next button, "you tell me whom I'm supposed to marry."

His fingers trailed a slow line from her throat, down the smooth skin her open blouse revealed, and rested on the next button. The blood began to pound in her ears. His eyes alone held her still as he spread her blouse apart. Slowly, his fingers roamed up the warmth of her skin, moving with casual possession over her. Her eyes clouded with growing need as he explored.

"Tell me who I'm going to marry, Samantha." His body shifted again, molding to hers. His shirt was warm against her naked flesh.

"L-Lesley," she stammered.

"No." His mouth lowered to the curve of her throat, his tongue teasing the vulnerable skin.

She felt the waist of her jeans loosen under his hand. His finger pushed away the material and moved along her hip. With her last claim to lucidity, she pushed against his chest.

"Please stop."

"Now I just can't do that, Sam." His hands teased the curve of her hip, trailing back up to the side of her breast. "I've waited a good long time to get you where I want you."

"I'm not staying... Did you say you weren't marrying Lesley?"

He frowned down in consideration, winding her hair around his finger. "Seems to me I did mention that. I don't know why you're always piling your hair on top of your head when it looks so good spread all over."

"But she was wearing your ring."

"Not mine," Jake corrected, still concentrating on the hair around his finger. "Your hair's gotten lighter these past few weeks, you haven't been wearing a hat. Les has a diamond, doesn't she? I told you once diamonds don't suit you. They're cold, and they don't have much imagination. But that's Les." He shrugged and began to move his mouth over her face again. "It doesn't seem to matter to Jim."

Valiantly, Samantha attempted to follow his words. Her head shook with the effort.

"Les is engaged to Jim Bailey. I'm sure you remember Jim Bailey, you spent enough time with him at the party."

"Yes, but..."

"No buts," he interrupted. "Les likes to have a couple of fish on the line, and when she got it through her head I wasn't in season, she netted Jim without a struggle."

"But I thought..."

"I know what you thought." He cut her off again and smiled. "Running away a few days early, weren't you?"

"I wasn't running. How did you know I was leaving?"

"Sabrina told me."

"Bree?" Samantha whispered. Bree did that?

"Yeah, yesterday. She came to see me while you were packing. I like this spot right here," he stated, planting his lips against the hollow of her throat. "I've had a devil of a time putting things in order since then, so I could take time for a honeymoon. Busy time of year for a cattleman."

"Honeymoon?" Her skin was trembling where his lips continued to taste.

"I've got a good foreman," he continued, as if thinking aloud. "I reckon he can manage things for a while. I could use another day or two. I had a nice long honeymoon in mind, someplace quiet." He brought his attention back to her stunned face. "You've never been to Bora Bora, have you?"

"Are you talking about getting your ranch in order so you can take time off to marry me?" She attempted to speak slowly and clearly while her emotions whirled like a summer tornado.

"Just being practical," he explained with a bland smile.

"Why you conceited, overbearing... Just what makes you think I'll marry you? You sit back and make all these plans and expect me to run off to Bora Bora with you like a passive little puppy. Of all the chauvinist—"

"How about Antarctica?" he suggested, willing to be reasonable. "Not too many people there, either."

"You're crazy. I never said I'd marry you. What makes you think..." Her tirade was cut off effectively as his mouth coaxed her silence. When he let her breathe, her voice had lost its strength. "That's not going to help you. I'm not in love with you."

"Seems to me I recall someone telling me she was a totally honest person." His gaze was disconcertingly direct. He held her chin, preventing her face from turning away. "You want to look at me and tell me that again? You've been fighting me all along, and I think I've just about used up my patience." His lips were teasing hers again, and his hands moved over her with more urgency. "Mmm, but you have a nice body. I can't take much more of this waiting around. Six months is a long time, Sam. I've wanted you from the minute you stood there ordering Dan to have his man tend to the horses."

"Yes, you let me know very early what you wanted." She no longer struggled, but lay passive in his arms.

"Gave you something to think about. Of course, you didn't know I wanted you to be my wife, too. It was easy to tell you I wanted you, but a bit difficult to tell you I loved you. Sam, look at me." She shook her head, but the fingers on her chin tightened in authority. "Look at me." She obeyed, her lids opening to reveal eyes veiled with tears. "You stubborn little idiot. Listen carefully,

I've never said this to another woman, and I've had to wait too long to say it to you. If you don't marry me soon, I'm going to lose my mind." His mouth took hers, spinning the world into nothing. Her arms flew around him as pain evaporated into unspeakable joy. "Samantha." He buried his face in the lushness of her hair. "It's been quite a race."

"I don't understand." She brought his face back to hers, needing to see the truth in his eyes. "Why didn't you tell me before?"

"I didn't think you'd believe that a man had nearly been knocked off his feet by a picture of a girl less than half his age, then had completely lost his balance when he saw the woman she'd become. If you hadn't been so wrapped up in Sabrina those first few minutes, you'd have seen how a man looks when he gets hit by lightning."

"Just like that?" Stunned, she traced the angles of his face to assure herself she was not dreaming.

"Just like that," he agreed, bringing her palm to his lips. "Then, after I'd recovered a bit, I knew I had to work around your dedication to Sabrina until you'd figured out there was room in your life for someone else. Then you stood there telling me you were going back home as soon as the baby was born. I nearly strangled you." His fingers tightened on her hand as he brought his eyes back to hers. "How was I supposed to tell you that I loved you, that I wanted to marry you, wanted you to stay in Wyoming? The night of the party, in the kitchen, I made up my mind I wasn't letting you go, no matter what I had to do to keep you."

"But I never wanted to leave." She shook her head in brisk denial, as if he should have realized it all along. "It was just that I couldn't bear to see you married to Lesley."

"You know, things might have gotten even more complicated if Sabrina hadn't come by and laid things out for me. She's got a bit more of you in her than I had thought." Laughing, he lifted his face from hers. "She told me to sit down and listen. She'd never seen two people run around in circles so long and get nowhere."

"It's not like Bree to interfere."

"She interfered beautifully. First thing she did was ask me what business I had getting engaged to Lesley. I must have stared at her like she'd lost her mind. After I managed to tell her I was definitely not engaged to Lesley, she let me have it with both barrels. Mixed with the buckshot was the information that you were miserable about going home, and that I was a fool for not seeing it myself. Then she folded her arms, stuck out her chin exactly like someone else has a habit of doing and asked me what the devil I intended to do about it."

Samantha stared up at him and shook her head in astonishment. "I wish I could have seen that."

He smiled and lowered his mouth. "Just look in

the mirror sometime." Flesh met flesh with no barriers, and with a small sound of desperation he savaged her mouth. The hard lines of his chest pressed into her breasts. "Let me hear you say it, Samantha," he murmured, unable to resist the curve of her neck. "I need to hear you say it."

"I love you." Her mouth searched for his, her arms urging him closer. "I love you. I love you." Her lips found their objective, and her silence told him again.

"I need you, Samantha." His mouth and hands continued to seek, growing wilder, possessive, demanding. "I never knew I could need anyone the way I need you. I want you for myself for a while, no distractions, no complications, just you. We've got six months of loving to make up for. I'm going to keep you fully occupied for a very long time." Lifting his face, he smiled down at her, running his hand through the hair spread over the grass. "A very long time."

She smiled back, running her hands up his chest to circle his neck. "I intend to keep you occupied, as well. Your cows are going to get very lonely." Removing his hat, she tossed it carelessly aside, then turned back to him with raised brows. "Okay, cowboy." Her arms lifted to lock around his neck, fingers tangling possessively in his hair. "Start occupying."

"Yes, ma'am." With a polite nod, he lowered his mouth and followed orders.

* * * * *

Introducing
the Stanislaskis...

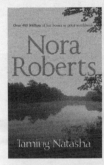
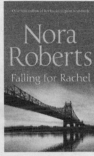
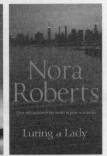
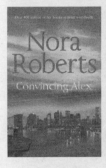
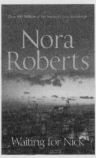
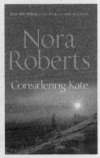

Get ready to meet the MacKade family...

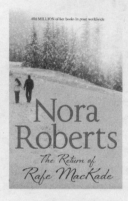

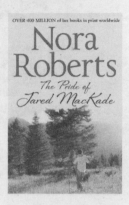

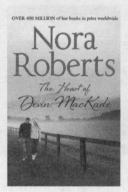

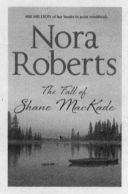

'The most successful author on planet Earth'
—*Washington Post*

www.millsandboon.co.uk

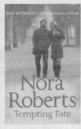
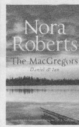
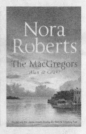
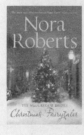
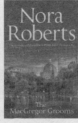
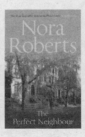
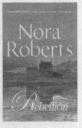

Snow, sleigh bells and a hint of seduction

Find your perfect Christmas reads at
millsandboon.co.uk/Christmas